LOVE
MONKEY

LOVE MONKEY

KYLE SMITH

wm

WILLIAM MORROW
An Imprint of HarperCollinsPublishers

FIRST EDITION

Designed by Adrian Leichter

Printed on acid-free paper

Library of Congress Cataloging-in-Publication Data has been applied for.

ISBN 0-06-057453-4

04 05 06 07 08 WBC/BVG 10 9 8 7 6 5 4 3 2 1

FOR MY MOTHER
AND MY GRANDPARENTS

It is awfully easy to be hard-boiled
about everything in the daytime,
but at night it is another thing.

—HEMINGWAY,
The Sun Also Rises

.

ACKNOWLEDGMENTS

Without the efforts of my super-duper agent, Harriet Wasserman, and my merely spectacular editor, Dan Conaway, this book would not exist, except as files on my hard drive, in which case you would have to come to my apartment to read it. That could be inconvenient for both of us.

Thanks to anyone who ever made me laugh, especially the Colonel, Der Spaniard und Die Austrian, Grover, Min, and J. Rack.

For their rah-rahs and whoo-hoos, cheers to Cutler Durkee, Larry Hackett, Gerry Howard, Jon Karp, Gersh Kuntzman, Stu Marques, Jill Schwartzman, and that cat-lovin' combat typist, Mike Hechtman.

LOVE MONKEY

y day.

8:00 A.M. Arise.

8:00–8:15. Light stretching. Don't forget those hamstrings. A few push-ups to warm the blood.

8:20. Out the door, hit Central Park Reservoir. Do six laps. Pace: seven minutes per mile. That's ten and a half miles in seventy-five minutes.

9:45. Back home. Shower, reread *The Brothers Karamazov* ("Grand Inquisitor" episode only).

11:45. Call Mom.

12:30. Lunch. Grilled quail, wild rice, spinach salad, fresh-squeezed oj.

1:00. To the Met. Check out Vermeer exhibit. Strike up conversation with cute twenty-five-year-old Dutch graduate student I meet standing in front of *Woman Wearing Doily Around Her Neck*; obtain her numerals, agree to meet for drinks at the Carlyle "early next week."

4:00. Back home. Work on my novel till dinner. One interruption: call from superagent.

8:30. Quiet dinner with a few friends at Le Bernadin. *No really, fellas, it's on me.* They all know about my huge advance. We laugh about it.

11:45. Village Vanguard to hear some jazz. Exchange dirty jokes with compadres, trade saucy banter with cocktail waitress who, as I sweep out the door, slips me her digits.

2:00. Cab back home, practice piano for half an hour, and so to bed. If can't sleep, read a chapter of that John Adams bio everyone's talking about. (Was he really cooler than T. Jefferson?)

That's what it says in my Yahoo! appointment book for today, anyway. But back here on Planet Manhattan, I creep out of bed as dawn breaks over Honolulu and skulk in the shower for forty-five minutes. (I know it was forty-five minutes because I had Pink Floyd's *The Wall* in my Raindance CD player, and I got all the way through disc one.) Then I pick, off the floor, a few more dead flower petals from The Dinner and plant myself on the sofa that still bears my ass print from last night, surrounded by my twenty-first-century entertainment- and sodium-delivery devices: four fiendishly over-complicated, girl-proof remote controls; two near-spent crinkly bags of salty snacks. There's a white crumb on the couch. I am too civilized to just leave it there, so I pick it up. And I put it in my mouth. Pfft. Dandruff. At *best.*

Some notes on me.

The name is Tom Farrell. I'm from That generation. You know the one I'm talking about. The one after the one that discovered the Beatles and nonbinding sex, the one before the one where seventeen-year-olds asked to be excused from Phys. Ed. so they could launch their IPOs. Yeah, that'd be us: the Lamest Generation.

Cultural anthropologists of the future will remember us primarily for nonblack tuxedos, Valerie Bertinelli, and Men at Work. Our grandfathers won World War II. We can't even tie a bow tie.

I'm not in great shape. I do, occasionally, complete one gasping lap around the reservoir. When I run, it's prose in motion. My abs are a one-pack. My arms are steamed licorice. My teeth are carved of wax. I've been compared to a redheaded Winnie the Pooh, an Oompa Loompa without the self-tanning lotion, a slightly elongated Teletubby. For one formative grade—fifth—I was known exclusively as "Doughboy." The first time some playground wit poked my tummy hoping to elicit a girlish giggle, it was funny. The 100th time it was less so. By the 500th time, I was developing a complex, and at 603 (I counted, oh how I counted), I entered therapy. At 607, my late father opened a glassine-windowed envelope, began a five-second argument with my mother ("What the hell is this shit?"), and therapy was concluded.

I'm defiantly average, studiously okay, the Gap of bachelors. You know how when you go into Duane Reade and there's a generic product next to the one with a logo and a memorable back story of amusing and informative TV commercials? IBUPROFEN. MOUTH-WASH. ANTIHISTAMINE. That's me: the man without a brand. The one you would never pick after you won the lottery. I contain all the same ingredients, and I'm a bargain. But I have no shelf appeal. If someone saw me in your medicine chest, you'd *die*.

I'm thirty-two, as healthy as any other Spam-raised American male. I look pretty young. Hair is disappearing from my scalp, but fortunately it hasn't deserted me: It's just relocating to my nostrils and ears. My face—my patriotic mug of red hair, white skin, blue eyes—is doing okay. I have no laugh lines (what's funny?). I'm not short, not really. I stand the Minimum Acceptable Height for an Adult Male. (Some celebrities I know to be shorter than myself: Redford. Stallone. Pitt.) But the only way I could ever be labeled tall would be if I became a Starbucks beverage. I don't play sports much anymore, so I compensate by watching extra sports on TV. Australian Rules golf, anyone? Need a rundown of the favorites at this year's Tour de Luxembourg?

I have a one-bedroom apartment, a refrigerator containing (solely) beverages and condiments, a Manhattan-sized mini-microwave deployed only for popping corn, a supply of Cheez-It crumbs that I store under my sofa cushions, stacks of dusty black stereo equipment, and an increasingly avalanchable Matterhorn of CDs. (Single women in their thirties accumulate cats; I stockpile home electronics.) I've got the requisite panoply of Banana Republic shirts in assorted colors (dark blue, light blue, blue). I own forty-three T-shirts. I watch *The Simpsons* 3.7 times a week, and I floss 3.7 times a year. When the house lights go down before a rock concert, I am often the first to shout, "Freebird!"

My most time-consuming hobby is collecting ex-girlfriends. When I'm feeling nonwhimsical, I call up selections from my personal torture jukebox. E-6: Tess. The girl I left behind after I worked at a stuffy newspaper in London for a few months. She hated America despite never having set foot here. She still hasn't, as far as I know. C-11: Judy. First girl I ever slept with, incompetently. She married a Japanese guy, moved to Kyoto, and had twins. Do you think I still have a chance with her? Then there's A-2: the one who almost did it to me. Betsy, my Betsy. Dated her up to and beyond (although not much beyond) the all-defining two-year mark. She knew me better than anyone else ever did. That was a feeling both excellent and scary. In the end I just couldn't handle the idea that my sexual scorecard would be stuck at four for the rest of my life. I was twenty-four. She's living with some guy now. He's an easygoing, jolly, kind-hearted fellow whom I would like to strangle in his sleep.

I've been thinking about this guy who wrote this book. It's about a regular, warm, flawed fella and his girlfriend. It goes into his longings and his needs and his fears and how he keeps screwing up in lovable ways. The whole story is told in Top Five lists. Every girl I know has read his book, and they all want (or think they want) to meet a guy like the guy in the book. More specifically, they want to meet the guy who wrote the book. What must a party be like for him? He must get home from the pub and empty his jacket pockets and go: whose phone number is this? And why is it written on a pair of panties? He wrote the world's longest personal ad and got paid for it. They even made a movie out of it: the movie consisted of good-looking people reading the Top Five lists from the book.

So I reflect for a moment about improving my relationships. About the secret sorrows of men and the stated needs of women. About longing and forgiveness and how wise people learn to love each other's imperfections.

And I conclude: I better get cracking on some Top Five lists.

I don't have a girlfriend now: I played the field, and the field won. This makes me slightly suspect. What's wrong with me? Am I gay? (I wish: nonstop guiltless action, plus you get to be good looking and tasteful, and all you have to do is wear a condom, which I seem to end up doing most of the time anyway. A lot of vaguely intellectual feministy New York girls seem to think the Pill is a male plot to give them cancer or something, a conspiracy they discuss over cigarettes.) Am I unable to share my deep feelings? Do I lack any deep feelings in the first place? Am I just picky? Possibly. But at thirty-two it starts to hit you: there is a fine line between picky and *loser*.

Despite my flaws I have had a more or less standard number of girlfriends. I have dated three different Jennifers, which puts me slightly below average for a guy my age, and two Asian girls: way below average. I have dated girls who quote Joni Mitchell and girls who quote Madonna. Girls who cry inexplicably and girls who go all Women's Studies on you if you call them girls. Girls who like to be taken to flashy parties and girls who like to stay home with Fred

Astaire. They all have two things in common. Every one of them was better looking, for a girl, than I am for a guy. And every one of them has improved me in some way. (A few personality renovations I owe to them: stopped wearing white crew socks with my khakis; began wearing belt every day; stopped wiping nose on sleeve when anyone is looking; learned key girl terms, such as mule, bias cut, empire waist, blowout, etc., essential to understanding most girl conversations.)

There are advantages to girlfriendlessness: no one to monitor alcohol consumption. Breakfast cereal: not just for breakfast! Can watch midget boxing if I feel like it. Very little time wasted discussing one's emotional issues and picking at one's family-inflicted scar tissue. If want sexual experience before I go to sleep, no need to be nice to hand all day. During, need not feel obliged to call out my name; afterward, not required to hold myself for one to two hours.

But then again. Boxing is boring. My hand never dresses up nice to get my attention. There is no one to make sarcastic comments to while watching TV. And in Singleland, you hardly ever get to ask: did you just fart?

About the emotional crap. I have no objection to talking about myself. (Why should I? I certainly have no objection to talking *to* myself.) And it's not like I don't have issues. They're just hidden in back. They're back issues. Would I be a more fully rounded human if I dusted them off once in a while? One of those poets they made us read in college said to know yourself was the highest achievement. What if your true self is a slimy little reptile? Is it really such an accomplishment to let it out to go slithering into the punch bowl?

Surely there is one way to find the answers for which I strive. TV.

Flick, flick. News on the latest local massacre, that scary sitcom about high school, Charlie Rose (is he on at all times?), the Argument Network, Always Pantiliner commercial, the Hitler Channel, Natural Disaster News, the Boring Channel (sea turtles and coral), the *The Breakfast Club* Channel, Tampax commercial (always reminds me of the old joke: Father says to his ten-year-old son, "What do you want for your birthday, son?" Kid goes, "Tampax." Father goes, "Why Tampax?" Kid goes, "Because then I can do anything. I can go swimming, I can go dancing, I can play tennis. . . ."), the Fishin' Magician (they still make those?), the Bands-on-Drugs-but-Very-Sorry-About-It Channel, what appears to be yet another MTV spring break show (wasn't spring break, like, four months ago?), the People-Talking-Very-Seriously-in-British-Accents Channel, and, ah!, wot's this then, gents? The Cartoon Network.

A Bugs Bunny retrospective. Bugs is standing on Elmer's head, rubbing the hair tonic in really good with his big rubbery bunny feet. The hair starts to grow. Elmer, observing developments in a hand mirror, is elated. Petals pop forth. No! That wasn't hair tonic, it was fertilizer! The kind that grows flowers on scalps! Now Elmer is very, very angry, and reaches into the back of his shirt, where he has been keeping his musket the whole time. How clever of him to have armed himself for his barber's appointment. But I know what's coming. In the next thirty seconds, Bugs will momentarily baffle him by dashing out of the scene, returning dressed as a girl (a girl bunny, though), and giving Elmer flowers and candy, thus wowing Elmer and causing him to present Bugs with a wedding ring, which in turn will inspire Bugs to don wedding regalia. Bugs and Elmer will find a minister and say their vows, but Bugs will carry Elmer up a stairway to their honeymoon suite, which of course will not be a suite at all but just a door leading into empty space. Bugs, lifting Elmer over the threshold, will then drop him to a nasty and violent death, which is really not very fair treatment for a guy who has just made a serious commitment to you despite the obvious hurdles involved in an interspecies marriage between a homosexual gun nut and a transvestite anthropomorphic rodent who barely know each other, at least within the context of this cartoon. That's marriage for you, folks. Who needs it?

Five hours later, Yosemite Sam is firing a cannon at Bugs when the phone rings. I am vaguely annoyed because I want to see what happens, although I admit that the smart money's on Bugs to find an even bigger cannon, catch the cannonball in his cannon, and fire the cannonball back at Yosemite Sam, leaving him with a singed mustache and soot-blackened face. I feel bad about this, but I plan to quietly rejoice when Sam recuperates the next second.

The phone. It could be an important news bulletin from an acquaintance. It could be one of several cute girls I know, although that's really stretching imagination to the warranty-voiding point. It could be a long-lost pal from high school. It could be one of the impossibly witty and lively guys I know, offering an outlandish good time.

But why take a chance?

And as the phone rings for a fourth time (my machine picks up; the caller hangs up), it hits me: twenty years ago on a Saturday morning, I would have been doing exactly the same thing, with only two crucial differences: 1) There was no Cartoon Network, so Bugs was only on from ten-thirty to noon, when my Hoover-wielding mother would forcibly evict me from the living room and urge me into the backyard where my psychotic older brothers awaited, day-dreaming of complicated tortures; and 2) I ate my Cocoa Krispies out of a plastic *Empire Strikes Back* bowl instead of the glass one on my lap right now. (Don't think I don't miss it.)

I'm thirty-two, only not. I'm a thirteen-year-old with a credit card. I am not a man. I am a manboy. Women know that boys will be boys; unfortunately for them, they must learn that men will be boys too.

I'm not the only one. You can be a manboy at any age, be of any nationality or race. Adam Sandler, Tom Hanks, Paul McCartney, Michael J. Fox, Bill Gates, Matt Damon, Robin Williams, Jackie Chan, Mickey Rooney, Chris Rock, John Cusack, Hugh Grant, Matthew Broderick, Jerry Seinfeld, Bill Clinton, *and* George W.

Bush—hey, two presidents in a row, first ones since Teddy Roosevelt (one of whose cabinet secretaries once said, I read somewhere, "You have to remember that the president is about twelve.").

So: manboys rule the box office, the White House, the Forbes 500. Why should I worry? Our day is at hand. And my life is my own. I'm the king of me. Nobody tells me what to do. I'm an independent soul, a wanderer, a questioner. Now if you'll excuse me, I have to call my mom.

"Hi," I say. "It's me," I say. Somehow it always feels necessary to add, "Tom."

My mom is fifty-eight. She enjoys costume jewelry, strip-mall yarn stores, General Foods International Coffees, and Derek Jeter. Despite the fact that I have toiled in the ink racket for years, the only publication she gets is the Sunday paper, which she buys solely for the Q-pons that she carefully files in a little gray plastic box. Her dream is to retire soon so she can devote herself full-time to her hobby, which is cleaning the grout in her bathroom. My mother's bathroom does not look like any human beings have ever been in it. It's a showroom from a soap-scumless Tomorrowland. You could manufacture microchips in it.

It would be fair to say that Mom likes things to go the way they're supposed to.

"Hi, honey," says Mom. "Weren't you going to call this morning?"

Yes. It's true. Yesterday I promised to call her this *morning*. She nailed me down via e-mail, which she uses as a global tracking device. For the first time since I was a teenager, Mom knows where I am every single day. She even makes me e-mail her daily when I'm on vacation, the rare adventurous weeks when I strike out for (and strike out across) Italy or England or France.

"Um," I say. "Did you just call?"

"Yes," she says.

"Why didn't you leave a message?"

"I asked you first why you didn't call me in the first place," she says.

"Honestly, Mother, it's because I don't like you very much."

I don't really say that.

"I'm sorry," I murmur.

"I just don't understand it," says Mom.

"I'm really sorry," I say.

"Tommy, you said you would call before noon!" Mom is like the bad guy at the end of the slasher movie, only instead of killing her three times, you have to listen to everything three times.

"Mom, I forgot. It's just that I've been so stressed out at work lately . . ." I allow my voice to tail off pitifully.

I've-been-stressed-out-at-work (or school)-lately is my bulletproof excuse, ranked number 1 (still!) after 562 weeks on my hit parade of all-purpose Excuses to Throw at Women Who Are Guilt-Tripping Me. Mom is a dental hygienist in Rockville, Maryland, and as such does not lead a terribly stressful existence. Generally speaking, you go home at a reasonable time of day and the work is predictable. Nobody ever says to a dental hygienist, "Dammit, you screwed everything up today. You're gonna stay till midnight. Every one of those patients are coming back so you can jam those suck hooks back in every one of their mouths, only this time, do it right!" There is rarely an emergency in the field of dental hygiene. (Code blue! We've run out of spearminty stuff to smear on the little circular power tool!)

Is it a little unfair to keep trumping my mother this way, to keep rubbing my white-collar job in her creased blue-collar face, reminding her of how much more successful I am at thirty-two than she will ever be?

Yes. It is unfair. On the other hand, isn't it a little unfair of her to expect me to call her every month just because she gave birth to me? I have a better idea: how about once a year? No, better yet: once a girlfriend. Then we'll have something to discuss.

Mom has nothing to say to me. I have nothing to say to Mom.

When Dad was alive, she always had lots to say: about how awful Dad was. She eventually tired of that topic, though, a mere five years after his death. I don't call my mother because there is no personality overlap. We haven't read the same books about seething young men careening around London or New York; we haven't seen the same movies about hyperverbal gangsters who operate impossibly large weapons while making remarks about comic books.

She thinks I'm a Good Boy. This is my role. It seems to work for her. When I was thirteen, I didn't swear around her. Now I can't. It's too late. I had an opportunity: that first Christmas break home from college. Then I could claim life-status change, renegotiate the terms of my son-ness. My swear window closed. Now she must honestly believe I don't curse.

"So what's new?" Mom says.

I hate it when people ask this question. Because absolutely nothing is new. My life is in a holding pattern. Or, to be honest, a holding-onto-nothing pattern. I own no car. Never have. I own no real estate. Never have. The most expensive thing I own is this leather chair: $1,099 plus tax and delivery. So basically the most momentous purchase of my life has been a cushy parking space for my ass.

"Not much," I say, dialing up Chipper Tone Number 3 for my voice. "So what's new with you?"

This is another risky stage of the conversation, because my mother's ears are not as sharp as they used to be and she always mishears this question. When I say, "What's new?" she hears, "Please furnish me with an itemized list of all the diseases currently striking our family members, mutual acquaintances, and people from your place of employment."

"Well, you remember Henrietta?"

"No."

"She's one of the girls from the office." Funny, when my mother says "girl," she means "fifty-nine-year-old woman with osteoporosis." When someone in Manhattan says "woman," she means "twenty-four-year-old girl with a Hello Kitty backpack."

"Uh-huh," I say noncommittally.

"Well," Mom whispers, "well, she has the leukemia."

And off she goes, leading me by the hand through a bright wonderland of sudden unexplained nausea. Bone-marrow transplants. Projectile vomiting. Tearful bedside vigils. Of someone *I don't know*.

"Oh, and I just talked to Grandma and Grandpa. Grandpa fell and broke his hip. Grandma is just getting over a cold."

My grandpa and grandma have been married since she was seventeen and he was nineteen. That's how they did things in those days. No Sixty Dates in Sixty Minutes. No love@aol.com. No Jewish singles night. No "And what do you do?" as you hand her a Heineken. Home for both of them was some dirt farm in Missouri, where if you were a man you'd be in a mine all week and then come out for air Friday night, change into your other shirt, and go dance in a barn and flirt with the pretty girls like there was no tomorrow. Because while there probably would be a tomorrow, it most definitely would suck. "Off to the salt mines," we say in Manhattan as we skip off to our air-conditioned, carpeted offices with candy bowls and whimsical desk signs. My grandpa worked in a salt mine. (Or a silver mine, I'm not sure. I recall dire shuddering mentions of excavation.) He and Grandma have been married sixty-one years and not only do they love each other, they don't spend a single hour outside of the other's company. They literally cannot get enough of each other.

It's kind of like that with me and Julia. Except instead of being married for sixty-one years, we "hung out" for five months. Oh, and instead of never spending a minute outside each other's company? We don't see each other. Except once in a while at work.

But she's here anyway. She never leaves me. She's there right now, sitting next to me, reading *The New Yorker*. I talk to her all the time in my mind.

"Whatcha readin'?"

"A Steve Martin story." She loves Steve Martin too. The only difference is that in my case, I want to see his movies. In her case, she wants to see his movies and then go home and have sex with him afterward. We once went to a "conversation" between Steve Martin and some schmo writer from *The New Yorker.* We stood in back and Steve, unscripted, kept firing off hilarious one-liner after woefully piercing observation after witty rejoinder. Julia was turning to butter next to me. She was wearing this little-girl flowery dress (she later revealed that she had specifically dressed cute in hopes of catching Steve's eye, even though she was far too shy to go up and talk to him) and she kept taking her left foot out of her khaki-colored sandal and rubbing it sensuously on her right instep. How am I supposed to compete with Steve Martin? On the other hand, in all probability she realizes that her chances with Steve aren't great. Maybe she'll settle for me. I could be a decaf, yolkless, edited-for-content-and-to-fit-the-time-allotted version of Steve. A mild and cozy guy.

"Funny?" I say to Julia in my mind.

"Yeah," she says. "But it's more sweet."

I'm sweet I'm sweet I'm sweet I want to say to her. But you never can, can you? You have to show, not tell. And once you show them, say, by preparing an elaborate dinner with place mats and everything, they start to think: *This guy is trying too hard.* I know because I've been there, grilled that. Got the place mats to prove it.

"Are you there?" Mom.

"Oh, yeah, Mom, I'm sorry, I just zoned out. So what's the next step for Henrietta after the bone-marrow transplant?"

"No, honey, I just told you the hospital sent her home. She could *go* any week now."

Looks like I'll never meet Henrietta.

"I'm really sorry about that. Were you good friends?"

I'm clicking the clicker: JFK and other black-and-white people. A clenched-jaw speech. That comedy Yankee accent. "We will bear any burden. We will pay any price." Meaning: We will do anything to stop Communism. Led directly to the Vietnam War. So this could be either a documentary or history's greatest bloopers.

"Wee-yell," my mother says in that Midwestern accent she still hasn't shaken after forty years in Maryland, "to be honest, I always thought she was a little bit of a back stabber. She used to spread gossip about one of the fellas who comes in here, and I happen to know it wasn't true."

So now I get it. We're talking about the impending death of a woman one of us doesn't know and the other doesn't like.

"Well, I'm sure she meant well." This is me in Good Boy mode. Always ascribing basic decency and humanity to people when there is absolutely no evidence of it.

"Are you seeing anybody?" she adds.

Wee-yell. I didn't see that one coming. Normally Mom and I have a gentlemen's agreement not to discuss anything serious, except if it's about our relatives. She only springs this question on me about once a year, and normally it's around Thanksgiving. That, of course, is when I most need a girlfriend. Because you must have someone to hold by the hearth when families gather to share a glass of cheer. Or, in my case, to use as a Mom-deflector device. She doesn't nag me when I shove a girlfriend at her. You can see how happy she is when I'm hooked up. *My son is normal* is written all over her face.

"Actually," I say, "I just broke up with someone," though this is not strictly true.

"I'm sorry, honey." How can she be sorry? She's never met Julia. I never even mentioned that we were together. (Correction. We were never together. We were just hanging out.)

"It's okay," I lie.

"I'm sure you'll find someone," she lies.

"I know," I lie.

"You're such a wonderful boy," she lies.

"True," I lie.

"It'll happen soon," she lies.

"Maybe," I lie.

When the endearments are concluded, I start feeling hungry. I assemble a repast of Ramen Pride noodles and two pieces of stale white bread smeared with poor man's pâté: chunkless Skippy. I know. A guy in my position should not be eating Ramen Pride, but the store didn't have any Ramen Shame.

Why do I eat thirty-three-and-a-third-cent main courses? I make a fair amount of money. *I'm saving it*, I tell myself. For the family I might have someday. My sons will be tall, not small. They will eat foie gras, not Kraft mac cheez. They will play lacrosse, not wiffle ball. No: *polo*. And not "Marco Polo" either: real polo, with *outfits*. Plus, having kids you can cherish means paying a lot of incredibly high fees to get them out of your sight: for nannies, private schools, summer camps in the Poconos. Things I didn't have. And didn't need, since I grew up in suburbia. The city complicates everything. Did my parents crunch these numbers? No, they just had me.

At some level I realize I am becoming the Rickey Ray Rector of bachelors. He was the death row inmate who was missing a third of his brain after a suicide attempt, when he was executed anyway in 1992. His last meal was baked chicken, fried steak, brown beans, cherry Kool-Aid, and pecan pie. He put aside his pie. "Why?" they asked. "For later," he told them.

I wash it all down with a glass of Nestlé's Quik, watch *The Matrix* for the fifth time, and have a glass of Scotch, which I chase with four glasses of Scotch. Then I pass out on my sofa. Nighty-night.

SUNDAY, JULY 8

*H*eadphones on, I'm leashed to the stereo. Playing excessively loud music. Like I said, I'm thirteen.

> *"That's Sugarcane, that tasted good,*
> *"That's Cinnamon, that's Holly-wood!"*

I'm doing the rock-and-roll chair dance, thrusting my head with each beat, thinking, as usual when listening to the words of Michael Stipe, both, This is brilliant! and, I have no idea what he's talking about! What is it this time? *Candy?* At least you can understand the words. In the chorus, anyway.

While I listen I paw through the tottering stack of CDs on top of the stereo. What's this? Must have had a Simon and Garfunkely moment last night, a little pothole for the streetcar named despair. I only require Paul's services when I'm feeling extremely, inappropriately, voluptuously sorry for myself. I am a rock. I am an island.

But which island? That's easy: England. Cold, rainy, and a hundred years past its prime.

Some albums I can no longer listen to.

- ❑ *Murmur*, **R.E.M.** Played it that time she came over on a Sunday afternoon.
- ❑ *Automatic for the People*, **R.E.M.** Played it that night, the night of The Dinner, the one with the place mats and everything.
- ❑ *Up*, **R.E.M.** From the same night. It was a long evening, begun while the sun was still shining, actually, and there was hope in the air. Long day's journey into blight.
- ❑ *Wish*, **The Cure.** Because she loves "From the Edge of the Deep Green Sea" and we both love "A Letter to Elise" and I think I played the album once—success!—as preparatory make-out music in my apartment. The whole album's pretty depressing anyway.
- ❑ *Parachutes,* **Coldplay.** Because "Yellow" was playing at Swift's the moment I found out that Julia didn't want me.

Later I awaken from a nice unscheduled nap on the floor. Down here with my cheek pressed into the carpet I have a nice view underneath the sofa, where I spend a few lazy moments blinking at the sinister furry mounds, the shifting dunes of dust. Someone should really clean it up. But I am nothing if not an optimist, and I truly believe there's a chance that it'll go away by itself. What's this black thing? Well, well. Ninety-two percent cotton, eight percent spandex, seventy-five percent caked in dust. Not too froufrou. 34B. It could belong to any of ten girls who've been relieved of their bras in this vicinity over the last couple of years. It's like finding Cinderella's slipper. Perhaps I should wander around Manhattan asking girls if I could slip it on them for size? That could take a while.

They all seem to be 34B these days. I remember once when I dated a 34C. I bragged about it for months. (What was her name?) Then there was that horrible incident with the 34A, the one who used advanced deception techniques to make herself appear, from the other side of her sweater, to be a 34B. Of course I never called her again. False advertising.

What time is it? Shit, five-thirty. Where did this day go? The six hours since the first time I woke up, anyway. Have I eaten yet? Oh, yeah: at twelve-thirty I confronted the concept of breakfast. Decided to dine on Tylenol and a gallon of water.

Enough of this sitting around my apartment doing nothing but feeling sorry for myself. I put on my shoes, grab my keys, and walk around the corner to Riverside Park. Where I sit on a bench feeling sorry for myself.

Gotta have something to watch. There are kids' playgrounds in the park, of course, but although observing little kids frolicking might lift the spirits, given the sketchy way I look right now, I'd probably get arrested if I happened to scratch my balls or something while in the vicinity.

No, I get a bench by the dog run. It's a dog singles bar, really. Dogs cheer me. Dogs have no trouble meeting, chatting, mating. Dogs do not ask what other dogs do: "Professionally speaking, I am a dog." Are their rituals less absurd than ours? Can I buy you a drink? May I sniff your butt? What's the difference?

I decide to get a copy of the *Times*, not because I have any desire to page inkily through its forty-seven sections but because I need the TV listings. Every Sunday I circle the best movies coming up on cable. This is one of the better parts of my week.

So I join the teeming weekend parade on Broadway, the Yupper West Side: where preppies speak hip-hop, child rearing has gotten more competitive than Rollerball, and Love is a pharmacy. I walk in to get some gum and a paper.

"Three seventy-five," says the lady behind the counter.

"What's this?" I say, picking up a small glass bottle filled with cloudy fluid.

"Bite me," she says.

"Excuse me?"

"It's called Bite Me. Put it on your nails, you don't bite them anymore."

She looks at my nails. Ravaged and bloodied around the cuticles, but only for the last twenty-five years. Over the course of my life, I have probably bitten off enough of me to make a new Tom, albeit one disproportionately composed of cuticles and nails; possibly this would be an improvement over the real me.

"Perfect," I say. "I'll take it. What's with the signs?" Big cautionary cardboard everywhere.

"This is our last month," she says.

Perfect. Love is shutting down. Going broke.

Paper in hand, I go back to the apartment. The smarmy professionals in my zip code make fun of "trailer trash" because our median household income is $86,000 but 90 percent of us could fit our entire living quarters on the back of a flatbed truck. Our trailer parks are vertical, that's all. In the trailer parks of Biloxi or Birmingham, they fry up a nice cat for supper. In our trailer towers, we just order Chinese takeout.

The sidewalk talent. Has there ever been a greater moment in history to watch girls? We have all come to an agreement on the hair: keep it straight, clean, neat, shiny, somewhere between chin and shoulder length. The hair. You can see your reflection in it, and the chemicals make it so natural looking. But if the hair is small, the tops are smaller. Some sort of T-shirt and tank-top manifesto has been signed out there in girl-land. Now every top comes in the same size: not quite large enough. Combine that with the low-riding pants and every time they bend over it's showtime. It's the summer of ass cleavage, and any girl who elects full body coverage quickly starts to wonder if she looks like a first lady.

Then there's upstairs. So much on display, so little on offer. Check out the top floor on that girl, the pair of them harnessed, pulled up, pushed together, tightly sheathed—she has a *shelf*, in a scoop-neck—make that two-scoops-neck—T-shirt. Julia's weren't that big. Yeah. Who needs her?

Time to pull myself together. I've got a date tonight. With Liesl Lang, that slender blonde I met at a party in Park Slope. She's sexy, but when I took her to lunch a couple of times she wasn't exactly encouraging. She made me fight her for the check, and she didn't reach for it in super-slo-mo the way most girls do; she really wanted to pay her share. It could be that she has an overripe sense of fairness, though. This girl is so honest, she would never make use of the pictures, descriptions, and accounts of a game without the express written permission of Major League Baseball. I have decided to warm her up by taking her for a nice mid-priced dinner. My plan, of course, is to fill her with alcohol. This is partly for her, partly for me. Because I also need warming up, because basically without booze I have no personality.

Liesl and I have these conversations. I try to make her laugh and she doesn't. She just waits. So I try again. Then she doesn't laugh again. She has a serious life, a serious job. She works as the head paralegal for one of those wild-haired downtown public defenders who sign up for any cause, as long as it's lost. They defend guys who try to blow up buildings, guys who decide God wants them to clean out a passenger car of the 5:33 to Garden City, guys who burn down entire nightclubs because it seems easier than waiting around to kill the ex-girlfriend inside. I have a slight problem with public defenders: why do these people think they're so noble? The night I met her I asked, "Uh, aren't most of the people you defend guilty?" She said, "They all are." Then of course she gave me the standard everyone-has-a-right-to-a-lawyer line. Sure. I understand. But shitty people have a right to shitty lawyers. What attracts good people to saying, "Oh, you've got some glassy-eyed murderers who need help evading justice? I'm there!" The KKK has a right to hold their spring cotillion, but you don't see any bright-eyed young Bryn Mawr grads applying for jobs on their decorating committee.

And anyway, she's not Julia.

"So why don't you just move on?" Julia's sitting by the window, smoking. I even miss her smoking. How can I miss her smoking? It fouls the air. It makes my eyes water. If she farted, would I be hiking through the Rockies and go, "Ah, the mountain breeze is nice, but not half as sweet as Julia's farts"? If she jabbed me with a steak knife every night as I slept, would I caress the scars?

Yes and yes.

"You're smart," she says. "You have a good job."

"Yes," I say, "but who wants to date a pasty-faced leprechaun shaped like a bowling pin?"

"I think you're quite handsome," she says.

"See, that's why I can't get over you. Who talks like that? 'Quite handsome.' Everything you say sounds innocently endearing."

"Oh, come on. You've gone out with a lot of girls. You even went out with other girls while you and I were, um, hanging out."

I never told her that last part, but Imaginary Julia knows everything about me. That way she can hurt me even more.

"That's true," I admit. Why not be honest when you're talking to yourself? "But it was only because I needed an air bag in case I crashed and burned with you."

See, then, I've scared her away again. Now I look at the window and all I see is the pane. Well, and the dirt on it.

I dial my friend Mike Vega, a guy who crossed over to the Other Side four years ago. Mike and I are friends because we once had a lot in common. We had lunch together every day at our Potomac high school, played soccer together, contributed shaky fiction to the school newspaper (my stories were about vampires, his about Euro-spies who seduced beautiful women). The intervening years, for him, have been the story of decreasing embarrassment about having money. Too late, I figured out that the rich are very, very different from you and me: they have more sex. The new Camaro that suddenly appeared in his driveway one senior day hosted more deflowerings than the bridal suite at beautiful Mount Airy Lodge. In those days he said he never thought of himself as rich—his parents had the money, you see, not him, all he had was the right to spend it—but money knowledge is in the genes and by the time we were twenty-six he had himself a law degree and a position at a top M and A firm. Now that he's happily ensconced with a wife, every day his little household corporation boasts a new acquistion—here a teak dining table or a digital TV, there a Tag Heuer, a Steinway, a Lexus. I keep wondering when he'll tell me I clash with his lifestyle and order me to get an MBA. Or at least take up golf.

He's not there. "Hi," he says on the machine. "We're at the hospi-tal having a baby, so we'll get back to you later."

Not that I have some sort of aching primal-chick need to have a baby or anything, but I do get the sense that Mike is accomplishing more than I am today. *Do something!*

So I flick on the TV. Bugs is in a wrestling match with this huge villain called the Crusher. The Crusher tries various ways to subdue Bugs (shooting himself out of a cannon—cannons are easily had in cartoons, there's always one in your hip pocket—or building a brick-and-mortar cube around his hand to slug Bugs with) and then decides to run him over with a train. So the Crusher ties up Bugs on some train tracks that have suddenly appeared in the wrestling ring and then goes off to conduct a train that apparently he keeps parked in the upper deck of the arena. The choo-choo starts up. The Bunny is scared. The Crusher is smiling maliciously. The choo-choo gathers steam. Bugs is really sweating bullets now. The Crusher can hardly contain his sadistic glee . . . then suddenly the film goes all wobbly and stops, as if it has come off the projector. Bugs walks onscreen, which is now merely a white background. He apologizes but says the film broke. He says he has no idea how it happened. Then, grinning rakishly, he brings out from behind his back a pair of scissors. Snip, snip.

Bugs is always doing pomo things like that. Not only does he have access to a limitless array of props, makeup, and costumes, but he also has this surreal godlike ability to simply step out of the situation and overrule everything that's happened. I'm kind of like Bugs. Bad things keep happening to me, mostly of my own doing, but I show no scars. I show up for work every day and go to parties most nights and I make conversation and trade remarks about characters in the popular culture. And, like Bugs, I am a permanent resident of the Valley of the Bachelors.

Can I just cut the film and start over please? This is not my life. It's just a rough draft. I'll get it right next time around.

The phone. It's Liesl. To cancel, no doubt. Girls can smell failure, even over the phone.

"I'm going uptown to see the Dance Theater of Harlem," she says in a cancellation tone.

"Uh-huh," I say.

"What time should we meet up, or?" she says hesitantly.

Betray no weakness. Cover up the stench. Rub on some broken-heart deodorant.

"Why don't you just stop by after the dance?"

Slick. Get her in the apartment.

I hold my breath as she makes pondering noises.

"Um," she says. "Okay."

Now relax. I practice the piano badly—really, it's a $99 electric Yamaha; Schroeder had a better piano—and then read without interest. I pick up the *New York Observer*. Throw away the articles. They're just the bread in the desperation sandwich. The meat is in the back pages. The small ads.

"Single white female, facial deformity, seeks man 29–40. 5'11" and above, in good shape."

This woman has a facial deformity, and I don't meet her height requirement. Us, afraid of commitment? Women can't commit to one drink with the greatest guy on earth if he's one inch shorter than they are. I read somewhere that Manhattan does not have the highest proportion of single people in America. We came in second. First place went to a county in Hawaii. Party town, USA? The place where moist young college grads come to celebrate panting youth? No: a former leper colony. Does Facial Deformity Woman place an ad, in, say, *Canker Sore Illustrated*? No. She picks the most upscale, Gucci-and-Harvard paper in the country for her personal ad, then she sits back thinking: *George Clooney will be calling any minute.*

Liesl buzzes me around five. I don't jump her, although she is sexy in a beige tank top with matching bra straps peeking out on the sides. And light makeup. This matters: it's a Sunday, and she's a feminist. Not a default feminist as in, "Well, I'm a woman so I guess I have to be one, don't I?" but a real one who writes angry letters to the *Times* to call attention to their insidious sexist language. This is the *New York Times* we're talking about, the paper that made "white male" a surprisingly effective insult.

I love the way she looks, all blue eyes, fair skin, medium-blond hair. She looks like the führer's wet dream, and why not? She's German. Half German, anyway. She was born here; her mother fled East Berlin in the fifties. I picture my friends—the Cohens and Rabinowitzes, the Meyers, the Shapiros, the Fleisch-, Good-, and Kuntzmans—freaking when they meet her.

"I like your place," she says, looking around as though she's thinking of renting it. "Oh, my. Those, *flow*ers," she says. "Time to change them."

I look at the windowsill: oh yeah. The flowers. From The Dinner. They look like I feel.

I'm in the middle of watching a Brian Wilson special on TV. I start to tell her about it. Maybe she's a fan.

"And who is Brian Wilson?" she says.

Who is Brian Wilson? He only wrote "Good Vibrations," "Wouldn't It Be Nice," and "Don't Worry, Baby." I can see not knowing who Brian Wilson is if you also don't know who Mozart was. But this girl definitely knows who Mozart was. And she grew up in the time of Brian, not in eighteenth-century Austria.

It gets better: she hasn't even heard of "Caroline, No."

" 'Caroline Knows'?" she says. "I thought it was 'God Only Knows.' "

At times like this, I look to a higher power for guidance. Luckily I have His image on the wall: Bogart. The poster shows him sitting at a typewriter. Next to him stand two guys pointing guns at him. He ignores them and keeps typing. That picture says it all. The film was called *In a Lonely Place*. He plays a jaded writer, a guy so hard-boiled that he cracks jokes when he finds out a girl he knew slightly has been murdered. My favorite line is when his detective buddy tells him he has recently gotten married. Bogey just says, "Why?"

Not only was Bogart great for the part, but the girl who makes him fall in love and confront his emotions for the first time is played by this withering blonde, Gloria Grahame. She was clever and hard, a girl who could say it all with a cocked eyebrow or a flared nostril. Bergman in *Casablanca*? Please. A clinging bore who fawns over that twinkle-toes do-gooder Laszlo. Where's the mystery in her? Give me Gloria any day. In every movie you get the feeling that she could be capable of anything. And in real life she was: she married the guy who directed *In a Lonely Place*, that weirdo Nicholas Ray. Then dumped him. Then she *married his son* from an earlier marriage. Now that's a woman who knows how to hurt a guy. And make him beg for more. Because he knows it'll take him a lifetime to figure her out. You don't hang on to the crossword puzzle after you've finished it, do you?

What would Bogart do with Liesl? He'd take her out to a cool dive. A mildly pretentious Frenchy cafe, the kind that makes girls want to drink because it's such a European thing to do. Luckily there's one right in my neighborhood. It's one of the main reasons I picked this apartment: I've closed many a deal at Cafe Frog.

We get a table in the sunshine. I give her the old, "Do you want to get a bottle of wine?"

"No," she says.

I get a half bottle for me. She orders one beer, makes it last. That scotches my evening right there. Never hit on a woman who could pass a Breathalyzer.

Mmmm. Scotch.

She agrees to come back to the apartment afterward. My arsenal is prepared.

Weapon number one: my baby pictures. This a) humanizes me; b) makes me look sensitive; c) makes her think we would make beautiful babies (I was one, after all); and d) shows me at my best, since frankly I looked stellar at five, but rarely since. Who doesn't look good in baby pictures? Clear skin, matched outfits, induced jollity. Plus your unbroken heart is in mint condition. Your hairline hasn't begun its retreat and your gut has not yet made the acquaintance of Messrs. Anheuser and Busch. Baby pictures are the Doomsday Machine of getting play. Press the button, it's all over.

There are pictures of my parents at Niagara Falls for their honeymoon, pictures of me abusing the seams of various Little League outfits (Why were they always too small, year after year? Couldn't they have just given me the next year's uniform ahead of time?), pictures of me in a Bugs Bunny costume, pictures of me arm in arm with my best friend, Bucky, both of us in white T-shirts and navy camp shorts. It is always summer in these pictures, or a holiday. I spot a pattern. There were the Gosh-Darned Adorable Years (0–6) and the Really Quite Acceptably Kid-Looking Kid Years (6–11). Then there were the Wonder Years (11–32), as in, I wonder how two such foxy parents managed to produce such a chimp?

As I hand each picture to Liesl for adoration, I realize she is meticulously putting them in chronological order. She is not even issuing the requisite "Awww's." Come on: me in a Donald Duck hat, age six? Who could resist?

"Wait, wait," she says as I give her a picture of my dad and me at Disney World circa 1979. I've got on huge plastic glasses and an Electric Light Orchestra T-shirt.

Liesl looks at this one, flips it over, peers at the date, finds the exact right place for it in the stack. I'm tempted to shuffle the deck on her to see if it will make her cry.

I take the Beach Boys' *Greatest Hits* off the CD player (I played it with manboy sarcasm; it contains both "Caroline, No" and "God Only Knows," but Liesl didn't seem to notice my point) and unsheath weapon number two: Cowboy Junkies, *The Trinity Session.* In times like these I always choose *The Trinity Session.* This is guaranteed stuff. Over the years it's fifteen for fifteen in delivering at least a gropefest. Don't think I don't keep charts for these things.

"What's this?" Liesl asks.

"Cowboy Junkies," I say.

"Is that a joke?" she says.

"No," I say. "It's actually their name."

"Is there anything on TV?" she asks.

After we watch a sitcom about (hint, hint) horny girls in New York ("I didn't think it was very funny," she informs me), I fetch her a glass of water (isn't that supposed to come *after* the sex?).

But we talk and chat and then we chat and talk and ponder and talk serious stuff about the future when all I want to do is taste the inside of her mouth. I can't, because she's still holding the glass of water. She takes a sip, and then *keeps it in her hand.* Who does this? The coffee table is right there! She takes another sip, continues to clutch the glass. She does this until she drains the entire glass. Then, finally, anxiously (the half bottle of wine has worn off so I'm all antsy again), I lean in and give her—well, not much, because I pull back at the last second and give her what turns out to be a peck. A mom kiss. Short and not particularly sweet.

"Umm," she says.

Here it comes. The let's-be-friends speech. Or worse: the I-don't-feel-that-way-about-you speech.

"Yeah?" I say, trying to hit the mute button on my ringing desperation. God, I need to prove I can get over on someone.

"Nothing," she says. Girls are always saying, "Nothing," but it's always something.

"Come on," I coax. Why do they always make you beg for bad news?

"It's just . . ."

"Yeah?"

"Could you . . ."

Rub your back? Kiss your ear? Remove your bra?

"Yeah?"

"Could you walk me to the subway?"

It's ten o'clock. It's ten fucking o'clock.

Off to the subway. A couple more pecks, but then she gives me a nice, long, warm hug. What does that mean? Maybe she wants to get busy. Maybe she wants me to be her brother.

Five minutes later I'm watching Bugs again, but after a while I decide I've had enough of this nonproductive behavior for one weekend. I stand up straight. I turn out the lights and program the CD carousel to play *Murmur, Up,* "From the Edge of the Deep

Green Sea," "A Letter to Elise," and "Yellow." I sit back down. It takes me five glasses of Scotch to get through them all and then I stumble into the kitchen to drink five glasses of water to cheat the hangover gods and then the couch seems so warm and friendly and inviting and . . .

And when I walk in the lobby this morning, whose is the first face I see? Hers. Not dream her; for-real her. We still work together, after all. Did I not mention that? I rarely bump into her, though, since her desk is on the far wing of the building.

Today it's her first day in a new job. She's been promoted from sub-blue-collar-wage-tryout-level deputy assistant flunky to, like, Officially Sanctioned Big-Time Media Factotum.

I kid around with her. Badly.

"So!" I say nervously. "Nervous?"

"Not really," she says.

Why would she be? She faces a long day of fax retrieval. It's 9:37 A.M., and already I'm ass of the day.

"How was your weekend?" I say brightly as we get in the elevator for the long ride to forty-two.

"It was all right," she says guardedly, in a way that screams: *I made screaming hot monkey love with someone other than you for forty-eight damp hours.* "How was yours?"

Oof. Checkmate. How was my weekend? How was Hiroshima? Blood runs for my cheeks. I'm a redhead. There has never been a redheaded spy.

I respond with a sound, but I'm pretty sure it's not an actual word. The cartoon thought balloons over our heads:

ME: *"I wish you would never leave me."*

HER: *"I wish you would leave me alone."*

ME: *"I wish this elevator would go to Saturn."*

HER: *"I wish I could think of a plausible excuse to get off thirty-five floors early and wait for another elevator."*

We ride up in silence.

On the other hand: we're together!

We work at a tabloid. It's a real tabloidy tabloid. Unlike the *Daily News*, with its hurrah-for-immigrants charts, its isn't-that-nice stories about entrepreneurs peeling a living off the streets of what well-off people no longer feel comfortable calling the ghetto, we make no apologies. We don't send serious journalists out to cover the ghetto. We are the ghetto for serious journalists.

Our newspaper was founded on the reasoning that if it took ten billion years for man to crawl out of the muck, then he's overdue to be dunked back in it. Our home deliveries once increased 20 percent when we hatched a cross-promotion scheme that enabled us to be hidden inside the *Times* on people's doormats. The other papers don't respect us, possibly because of the name of the paper: it's called *Tabloid.* (Motto: "America's loudest newspaper.") Old folks understand what they're getting, wide-pantsed hipsters love the cheeky self-referentiality of it. Internally, we call it the comic: we work here so we can laugh at the world. Everyone has to believe in something, so we placed our faith in skepticism. We weren't the first to discover that the world is a toilet. We just give you something to read while you're sitting on it.

Three years ago I was the youngest hack on rewrite. The four of us were lashed to consecutive cubicles, a whole squadron of back-of-the-class smart-asses thrown together in the front row facing the Desk, within doughnut-flinging distance of Max, the screaming, insane city editor. Occasionally some aged hack would refer to "the rewrite pit," and though we were on the same elevation above sea level as everyone else, we loved to think of ourselves as a feared four-headed monster, waving our tentacles at our betters.

By unspoken rule, once settled for the day, rewrite doesn't leave the office. Rewrite doesn't do lunch or go to the gym or meet "sources" for drinks. Rewrite never knows how long it'll be at work; true soldiers of smudge never want to leave. Every day is spent abusing three drugs: caffeine, MSG, and information. Rewrite knows everything that happens before it's finished happening. You had to: a breathless reporter in the field could call in at any moment with a new bump on any story that ran in the paper in the last month—genocide in the Balkans, a hot-dog-eating contest in Coney Island—and you had to come up with the right questions to caulk up all the holes in time to write it up for edition. Rewrite studies every wire story, absorbs every TV news broadcast (not hard: they steal all their stories from us), gobbles up every newspaper.

Sucking in coffee, spitting out wisecracks, rising to every gruesome moment with hard-boiled nonchalance, we four deadline poets wrote pretty much the whole news hole. We worked strictly for our own amusement, the outside world's opinion mattering somewhere between diddly and squat. Max pushed our buttons—"Stir up a little outrage," he would order, his eyebrow cracking like a whip—and out came the headlines, backed up by the usual dubious quote-whore suspects ever ready to spew anger on demand. It isn't hard to find somebody who is famous, or has followers, or holds office, or used to hold office, or at very least has "association" on his letterhead and a membership of one or more—who is up for a nice game of controversy. Our Rolodexes burst with their names. We had their home numbers. We could find them on any weekend and any night. The numbers were our buckshot, which we would take into the forest and fire at the truth, hitting sometimes, missing most, but when you return for the evening with dinner for your tribe, no one asks you how many bullets you had to fire.

When things were breaking our way, Max, this anonymous figure, a guy whose face never turns up on TV shows or in syndicated columns, whose name doesn't appear in any paper, even ours, a guy who is no threat to be recognized at a soiree where people swarm around the fops who run *Forbes* or *Vanity Fair* (not that he even goes to those six-to-eighters in the first place; he's always at work till ten) was the most powerful journalist in America. And when he roared, the republic waved a hand in front of its face and wilted before his halitosis. Under his bidding we judged the judges, vetoed the politicians, and bounced the basketball coaches we didn't like. We were the double espresso to the heartbeat of the city, our gibes providing excellent graphics for TV news. Even the respectable press, too timid or too dull to marshal its own attacks and making everything look more complicated than it was, would wistfully issue reports of our crusades. To us they're just an empty canyon begging to be shouted into. It's our America now. When was the last time you saw the front page of the *New York Review of Books* on *World News Tonight*?

To rewrite, there is one unforgivable blunder—the one whispered about darkly in drowsy two A.M. heavy-news-day conversations when everyone's thoughts turn to the nearest drinkery; the one rewrite parents warn their rewritten children never to do: *Pull a Hymietown.* Hymietown is the word once used to describe our city by a major presidential candidate in the 1980s. The candidate casually dropped this municipal pet name into an interview with a *Washington Post* reporter who, confronted with the scoop of the year, the one that would reverse the tide of the presidential campaign and vaporize a figure who had a shot at the top, promptly buried it in the thirty-seventh paragraph of the interview. Since no one outside the journalism industry has ever read to the thirty-seventh paragraph of any newspaper story (ours never run more than one-fourth that length), the remark would have had the shelf life of a banana if *Tabloid*'s zombie-eyed rewrite man, a night prowler skulking in the graveyards of words, hadn't scoured every sentence of the *Washington Post* wire at one A.M and plucked out the one noun that mattered in a two-thousand-word story. As though he'd found a wounded bird in a trampled nest, he gave it the care and nurturing it deserved by resettling it in the hot incubator light of our page one. So ended the candidate's chances of winning the New York state primary. To this day, J schools will teach you that the *Post* broke the Hymietown story. Yeah, they broke it. We fixed it.

When the outside world was behaving too well, we got bored and gave the rewrite treatment to everything that was happening at the comic. You could fill another newspaper with our staff vendettas and petty crime, with the intraoffice exclusives we broke by reading the editorial lips that flapped behind silent glass walls or by liberating confidential memos from the trash. Since all of our training worked to shorten the time between discovering and telling, none of us ever tried to keep a secret; no news is bad news. We gave long shrift to all of the pressing questions. Who got fired? Who got divorced? Who got pregnant? Rewrite knows, and rewrite tells. When dish is gold, you get extra points for feeding the needy with gossip, so those colleagues who lived their lives in technicolor were objects of awe. The newsroom never disappointed. It's a Louvre of eccentricity and turpitude. Behavior that might be frowned upon at other major international corporations (or so I've heard; I've never worked anywhere else), was lustily cheered on rewrite: excessive drinking, getting arrested, or being discovered in compromising circumstances with a person not your spouse—or, ideally, all three— made you a hero for months, inched you closer to the ultimate accolade: the title of *legend,* which upon being earned would invariably accompany your name whenever one of your colleagues, fellow tribesmen, introduced you in a bar.

It was combat. Behold our names; we even sound like cannon fodder in a World War II movie: Rosen, Burke, Feldman, and Farrell. The women, Rita Rosen and Liz Burke, are still there, returning to work every day the way Nicole kept going back to O.J. Feldman responded to twelve years of Max's lash by throwing his computer through a window. After that no one would hire him except *US* magazine. I ducked the shells of three deadlines a day until they started a Sunday edition. Somebody had to become weekend features editor. My hand was the first one up.

There was no increase in salary, but I gladly accepted a 10 percent cut in my pulse. Now I edit the movie reviews on Friday, the starlet interviews and hot-bars blurbs for Saturday, the best-in-town stuff for Sunday. At the time I thought, This is success. I felt it important to succeed for the same reason everyone does: because I secretly hoped to be able to lord it over my classmates at some imagined high school reunion. But it's been a couple of years since I was last called an up-and-comer, and at some point even wonder boys awaken to discover they've become middle management.

I've made the stuff so light that the ink nearly floats off the newsprint; mine are the pages that don't slam or rock or ooze or indict; the stuff, in other words, that we can close four days in advance to make our production schedule. If I come up with something too newsy, it gets taken away from me and put in the daily paper. Which creates a hole in the Sunday paper that I will then have to scramble to fill with something commissioned on the fly. My job therefore is: don't do your job too well, and mediocrity is my middle name. Ten best places in the city to get your nails done? We did that one last month. Also in November, January, and April.

Tabloid's frosted gray 1940s-style-private-eye glass doors—even our entrance is hard-boiled—open into the city room. Under the all-night bug-zapping fluorescent burn, tough guys and the women who don't mind them make dirty jokes, yell insults at each other, cluster in front of TVs. Wastebaskets overflow, the smell of fried food clouds the air, phones ring, empty pizza boxes form unstable skyscrapers. Add a couple of bongs and it could be Delta House at any state U.

At the bank of TVs by the window a guy dressed entirely in mail-order casual clothing is watching New York 1 news. He is my rarely sighted archfoe Eli Knecht. At one time he was my archfriend, a fellow drinkslayer whose stucco complexion, unpressed 60/40 shirts, and inner-tube waistline, I thought, provided a constant subliminal reminder to women that they could wind up with someone even less attractive than me. Eli grew up in a small town in upstate New York hungering for big-city hackdom, skyscrapers glinting in his irises, his broad-beam forehead aching to butt down doors. All he ever wanted was the honor of a cheap suit. Not only couldn't he wait to grow up, he couldn't wait to grow *old*, to own the weary staff of knowledge so he could club people with it. The guy is my age yet his conversations are full of casual references to dead mayors, ancient work stoppages, forgotten scandals. Rewrite has long whispered that he is bald as a friar on purpose, to live up to the look of someone old enough to remember the 1965 mayoral race. Now Eli is our third-string City Hall reporter, devouring every zoning decision and PAC donation so he can prove without a doubt that rich people have more political influence.

When I started, he introduced me to the street. Unlike a lot of reporters, he was generous with his knowledge and taught me a few things when, years ago, I took my first trembling steps onto the long carpets of broken glass that invariably mark a neighborhood where crime is the leading industry. Eli knows more tricks than a forty-dollar hooker: always carry a pencil because pens always explode, run out of ink, or freeze; don't bother with a tape recorder because then you'll spend half your day transcribing (a suggestion seconded by our lawyers—who can prove you misquoted someone unless there's a tape?); and keep your press pass in your pocket, not dangling around your neck, unless you want to spend the afternoon parked behind a sawhorse with the I-got-a-journalism-degree pretend reporters in a designated "media courtesy area" half a block from the cooling corpse getting tucked under the covers while stealthier journos posing as real people who just happen to live in the building glide in unnoticed and get the story.

For years we used to go to South together for pitchers and peanuts, him and me and Hillary from the editorial page, a girl whose hotitude was so off the charts that there would have been as little point in flirting with her as there would have been in showing up at Yankee Stadium with glove and cleats, saying, "Hi, mind if I try out for first base?" I once saw her walk by a construction site on Broadway. The hard hats didn't whistle. They didn't shout dirty words. Instead, moving as one man, they stood and bowed their heads. Besides which, there was the matter of the hardware she lugged around on the third finger of her left hand. I got to thinking of her as one of the guys, albeit the only one I often pictured dressed only in Reddi-wip, and so we'd all drift over after work to take turns shooting pool or trying to belch "Hotel California" (she once made it all the way to "warm smell of colitas"). Rewrite would joke about our little ménage à trois, but suddenly there was only one of us and nobody was talking about my ménage à un. You know you're pathetic when even rewrite orders a cease-fire.

Now Eli's in the Zone with Hillary. I confronted him about it one night. They had been making cute little call-me-later gestures at each other across the newsroom as I was stuffing my backpack with stolen office supplies, and when I left, he and his gonna-get-some-tonight smirk followed me onto the elevator.

"You in the Zone?" I said.

"I may be. I may be in the Zone."

"When?" I said.

"Could be a year, could be more."

"You know this?"

"She's dropping hints. Let's just say we've started making trips to Bed Bath and Beyond."

Fucker. "Nice," I said. He'll never invite me to the wedding, which sucks because I want to make a big thing out of not going.

"Yep," he said.

"And the other guy?" I said.

"Oh, *him*," he said. "Never existed. She had to wear an engagement ring to keep *lo*sers from hitting on her. It was made of *glass*, Tom, didn't you notice?"

Fuck. Checkmated by my jewelry ignorance.

I couldn't bear to deal with him after that. It was like he graduated, went to Harvard, and left me behind in kindergarten, eating paste. Today I just give him a nod.

"Hey, Ignatz," I say. For some reason neither of us can remember, I always call him Ignatz.

"Hey, Pappy," Eli says, his go-to-hell tie slung completely unknotted around his neck like a flying ace's scarf. For some reason neither of us can remember, he always calls me Pappy.

I slither off down cubicle way, passing two side streets of gray sound-deadening uprights and the interior fishbowl offices reserved for the muckety-mucks. My house is right where I left it, at the corner of Jaded and Cranky.

Another day in my cave, my cube: ten years in the business and I have never had an office. Sitting on my chair where I specifically ask the copykids not to place them—those unsightly black ass stains—is the usual heap of today's papers.

Hit the button and the computer starts humming. This is what I do: I spend my life at three keyboards. One I play pretty well. I slouch in front of it with a beverage and words come out of me, often before I have even thought them.

One I'm still studying. It has about eighty-eight keys. You have to learn how to push this and hold that, execute complex tasks with one hand while the other is doing completely different things in an entirely different area. And through it all, you have to stay in rhythm and listen for the climactic moment.

The third one is the piano.

I start to type. Type, type. Today I'm doing headlines. The heds. Screamers. They're meant to scare you and make you laugh at the same time. Kind of like Mike Tyson. And like Mike, we enjoy duking it out with the mighty, but sometimes we're just as happy to gnaw on somebody's ankle.

There's a story about the sexploits of Tommy Lee and his former bandmates: "COCK-A-DOODLE CRÜE," I type.

Here's one about the future of topless bars: "THE STRIPPING NEWS." Writes itself.

We're doing another piece on *The Producers* hype. It's the biggest smash on Broadway. You can't go wrong with Nazis in dresses. We've already done six feature articles on it. This one is about the costume designer. "STURM UND DRAG," I write.

A new offshoot of Judaism that attracts lots of young professionals back to temple. "SECTS AND THE CITY," of course.

And the one from our Hollywood stringer, who has seen and enjoyed an early cut of *Jurassic Park III*. Well, not enjoyed, exactly. His words to me on the phone were, "It sucks less cock than you would expect, considering Spielberg didn't direct it." I rewrite the story to make it more enthusiastic, for one reason: I've always wanted an excuse to use the hed, "IS IT GOOD? YOU BET JURASSIC."

I'm good at this job. Yes, I am the one who imported "Wacko Jacko" from the British press. And I was the first headline writer ever to describe Hugh Grant as "overblown." I still remember with pride the time I saw a pretty young thing with that page of the newspaper on West Eighty-second. She was using it to pick up her Airedale's giant Mississippi mud pies. You can't say I'm not a man of strong words. Absorbent ones too.

At five-thirty a gentleman wobbles up to my desk looking like the world's best-dressed derelict, an apparition held together by hairspray and gin. His chalk-striped double breasted is about a hundred years out of style and it hangs on him like a bedsheet on a hat rack. His skin is parchment. You could open an envelope on his cheekbones, or on the silver prow of his proud pompadour. If he showed up at a wake, people would tell him to get back in the coffin. There are only two jobs this guy could do: vampire, or journalist.

"How are you, mate? Name's Rollo," he says, proffering a talcumed pink claw.

"Tom," I say, adding, for old time's sake, "we've known each other for three years."

He puts both hands on the edge of my cubicle and hangs on, doing what appear to be involuntary deep-knee bends, absorbing this new information, looking for his sea legs. His faraway eyes whir into focus. His wedding ring is like a hula hoop rattling around his skeleton finger.

"And your position here, lad?"

"I'm your editor," I tell him.

London grown, Sydney reared, Rollo Thrash is the Obi-Wan of hacks, chief revenue stream for Elaine's and Langan's, foremost defender of the voodoo tabloid faith in an age when journalism has started to act like a kid born in a whorehouse who grows up to preach chastity and temperance. He could drink you under the table, through the floorboards, and into the basement, where he would call down to prompt you to stop mucking about and fetch him up another case. No one has ever seen him eat.

Best Rollo story—and the best ones don't even come from Rollo, they have to stew in Langan's for a while, slow-cooking in entirely implausible detail—is the one about how he's in Hong Kong, sent up from one of the Sydney rags to cover some Sino-Australian dissident who, after his imprisonment on ludicrous charges caused a diplomatic uproar, is finally being released. This is when it was impossible to get a visa into China. So they let the prisoner out at the China–Hong Kong border. He walks across the border. Up pulls a black stretch, tinted windows, uniformed personnel at the wheel, security guards with hip holsters, Australian flags on the buffed fenders, the works. The dissident waves good-bye to the brownsuits, so long, suckers, gets into the car. Car drives away. Ten minutes later the real Australian ambassador shows up with a confused map-wielding driver and a battered Mercedes, asks the People's Liberation Army where the dissident went. The soldiers shrug. Not our problem anymore. Meanwhile, in the black stretch, which Rollo has rented and decked out for the day, Rollo is not only getting the exclusive interview, he's whisking the guy away to hide out in a luxury Kowloon hotel under a false name so none of the other hacks will be able to find him, at least not until after edition.

"Tom," he says now. "Not much of a word picture. Where's the sting of poetry, the glow of fire? What word will conjure the man before me: the hang of the face, the lie of its aspirations? We stand confronted by a categorical imperative—the indispensability of a nickname," he says, in a more-in-sorrow-than-in-anger sort of way.

When the drink is on him, he begins to declaim voluptuously. Among the nicknames he's already given me: Peabo, Sly, T-bag, Piss

Boy, Atomic (as in Atomic Bomb: rhymes with Tom), and the most enduring, Frogfucker, in kind remembrance of a well-shod Parisienne I dizzily pursued with Brie and Beaujolais. But not only did I not sleep with her, I never even kissed her in her national manner.

"How about the Duke?" I say.

"Not a chance," he says, rapping his ring on the metal top of my cube fence.

"Kong?" I say. "Bogie?"

"The boy who never grew up, who was it?" he says. He speaks loudly, possibly to drown out the volume of his tie.

"Michael Jackson?" I say.

He lowers his forehead and, astonishingly, for a face that already bears a line for every pub between here and Sydney, manages to create even more furrows. I swear I hear a faint crinkling, like someone opening a bag of potato chips down the hall. His brain begins to work.

"Peter Pan. Cathy Rigby. Eleanor Rigby. Paul McCartney. That's it," he says. "From now on, you're Ringo."

"Ringo?" I say.

"That'll do nicely."

"Did you write that movie review you owe me?" I say, thinking, I could write movie reviews. When people ask me what I want to be when I grow up (and they still do: that uncooked manboy quality), I always say, "You mean besides write movie reviews?" I mean really, what could be better? The movie critic is the superstar, the one who gets the giant photo next to his byline and the most-expenses-paid trips to Sundance and Cannes and Telluride; the one who sees his name in the newspaper ads an inch high, the one who doesn't have to come into the office even though, at the office, he *has an office*, a refuge, a soundproof shelter from the shouty people who stalk the forty-second floor. Rollo has worked for various newspapers associated with this company for forty years. With a suit his only equipment, he has sauntered into the midst of assassinations, invasions, and

atrocities on four continents, always bellying up to the abyss, ordering a shot and a lager and telling a dirty story until the abyss snorts
seltzer out its nose. On countless occasions he has written the first, or
incorrect, draft of history. To me, he's a superhero. Like 007, he can
breaststroke his way through a river of fire, shuck off his wet suit, and
emerge in black tie, ready to command a waiter or unzip a little black
dress. Today, in his dotage, he has elected to put his camouflage
fatigues in storage and decorate our pages as our senior film critic.

Rollo's reviews. Dire communiqués about the undoing of the
American moral fabric, phoned in from a bar stool by a degenerate
Aussie hack. I wring the gin out of the clauses, make his woozy sentences sit up straight before a pot of coffee. Then I use the result as
a rough draft, which I completely rewrite. To a well-lubed Rollo,
every politician is a mountebank, every fib a rodomontade, every
crook a desperado. Sometimes I leave in the whoop-de-doo and
brimstone, but other times I have to tweeze away words unknown to
my readers, or to Webster. I cultivate few standards as an editor—it
keeps my life simple—but I try to avoid printing words not actually
in the English language. "Sperd"? "Pring"? "Whinge," it turned out
in a bet I once lost, is a word—it means "whine," but only to those
kidney eaters across the pond.

His talent for uttering truth and falsehood with equal, swagger-
ing omniscience turned out to be a useful trait for a critic, and he is
today a figure of renewed renown. The fifteen-year-old photo byline
has freshened his face, which seems to be aging in reverse to catch
up; reality, after all, is always trying to catch up to tabloids. He's
become a starlet himself; I'm just the schlub who holds his coat
while he waves to the cameras. Occasionally I'll spot his name on a
movie poster adhering to some bus shelter or video-store window
and cringe when I notice that the words between the quotation
marks are my own.

"Film review? It's done, Rimbo."

"I asked you to rewrite it a bit, though, remember? You just gave me seven hundred and fifty words on Reese Witherspoon's mouth."

"Right, Limbo, right," he says. "Forgot her tits." And he walks away choosing his steps, like a poodle on a patch of ice. He's not heading for his office, the one whose floor-to-ceiling windows are papered with randomly spelled lunatic-sent hate mail (so displayed to make us jealous, and also to provide emergency napping cover). He's going out the way he came in.

"Can I reach you at Langan's?" I say.

He shows me the back of one balsa-wood hand.

I'm shutting down my computer for the day when the Toad's crazy white Einstein hair appears over the superwide central cubicle surrounding the Desk. His giant golden wire-rims—never in style, not even in Europe, not even ironically—are the size of hubcaps, giving an outline of craziness to eyes aflame with sarcasm, eyes of Aqua Velva blue. His tie looks like a specimen slide for Fu Ying Chef Special Lunch Platters 1–8. He bobs like a prizefighter, or a peg-legged pirate, due to some ancient botched surgery that requires him to wear orthopedic, stupendously uncool sneakers. He parks his collegiate nylon book bag and comes shambling this way. Lucky me: he always stops by on the way to the bathroom, radiating cheerful cynicism.

"Hi, Tom," he says. Shuffle, shuffle. "You look like shit." His voice is like a taxi honking in crosstown traffic. His breath is like a spritz of Mace.

"Yeah?" I say. "What are you? The Sexiest Man Alive?"

"Seriously, though," he says. "Did you spend the weekend in jail or something?"

I think of my maximum-insecurity facility, the solitary confinement, the bad food, the lack of exercise and fresh air. Throw in a few butt rapes and some pontificating about racism, and I've built my own personal *Oz*.

"Kind of," I say.

Irving T. Fox, deputy city editor, is a sixty-year-old Jewish man with three cats, two ex-wives, and no TV. He is my best friend at this newspaper. Rewrite started calling him the Toad because of his quick tongue. That's what we tell him, anyway. It's really because he has buggy eyes set on either side of his wide warty head.

"So what're you working on?"

"Need a hed for this thing on celebrity stalkers. I'm thinking, why do it from the perspective of the celeb?"

"So do it from a worm's-eye view?" he says. "Perfect. Our readers will identify." He doesn't have to mention the old joke about why Macy's won't advertise in our paper: supposedly the chairman of the store told our publisher, "Your readers are our shoplifters."

"So what do you think of 'Stalk This Way'?"

"They'll never go for it," he says. Although we have the honor of being the most-sued daily newspaper in these United States, we do have a staff of libel lawyers reading everything we say. Otherwise we'd really have some fun. A headline that is seen as encouraging crimes against celebrities is likely to get ICM's shysters on the phone toot sweet.

"The best ones never make it," he says with a dreamy look in his eyes, as if he's remembering being married to Marilyn Monroe or something. "One time there was this guy who was arrested for killing stray cats. He was gassing them to death in his oven." Irv's empathy for soft whiskery pals is his known weakness, which is why rewrite is constantly lobbing dead-cat jokes at him.

"Horrible person," he continues. "So for a hed I wrote, 'Meow-schwitz.' They wouldn't run it," he says. Still smarting.

"You told me that before," I say. "Wasn't that, like, fifteen years ago?"

"Or the time that violinist for the New York Philharmonic got killed? By that psycho who took her up to the roof of the Met and pushed her off?"

"I know," I say. " 'Fiddler off the Roof.' "

"Hey, wanna join our shortest-joke-in-the-world game? The copy desk started it. I'm winning."

"With what?"

"Italian army. Eleven letters."

"Good one," I say. "Hmm. Nazi disco. Nine letters."

Hillary comes by to give the Toad some faxes. Even among six-foot Swedish/Dutch blondes with impossible bodies, she looks good.

"Hey, Hillary, want to play shortest joke in the world?" the Toad says. "I got one. Gay porn. Seven."

"Perot," I say. "Five."

"Zima," says the Toad. "Four."

"XFL," I say. "Three."

Hillary looks at us as if we're idiots, and promptly beats us both. "L.A.," she says, and we are forced to concede victory.

From the Desk comes the usual deadline mayhem. Max, the city editor, and the big-boss editor, Cronin, who reacts to him the way orange juice reacts to your mouth after you've brushed your teeth, are inviting each other to perform anatomically unlikely feats. Cronin's the editor in chief. The guy whose job Max wants. The guy known to rewrite as Cronie because he's palled around with Tyrone Rutledge-Swope, our ruthless, hedgehoglike Aussie owner, since both were on their first newspaper. By the windows, weeping pitifully, slouches one of the interns, a twenty-one-year-old Wellesley girl whose Scarsdalian mother, Max is just discovering, has forbidden her from doing any journalism requiring her presence in our northern sister borough, the Bronx. Rewrite says Wellesley's mother is one of Cronin's mistresses, though, which is why we're stuck with her. Someone ducks out of the way of an airborne phone, which lands with a splitty sound on a radiator.

"You've worked at this paper for twenty-five years," I say to the Toad. "How?"

"Dja ever read *I, Claudius*?" the Toad says.

"No," I say. I thought about renting the videos once, but I went with a Bill Murray movie instead.

"After all the emperors of Rome scheme and stab and poison each other, who's left to rule the civilized world?" he says.

"Who?" I say.

"The guy who drools on himself," he says. And he goes lurching off to the bathroom like a cowboy in snowshoes, one shirttail slow-leaking out of his Wranglers.

*G*et off the train at Broadway and Fiftieth. Right outside the entrace, at one of the busiest intersections in the city, is stationed the beggar Nazi. He's like an armored personnel carrier, with a long line of big ugly metal newspaper boxes chained together guarding his right flank. His dirty camouflage-patterned pants scream *Vietnam veteran* or, more likely, given that the war ended twenty-six years ago and he appears to be no more than forty, *Army-Navy shopper*. Like every good Nazi, he even has a German shepherd (ABUSED PUPPY, reads a calculatedly unverifiable handwritten sign). He has made it impossible to pass without a lengthy detour. So we have to go right into the maw of his mechanized begging, right by the sawn-in-half Tide bottle filling with coins, which he shakes like a grubby maraca. In the fifty seconds I wait for the light to change, I see people give him about seventy-five cents. That's ninety cents a minute. Times eight hours. The guy is making four hundred dollars a day, tax free. Sometimes he decides to cross the street for a cup of Dunkin' Donuts coffee. To minimize his time off the clock, he doesn't bother to pretend his legs don't work at these moments; he zips along in a sort of seated run, pushing off with his feet while he hangs on to the leash with both hands. Mush. The dog bolts through the crowd of speed-walking office drones. Only by skipping sideways do I avoid unsightly tire tracks on the back of my shirt. But I don't let him get away with it. I shoot him a really nasty glare after he passes by. People ahead of me scatter as the guy thunders through like a sawn-off Ben-Hur. They turn around angrily and see: a guy in a wheelchair. They're so ashamed of this feeling that they resolve to vote themselves another tax increase the next chance they get.

I arrive at work feeling mean. Meaner than Saddam, meaner than Stalin, meaner than a French waiter. Get in the elevator. A familiar crone with a bald spot and a cloud of Eau de Decay perfume is the only other passenger. Is she a copy editor? A librarian? Someone I dated?

"Hi!" she says.

"How's it going?" I mutter.

"Pretty good!" she says.

And I can feel it coming. The weather conversation.

"Wasn't that a beautiful weekend?" she says.

A conversation is a workout, an exercise in discovering a topic that interests both of you. Weather is pretty much the broadest thing people can possibly have in common, isn't it? It's just one step removed from, "I've noticed we both live on planet Earth. Isn't it a great planet?" As for weekend nostalgia: it should expire by noon on Monday.

"Yeah," I say, ransacking my backpack for a magazine to occupy me for these final forty seconds.

"It was warm," she analyzes, "but it wasn't sticky at all!"

What do people in L.A. talk about in elevators? "I wonder if it will be seventy-five and sunny today?" Then again, to the kind of people who gave us the USA Network, this might qualify as snappy banter.

"Sure was!" I say, importantly flinging open a leaflet from the Learning Annex someone (okay, a girl with smiley eyes and a white oxford shirt on which only three of the seven buttons were in active service) shoved into my starstruck hand at Eighty-sixth and Broadway. I smear a look of fascination on my face and pretend to read an article about male breast cancer.

Ding, says the elevator, and I'm free.

Another bright morning at the comic. Today's assignment: write a book review. That new John Adams book by David McCullough. As a critic I must remain scrupulously neutral, fair, unbiased. To keep my mind absolutely free of prejudice, I haven't read a word of it. Instead I'm reading NEXIS clips of all the other reviews. My review will therefore be a sort of metareview. A review of reviews. As we often say at the comic: "It's only a tabloid." I crack open the book at random:

> There was silence from the floor, until Oliver Ellsworth, considered an authority on the Constitution, rose to his feet. "I find, sir," he said, "it is evident and clear, sir, that whenever the Senate are to be there, sir, you must be at the head of them. But further, sir, I shall not pretend to say."

Yes, sir, it's a spine tingler. But I'm going to give it a good review. Everyone else has. Plus, no one's ever going to accuse you of not having read the book if your review is a valentine. A book like this has only one purpose: to give your dad on Father's Day. He'll smile ("My kid thinks I'm intelligent!"), you will smile ("I'm thoughtful and patriotic!"), Mom will smile ("It'll make a good coaster!"), and Simon & Schuster will be $35 richer.

The phone. It's my close personal adviser Shooter. There is no salutation. We join this rant already in progress.

"The problem with women," Shooter begins, "is they don't know what they want. Remember that Mormon guy?"

"Uh-huh," I say. Rarely do I require any other words in a conversation with Shooter.

"They sent him to prison for bigamy. Prison. For having ten wives. It's not illegal to have ten *girl*friends. It's not illegal to be married to one girl and fuck ten others. It's not illegal to fuck ten girls *in one night*. But if in addition to fucking them you actually agree to give them something in return? Make a solemn public vow to take care of them, feed them, listen to their problems, give them a place to live? *That's* illegal. Isn't women's big thing that we can't commit to even one girl? This guy is the Superman of commitment. So they chuck him in the joint. What kind of fucked society are we living in?"

"Uh-huh," I say. I remember one night Shooter and I were out having drinks with my friend Nick DePuy. Nick is smooth chested. He smiles while he's talking to you. He reads *Details*. Enough said. The next day Shooter asked me which side of the street Nick drives on. I spoke honestly: Nick is a guy who can't throw a spiral. Nick likes movies about gladiators. If he were any more gay, he'd have to marry Liza Minnelli. "Yeah, I figured," was what Shooter said at the time. "But you know what? I really respect that. Because I fucking *hate* women." That made me wonder: is success with women a direct result of not liking them? Because Shooter goes through girlfriends the way Richard Gere goes through gerbils. If you like a girl, what happens? You're nervous with her. Because you're worried she might not like you as much as you like her. She looks at your nervousness and she doesn't think, *Aw. So sweet. He likes me.* She thinks, *This guy has no confidence.* Why would I be confident with a girl I think is spectacular? I don't think I'm spectacular. Girls go for the cock-wagging oafs, the guys who speak loudly and carry a big prick, and then six months later it's "Why is he so selfish? Doesn't he care about *my* needs?" Girls, in other words, go for guys like Shooter, which is why he's my close personal adviser.

"Here's why this is a decadent society," Shooter says. "Manhattan today is the first advanced civilization to be completely controlled by women. What are you wearing?"

"Huh? Black pants. Gray shirt. Black shoes."

"Why?"

"I don't know. Trying to look somewhat cool."

"Exactly," Shooter says. "It's eighty-five degrees out, yet you think black is cool. Why is black cool? Because women think it hides their fat. To shave tonnage. So black becomes cool among women. And since cool is whatever women say is cool, you have to wear black—you have to dress like a woman!—to look cool."

It's been a long time since black became cool. Can you remember when it wasn't? I can't. Every season, black turns out to be the new black.

"Don't they dress to impress us?"

"In the eighties women wore shoulder pads," Shooter says. "Giant ones. Did you tell them it looked good? I didn't. No *guy* ever did. They don't care about us. They told each other it made their waists look smaller. In fact, their waists looked exactly the same and their shoulders looked like they were trying out as linebacker for the Pittsburgh Steelers."

"At least we have all the money," I say.

"That's just it! That's just it!" Shooter says. "Why do we have the money? Why do we work all day?"

"Tell it."

"So we can spend it on them! Walk by Saks Fifth Avenue in the middle of the day and what do you see?"

"Women. Buying fifteen-hundred-dollar handbags."

"So whose money are they spending? Can't be their own: if you can afford to drop fifteen bills on a Fendi bag, you'd have to work all day. No, women spend our cash. They have the fun. While they're out shopping and having lunch and seeing shows, we're invisible. In our offices. Selling stocks. Writing books. Designing buildings. Men are *dy*ing, you know. We kill ourselves. Women live *ten years* longer than men, did you know that? And still every newspaper and magazine runs a story every week about how women's health care is being neglected. They're beating us by ten and they're trying to run up the score! As we get crushed by the stress of our incredibly demanding jobs. We only work for one reason: to get laid. So we can fling woo at beautiful women. So we can say, Look, I can take you to any restaurant you want! Look, *I've sold my youth to Wall Street for bucks deluxe!* Look, I built this building *for you!* I went to war *for you!* Beautiful women don't need to have high-powered jobs. They don't need to do anything to get laid. All they need to do is show up and look good. So they have to get their hair done a lot. So what? Which is more fun, chatting with François at the beauty factory or being a corporate troll for the Man? They don't need their own money. If they get a job, they work in *pub*lishing. They teach *kinder*garten. If you see women actually working hard, being big-firm lawyers or something, they're either, a, too ugly to get a man, b, dykes, or c, just killing time until they marry a senior partner."

"When was the last time you worked?" I say, knowing the answer: 1991. Shooter's life is a riches-to-riches story. His father owns a big business. You have to take everything he says with a grain elevator of salt.

Shooter doesn't answer. Shooter is riffing.

"So every book that gets written, every movie that gets made, every rock band that rocks, it's all for some woman."

"What about girl groups?"

"There are about *five* of them. The only other girls in music are the singers. Why? Because the singer is the one everyone looks at. Girls want to look good. They don't want to slave away behind the drum kit. Some *guy* is back there. Trying to impress the girl with the mike. Everything we do, we do it for the women, and it still isn't enough."

"Uh-huh," I say.

"Murder!" he says.

"Yeah?"

"When *men* kill, they kill their wife or their girlfriend for leaving them. Or a liquor-store owner so they can get money to spend on some girl. Then they get the death penalty. When women kill, they kill their kids. They get three to five and a shrink."

"Maybe not in Texas."

"Now, I'm not saying murder is okay. But which is worse: killing some evil bitch because she fucked your best friend or a helpless little kid because he shit the bed?"

"Speaking of crap," I say. "Gotta edit some stories now."

"Oh, okay. What time is it?"

"About eleven."

"Whoa," Shooter says. "Been a long night."

I turn back to the review for a while. I get to the point where I want to quote something no one else has quoted, to prove I read a book I didn't read. So I flip around and discover this little tidbit: when John Adams was declaring revolution and all that in Philly, his wife, Abigail, was writing him from Boston, "in the new code of laws which I suppose it will be necessary for you to make, I desire you would remember the ladies, and be more favorable to them than your ancestors. Do not put such unlimited power into the hands of husbands."

Adams wrote back: "You are so saucy." He really did. He went on:

Depend on it, we know better than to repeal our masculine systems. Although they are in full force, you know they are little more than theory . . . in practice you know we are the subjects. We have only the name of masters, and rather than give up this, which would completely subject us to the despotism of the petticoat, I hope General Washington and all our brave heroes would fight.

So, 150 years before women *even had the right to vote*, the panty posse was running the show. Despotism of the petticoat? That's 1776-speak for *whipped*. And this is a president talking. A founding father. What chance do I have?

The phone.

"Tom?"

"Yeah," I say.

"We just had our baby on Saturday," says Mike Vega, my fertile friend. The proud papa. How come married guys are *proud* but single guys are *cocky*?

"Hey!" I say. Of course I know this already; his answering machine told me. Sound enthusiastic. Possibly he's mad at me for not calling to congratulate sooner. "Great! Nice! Um, beautiful!" I'm trying to think up superlatives, but really: "MAN, WOMAN BECOME PARENTS OF CHILD"? It's not much of a story, is it?

"What is, uh, it?"

"A girl. We're calling her Alexandra."

A girl a girl a girl. And an Alexandra: third baby I know named Alexander or Alexandra. I try to drill this information into my brain. I have noticed that people expect you to keep track of the genders of their offspring, information I have on several occasions been forced to punt around by asking dreamy-eyed couples, "So, how is your little, um, one?"

"How big?" I say. He tells me. And that's it. Those are the only questions I can think to ask about the situation. But I hear more. Details I don't want to know. Real horror-movie stuff, bodies splitting open, gushing fluids, eight and three-quarter hours of screaming agony. Childbirth sounds a lot like *Alien*. I'm invited to meet the kid today at lunchtime, though Mike will be at work.

That my friends are having kids makes me even more of a kid. With all the man-jam I've sent spiraling down my shower drain, I could start a sperm bank. A sperm Switzerland. Isn't this a bit childish of me? Shouldn't I be using those sperm for something? Shouldn't I have someone other than myself to worry about by this point in my life?

Not that I blame anyone but me. The reasons my last five relationships ended:

1. I acted like an asshole.
2. I acted like an asshole.
3. My UK work visa ran out and I had to move back to New York.
4. I acted like an asshole.
5. She acted like an asshole, but only after I tormented her for six months.

I miss them all, of course. Take last summer's girl, Maggie Kelly. Met her at someone's birthday party. She was adorable. Smart. Fun. Self-confident. Loved to laugh, eat, drink, screw. We went out to her mother's house on Memorial Day weekend. Dad wasn't there, having moved in with his new mistress in the city a couple of months prior. Looked like Mom was going to have to sell the house. It was a beautiful one. Immaculate maintenance, double-hung windows, extreme gardening, the works. Her kids were grown, she didn't have a job or any job skills. She was getting old and life was turning out to be a major bummer. She made us soup and we chatted for a while. I was on my best behavior, trying to be cheery. I nodded a lot. Complimented her cooking. Complimented her daughter. Asked about her garden. Didn't mention dad's mistress. In short, I scored the max. I was ideal.

Couple weeks later Maggie is giving me the rundown on her family's troubles.

"My sister didn't get that understudy part," she says.

Her big sister, Stephanie. Actress. Her claim to fame: she once auditioned for *The View*. She didn't get it. Scuttlebutt was that they were "going ethnic." She's cute, but not actress cute, and she's thirty-five. It would be rude of me to point out that no woman ever started suddenly getting prettier at that point.

"That's too bad," I say. "What's she doing now?"

"She's looking for a waitressing job," she says. "She's talking to a sushi place."

"How's your mom?" I say.

"Dad's being such a jerk," she says. "She's going to have to hire a lawyer."

I wait for a polite moment to get to the point.

"What did she say about me?"

"She said you seemed *sad*."

Sad. From a woman whose life was falling apart. Those three letters ricocheted around my brain for weeks. "Depressed" implies it's not your fault: those pesky chemical imbalances. "Sad" means, *Buddy, you're just not trying*. And after a while I made Maggie sad too.

Before Maggie there was my Besty. Besty who loved cats. Besty who got me interested in Audrey Hepburn movies. Besty who was so quick and lively and lovely and serene that I had to break up with her.

We'd make up fairy tales after sex.

"Tell me a story!" This from somewhere in the $139 futon that was my bed for three years.

"Once there was a fair princess named Besty," I began.

"Only fair?"

"Once there was a slightly above-average princess named Besty," I said. "Ow. And she was heralded throughout the land for her ability to fell evil beasts by poking them in the most sensitive part of their tummies."

"Did she have a boyfriend?"

"Her only boyfriend was a gecko lizard named Tom," I said. "Tom met her in the amphibian singles bar."

"Because she was used to dating guys who were basically reptiles."

"Exactly. And Tom the gecko told Besty, 'If you do tequila shots with me and give me a kiss, you will see a magical change come over me and also you will get a commemorative Jose Cuervo T-shirt.'"

"And did she?"

"She had a few shots to steel herself for the challenge."

"Did she kiss him?"

"She looked at him. She saw that he was a kind, quirky, friendly, harmless creature, and then she decided. She closed her eyes. She leaned over. And she asked the bartender for some more tequila."

"And then did she kiss him?"

"After enough liquor to knock down Robert Downey Jr., she finally puckered up."

"Did he turn into a handsome prince?"

"No, he turned into a gila monster. But she did get the T-shirt."

She moved even closer. We braided our arms and legs together.

"Hey," she said.

"What?"

"Nothin'."

"Oh."

A minute passed expectantly.

"Hey," she said.

"What?"

"Nothin'."

Uh-oh. Paging Mr. Sandman. Carry me away.

"Hey," she said.

"Yeah?"

Pause.

"I love you," she said.

Something twanged deep down within me and for a few seconds I forgot to breathe. I carefully considered the situation, ran through the options, weighed some choice responses, and then did what I always do when confronting difficult choices. Nothing. Good thing I wasn't Sophie in *Sophie's Choice*. Which kid should I save from Auschwitz? Mmm, let me see about that. Uh, yeah, I'll just weigh the pros and cons for a while, this one's health against that one's intelligence, this one's lovely personality against that one's essential courage. Oh, time's up? So you're taking them both? Whew, that's a relief.

Tick, tick, tick. I wanted to say something. But I didn't.

So I hugged her and kissed her for a while. Thinking, Maybe she'll forget about this awkward little moment?

With the next girlfriend, I won't be sad or weird or distant. I'll give her everything she wants and more. An emotional AmEx card. No preset intimacy limit.

But first I have to go celebrate a baby not my own.

Mike went back to work today, but Karin's still at New York Hospital. The thing is two days old; it looks like a rough draft of a human being. I am expected to say how cute it is, but I resolve to stay noncommittal on these things. Must keep my options open.

"Is it the cutest baby ever?"

These are the first words out of Karin's mouth. Her whole face is shiny, as if someone went over it with a belt sander and a coat of Turtle Wax. In the last two months of her pregnancy, she grew scarily large. She was getting worried too. You could tell. I said nothing, but privately I wondered if she was going to deliver a VW.

A grin is oozing all over Karin's face. Even her hair is smiling.

"Isn't she?" she prompts.

"I don't know. I'll just stroll over to the nursery and do some comparison shopping."

But I don't say that.

"Of course," I say.

"Great baby," I say.

"Good job. Uh, giving birth. And all," I say.

I'd always heard that parents undergo this weird brain rewiring that makes it impossible for them to think their baby is not the darlingest diaper filler that ever lived. I keep waiting for evidence to the contrary, but there is none. I have a lot of smart friends, investment bankers and doctors and so forth. Theoretically, they're smart enough to have figured out that just about half of all babies are below average. Yet to date I have never heard one new duh-duh or maw-maw say: "Don't you think our baby isn't as cute as most? Frankly, I'm disappointed with the outcome. Then again, look who I married."

I ask no questions about bodily functions, except, tentatively, "So, um, how was the, uh, labor, uh, thingy?" It seems impolite not to give her an opportunity to chat about what is, after all, the most memorable experience of her life, though it is completely without interest to me. It's the only question I ask on the subject. There is a reason: *I don't want to know.* Yet somehow in the next twenty minutes, just by being polite and nodding my uh-huhs, I will discover:

1. Karin had to have doctors cut a huge hole horizontally across her abdomen.

2. They then had to make another huge slice, this time vertically, in her womb.

3. She is currently being held together with *staples*.

4. She has not farted since the delivery, which apparently is a bad thing.

5. The baby's sole source of nourishment for the time being is whatever it sucks out of Karin's breasts.

"Do you want to hold the baby?" she says.

No. Why do women always ask this? Do they not realize that the feeling *they* get from holding *their* baby (i.e., unsurpassed joy, love, and pride at not having given the kid spina bifida or anything) is different from the feeling *I* get when holding *someone else's* baby (i.e., nothing). I like Electric Light Orchestra (still) but I never make anyone else listen to them.

"Yes," I say.

I'm holding the baby. I'm supporting its head and thinking that it's about the size of a loaf of bread. No wonder they say, "She's got a bun in the oven." Karin goes to the bathroom (is she just passing gas?), and when she's gone I surreptitiously feel around the kid's head looking for the soft spot. It feels pretty hard to me, though. I thought their heads were supposed to be like week-old bananas. Yet another letdown.

"What are you doing?" Karin is back. She has caught me groping madly around her newborn's skull.

"Uh, just, I don't know." *Change the subject. Punt!* "She's just so, uh, cuddly!"

"Talk to the baby!" she commands. "It's good for them!"

I picture the kid in eighteen years, getting the thin envelope from Stanford. Maybe even from SUNY Binghamton. Because I didn't develop her brain enough during the four minutes I spent silently with her when she was three days old.

"Uh," I say. "Hello, baby. You're really . . . small, there. How was the birth? Nice baby. Good to see you. Hope you're feeling well."

I make my apologies ("Stressed at work," I murmur, and what do you know! First time I've ever used this excuse on an infant) and make good my escape. I have to walk by Sloan-Kettering, the cancer hospital across the street. There's a homeless woman. Well, not homeless, exactly; she appears to be a permanent resident of a cement overhang, an alcove tenant. She's just lying there completely prone, facing the building. Her pants are pulled down so as to expose her mottled, bleu-cheesy haunches: kiss my ass, world. It must suck to be living outside a cancer hospital. Then again, better to be outside it than inside. On the street a woman walks by. She is missing her left arm. These are people who truly have cause to be miserable, and are they?

Well, yes, they certainly appear to be. I, on the other hand, have absolutely no reason whatsoever to be miserable. Yet I am. Which in turn makes me even more miserable. Plus now the misery comes with a little garnish of guilt too.

After work I get home feeling fat (I think I'm starting to get cellulite in my *chin*) and throw away everything bearing the evil names of Keebler and Hostess, not to mention that slut Little Debbie. I'm thinking about tomorrow. Julia's thing is tomorrow. She knows I want to go. I've hinted at it. (Example of my hinting: "Hey, can I go to your thing on the fourteenth?") But she hasn't mentioned it this week. Maybe she'll call. Probably she won't.

It's a Friday night, so I celebrate by turning on the baseball game. And a CD. Plus I open a window. I need noise to drown out the sound of my Julia thoughts. I am reminded of her, on occasion: every time the phone rings, every time the e-mail at work doinks, every time I hear a song she likes, every time I find myself sitting in front of the TV watching a movie we've talked about, and pretty much every other moment of every day.

As for the apartment, well. Normally it has a lived-in look. At the moment it has a died-in look. Some cleaning up is definitely in order. Luckily, it's a small place. Spraying everything in sight with foamy toxins and wiping them off again doesn't take as long as I'd feared. The lemony scent begins to waft, only somewhat gaggingly, through the apartment.

The phone. It's 8:55.

I flop sideways in my big leather armchair, slinging my legs over an arm. My stack of black plastic shines dustlessly. I issue a tentative hello. I hate it when I answer the phone with a big friendly voice and it's a telemarketer. Makes me feel so used.

"It's me," says the voice that I most, and least, want to hear.

Shit. It's Friday. She's caught me at home with nothing to do.

"How's it going?" I say.

"It's going okay..." she says. Many of her remarks end with ellipses. Julia is a big believer in words unspoken. Every conversation with her is like an Easter-egg hunt. Well, a Satanic Easter-egg hunt, in which you search wanly for an egg and find a rainbow-striped grenade.

"What are you up to?" I say, as I always do.

"Nothin'," she says, as she always does. "What are you up to?"

Now I run through the options silently.

1. The truth: I have been cleaning in a way that would startle and delight my mother. In fact, if my mother were here right now, we would have something to talk about for the first time since 1984.
2. A really weak, unprepared lie.

"Just, having some friends for dinner," I say. Yeah, Dinty Moore, Uncle Ben, and Sara Lee.

I inhale, preparing for follow-up questions.

"I was just wondering," she says, backing into the point as always.

And when she backs up, I'm always the guy standing behind the truck, looking the other way. Beep! Beep! Beep! "What are your plans for tomorrow?"

I exhale. Tomorrow is her thing. Her dance recital. She and the rest of her dance class, most of them little girls, are putting on an amateur performance at a junior high school in South Norwalk tomorrow night. Julia is going to perform in two of the pieces and she is so beautiful when she's just sitting around that I would give my left nut to see her dance. Well, I may need my left nut. My spleen, though. My pancreas. Any of the B-list organs.

But she's going to tell me: Please don't come.

She's going to tell me: Duane is going to be there. (And he's taller than you.)

She's going to tell me: Can't you see it's all over?

She's going to tell me: Quit hanging around me.

"I'd kind of like to see your dances," I say, exploratively.

"Are you sure?" she says.

"I think it might be fun," I say.

"But it's going to be so lame!" she protests.

"I don't believe that," I say. "I think it'll be lovely." Did I just say "lovely"? This girl gets me to say words like lovely.

"You're going to get all the way up here and think, 'I wasted a perfectly good Saturday afternoon.'"

There is no such thing as a perfect Saturday afternoon unless it involves her.

"I've got nothing better to do," I lie. I've already declined a christening and a wedding for this. Of course, I couldn't tell friends I've known for years that I was missing these once-in-a-lifetime events on the off chance that a girl I like might let me watch her dance in a linoleum-and-concrete auditorium. So I told everyone I couldn't go because my mother has an ovarian cyst. (Lesson one when lying: effort counts. Be so specific that you couldn't possibly be lying. Lesson two: choose a lie thesis that people don't want to discuss at great length.)

We discuss train schedules, rendezvous points. The trains back to the city don't run all night, so she tells me to bring an overnight bag. I can stay at her parents' place in a pinch.

"I'm kind of excited you're coming," she says.

Hmmmm.

"By the way," she adds. "Duane might be there . . ."

"Oh yes?" I say.

"Is that okay?" she says.

I chase the question with a grunt. Then I put down the phone and sit there listening to the evening's symphony of car alarms on West Eighty-third.

REWIND

But let's go back. To how we first got together. They weren't dates so much as doses. Powerful ones, unregulated by the FDA.

FIRST DOSE

I'm sitting at my cubicle at work in the bleak of February, a phone to my ear. Am I asking for trouble? No. I'm asking for General Tso's chicken. It's eight o'clock at night and I'm ordering my fourth meal of the day. On my desk: menus, mock-ups, magazines, and my size nine and a half Oxfords.

"And pork fried rice," I say. "How long?"

"Ten minute?" says the girl on the phone.

I hang up and go back to my editing chores. Just minding my own business. Actually, I'm minding the business of celebrities and criminals.

"Here's where Tom Farrell sits," says Hyman Katz, the world's oldest copyboy, a man so at home in himself, so dedicated to the 24/7 task of Hyman Katzness that he is referred to only by his full name: *HymanKatz*. For thirty years he has worked at this newspaper, delivering faxes and answering phones and—whatever they did in the old days, transcribing Morse code, stirring vats of ink—as well as schooling succeeding generations of copyboys and -girls in sophisticated metropolitan bitterness. Today he's with a new copygirl. She peels a fax off her stack and gives it to me.

I look up. She smiles. Her face hits me like a beauty bomb. My eyes are as big as a muppet's.

Then Hyman Katz leads her away.

Whoa.

The fax in my hand is my only connection to her.

HJB ASSOCIATES INC.
_____

To: Editor/Producer

From: Cheryl Wang, VP publicity, 525-9411.

FOR IMMEDIATE RELEASE

Randy announces search for most beautiful woman in the world 2001.

After that I don't see her in the office again. I don't know her name. I'm not even sure what department she works in. And if I see her again, what'll I say to her? "I'm Tom. And you're . . . incredible."

SECOND DOSE

A week later. It's Valentine's Day. I'm at Langan's after work with Bran Lowenstein, my default date for a couple of years. We know each other excessively well. Many times we've revealed intimate things about ourselves in long discussions that took place in bed at two A.M., except she was in her bed on West Eighty-seventh Street and I was in my bed on West Eighty-third.

Bran's eyes, her hair, and her sense of humor are equally black. The thing that makes you question her attractiveness at first is her nose, which I once playfully but not inaccurately referred to as a "beak." She did not react well. No matter how well calibrated her sense of humor, no girl can stand having any part of her body made fun of. Really. Even her feet. Girls think it's unattractive to be well endowed below the ankle. They're convinced guys sit around in bars saying, "That Rebecca Romijn, she's all right I *guess*, but I hear she wears size-eleven pumps." "Eww, no! I can't believe you said that, dude! I'll never look at her again! All that's left are her perfect face, hair, tits, belly, and ass!"

Bran's feet are gunboats, by the way. But as for her nose, after you've known her for a while, you realize it's her best feature. It makes me smile every time I see her. We meet up once in a while to attend movies—she makes a big feminist point of paying for every third one—and complain about our current boy/girlfriendlessness. I don't see her that much because a lot of the time she's on the road chasing a story. She's a producer on one of those prime-time newsmagazine shows, the ones that say frozen yogurt isn't really low fat or your can opener can kill you or whatnot.

Being with Bran is a free upgrade in my masculinity. It always gives me this feeling of being a wolf in wolf's clothing instead of a sheep in sheepish clothing. She's an inch taller than me, so she forces me to stand up straight. She thinks at least as fast as I do, so I have to pay attention. I saw this movie once where a kid with a deformed face stops in a fun house. The mirror that wildly distorts everyone else makes him look normal. Bran's my fun house.

"You look—" she says.

"Yes?"

"Like you actually thought about how you look," she says. "For once."

Bran doesn't carry a chip on her shoulder; she carries it in her hand, so she can jab you with it. I blame it on her name: Brandy, Brandy Lowenstein, maybe the only Jewish girl on Long Island with that particular handle. She has issues about this. When your parents name you after a beverage, people start to make assumptions. And brandy, as I never fail to remind her, is a Christian drink.

"Clothes look good on me," I say. "Not to brag, but I have the build of a professional athlete. A sumo wrestler."

My hair is long and wild, which gives me the quality of a rock and roller, or possibly a lone gunman. But I'm working it with the outfit: checked brown houndstooth jacket with taupe—"taupe," another term I picked up from girls, along with "sage" and "celadon"—shirt and solid tie of royal blue. Yes, I wear a jacket most of the time. Gives me the illusion of shoulders. Surgical shoulder implants: could be huge. I've got the cool black pants, the polished Kenneth Coles. At some point in my late twenties I discovered: whatever else we may have going for us, all guys are subject to immediate disqualification by reason of footwear.

"I can't believe I don't have a date," Bran says.

"I love you too," I say.

"What kind of date are you?" she says. "You didn't even embarrass me at work with a huge fucking bouquet."

"Maybe I'd send you flowers if you boinked me," I say.

"Maybe I'd boink you if you sent me flowers," she says.

"I guess we'll never know," I say.

"I hate Valentine's Day," she says.

"I love Valentine's Day," I say. A petite brunette elbows her way next to me at the bar. Gives me a shy smile. I have to admit that whenever I'm with a girl, my natural impulse is to check out all the other girls to see how mine matches up.

"Hello, gorgeous," I say, to piss off Bran. "Love the shoes." All girls believe that their shoes are great, but they're so unused to guys noticing the things they're most proud of that sometimes you can get a solid three minutes' conversation out of this line. Also, as a bonus, a lot of girls assume you're gay if you're scoping their footwear, so sometimes you can catch them off guard and wing your way into an in-depth conversation before they know what hit them. Fly under their gaydar.

Something in the little brunette's face switches on. She starts to say something, but Bran cuts her off.

"You're sick," she says with unneccessary volume.

My little brunette and her face move away.

"No really," I say. "Look around."

Little misery clots of single women are packing the place in co-supportive pairs and brave, nurturing triplets.

"At what?" she says.

"This bar," I say, "it's your normal wood-paneled sports-on-TV-over-the bar Irish joint. It doesn't have a 'look,' it doesn't have a 'vibe,' it doesn't have idiotic chung-a-chung-a-chung Euro-house trance music blaring over the stereo. This place is about alcohol and the men who love it. Yet even here there are many fabulous babes. On a normal night you never meet a great-looking girl who doesn't have a boyfriend. Tonight, though, all the women who don't have a boyfriend are thinking, I have to be strong! Someone take me away from my Kleenex and my *Pretty Woman* video! So they've all come out to play. Moreover, you know any woman you see tonight without a guy must be single, so you don't have to worry about wasting half an hour chatting up some honey before she drops the B-1 bomb on you."

"The B-1 bomb?" she says.

"The boyfriend bomb."

"Too bad you're stuck with me," she says.

"Maybe I'm stuck on you," I say.

"Oh stop," she says.

I'm not sure if I have a crush on Bran. Every time I serve up the possibility, I can't resist adding a side dish of sarcasm. What I do know is, when I'm out with Bran in a bar full of hungry-eyed women, girls look at us. They're thinking, He's already girl-approved. Certified pre-owned. Say there are five single girls in a bar and they meet five guys. Four of the guys are single. But the other one casually manages to convince everyone that he is dating a supermodel. All of the girls will fight over the guy dating the model.

That's when Laurel, a slightly nervous junior reporter from the City Desk, comes in munching her hair and glancing around.

"Hello," I say, leaning in with the obligatory welcome peck. I never know if I'm supposed to actually make contact and risk messing up their makeup. Or just be a total phony and whoosh by it. Then there's the whole saliva issue, plus which I'm drinking beer, which moistens my lips and could be misinterpreted as wayward spit. You really don't want the peck to lead to the wipe.

I introduce Bran to Laurel.

"Hi," Laurel says. And she turns to pluck someone out of the crowd behind her. "This is Julia."

That's when I notice the cutest little fax deliverer I've ever seen edging her way through the crowd at the bar. She looks excessively small, overwhelmed, bruised by the city.

"I'm Tom," I say, as though I've never noticed her before, and our dippy little handshake is the first time I ever touch her. When did it begin, this handshaking with women? Do I go with the firm manly handshake the way I would with a guy and risk crushing their unsuspecting little sparrow bones? Or give them the soft touch and permanently burn the word "wuss" into the backs of their brains? Let's face it, nothing's simple when it comes to women.

Julia says nothing. Bran and Laurel immediately begin commiserating about Valentine's Day. Laurel is killing time before she's supposed to meet her boyfriend, who despite having dated her for a year, didn't send her flowers today. The message couldn't be clearer if he had taken a long lease on some outdoor advertising: he isn't going to marry her. Laurel and Bran launch a lengthy school-of-Athens style debate on the subject. Every time they get too close to the obvious lesson, they shy away from it. Instead, they conclude that Laurel's best strategy is to guilt him into giving her some expensive gift. That way she can have a pleasing symbol of the feelings that he plainly does not have. Which will be suitable for ironically hurling in his face the day she finally goads him into breaking up with her.

"But maybe I'm just fooling myself," Laurel says.

"He sounds like one of those worthless daydreamers who has absolutely no ambition," says Bran. "Oh! Sorry, Tom."

I'm not listening. I sip my half pint of John Courage and take a big swig of Julia. She's a merciless sight. Her skin is a Bain de Soleil ad. It looks as if it's been given a light rubdown by the Mediterranean sun every morning. Her lips are like the first bottle of wine you ever got drunk on. Her ash-blond hair falls expensively to her shoulders, dips ruthlessly over her eyes like a river of lust. I want to bathe in her hair. And those green eyes, as warm as a Christmas Eve fireplace, with dark accents in the hollows around them. They're soft needy poet's eyes, patient quiet eyes, the eyes of slight but perpetual disillusionment, eyes that say, *Sometimes I like to be hurt.* They've got real eyebrows above them, not those absurd penciled parentheses of the ritually overplucked. I don't think she's wearing any makeup except lipstick. The point of makeup is to look the way she does without it.

But after a while the evening turns strange, crazy patterns form. Laurel just leaves. Goes to hunt down her BF. And Bran, proclaiming that there is no potential BF for her in the bar, begins to make noises about going home to watch the *Pretty Woman* marathon on cable, so I walk her to a cab. All these fabulous babes and I'm no one's BF. I haven't had a BJ since B.C.

Then an even stranger thing happens: Julia, that darling little critter, lingers. What are the odds on that? Then again, what are the odds of three unrelated Taylors all winding up in Duran Duran?

"Can I buy you a drink?" I say, stupidly. I am the kind of guy who never says, "Can I buy you a drink?" I sound like a Martini & Rossi commercial from 1979.

But she says a beautiful thing.

"Yes," she says. It's the first word she ever says to me.

"I think I'll have a gin and tonic," she says, but she doesn't take off her darling little yellow overcoat. "Darling"? Did I just say darling?

While I get the beverages, some barfly is chatting me up.

"You look like a writer or somethin'," says the guy, who looks like every guy I've ever met from Long Island except he's approximately two-thirds the size. "Sophisticated, right?"

"My socks match," I say.

"You probably know all that stuff about similes and metaphors, right?"

"Sort of," I say.

"So what's a metaphor, when you compare something using like or as, right?"

"That's a simile," Julia and I say together, and we share a smile. I am endlessly impressed by a girl who knows grammar.

A thought: maybe I can keep her smiling. And by talking to this guy instead of her, I will be ignoring her. Being cool. Cool is the thing I am worst at. My close personal adviser Shooter is always telling me: *Act like a guy who talks to hot girls all the time.*

"I'm John," the guy says.

"Tom," I say. "The silent lady is my new friend Julia."

They shake hands. Shake, shake.

"Thanks for the drink," she says, lighting a cigarette and taking a sip of her G and T. "I'm going to quietly enjoy it."

I don't smoke. I don't like smoking. I do like smokers. Most of the most interesting conversations I've had in this town could have been scraped out of my lungs the next day.

"You work at the *Times*," John guesses.

"No, *Tabloid*," I say. "Sorry about that."

"Why not the *Times*?" he says, disappointed.

People often ask me this question. Why not the *Times*? I do all right. Make enough money. Does it really matter if I work for a paper whose first edition is so rife with typos that in-house wags call it "the rough draft"? Does it matter that the ink of the heds comes off on your hands so smudgily that you literally (as well as morally) feel as if you need a shower after reading it?

No, none of this matters: I do it for the love of the adrenaline, the freewheeling personalities, the take-no-prisoners attitude. Plus the *Times*'s editors won't return my calls.

"The *Times*?" I say for Julia's benefit. "Why would I want to take a forty percent pay cut?" Shooter say: *Poor men don't get laid.*

"I thought you guys were kinda low paid," John says.

"The *Times* pays you in prestige. You can't eat prestige," I say, although I have no idea what the *Times* pays except I'm pretty sure it's more than what the cash-strapped Australian tax dodgers who own our paper pay. But Julia is new to this racket and for all I know, she thinks I get paid like a corporate barracuda.

"Oh, *Tabloid*'s a good paper," the guy says, nodding. "I read it on the train."

"Everyone reads it on the train," I say. "As long as people shit and use mass transit, we're still in business."

Julia laughs.

"What do you do?" I say.

"Guess," the guy goes. He has the striated arms and overdeveloped neck of a construction worker. The cast-iron palms of a construction worker. The sun-hammered skin of a construction worker.

"Interior decorator," I say.

Julia chuckles.

"No," he says. "Guess again."

"Oh, sorry. How could I have been so dumb? Interior de*sign*er."

"Nah, something totally different."

"Symphony conductor."

Another giggle from Julia.

"No," John says. "Come on."

"Tae Bo instructor?"

"Nah. Come on, I'm the foreman of a construction crew."

"You put up buildings," I say.

"That's right."

"I respect that," I say, and I do. "You're going to be able to walk around this city with your grandchildren and say, 'I built that. I built that.' But every word we wrote in the paper this whole year will be forgotten."

Julia seems to approve of this. She's done with her drink. I order her another.

"More of the Courage for you?" says the barkeep.

Sure. For all Julia knows, I could be an impressive individual. Forthright, sincere. A wit, keen dresser, and friend to the working-man. Now all I have to do is work in a few lines about my love for animals.

"Hey, where you from?" John says. "You're from Manhattan, I'll bet. I'm from the Island."

"Actually, I'm from D.C." I always tell people this, to make them think I'm a senator's son from Georgetown, when in reality my dad was an air-conditioner repairman in Rockville, Maryland, a man who considered french fries to be vegetables. I had to pretend to live with my rich aunt so I could attend the Potomac schools, where the kids appeared born in their Tretorn sneakers and Benetton sweaters. Mr. Farrell's wardrobe? Exclusively by the Husky Boys' department at Sears, right down to the tan work boots that said "maximum dork" then and yet would become inexplicably cool with this city's fashion-wise uptown kids by the time I hit thirty. (I, of course, can never wear them again, or corduroys, or flared-leg jeans—which means my cycle of uncool continues.) We couldn't even afford real Oreos: we were one of those Hydrox families. Every drinking glass in our house bore the image of Hamburglar or Mayor McCheese. (Whatever happened to Grimace? Was he too gay? Or did he just reinvent himself as Barney?) Senior year of high school, I hoarded the ten-dollar bills my dad gave me every time I mowed the lawn and traded them for a cut-price Member's Only windbreaker, only to discover that they had become about as fly as the canasta tournament at the Topeka Country Club. Thus did I learn my first lesson about fashion: by the time I can afford it, it's over.

"So what'd your father do?" John says, calculating the size of my trust fund in his head.

"That, I'm afraid," I say, "is a national security issue."

Julia laughs.

And my hard-on is clanging in my pants.

Time for a break.

In the men's room, I look at the mirror and think, It's been an hour and a half. Julia is sticking. She could be planning to leave any second since she still hasn't taken her coat off, but we're kind of near the door and it's kind of chilly and anyway *she's sticking*. My God, my God: do I actually have a chance with this girl? The thing is, when I first saw her, I thought, No biggie. Just another beauty in her don't-touch-me force field. She didn't get to me that much. But now I'm thinking: this is it. Maybe every guy gets one chance.

Time for a chat with the man. The top dog. Mr. Underneath. My A-Rod.

—So.

—So.

—How do you feel?

—How do I feel? How do I look?

—You're plumping like a Ballpark Frank.

—Swelling often accompanies fever.

—Settle down. That's not what we're here for. I can't if you're in that mood.

—Bullshit. We're put on earth for one reason.

—This isn't earth. This is a urinal.

—Get me in her mouth. Do whatever it takes. That's all I ask of you.

—"All I Ask of You." That was in *Phantom of the Opera*. Streisand sang it.

—You fucking pussy.

—Just trying to do a job here.

—I mean, have you checked her equipment?

—Mmmm.

—The lips on her? Dual air bags, amigo. So ripe they're about to burst. And the softness. That color. Can you imagine how good I'd look wearing those lips as a sombrero? O-fucking-lay!

—You're Ballparking again.

—I need, I need.

—I'm laying the groundwork.

—Lay the girl.

—Jump her?

—I would.

—You're a dick.

—I will never ask you for anything again.

—Wrong. You'll keep asking again and again. You're never happy.

—I'm only human.

—Nothing's happening here. She's going to think I'm stroking you.

—*Would you? It'll only take a sec.*

—Not appropriate.

—*Bitchtalk.*

—It's a woman's world. We play by their rules.

—*Take her.*

—Calm down. Barbara Bush.

—*Ow. No.*

—Hillary Clinton.

—*Ugh.*

—Camryn Manheim. Rosie O'Donnell. Oprah.

—*Uma.*

—Oprah.

—*Uma!*

—That's it. Liza Minnelli.

—*You win. You fucker.*

—Ahh. Thanks.

Tinkle, tinkle little stud.

—Anyway, I can't just jump her. What if I get slammed?

—*Failure is not an option.*

—You're quoting Ron Howard movies?

—*He did* Night Shift.

—Shelley Long.

—*That scene in her* panties.

—You're Ballparking.

—*Her ass when she's reaching over the counter.*

—Ballpark. Stop it. Bea Arthur. Nancy Reagan.

—*Jackie Kennedy!*

—Jackie Mason.

—*Faggot.*

—It worked.

—*The only constant is acting like a man.*

—You have to be smart.

—*A man doesn't need brains. He needs balls.*

—You need brains to earn money to spend on her.

—*Stephen Hawking has brains. Hugh Hefner has balls. Who'd you rather be?*

—You have too much balls, you wind up in prison, then you're somebody's girlfriend.

—*Do not fuck it up.*

—Doing my best.

—*Your best? Like that time with Sabrina Klein?*

—I know.

—*You had her right there.*

—I was being a gentleman.

—*On her couch. In her bathrobe. She put her head on your shoulder.*

—She was sick.

—*You're sick.*

—I'm supposed to take advantage of a girl who's been in bed all weekend?

—*Her head. Your shoulder. The body on her. I would have gotten so deep in her I would have tickled her liver.*

—I figured it would pay off in the long run. Being trustworthy.

—*Trust, yeah. That's fine. If you want to be her* sister.

—She might have just slapped me.

—*Her head. Your shoulder.*

—You can't tell with girls. Sometimes they're offended if you make it a sex thing.

—*Everything's a sex thing.*

—To you, maybe.

—*I am the most powerful force in the universe.*

—What about God?

—*Yeah, but I actually exist.*

—How did I miss with Sabrina?

—*How close was the belt of her robe to your hand? One fucking tug would have done it.*

—Oh God. Angela Lansbury. Ethel Merman. Jean Stapleton. Janet Reno.

—*Okay, okay. We'll talk later.*

—When?

—*About ten seconds after you get home.*

—Right, buddy, done. Time for me to tuck you in.

You are not my friend.

Back in the bar, John has wandered off. Julia hasn't. What's her last name?

"Brouillard," she says, taking a puff of her Camel Light.

"French, huh?" I say.

"*Un peu,*" she says, exhaling.

"So what'd your boyfriend get you for Valentine's Day?" I say. All casual like.

"Nothing," she says.

I look at her. She looks at me. She doesn't elaborate.

There's a scene in *Fort Apache, the Bronx* (number four on my list of Greatest New York Movies, right behind number three, *The Warriors*; number two, *Midnight Cowboy*; and of course number one, *Dog Day Afternoon*) where Paul Newman is sitting in a car in a crappy neighborhood in the Bronx with this lady cop (who turns out to be a junkie, of course) he's been flirting with. She asks him why he hasn't hit on her. "I don't go to parties where I ain't invited," he says. "Do you want an engraved invitation?" she says.

The mail has arrived.

Shooter's ninja combat training is kicking in. Shooter say: *As soon as you get a Moment, get her out of there.* Just leaving a place and going to another place with her raises the stakes.

"I told a friend of mine I'd stop by his bar. Do you want to come with?"

"Yes," she says.

Well that was easy.

On the way over she casually drops in a mention of how she "and my boyfriend" used to work at the Bridgeport, Connecticut, paper. It is unclear whether going out with the boyfriend is part of the "used to." And Bridgeport is like the Bronx of Connecticut. So I just say, "Uh-huh."

Shooter say: *All hot girls have a "boyfriend" hanging around somewhere. Ignore this information. The brain of the hot girl is not wired to handle the concept of being without a boyfriend. So they hang on to the old until they begin with the new.*

She doesn't elaborate. I don't press her.

Luck is on my side again at South, a ramshackle underground alcohole on Forty-ninth. Pete is on the door. He acts like a big friendly slobbering bear, as usual. Gives me a manhug (no contact below the chest, which necessitates sticking your butt out, which is an incredibly gay-looking pose, which is why the straight manhug is an exceedingly rare beast, the did-you-see-it-or-didn't-you Sasquatch of social gestures). He's the only bar owner I know in this town. Julia doesn't know that. Pete loves journalists, always treats us to free drinks. We treat him to free stories in our papers. We would do the same for any saloon keeper. Why haven't the rest of them figured this out? I get some drinks. Pete won't let me pay. I don't try very hard.

Time to show her the back room.

Hardly anybody hangs in the desolate overlit back, the empty place where the barbershop and shoeshine stand used to be. I let her pick three songs from the juke (an obscure Nirvana track, some Nick Drake, and Jane's Addiction's "Then She Did"). It won't occur to me for months that two of these songs are by dead people and the third sounds like an extremely exhausting heroin trip.

We sit on a tattered orange sofa big enough for two, and only two. The light is garish but we're completely alone in the room.

"What were you like in high school?" I say.

"I was such a dork," she says. "No guys would ever go out with me. Till I was, like, *fifteen.*"

"You seem like a loner," I say.

"I always have been," she says. "I'm just, I don't know. A geek."

"You have very nice eyes for a geek," I say.

She smiles. "I don't know if I'm ready for the city," she says.

"Where do you live now?"

"In South Norwalk. Connecticut."

Wow. Now that's a commute. "You can't do that much longer," I say.

"I know. It takes me an hour and a half to get to work. This week I've been staying with that girl who works in reception."

"You can find an apartment here," I say. "Just so long as you're okay with urban squalor."

She laughs. "That's the thing. I don't mind living in a dump, it's just that there are too many people here. I'm a small-town girl. I just want to read books," she says. "And be able to drive my car."

We talk about old girlfriends. Mine. Hers. She had the Obligatory Lesbian Affair. And she's not just saying it to turn me on. Her life is more interesting than mine. She's so much younger than me, and so much older. Her face is at that age when girls have just lost their baby fat but haven't yet put on the adult fat. Post-zit, pre-wrinkle. Her skin is perfect. Yet she's about as young as Yoda.

I ask questions about the things that made her. All of our personalities are just hot dogs crammed with bits and pieces of books and movies and songs, aren't they? That thing you said because it sounded like something Bogart would say. That thing you wore because it made you feel like a character in a video you saw when you were fourteen. She loves *Blue Velvet*, but also *Meet Me in St. Louis*. *The Virgin Suicides*, but also *Powerpuff Girls*. She has read Sylvia Plath but never interpreted her writing as a call to stop shaving her armpits. She's on antidepressants but doesn't brag about it. She does not wear glasses but she wishes she did. She does not say, "You do the math" or "at the end of the day" or "don't go there." She lost her virginity in a tree house. I want to buy her books, and jewelry.

Being with her is weird and familiar at the same time, like a memory of the future. You know how when you're young you always think you're going to meet your Ideal? You know, a woman with great hair and clothes who doesn't talk about her hair and clothes? A woman who does not believe "Whatever" is a sentence? A woman who eats steak? A woman who isn't trying to meet Wall Street guys? A woman who neither hates her mother nor is obsessed with pleasing her?

"You should at least try living in the city," I say, expressing my empathy with a sidle. "It may break your heart, but it'll never bore you."

She considers this, motionless as a cat on a warm windowsill. You couldn't slide a Saturday edition of *Tabloid* between us. And, ladies and gentlemen, she. Is. Sticking. But she's also lighting a cigarette.

I'm starting to be aware of my breathing. My pulse. My schlong. You know how a cute girl looks through extra-strength beer goggles? That's how she looked when I was stone-cold sober. Imagine how she looks now that I've drunk a gallon of Courage.

"How old are you?"

"Twenty-two. How old are you?"

"Thirty-two." Don't act old. Don't give yourself away. Most girls like slightly older geezers. More mature and that. Keep looking right into her eyes. Giving her a few signs of interest. Basking in her eyes and hair.

That was her last smoke, so I go back to the bar to see if Pete's got some. He doesn't sell, but he scrounges up a few singles and sticks them in my jacket pocket. I score some matches as well.

"Zat your girlfriend?" he wants to know.

"Not yet," I say.

"Ooh, look at him," Pete says. "Don Juanabee."

"It's going ridiculously well," I say. "I just met her."

"Best thing you can do?" he says. "Say good night and walk away. She'll go nuts."

I can't do that. This is the most beautiful girl I've ever gotten this far with. She's laughing at the right moments. Looking serious at the right moments. She's still wearing her little yellow coat and just thinking about what's under there is making the mercury rise in my thermometer.

So here it is. I'm drunk on the night air. I'm drunk on her face. I'm drunk on alcohol. She's matched me drink for drink. Five. Six. We've spent three hours together, maybe more. We're sitting side by side with cool moody alternative music playing, the kind she used to make out to in high school.

Give her a cigarette.

"Thanks," she says. She fumbles around in her coat. I'm already lighting a match. Although I hate cigarettes, I love to light up pretty girls. Because.

"Lighting up a girl, there's something, sexual, about it," I say, waving out the match.

"*Defi*nitely," she says, shooting a plume in my direction.

I move closer. She doesn't flee. I move closer still. She's sticking. Now she's in my kissing radius. I look at her. Straighten your posture, man. Your posture is always bad. I look away. Look around the room. Check out the juke. Stare into the yellow light of this grungy subterranean grotto. And then: lean back toward her. And I go in.

And she sticks. Relief wells up in me. Surges. A wave of calmness.

I am liked. Meeting this girl is like cleaning behind my refrigerator: a once-in-a-lifetime thing. Bachelorhood has had a long run, there have been several girlfriends who were almost perfect. But this could be the last girl I ever kiss.

We kiss. We pause. We kiss some more. Her hand is on my shoulder.

Then I pull up and put my mouth up next to her ear and very softly I say exactly what I'm thinking.

You should never say what you're actually thinking.

You should especially never say what you're actually thinking if you are in danger of giving up the secret you, the one it should take six months of hard-core dating to uncover.

You should extra-super-especially never say what you're actually thinking if what you're thinking sounds like dialogue from a 1968 episode of *Days of Our Lives*.

But here's what I say. I say, "Where have you been all my life?"

She just gives me a crooked little smile. I've never seen anyone smile like that before. Half of her mouth is delighted. The other half is worried.

Then she gives a little laugh.

And I am filled with hope.

THIRD DOSE

We make a date for Thursday to see a movie about jujitsu and boxing and sword-fighting and love. All of your basic forms of combat.

"There's an eight-thirty," I say. "There's also a six."

"Maybe eight-thirty," she says. "No, wait. Shoot. How about six?"

I show up at 5:50. She isn't there. She isn't there at 6:15. Go to the Mexican restaurant next door. Change for a dollar, please. Call the office. Call the house. No messages.

I'm paralyzed. Surely she wouldn't go in without me. So I wait.

Six-thirty. What the hell. I'll just wait till the eight-thirty showing. See what happens. Say she shows up at eight-fifteen all is forgiven.

I cross Forty-second Street to the HMV store and stew a bit. Check the office machine. Check the home machine. Check 'em again. Wait ten minutes and recheck. I'm frantic, running over the possibilities. I once read this article about Occam's razor. It's a theory: the simplest explanation is the likeliest. The simplest explanation is, she has simply lost interest.

I sit through the film anyway. I really wanted to see it. But it's so poetically sad and lyrically pained and tragically tragic that it's like seeing my psychic X rays blown up forty feet wide. I leave before the end. I just know somebody's going to die.

I have this problem. Sometimes I go overboard. But I don't just go overboard. I go overboard without a life jacket. In shark-infested waters. With a vicious nosebleed. And I just remembered to forget how to swim.

I call in sick on Friday. No messages. Call Julia at the office. It rings. Someone picks up. The line goes dead. I don't call back. The weekend passes. I call in sick on Monday. Call her at the office. She doesn't answer. I leave a message. "Uh, hi. It's, uh, Tom? Could you call me?" But she doesn't.

I'm mad at myself, mainly. I saw a yellow light, or a yellow coat, and I stepped on the pedal. Right into a buzzing intersection.

Tuesday I go back to work devising excuses. No one tells me I don't look sick.

I feel like ten pounds of nothing in a five-pound sack at the office that whole week. I don't see her around. *She might be out covering a story. She could be sick!* Too sick to operate a phone? It could happen. I picture her lying in a soap-opera hospital room with swaddled head muttering her "Who am I?"s to teams of mystified doctors.

The following Monday. Ten days since she blew me off. In my cubicle there are stacks of newspapers, layouts, magazines, all the crap of my crap existence. Hello, I'm Mr. Crap, who are you? Oh, you're Mr. Calm, Secure, Married Guy? I guess you don't worry about where your next lay is coming from. Or, your next cuddle. Because even guys get tired of fucking. Yeah, it's pretty easy to find someone to fuck. Actually, it's incredibly hard to find someone you want to fuck, but it's even harder to find someone you want to wake up with.

At the bottom of the stack: a note. No envelope. Thick, unlined white paper. Folded in thirds. My name in cursive.

Tom,

I can't tell you how sorry I am about last week. I don't think I can even give you a reason that doesn't sound like a lame excuse. The truth is that I've been having a rough few weeks, and I haven't quite been myself. This is no excuse for not simply picking up the phone and calling you, I know.

The thing is, I really liked hanging out with you, and I would like to try it again. Of course, if you think I'm a complete jerk/psychopath, that's understandable. Anyway, I just wanted to tell you I'm sorry.

Julia

God, even her handwriting is beautiful. It's neat, it's readable, but it's kind of cool and smart and tragic: tight, angular, brooding. Not like girly handwriting with its fat loops, its smiley faces in the girly dots of the *i*s. Now she's really done it to me.

I don't call her until I'm getting ready to leave at the end of the day. "Hey," I tell the phone.

"How are you," she says. Other girls' voices rise? Like, at the end of every sentence? Not hers. Her voice is all low and smooth and soothing and sexy. Talking to her, you expect to be charged $3.95 a minute.

My other line is ringing.

"Got your note," I say.

"Yes," she says.

"How about we start over?" I say.

"I'd like that," she says.

And I pick up the other line to deal with this hour's story of the century.

THIRD DOSE. SECOND ATTEMPT.

I tell her to meet me at one of those nouvelle Mexican places. It's a lot like the oldvelle Mexican places, except there is a little jar of crayons for doodling on the butcher paper that covers the table-cloth, the loud music is soul instead of salsa, and the margaritas have flavors like pomegranate and kiwi-kumquat. Also, for what each of them costs you could go on a three-day bender in Tijuana. Shooter say: *Let her see you waste money.*

"I'll just have a regular margarita," she tells the waitress. She is perfectly still in her cute yellow coat. I imagine everyone is looking at her. And I don't have much imagination.

"And for you?" the waitress says.

"The watermelon. Is that seedless?"

Julia laughs. The waitress doesn't. New York waitresses don't laugh.

"Actually I'll just have the strawberry-mango," I say. It occurs to me a moment too late that this is perhaps not the manliest drink in existence. I should have said something like, "Whiskey and soda. Hold the soda."

The waitress rolls her eyes and leaves without a word.

"Missed you the other night," I point out, picturing Shooter slamming a glass on the table and bellowing, "WHERE THE FUCK WERE YOU?" Should I be more like Shooter, or more like me? And if the latter: who the hell am I?

"I'm sorry," she says.

"What happened?" I say.

She doesn't say anything. She just makes a lost-doggy face and lets her shoulders droop. I can see words forming in her green eyes. She can't get them out of her mouth, though. Then something occurs to her. She rootles through her purse for an answer. And finds her cigarettes.

"That's your reply?" I say.

"It's just, boyfriend things," she says.

I light a match for her.

"Things," I say. She leans into my flame.

"Things haven't been so good lately. I don't know what's wrong with me. You know?" She blows smoke out of the side of her mouth. Her coat is still on even though it's warm in here. She looks as if she could run away at any moment.

"Can you tell me what things?" I say.

"Not yet," she says.

Little does she know. I'm a sucker for a good mystery. Or even a bad one, if it has green eyes. One of which is partially hidden by that gorgeous hair. She's a riddle wrapped in a mystery wrapped in a truly excellent body.

When I was a kid, my older brothers would scamper off on a Sunday afternoon while my parents dragged me around to flea markets. They were there to rescue woebegone furniture, begrimed wooden survivors that reminded them of stuff their parents had had around the house when they were kids. These soapboxes and pedestal tables they planned to tote back home so they could spend several devoted days lovingly stripping off the paint in order to unveil the battered piece of junk that always lay underneath. At the flea market I'd mope listlessly through the piles of scratched records and clothes that smelled like somebody else's house. Did I want anything? my parents would ask. No. The macramé lady, the tube-sock king. Did anything catch my eye? No. The hard-candy booth, the land of hand-painted ceramic farm animals. Couldn't they get me anything for being such a Good Boy? No. Until we stumbled upon some merchant-wizard who had a barrel filled with lumps of undercover merchandise in brown paper sacks tied with ribbons. A Magic Marker question mark was their only label. GRAB BAGS, the sign would say. Only a buck. I had to have one, every time. By the time we got home I would have thrown away the Bakelite candy bowl or wooden duck that always lay within.

The waitress comes back with our drinks. At the next table two white guys and a black guy sit down and start arguing about sports. One of them, the biggest, is wearing a backward baseball cap. It's a look that says, "I'm so proud to have made it to the first rung of Wall Street that I'm prepared to spend up to fifty dollars tonight." The big guy banters strenuously with the waitress. I watch. I love seeing other guys strike out.

Julia lets out another puff of smoke. It corkscrews over her head. Everything she does has this style to it.

"So how was the movie?" she says.

"It was okay," I say. "I like old movies better."

Her eyes widen. "You are so right. I don't understand why there's one theater that shows old movies and a hundred theaters that show new movies. Isn't that so ass backwards? I mean, if you go in a bookstore, they have a table full of new stuff in front, and the whole rest of the store is old books."

"Same with CD stores."

"Does everything have to be so relentlessly *now*?" she says. "I wish everything would slow down. I wish time would start moving *back*wards."

"Well. As Woody Allen said, that would mean I'd have to sit through the Ice Capades again."

"I like getting older," she says. "I just want history to go back. There's a lot of stuff I missed. The Beatles. JFK."

"Let's fight it."

She smiles. "Yes, shall we? But how."

"Never read a book that's less than ten years old." Easy for me. I don't read much anyway.

"*Yes.* And only black-and-white movies."

"Unless they have Steve McQueen in them."

"Mmm," she says. "Or Hugh Grant. Or Jack Nicholson."

"You can't like Hugh Grant and Jack Nicholson," I say. "That's like me saying I want to marry either Audrey Hepburn or Marilyn Monroe."

She shrugs. "At least I want to sleep with the *liv*ing, Grandpa."

"Maybe you don't know what you want."

"Sure I do. Somebody who's like Hugh when I want him to be like Hugh and like Jack when I need that."

"Uh-huh," I say. "And how are the young bucks supposed to figure out today's mood?"

"That's just the thing," she says, blowing more smoke. "If you can't *read*, don't pick up the book."

She looks exactly like Gloria Grahame when she says this. The turned-up nose schooled in long-distance bullshit detection. The way she cocks that eyebrow of hers. You should never cock a weapon indoors. Somebody could get hurt.

"Do you know," I venture, "who Gloria Grahame was?"

She half-closes her eyes. Her mouth falls into a lopsided grin. She looks as if she's entered a trance. "She was the haunted drunken diva in *The Bad and the Beautiful*. She was my favorite character in *Oklahoma!*, for God's sake. The Girl Who Can't Say No. That was the *best* song. 'Every time I lose a wrestling match, I get a funny feeling that I won.' She must have been the first character ever in the history of the movies to make it okay and fine to be a total slut. She didn't have to pay for her sin in the end. She didn't go crazy or get killed."

"You kind of remind me of her," I say.

"Do I now?"

This earns me another drink.

"I could never figure out Gloria Grahame," I say. "You always got the feeling that she could end up marrying the hero, or—"

"Or garroting him," she says. "She was like a more fem Lauren Bacall. Oh, *oh*. Do you know *In a Lonely Place?*"

"Know it? Memorized it."

"That little speech he gave her, do you remember it?" she says.

"Sure. In the car. 'I was born when she kissed me. I died when she left me.'"

"And," Julia says, taking a big philosophical drag, "'I lived a few weeks while she loved me.' I love hard-boiled despair."

"The look on her face when Bogart tells her that," I say. "That face could imply anything."

"So right. Why speak when you can imply?"

Spoken like a true grab bag.

"What are you doing at *Tabloid?*"

"Please," she says. "The *Southeastern Connecticut Poetry Review* doesn't pay."

"Maybe there's poetry in what we do. We're just trying to get the rhythm of the massacre. The song of squalor."

"I'll bet you can write," she says, lighting another cigarette.

"I earn a nice living at it," I say.

She raises an eyebrow.

"What?" I say.

"No. I mean, *write*."

Poof. A little guilt dart hits me in the throat. There are times when I've thought about growing up, cashing in however many talent chips I have, getting down to work. But there's always something good on TV.

"Maybe I will, sometime," I tell her.

"Will you write a story about me?" she says.

"No," I say.

She looks hurt.

So I say, "You could only be a novel."

Save! And the crowd goes wild. I've won another drink. I catch her looking at me in a different way.

"What's with that look?" I say.

"Nothing. It's just, I don't know. You're one of the few redheads I've met who doesn't have that disgusting orange hair."

"Umm, thanks?"

"No offense, of course." She puts a hand on my hand and gives me the look of the big-bucks newswoman in the primary-colored jacket who gets paid to make people cry.

I look at her hand, hoping it'll stay there a while. "You wish you had it," I say. "Don't you." My hair would look much better on a girl. All girls wish they had red hair. Sometimes I think the only reason any of them ever go out with me is that they're plotting to shear me in the night and make a run for it to the wig shop.

She laughs. Reclaims her hand. "I could do a lot with your hair."

"You're looking at me like a German shepherd looks at a steak."

"I like your nose, too," she says.

"Oh. Well that, you can have."

"Okay. Now you have to pay me a compliment."

This throws me. Where do I begin? With the *a*'s?

"Why?" I say.

"I just gave you two of them."

" 'Not disgusting' is a compliment?"

"Sure."

"Okay," I say. "Let me think about this." I look at the floor. I look at the ceiling. I tuck my chin down and look up at her shyly. "Julia," I say. "Honestly? I have to be serious for a second. Of all the girls I've known—"

I think she's holding her breath.

"You're one of many who does not make me puke."

She laughs. But she looks a little relieved.

"You still owe me one, you jerk," she says.

"And you have mysterious eyes," I say.

That half smile again. As she starts to doodle with a crayon.

"That'll do," she says.

"Draw a picture of you," I say.

"Okay, but you have to do one of you," she says.

I take a crayon out of the little glass jar and start sketching out an epic. I can't draw. There are a lot of things I can't do. This does not stop me from trying to do them.

I'm trying to see what she's doing but she's blocking me.

"Uh-uh-uh," she says, without looking up from her work.

I'm drawing a massive stadium. A cheering throng. The perspective always kills me. I need an eraser.

She's switching crayons. "Gimme a yellow," she says.

"Almost done with it," I say. "What are you drawing?"

"Shhh," she says. "Genius at work."

The guys at the next table are looking. The closest guy to me, a guy in a snazzy suit and overly shiny shoes, taps me on the elbow.

"Excuse me," he says, with four-margarita authority. "I have a question for you."

"Not now," I say.

"Just one question," he says.

"Leave us alone," I say, giving him a look. "*Seriously*. I mean it."

"Can you tell me how to get, how to get to Sesame Street?"

Big laughs from the I-can-tie-my-own-tie table.

Julia looks up.

"Hey," says the black guy. "Didn't I see you at recess?"

They laugh some more. This time they all slap each other's body parts. Julia keeps her head down.

"Please," I say.

"Buddy," says the third guy, a really huge piece of meat. "Ask your little daughter if she wants to suck on my lollipop."

Julia pretends not to hear this either.

"Enough," I say. Looking the third one in the eye. The big guy.

"Ooooh," he says. "Whatcha gonna do?"

I don't say anything. I keep drawing.

"Done!" Julia says.

"Let me see," I say.

"You first," she says.

So I show her. Me with rippling muscles, calf-high boots, a shield, a sword. Long red hair flowing out underneath my helmet. The crowd adores me. The lion and the tiger are in midleap. I don't look worried. I smile the cruel smile of a hardened killer.

"That's *exactly* how I see you," she says. "Only why do you appear to have a learning disability?"

"That's my rakish grin," I say.

"I'd say more of a maniacal leer," she says.

"Guess you don't know steely-eyed determination when it's staring you in the face," I say.

"Goofy-eyed, with possible lack of bowel control, is what I'm seeing," she says.

"Hey," says the black guy at the next table. "Hey. Pi*cas*so."

I ignore them. Julia looks uncomfortable.

"Hey, *Rem*brandt," says the suit.

"What?" I say. The drinks are settling in. Feeling a bit feisty.

"You do nudes too? Of her?" says the suit.

Julia looks deeply uncomfortable.

"You're being rude," I point out to the gentlemen.

"Hey," says the big guy. "Hey, *Shakes*peare. Can I have your autograph?" he says.

Shakespeare?

"Sure," I say. I lean over to the table of mirth and take one of their crayons out of their little jar. On their butcher paper, I write, in the most elegant and painterly script I can manage, "Gogh."

" 'Gogh,' " says the big oaf. "That's it? You only got one name?"

"Oh, I'm sorry," I say. "I forgot the rest of my name." And I lean over and add, "Fuck yourself."

You can probably guess what happens next.

"What's that supposed to mean?" says the big guy.

"Pardon my French," I say.

Now Julia looks afraid. All three of the guys stand up. I stand up too.

"Listen, buddy," says the suit, poking me in the chest. "Don't you see us? Can you count to *tres*?"

The suit and the black guy are about my height. I look from one to the other. "Maybe," I say. "Why don't we step outside and discuss it?"

The three guys confer for a second. And then they laugh.

Julia looks alarmed.

"Yeah," I say. "You'll probably win. Eventually. But I guarantee that by the time it's done, I'm going to put one of you in the hospital. Who's it gonna be?"

They just stand there for a second. I sit down and have another sip.

They sit down. "Why don't you just chill," says the suit.

"We'll just forget all about it," I say. "Right after you apologize to my friend."

They grumble a little. Julia gives me a crooked smile of relief.

"Yeah, you're right," says the suit. "We were outta line." And they go back to advising each other on how to manage the New York Mets.

Julia's eyes widen. She exhales as if she's been underwater for several minutes. "Well!" she says. "Do you know where the bathrooms are?"

I point the way. She passes behind me. Then stops and puts a hand on my shoulder. She leans over till I can feel her breath settling on my earlobe. "You *brute*," she whispers.

As soon as she's gone, the suit nudges me. "Hey," he says.

"So great," I say. I swear my eyes are warm, as if I've been staring into a fireplace all evening.

"She's hot," says the black guy. "What do you think, Mike?"

"Most hot," says Mike, brushing something invisible off his suit.

"She's okay," says the big guy.

I glare at him.

"Ned, this is Tom," says Mike.

"So," says Shooter. "You getting this tab or what?"

"I said two rounds. For you and *one* accomplice. You almost blew it with the gorilla."

"What are you talking about?" says Shooter.

"You don't think it looks a little ridiculous, me offering to take on two guys my size plus King Kong over there? You oversold the gag."

"It's called *atmosphere*, Tom," Mike says. "He was in my brother's frat."

"I thought he'd be perfect," says Shooter. "Look at him. The man exudes Wall Street dickhead. Christ, he even went to Florida State."

"Florida," says the hulk.

"I can tell he went to Florida. That's not the point," I say.

"How do you know I went to Florida?" says Ned.

"Your baseball cap," I say. "Your jacket. And is that a gator on your watch?"

"What's wrong with Florida?" says Ned, who looks even bigger now that he's standing.

"Sit, you animal," Shooter says. "What was *up* with that Shakespeare shit?"

"All right, all right, everybody," Mike says. In college, he used to tell everybody he was going to be a UN diplomat someday. He always wanted to charm his way out of violence. Which is why Shooter and I have long considered him a bit of a pussy.

"Don't blame this on the gorilla," I say, slipping Shooter two twenties. "You're the one who brought him. I had a plan. You and Mike I can trust."

Now Ned is over on this side of the table. How'd he get here? Did somebody give him a map?

"Hey," says Shooter. "Hey, hey." He's coming over too, but the tequila has slowed him down.

"I'm nobody's ape," Ned says. "Maybe *you*'d like to step outside?"

"Come on, Magilla," I say. "Let the grown-ups discuss this."

Ned has me in a headlock and Shooter is pounding on his back and screaming gibberish when Julia comes back. Mike has disappeared somewhere below table level. I think he's gnawing on Ned's ankle. The waitress, demonstrating for the first time all evening her ability to move at a speed greater than the feckless Euro drift, is dashing madly behind the bar and yelping girlishly. Tattletale. The bartender doesn't look happy. Now he's coming over. He's bigger than me too.

"Czzzzech pleeeeeease," I say through my crushed windpipe.

Fortunately, I have the privilege of being thrown out first. The guys are still inside arguing over the check when Julia and I hit the night air.

"Lovely," she says. "Drinks, *and* a show."

Does that mean phonier than a Kansas City dinner theater production of Cats? I wonder as I rub my neck. I read somewhere—or was it merely a tabloid invention?—that when the ancient Greeks used to do *Oedipus*, they'd force a slave to play the title role. So that way, at the end, they could really stick hot pokers in the guy's eyes. And De Niro thinks he invented method acting.

"My brave gladiator," she says. "Here."

And she starts massaging my neck.

"Next time," she says. "Can I pick the place?"

Next time. I like the sound of that.

She has an hour to kill until her train to Connecticut, so we stumble around the Upper West Side for a while, not saying much. She looks small and shivery in her yellow coat and white mittens. The cold is stinging my eyes. Up on the corner I spot inspiration. The all-night grocery store with its beckoning fruits and vegetables. Sometimes the fluorescent light strip over the produce aisle browns out. It was like that yesterday. This creates possibility.

"Come on," I say.

The light is still out. The produce aisle sits under a canopy of incongruous barroom darkness. Word has gotten around. A tall preppie in a fishing hat and his little Korean girlfriend are in a dim corner laughing over their stolen grapes. Two gay men and their little gay dog loiter suggestively among the kumquats.

"You're *so* bad," Julia says as I put a wild blueberry in her mouth.

"Shh," I say. "No one will know if we eat the evidence."

We almost bump into another couple, a fresh-faced blonde and an artsy-looking guy, both wearing identical chunky glasses, laughing dirtily. We let them pass before resuming our crime spree.

"I love the feel of things," she says, cradling an orange in both hands, testing its pebbled skin. She holds it up to her nose and takes a long whiff. "The smell, the color. The way something can be so rough and rubbery on the outside and so tender under the skin."

It's true. I usually motor right past this aisle to the things that come in cans and packages. I haven't spent more than two minutes

in this aisle before. But through her eyes it all looks saucy and flir-
tatious. Broccoli is stacked like a wall of bush. Stalks of corn await
circumcision.

"Smell this," she says, holding a lemon under my nose.

I draw in a deep breath, feeling the citrus writing its name in my
brain. It makes me a little bit drunker.

"It's like the porno section of the video store," I say. "Everything's
so round and juicy and ripe. It should all be hidden behind a curtain so the children don't stumble on it." The permanent excitement
of the bananas and cucumbers reminds me of myself in eighth
grade; the heads of lettuce look born to strip. I try not to contem-
plate the fuzzy ovular kiwis. Just thinking about some perv walking
up and giving them a squeeze makes my balls ache.

"Oh my God those *strawberries*," she says.

I take one out of a box and eat half of it.

"Gimme," she says. She makes a grab for it.

I yank it out of reach.

"Uh-uh," I say.

She just watches me.

"Close your eyes," I say. And she does. Her lips seem to part
involuntarily, waiting. I rub half a strawberry across her top lip,
down and around and on to the bottom lip. Then I do another lap, at
half speed. And another, even slower than that. Years are going by.
Her mouth widens a bit. Her eyes seem to shut tighter. Then I give
her the berry and she takes a little bird nibble. And another. Making
it last. She still doesn't open her eyes. She holds my hand as though
I'm lighting her cigarette. She flares her nostrils in fruity rapture. A
little stream of juice runs down her chin. It takes her five languid
bites to get through a berry. And then she kisses my fingers.

She looks up at me with big mischievous eyes. "Come here," she
says. And I lean in for the kiss.

I don't get one. She does a smart about-face and leads me down the aisle. There are big open barrels of coffee beans sitting there. Arabica. Sumatra. Colombian espresso. "Try this," she says. "This is the best feeling." She shrugs off her coat, hands it to me. And she plunges her right hand into a barrel of French roast. All the way up to the elbow. She turns her arm this way and that. Working her muscles.

"It feels so weird when you clench and unclench your fist. And rotate your wrist. It's like entering a different atmosphere," she says. "Another planet. I could take a bath in this stuff and just, disappear. The funny thing is, I don't even like to drink coffee."

"No, you just like to molest it," I say.

"Sometimes," she says, "I make a pot of coffee, just to smell it. I always throw it away. Doesn't it make the air so rich?"

I bury my left hand in the barrel. It's a workout. You can't force it. You have to insinuate yourself, picking aside one layer of beans at a time, tickling them out of the way with your fingertips. My hand keeps slithering and twisting, plunging down and down, fighting through the resistance. Our hands touch halfway down the barrel. I run a forefinger down the soft underside of her thumb. She presses her hand into mine.

"Nabbed," she says, and peers up at me under the canopy of her eyelids. Watching to see what I'll do next. Daring me.

"Did I catch you, or did you trap me?" I say.

"Maybe," she says.

"Maybe which?" I say.

"Maybe you should figure it out yourself," she says.

I pull her mouth into mine. It's a nice long kiss. The loaminess of the coffee smells like something primal, as if every bean has been mined from the center of the earth. It's so thick it's as if we're all alone, hidden or sheltering in a caffeine cloud.

FOURTH DOSE

She cancels twice. No reason given. Then she picks a French place on the East Side. The sign over the door says two maggots or something. These French names, they're a little freaky. She's five minutes late. Which in girl time is ten minutes early.

It's a Thursday night in March. Winter is screaming its closing remarks at the door. We get a banquette along the wall in the back room. Go for the steak frites. Shooter say: *Always get the most expensive thing on the menu and insist that she do the same.*

I look around, make a mental note: chick heaven. It's got that we're-trying-really-hard-to-be-French vibe so few places have. The waitresses talk like Pepe Le Pew.

"Steak frites, medium rare," I tell the waitress.

"*Moi, je prends la même chose,*" Julia says, bundled in her yellow coat.

Memo to self: learn French.

"What ninety-nine St. Émilions do you have?" I ask. Shooter made me memorize this line.

The waitress looks impressed, offers me her fave. I order it without asking for the price. Class. That's me.

"You speak French," I say.

"Not much," she says. "I was mostly in it for the naughty words."

"Julia Brouillard," I say, tasting the words. "What's that mean?"

"Fog," she says. "I kind of like it. Makes me feel like I can hide. Alone in my haze. That no one can penetrate."

"What's Les Deux Magots then? Two maggots?"

"Slang," she says, already on her second cigarette. "For two ugly guys."

"So I make you think of ugly guys?"

She laughs. "The one in Paris used to be frequented by Verlaine and Rimbaud."

"Hey, I know them," I say. "They're in a Bob Dylan song. 'Situations have ended sad, relationships have all been bad. Mine have been like Verlaine's and Rimbaud's.' "

"Uh-huh," she says, peeling off her coat. A big Irish sweater under it. "From 'You're Gonna Make Me Lonesome When You Go.' That's how I got interested in them in the first place."

"I gather it didn't work out between them," I say.

"No, they were pretty much doomed," she says. "Beautifully doomed. It would make a good movie."

I beat down the urge to make a joke about how Stallone should play Rimbaud.

"Verlaine was married," she says. "Rimbaud was just a teenager when they met. He was like Verlaine's . . . Lolita."

"Now that's a dreamy smile," I say.

"Can you imagine the power of being Lolita?" she says. "I loved that book."

I never got around to it. I know it was a big tabloid story in the fifties and all, but "OLD MAN WRITES FILTHY BOOK"? Not so shocking these days, is it? Tabloids, like medicine and rocket science, have moved far beyond what was ever thought possible.

"You never showed me your drawing of yourself the other night," I say.

"Oh," she says. A hand flutters automatically to the clasp of her purse. "It was pretty dumb."

"Ah-ha," I deduce, all Sherlockian. "You still have it."

"No," she says. "Yes."

"Come on," I say. "I showed you mine."

"It's just, stupid," she says. She takes it out and unfolds it in her lap as the waitress puts our steaks in front of us.

I pick up a fry and look at the picture. Big pointy skyscrapers. They all look like the Chrysler building, daggers stabbing the sky.

They line both sides of the street as a tiny lone cab putters by. Only the buildings look like monsters. They're full of sharp angry angles and they bend together over the street, blocking out the sun. Their windows look like gritted teeth. In the cab a very small, very pretty face looks out the window, looking overwhelmed by it all.

"This you in the cab?" I say.

"I know. It's lame," she says. "I was trying to be all artsy."

"I like it," I say, though I'm not sure that I do. "The New York City visitors bureau could use it in print ads. There are way too many tourists here anyway."

"I didn't say I could draw," she says.

"What are you best at?"

"Nothing."

"I'll bet not."

"Okay," she says, conspiratorially. "Just between us? I dance."

I dance. Are any two words more guaranteed to stoke my engines? Besty used to dance.

"What kind of dance do you do?"

"All of 'em," she says. "Modern, jazz, ballet. Not tap, though."

"I'll bet you're beautiful when you dance," I say.

A shy smile. And then she stands up and peels again. The big sweater down to the hips goes. Underneath it she's wearing an abbreviated skirt with ironic ruffles and a go-to-hell black sleeveless shirt, tight, with a glittery silver heart in the middle. She sits back down, watching me watching her.

"Can I see you dance sometime?"

"Actually," she says, "we're putting on this recital. In July. It's me, my friend Carla, and some girls from our studio in South Norwalk."

"I'd like to see it."

"You," she says, pointing a fry at me, "should come."

By the time dinner is over and we've each put away three glasses of wine, we're getting a little loopy. So we each order another. It tastes like mother's milk. Better, actually. My mother's milk was full of tar and nicotine. I'm liking her so much I haven't even planned any skits.

"So I found a place," she says.

"In the city?" I say.

The busboy is clearing the table. Suddenly we're almost the only ones here. I look at my watch. Four hours have evaporated.

"It's in Harlem," she says. "Well, 121st Street. Up by Columbia. I'm moving next weekend."

"That was fast," I say.

"Someone I used to work with at the Bridgeport paper needed a roommate," she says.

"She a friend of yours?" I say.

"It's actually a guy," she says.

Something in me flinches, something low down. My pancreas does a stutter step, my bile duct farts. But it isn't unusual for people to have roomies of the opposite sex in New York. The housing crunch is permanent here. I could name half a dozen girls I know who have male roommates they aren't involved with. Some of the guys aren't even gay.

"It'll be good to have you in town," I say.

"I'm excited. The commute was killing. Three hours a day."

"You'll have lots of fun here," I say.

"I hope."

"Come over here," I say.

"Okay," she says.

And she gets up and sits next to me on the banquette. We cuddle for a while.

"I need you in arm's reach at all times," I whisper in her ear.

"Okay," she says.

"The French," I whisper, "have this special way of kissing."

"Oh yeah?" she says.

"*Oui*," I say. And by the time I'm through kissing her, we are the only customers left in the place. There are about ten waitresses and busboys lingering nearby. The music has changed. Edith Piaf has yielded to "Total Eclipse of the Heart." At frightening volume, I make faces of outrage and despair. Julia laughs.

"Any minute now," I say, putting down a credit card that disappears in seconds, "they're going to turn the house lights up."

"I have to go anyway," she says. "The last train's in twenty minutes."

They've already brought the bill. It's about a week's rent. I overtip. Then I walk her to Grand Central. It's beautiful and quiet inside at this hour, now that it has spit its throngs back to Connecticut and Westchester.

"Want to see my favorite spot?" I say.

"Sure," she says. "By the way, I've had a lovely evening, *monsieur*."

"*Mamselle*."

"I think I should have been born in France," she says as we walk downstairs. Well. I walk. She sort of dances all the way down. And at the bottom she twirls around on one leg with the other pointed straight out behind her. She looks at me with pursed lips and her tongue poking her cheek like an insolent child. "I like the way the language works. It's a very foggy tongue."

"Foggy?"

"Imprecise. French has a lot less words than English, so words do double duty all the time. You always have to read into it, figure out the context."

"Example."

"Depending on the context," she says, twirling, " 'like' and 'love' are the same word. 'Kiss' and 'fuck' are the same word. 'Malicious' and 'clever' are the same word."

"Sounds like an ideal medium for miscommunication," I say.

"Yeah," she says. "In the musical-comedy, mistaken-intentions sense."

In front of the Oyster Bar there's this stone archway with a vaulted ceiling.

"Here," I say. I put my hands on her shoulders and put her in the corner next to one side of the arch. "You stand here. Face the wall."

"Why?"

"Trust me," I say. And I retreat to the opposite corner, fifty feet away. I turn around to see if she is cheating. She is. She's sort of facing the corner like an unruly infant, but she's mostly peeking over her shoulder.

"Ready?" I say. "Turn around and face the wall."

She does, tentatively.

I face my corner and start whispering to the wall. "Juuuulia," I say.

Her laugh ricochets up her corner, across the ceiling and down to my corner, clear as fiber optics. "That was awesome," she says. "Do it again."

"Try whispering," I say in the lowest voice imaginable. "It's a whispering corner. It picks up everything. Especially secrets."

"Thanks for dinner," she whispers. "Thanks for . . ." Her voice trails off.

"What?" I whisper. "I didn't get that last part."

"Maybe you weren't meant to," she whispers.

There's puzzling, there's cryptic, and then there's French.

"Julia," I whisper. "I would like to kiss you because you're clever."

She laughs again.

"Do you know what they call a love affair in France?" she whispers.

"What?"

"*Une aventure.*"

"An adventure?" I say.

"Oh yes," she says, so softly.

I guess that makes me Indiana fucking Jones.

"Don't move," I say. "Keep facing the corner."

She does. But by the time I sneak up behind her and put my hands on her waist, I'm pretty sure she knows what I'm up to.

S U B S E Q U E N T   D O S E S
L E A D   T O   A D D I C T I O N

I take her to a movie. Afterward we get loaded on gin at McHale's. I take her to a play. Afterward we get smashed on flavored vodka shots at Russian Samovar. A week later I take her to a premiere at Radio City. Afterward we get blitzed at the giant dinner reception at the Hilton. I take her to a Knicks game: some friends of mine had an extra pair of luxury box tickets. A parade of waiters brings an unending supply of G and Ts to our seats. I am not actually this wonderful, but I'm willing to pretend for as long as necessary. Afterward we build on our drunk at Swift's.

A grinding guitar line on the speaker system. A guitar like things falling and breaking. It's Coldplay. "Yellow."

"What do you see in me?" I say over my Bass. It's been more than a month, and the unanswered sex question hovers between us like a fly you want to squash, just to stop the distraction. Every night ends with an increasingly naughty grab session in the back of a cab as it pulls up to my apartment. "Come up," I say to her ear, every time. "I can't," she says, every time.

The thing I like about the Coldplay song: the aching tiredness of it. As the guy is singing about how much he likes the girl, and how great she looks, about how she reminds him of the stars, you can hear the exhaustion dripping off him, like sweat off a boxer. A boxer who has gone about nineteen rounds.

"What do you mean?" she says.

"I mean, why do you hang out with me?"

We listen to the guitars rumble and claw.

"You're smart," she says. "You're kind. You're funny. I like you," she says.

"I'm the man of your dreams, then."

That one merits half a laugh. No comment. Julia would have made a good White House spokesperson.

"I've been meaning to tell you something," she says.

I nod. Uh-oh.

"The night we met," she says. "I told you I had a boyfriend."

"The one who works in Bridgeport," I say.

A nod. "When I was living in Connecticut, it was, different. But since I've been in the city . . ."

The unfinished sentence hangs in space for a while, and then it just falls on the floor with the spilled beer.

"It's gotten more serious," I say.

"Yes," she says. "So. About us? I'd like to keep things—"

You know the word is coming before it arrives. You can hear it screaming down the tunnel like a 2 train at rush hour, showering sparks over the rails, busting into the station with a hundred tons of lethal momentum.

"—platonic," she says.

Keep it platonic. I've kissed about 40 percent of her body. Who was Plato anyway? A guy who didn't need to get laid? This makes him a hero? Or was "platonic" the word he invented so he could beg off taking girls up to his apartment and go back to fooling around with little boys? And who says he was so great in the first place? Three thousand years later and his country is known for, what? The gyro and the design on disposable coffee cups.

I don't say anything. I just nod. Play Understanding Guy. Try to cover up Cardiac Arrest Guy underneath.

"Whatever you want," I say.

Coldplay say: *"For you I bleed myself dry."*

She takes my hand. Drops her shoulders with relief. She knits her eyebrows. This all makes her even more beautiful, which seems unfair.

"Thank you," she says.

"So," I say. "What's his name?"

She doesn't say anything for a long time. She tries to half-laugh her way out of it. My eyes don't leave hers.

"Duane," she says.

I don't say anything. Because I'm unflappable. Insouciant. Non-chalant.

"How do people stay interested?" she says, looking down. "Don't people get bored with each other?"

"You're bored," I say.

She nods.

It strikes me for the first time that "Yellow" is both a warning and a conversation. The warning is: Guys, do you really have the stamina for this? The conversation is: The singer pleads, then the guitar, playing the part of the girl, answers. But it doesn't say much, that guitar. It just saws and gnaws away.

And I can't ask the next question. Because I'm flappable. Souciant. Chalant.

We go outside and hug. I punch the air until a cab stops. And I don't ask the question: are you bored with him or me?

Back at my place I climb four flights alone. I have had much to drink tonight, but not nearly enough. I pour myself a large glass. I want to crawl inside it and marinate in my longing. Things shouldn't be this complicated. Things weren't always. Were they? I still have the same worries I did when I was thirteen. Except now I'm slightly better dressed, I have a lot more money, and I'm a lot closer to the point where it is severely abnormal to be single.

My top ten favorite things when I was thirteen:

1. whacking off in the bathtub with a dirty magazine;
2. *The Empire Strikes Back*;
3. beating Bucky in tennis;
4. Steve Martin;
5. throwing things at each other in Bucky's pool while quoting *Caddyshack*;
6. three-on-three football games at the high school with Bucky and Clint and John and Jim and Ralph on misty days in the fall, when you could smell the fresh decay in the air and the leaves made cool crunchy sounds underfoot in addition to being fun to get tackled on;
7. the guitar solo in Boston's "More Than a Feeling;"
8. a come-from-behind victory by the Baltimore Orioles;
9. playing Intellivision with Bucky;
10. feeling like I had a bright future.

My top ten favorite things now:

1. real, actual, official sex, the kind that counts in all scorebooks;
2. getting a blow job (used to be number one, but let's face it, girls these days are giving them away like sticks of Dentyne. Or Big Red. There's a potential new product: "Give your breath long-lasting freshness with Big Head!");
3. meeting a girl for the first time at a party and flirting with her and making her laugh;
4. getting pleasingly drunk (as opposed to desperately, you've-got-a-problem drunk), preferably on the same night as 1), 2), or 3);
5. whacking off with a Victoria's Secret catalog (if I keep waxing the cuke, will it get all shiny and worn like a

baseball glove? When will they come up with schlong transplants anway?);

6. somebody cute coming up to me at a party and quoting one of the witty remarks I've made in some article I wrote (never happens, but would be cool if it did);

7. Hanging out at Shooter's pool in Amagansett, not throwing things but still quoting *Caddyshack*;

8. getting comped to a Dylan concert or a cool movie premiere;

9. thirty minutes of extreme sweating in a cedar sauna;

10. the joke section in *Randy*.

Let's see. What hasn't changed? I still like a joke and an orgasm. Still like a movie, and, hmm, seem to like being damp. What happened to hope for the future?

At work I read the papers and script a conversation. I plan my spontaneity down to the last detail. I make *notes*. Then I call her "just to say hi." I don't want anything. Who me? I'm just a great guy, saying amusing things about topics of the day. I do not ask her out.

I call her the next day, same thing. Aren't I the best? I'm a pal. We talk about her brothers. We talk about her mom. We talk about various books we're reading. Well. Books she's reading. I do not ask her out.

Then we're on the phone on a drippy Friday in April. There's always a hint of dreamy farewell about these Friday-afternoon chats: she goes home for the weekend on the 8:52, and I know I'm not going to see her again until Monday. I don't ask about the details. It's understood that we don't see each other on weekends.

"What are you doing this weekend?" she says.

"Not much," I say. "And you?"

"Same old," she says.

"Wanna get some air?" I say.

The rain looks like it's stopped (the only way I can tell from this floor is to gaze down at the street five hundred feet below: if you can't see any umbrellas, it's clear), so I put on my blue blazer, the one some people Julia's age think is dorky, but which she thinks is kind of retro-prepster-cute. (I don't tell her I bought the jacket in an entirely unironic state, because I thought it looked grown-up and needed something to wear to all of my married friends' increasingly frequent semi-stuffy Sunday brunches.) We stroll down Seventh, all the way down to Penn Station, talking about Audrey Hepburn. *Breakfast at Tiffany's* is her favorite film, of course.

"*Charade* is much better," I say.

"*Lovvved* that," she says.

"Did you see *Sabrina*?"

"You mean she played the Julia Ormond part?"

"Funnee," I say. "What about *Two for the Road*?" My favorite obscure Audrey movie: but she's seen that one too. And loved it. It's all about a love affair between Audrey and Albert Finney, and they're wisecracking newlyweds kicking pennilessly around Europe in the sixties, and Audrey always wears dresses by (another thing I've learned from hanging around women) Givenchy, which (as a girlfriend once taught me), is a name that may only be pronounced with maximum pretension: "Zhih-von-shee." The movie is all mixed up in time, skipping back and forth between good and bad moments in their relationship.

"It's cool how it keeps you off guard," I say.

"Yeah," she says. "It preserves the mystery of it all."

"The mystery," I say, chewing it over. "Good word. Speaking of."

I nod at the Kmart across the street.

"Nooooo!" she says, doing her best take on the girlfriend of the action-movie hero as he races toward the ambush.

"Come on," I say. "Daddy needs some lightbulbs."

Today I'm dressed just okay for a New Yorker but here I look like the king of Monaco or something. Plus, here among the Kmart shoppers, I feel well above the Minimum Acceptable Height for an Adult Male. Poor people aren't just short of *cash*. Maybe I should look into a Kmart Kareer.

"Excuse me?" An enormous Latina woman of about fifty, wearing her makeup in thick layers. In her shopping cart is economy-sized, cheap-branded everything. She looks exhausted by life.

Julia and I ignore her but the woman is tugging my sleeve.

"Excuse me, do you work here?" she says in hesitant English.

I give Julia a look.

"Yes," I say.

"I have to find baby formula," she says. "The guy, the *kid*, he tells me it's over here, but he don't say where over here. I been looking for ten minutes."

"I don't know where that is," I say.

"You what?"

A kid in a red vest comes by wielding a price gun. He's moving as if he's on wheels.

"That's him," says the lady. "Excuse me! Excuse me!"

The kid hears nothing. Get out of his way. He's got a price gun.

I stick a hand out.

"Tom Farrell, regional sales," I say. "Jerome?"

The kid stops short, bewildered, as though I've read his mind instead of his name tag. "Yeah?"

"Can you help this nice lady? She needs baby formula."

"It's over—"

"Jer*ome*. What's your last name, Jerome?"

"Carns?" Now he looks scared. I've got his last name.

"Do me a favor," I say. "Take her there and show her. I'll remember you when I'm doing the Christmas bonuses."

The kid, it is plain, has never gotten a Christmas bonus in his life. Of course, he probably never will.

"This way," says the kid, and darts down an aisle.

"Thank you," says the lady, kissing her fingertips.

Julia is smiling at me.

"That," she says, "was *awe*some."

We go back to the office and get an elevator to ourselves. I take up a strategic position in one corner, my hands behind my back. She is in the far corner. I want to grab her. She wants to be grabbed. There are security cameras. We stand our ground, smiling at each other. After a while we start trading funny faces. The ditzy girl. The *Sling Blade* guy. The fainting duchess. The skeezy pickup artist. Ding. The door opens.

" 'Bye!" she says and skips out. She literally skips out. And she trips a little, over nothing. "Did I mention," she says, "that I dance?"

I go back to my cubicle but I don't call. When it's about time to leave, I simulate a rush to begin my madcap bachelor weekend, when in fact my slate is bare except for a planned Friday evening at the apartment of Karin and Mike, formerly autonomous human life forms who now say things like, "*We* don't like those kinds of movies" (about *Boogie Nights*), "*We*'ve never heard of them" (about Radiohead, or any other band since the Thompson Twins), and (late last year) "*We*'re pregnant."

The phone. Her name on the LED readout.

"Hey," I say.

"Hey," she says.

"Have a great weekend," I say.

"You too . . ." she says.

"I heard that ellipsis," I say.

"I was just wondering," she says, "if you'd care to have brunch on Sunday."

And my ever-uneasy mind settles into a nice little hum of contentment. She was just wondering if I'd care to have sex on Sunday.

"How about Cafe Frog?" I say.

"Around noon?" she says.

"I'll see ya there," I say.

I look at my watch: first down, forty-two and a half hours of sweet anticipation to go.

The day of. I'm springing out of bed at eight, flinging open the blinds. Sex is doing a drum solo in my veins. My pulse goes: "sex-SEX sexSEX sexSEX." Wash the face (sex). Brush the teeth (Sex). Take a shower (SEX! SEX! SEX!). Get dressed in a way that says: I am not trying for sex in any way. Jeans (sniff carefully—do they smell sexy?). Clean T-shirt. Ragged go-to-hell long-sleeved shirt over that. Unbuttoned. Casual like. Cologne? Don't. Well, maybe just a little. Dab, dab. Sniff, sniff. Too much! I stick each earlobe under the faucet. Which gets water running down my neck and into my shirt. But better to smell like nothing than to smell like a guy who wears jewelry.

Get there a little late. She's later. Cars whooshing by on the drizzle-covered streets. Ten minutes late. Fifteen. I just stand on the corner glowering, thinking, If she stands me up this time, I'll . . . I'll forgive her quickly and go back to telling her how beautiful she is. She can do anything she wants to me. She should not be allowed to realize this. But I won't need to hide myself from her much longer. After today, things will be different. I will have a freshly minted girlfriend. And New York—waterlogged, filthy-puddled, unnecessarily cool-yet-humid April New York? New York will be minty fresh. So will I. Knowing this girl, it's like a soul gargle. All that emotional plaque is coming off.

She's here. Disentangling herself from the backseat of a taxi.

"Sorry sorry sorry sorry!" she says. "It's really hard to get a cab in the rain."

"Not a problem," I say, cheek-kissing her.

"Shall we?" she says.

And in we go. We're looking over our menus when she gives me the once-over.

"So," she says, "this is what you look like on weekends."

"How do I look?" I say.

"You still look pretty good," she says.

There is a slow unfurling in my lap. We eat slightly more quickly than is necessary, talking about nothing.

"So what do you want to do?" I say. "There's a flea market across the street." Shopping for things other people have thrown away. Yeah, *that's* why we're here.

"I'm actually kind of tired," she tells her plate.

"Wanna take a nap?"

"I could take a nap," she says to her shirt.

Blood leaving my brain. It's needed elsewhere.

"Check?" I tell the waiter.

Walk slow, I tell myself as I lead her back to my lair. Just lollygagging. Strolling. Admiring the flowers popping up in the little caged patches of grass around the trees. Overdressed people walking home from church. Suckers. They believe in God. I believe in hot little dancers.

No hurry at all. *Four blocks.* (Baby carriages are so slow. Pass them.) Just taking in the day. (This hand-in-hand couple sauntering down the sidewalk like they own it. Let's just take a detour into the street. Splash through this puddle here.) Yeah, I could spend hours just wandering aimlessly. (This jogger is practically going backward, let's just squeeze between him and the brownstone, oops, scraped some skin off the elbow, that's okay.) *Three blocks.* Such a lovely day to be outdoors. (I thought Rollerbladers were supposed to be speed addicts. Yet we seem to be catching up to this guy in the skintight racing suit.) *Two blocks.* Yes, me and my girl here are just lingering in the afternoon (tripping over dogs and children). *Last block.* Did everyone on the Upper West Side take six Valiums with their coffee or is today National Slo-Mo Day?

Carefully, carefully. I don't put my arm around her waist. I don't kiss her at the red light. We just look straight ahead, stepping around puddles. On Broadway Love is still in business. Up the four flights to my apartment. And.

She sits on the couch. I go to the stereo. Put on *Murmur.* And though I hate to be one of those their-first-album-was-their-best guys, in this case it happens to be true. Except for "Radio Free Europe," which is the worst song but also the first, so I always skip it.

"I *love* this album," she says, closing her eyes.

"Michael Stipe was so much more interesting when he was speaking in tongues."

"I *know.* 'This One Goes Out to the One I Love?' Please."

I sit next to her. Reasonably close. Chummily close. I don't touch. I just listen.

Michael say: "Rest assured this will not last."

" 'Pilgrimage' is such a great song," she says.

"Best song on the album?"

" 'Perfect Circle,' " she says.

"I was hoping you'd say that," I say. "You know, I never heard this album till freshman year of college."

She just looks at me.

And I'm remembering a particularly loud show I once watched on my employer's sister organization, the Argument Channel. It was called the *Gaffe Guys.* It was a political news wrap-up that played clips of elected officials making comments they would later regret.

Whenever the show caught an inappropriate remark, there would appear superimposed on the screen a giant red balloon with the word "GAFFE!" on it. One of the Gaffe Guys said a gaffe is defined as the moment when a politician in desperate evasion of the truth accidentally reveals what he truly believes.

Forgive me, Father, for I have gaffed. A thought, a disturbing thought: this must be some kind of *oldi*es album to her. Is Michael Stipe her *Sinatra*?

"Wanna see some pictures?"

"Yeah!" she says.

All part of the plan. I keep my pictures in purposeful disarray: they're all in the envelopes they came in, jumbled in a haystack on one of my bookshelves. I don't put my pictures in albums. If I did, one could leaf through them and notice that the date stamps over the last few years could—not frequently—raise issues of girlfriend overlap. All of which is behind me now. When things are set with Julia, the (exceedingly rare) problem I had with other girls will vanish. The most beautiful woman in the world is here on my couch. Waiting.

I take the three harmless envelopes I placed atop the stack last night with lust aforethought. Despite the (really almost nonexistent) overlap thing, it proved depressingly easy to find envelopes that were entirely girlfriendless.

I show her some aww-shucks pictures of me playing with my friends' babies. Me at my friends' weddings. Me clowning in a two-horned Norseman's helmet like the one Elmer wore in "What's Opera, Doc?" Me in black tie. All pictures carefully selected to say: I am fun but dependable, popular and loved, well traveled and full of surprises. It takes the entire length of the CD and then some to get through them all. We're hearing the fourth track again when I return from putting the pictures back in the bedroom.

"That was fun," she says. "Like, *Tom Farrell: The E! True Holly-wood Story.*"

Michael say: *Talk about the passion.*

And then the kissing begins.

And then the touching begins.

And then the undressing begins.

I know when I unbutton her shirt. The bra. It isn't a bra meant for wearing. It's a bra for removing. Sex bras are always brand new, lacy, and red or black. (In advanced scenarios, they can be white. Only the really clued-in girl knows the effect a white bra has on a man. The first bra we ever see is usually white: mom's. In the olden days, underwear was federally required to be white. Thus every white bra brings back that first accidental glimpse while mom was getting dressed, or that heart-stopping debut glance in the forbidden underwear drawer.) This one is bright, wicked scarlet.

"Did you wear this hot bra for me?" I say.

She laughs. "But I don't match!" she says.

"Let's see," I say. Zip. Lime green.

I take it slow. She stops for a second.

"Your kisses are so soft and gentle," she says.

I smile.

I use the R.E.M. record for rhythm. Work on one erogenous zone per song. But I can't. That's four minutes. Hell. By the time "Perfect Circle" comes on, I'm taking her into my arms and carrying her into the bedroom. Well. I'm stumbling a bit. It's awkward, carrying a girl, you know? Plus I almost crack her head on the doorjamb.

I toss her on the mattress. She turns over and waits, lying hotly on her tummy in her hot underwear. Look at her. Her panties should carry a warning tag: "Caution: The Girl You Are About to Enjoy Is Extremely Hot."

This is going to be incredible. This is going to be like nothing else has ever been. Except. You know how everyone thinks they have a good sense of humor, are good drivers, and are good in bed? When there's a break in the conversation at a party, I can never think of a good joke. I was in three non-minor traffic accidents before I turned twenty-five. And—

SATURDAY, JULY 14

But that was almost four months ago. Today is the day of her dance recital. I'm up early. I don't want this day. Can we skip over to the next day, please?

I piece myself together uncertainly. "Suave," says my shampoo. "All-purpose solution," says my contact lens cleaning fluid. "Total control," says my styling gel. "Cool," says my antiperspirant. I am not living up to the expectations of my toiletries.

I picture me sitting next to him in the front row, all civil like. Then I picture him getting in a seething jealous rage over me and yelling at Julia and squealing off into the night in his two-cylinder 1986 Hyundai Muskrat, sending Julia caroming neatly into my arms.

At the flower store for the long stemmed. Would red be sending a signal? I get yellow, the rose of caution, the rose that goes slow. The rose that reminds me of her yellow coat. The guy talks me into getting a glass vase to go with. Very schmancy. Whole thing costs me sixty-eight bucks. I don't care.

She told me I could stay overnight at her parents', so I pack a pair of shorts and a T-shirt to sleep in and a change of underwear, and while I'm in my underwear drawer . . . heh, heh, what have we here? Hello, my latex friends. (These guys could use a quick splotch of Endust too.) Never hurts to have one (or five!) of these around, does it? I pick up a couple, start to put them in my bag. Then I put them back in the drawer: what if she found them on me? Might look a tad presumptuous. On the other other hand, what are the odds that this intensely non-nosy person is going to go rootling around in my stuff? I start to put them in the bag. Then I think: being caught without a rubber is the last thing I should worry about. Back in the drawer they go.

On the subway I sit with my giant bouquet concealing the hard-on in my lap. Women look at me approvingly. Nod, smile. A guy bringing pretty flowers to his lady. I make a mental note: *good way to meet women?* All I have to do is shell out sixty-eight dollars every Saturday and ride the subway all day. Of course, if anyone asks, they're for my mother. *No, it's not her birthday. It's just . . . because.*

"Beautiful flowers," says one woman on the platform in Grand Central. A blonde, nice eyes. Okay, she's fifty. This is the most action I've had all week.

So I leave New York and take the train into America. CBS-watching America. JCPenney America. Souvenir-plate America. Daytime TV America. Bumper-sticker America. SUP R STOP N SHOP America. Salad bars and lawn mowers. Lyme disease and strip malls.

On my headphones I'm revving for the challenge: Radiohead's *OK Computer.* This would be really hot sex music. Then I remember her telling me she loved that album. Or maybe she's been loved to that album. I try not to think about it. I fail.

I'm replaying my favorite Julia moments. The time in Swift's when we were looking at the jukebox and she was looking for "Rikki

Don't Lose That Number" for some reason and my arm discovered her waist and I pulled her to me and kissed her hair. "Mmm," she said. "You do smell *nice.*" I mentally ran through the list of things that had been on or near my body that day. Shampoo. Conditioner. A little Ivory soap for the pits. Deodorant. Trying to reconstruct my smell.

That time at Russian Samovar. It was eleven. We were both in a good mood. We did lemon-vodka shots, horseradish, coconut, watermelon. We did a lot of shots. She hadn't eaten. We told each other secrets and then messed around in the cab. She wouldn't come up to my place so I sent her onward. Later she told me that when the cabbie was dropping her off at her place, she quietly leaned over and upchucked in the backseat. She was too embarrassed to tell him. She was a puke scofflaw. I told her that from now on I wanted her to think of me every time she puked. She laughed.

That time after the National Book Critics Circle Awards. The evening promised to be dull, and for once something lived up to expectations. The ceremony took place in a grim little high school–sized auditorium down at the NYU law school. I hadn't read any of the books. I didn't see anyone I knew at the after party. And book people are ugly little trolls. I fit right in there. But I left early and called her from a pay phone on a windy Monday night unfairly cold for mid-March. She was still at work. She was about to get out. Was she up for a drink? She was. I told her to meet me at this sleek bar on West Forty-eighth called Mystery. It's one of the few vaguely cool places near where we work. She stood me up. I waited there for half an hour thinking, Should I call her cell phone? But I didn't have a quarter. I'd have to go to the bar. Beg one of the glamazon waitresses for change. I'd look like an idiot. I'd look like a guy who'd been stood up. Forty-five minutes. Nobody wants to look like what he actually is. Finally I got some nerve, got some change. Called my home machine. Got this message.

Hey, um, it's me. I am probably just an idiot—it's eleven—and. I. Couldn't seem to find the place you were talking about, so. I went to West Forty-eighth. But. No one can seem to help me find it. I. Guess. I'm. Gonna. Go. Home. I'm really sorry. 'Cause you've probably spent a good deal of time sitting there just thinking that I flaked out on you again. Which I didn't! So could you call me? On my cell phone? Or house phone? When you get this message? And, um, just let me know that you don't hate me. So. I'll talk to you soon. 'Bye!

Adorable. Poetry. My anger just slid right off me. I got her on her cell.

"The bar's kind of hard to find," I say. "There's a sign. But it's a small sign. The rule in New York is, if you want lots of customers, hide your bar."

"I'm such an idiot," she says, sounding really nervous. "I can't believe it."

"Shhh, sweetie," I say. "It's all right. Meet me outside. Southeast corner of Forty-eighth and Eighth. My mistake for picking such an obscure place."

Five minutes later I'm standing at the southeast corner of Forty-eighth and Eighth. There's a parking garage there. It's freezing. It's the middle of March! It's the endless winter of '01. Where is she now? I look across Eighth. I look across Forty-eighth. I wrap my scarf around my neck. I put my gloves on. Something makes me turn around, toward the Forty-eighth Street entrance of the garage.

She's sneaking up prettily behind me on tiptoe in the yellow coat that is much too thin for the weather. She has a cartoon look on her face. I'm Elmer. She's Bugs.

The expression on her face. *Caught! Foiled! Oh no!* I grab her in a bear hug and I pick her up off her feet and I hold her as tight as I can and we twirl. She laughs and laughs. Folks, tonight's happiness scores are in. Every other guy in the world is competing for second place.

Get off the train in South Norwalk. She's not on the platform. She's downstairs, wearing glamour-girl Hollywood oversized bug-eye black shades and a denim dress, the kind with no zip up the back (I check). You just throw it on over your head, on your bare skin. She's not wearing a bra. She looks incredible. She looks like the encyclopedia of sex.

"Hi," she says and laughs her half laugh. Julia is big on nervous laughter. It fills in all the spaces for her, spackles over the perpetual mild embarrassment of existence. She reaches up to give me a sister peck on the cheek. Mwah.

Only then does she notice what I'm holding. The giant glass vase is all wrapped up in cellophane and there are little extraneous sprays of supporting-act flowers and the whole package looks mighty impressive.

"Oh, *my*," she says. And she laughs her nervous laugh.

"Found these on the train," I say.

"Oh my," she says, her sentences getting shorter.

"Really," I say, "it was just lucky someone left them there."

At her house I meet the parents (dad sullen, mom breathlessly emotive) and the brothers (know-it-all seventeen-year-old, deeply confused college junior). You can tell this is a family that has seen more fights than Madison Square Garden. More circuses too.

"Look at those!" says mother. "*Very* hoity-toity. Where did you get them?"

"Oh, these? Found 'em on the train," I say. Aren't I charmingly self-deprecating? But I'm thinking, Should have brought something for the mother. *Always bring something for the mother.* Unless Julia's the kind of girl who specifically dates guys calculated to irritate the maternal unit.

The younger brother slouches into the room, the teen who just got into Wisconsin: Al. Al doesn't say much.

They've laid out a real spread for me: iridescent blue-green plastic throwaway plates, matching cups. The full bounty of the Oscar Mayer aisle, an archive of luncheon meats. The plastic forks and knives are translucent, ostentatiously heavy, as if to say, this is *quality* disposable flatware. And to drink: they've got six liters of popular carbonated beverages. Most of them are caffeine free. This is okay. My blood is surging, my nerves are frying in a pan of butter, my hormones are ringing like a gong as one message chug-a-chugs through my power grid: JuliaJuliaJulia. As addictive as java, and worse: not only do I need her when I get up every morning, I need her when I go to bed every night.

We eat spiced ham and pimiento loaf and make small talk with the grandmother and the aunt, who just showed up. They're both proud, wide women with grooves carved into the rubber of their faces. Julia therefore will look like this in thirty years. So it's no big thing if I don't wind up with her. Right? This is what I keep telling myself. It must be true.

The mom ("Call me Charlotte!") fusses, getting ice, grabbing bottles of soda, deplasticizing more processed meats. She is largely implied throughout the meal. Occasionally her voice ricochets in from the Formicaed kitchen. At one point she sits and eats a rolled-up piece of bologna, but then she disappears again on a mysterious errand.

The dad sits at the head of the table chewing. He says nothing.

After lunch we go over the family albums and make fun of Julia's large high school hair. There's a loud Frankenstein's-monster thump on the door.

Brother Gary, the college student, answers. "Hi, Duane," I hear.

Hi, *Duane.* Normally the only time I wish ill on anyone is when reading my college alumni notes.

There's a lot of Hi, Duaneing going around the house. He is not unknown here. In fact he acts as if he has been here hundreds of times.

The Duane goes to kiss Julia; she gives him her cheek and an awkward little rub on the back. No making out in front of me, at least.

Duane is tall, five inches taller than me. A storky dork, all elbow and knee. I suppose girls would say he's dreamy to look at, but let's break him down, shall we? He has nondescript brown hair and blue eyes and a fiercely nonhumorous face, a face the texture of meat loaf. And he has an earring; not an interesting one. It looks like the little circular paper clip they put your new key on when you get a key made. What kind of heterosexual man wears an earring in 2001? He's wearing blue jeans and a green T-shirt, sneakers. Your basic auto-mechanic look.

He's getting the check-in cheek kiss from the auntie and the grammy and the mommy, another casual, "Hi, Duane," from the dad, as if he's a welcome presence instead of the prince of darkness. They are treating him like the son-in-law. I'm the son-out-of-law, the son out of luck.

Duane and I size each other up.

"Tom Farrell," I say.

He glares. "What kind of name is that?"

"It's, um, Irish."

Drunken potato-eating bricklayer, say his eyes.

"What's your last name?" I say.

"Feinberg," he says, aggressively.

Uh-oh. A Jew. He's probably pretty smart. And funny. And his dad was probably a cardiothoracic surgeon instead of an air-conditioner repairman.

The brothers are asking Duane to go play Frisbee. As if they've done it a hundred times before. *They're all friends.*

"You wanna play Frithbee?" Duane asks.

Let's see, do I want to play Frisbee with the guy who is having sex with my woman? No, not particularly. I have not played Frisbee in years. Possibly I might toss more than my share of wobblers, and I try not to do anything I'm not good at around a girl.

Duane does not subscribe to this philosophy; for instance, he speaks despite having nothing to say. Conversation involves a certain amount of treading water until your wit window opens. With him it's all treading water: the traffic, the weather, what time he got up, what he had for lunch (matzoh ball thoup at his mother's; she's having a delayed Pathover, apparently). He is a boring guy, precision measured and custom fit for a boring suburb, a guy built to serve one purpose: to be a dodgeball target.

"Where you from?" he says.

"Rockville, Maryland," I say.

I gracefully allow him a response window. He has nothing to say, though.

"Where you from?" I say.

"Pithcataway," he says.

"I'm sorry?"

"Pithcataway. New Jerthey."

"I love New Jersey town names," I say. "Ho-Ho-Kus? Weehawken?" She laughs.

"When you look at the map, they're all absurd. Were their founding fathers a bunch of DKEs hunched over pitchers of Schlitz? There's probably a town called Dicksmawken or Tu-Tu-Tuchus."

Julia throws her head back and laughs. Duane gives her a sharp look. That's right, buddy. Deal yourself right out of this game.

"Actually," Duane says, "they're Native American named. Not a joke to them."

The look on his face is blank, earnest, serious. How many unfunny Jews have you ever met? Not counting the pros, the ones who go moping down the street in their all-black look-at-me-I'm-Jewish costumes.

We all look at the mom's fiftieth birthday party pictures. Julia's hot in a deep V-neck sleeveless top, giving a shy toast or mugging with her brothers. In every picture Duane lurks buffoonishly in the background, always with the same expression on his face: I am Stable, I am Sober, I have a two by four up my Sphincter.

There's a picture of Julia, her tongue leaking epileptically out of the corner of her mouth, awkwardly trying to applaud-catch a Frisbee between two flat hands.

"She always tries to catch it like that," Al says, shaking his head.

"The grace. The poise," I say. "Are you by any chance a dancer?"

"Shut *up*!" A right cross to the shoulder.

"You could really do something with this picture, though," I say. "Could be on a poster for the Special Olympics."

"Isn't that where you go to hit on girls?" she says.

"Tried to. The competition was too fierce, though. I got beaten up by a paraplegic."

"And how did your pick-up lines go over with the deaf girls?"

"The ones who couldn't talk didn't really like being referred to as 'dumb.' "

"See, now, I would've thought you're an expert on dumb."

Speaking of: Duane isn't saying a word. His eyes dart wildly between us. Mother turns to the next picture in the stack: it's the money shot. Topless Julia, scampering madly on the beach, age approximately four.

"Oh God!" she says. "Moth*er*!"

"I found this the other day," Charlotte says brightly. "I just threw that in there while you were eating."

"It's so nice to see there's a couple things about you that haven't changed much over the years," I say.

Charlotte laughs. "She was always so flat chested," she says. "She didn't get them from me!" Then, for emphasis, she places hands on herself. Plumps herself up for inspection. Yep. Can't miss 'em.

"Okay," Julia says. "Barf bag, *please.*"

"You were so adorable," Charlotte says.

"Were?" Julia says.

"Of course you made me a copy of this?" I ask Charlotte.

Duane is silent. The plan has been to show her, one on one, that I'm better in every way: okay, he might be a smidge better looking than me. But aren't girls supposed to care less about that kind of thing? And though he's a lot taller than me, I'm a lot taller than Julia. On conversation, I've got the guy beat. Surely she is noticing. I've made her laugh half a dozen times. Duane is ringing up a big bagel.

We drive over to the recital together, papa bear, son bear, son-in-law bear, and me: Barely Tolerated Bear. The performance is in a junior high school auditorium. On the way over, Duane pushes banalities at me like a mother offering a bowl of candy. He attempts to begin every sentence with "So," which is an unwise strategy for him.

"Though, what do you do at the paper?" he says.

"Though, how long have you been in journalithm?" he says.

"Though, what'th the latht movie you thaw?" he says.

I feel like setting things on fire.

At no point does he say, "Though, have you ever had thex with my girlfriend?" Despite knowing the following:

1. I bought her an expensive bouquet, *with* a glass vase;
2. I rode a train for an hour to see a bunch of amateur dancers crash into the scenery and each other;

3. I hardly ever make eye contact with her when we're all in a group together.

Yet he asks nothing. What kind of reporter is this guy? A small-town reporter, a guy who retypes the press release without picking up the phone, a reporter who doesn't ask what he doesn't want to know.

At the auditorium, I look at the smudgy xeroxed program. A crude drawing of skyscrapers twinkling in the night. Fat childish lettering heralds A SALUTE TO NEW YORK CITY.

Put on by a group of people who live sixty minutes from it. Yet they're right. In this place, the city seems as exotic as Bangkok.

Curtain up. A guy standing in front of the stage actually puts a record on a turntable. The record hisses over the Korean War–surplus speakers.

The scenery is a series of cardboard decorations affixed to the rear curtain: a slightly lumpy five-foot-tall red apple covered in glitter. Ten white stars arranged to the side in a wedge formation. The big apple I get. The stars mystify me. Two for each borough?

The first dance is "New York, New York" from *On the Town*. The dancers—these are the intermediates, the fourteen-year-olds—lip-synch along to the crackling lyrics. They point up to the Bronx. They point down to the Battery.

More time-warp numbers. "Give My Regards to Broadway." "I'll Take Manhattan." Every number runs embarrassingly long, *with a reprise*. Tubby dancers stepping all over each other and little girls and housewives inexplicably commingled with the few girls who can dance. No two dancers are exactly in rhythm as they cavort across the stage. One number involves hats: they take them off, they spin them on their hands. They lie on their backs and point their chubby legs up and spin the derbys on their feet. Gradually dancers lose their hats. Soon the stage is littered with them. Those who have dropped their hats continue to do the number with make-believe hats, which is easier for all involved. Possibly they could have extended this idea a bit further: what if the girls and the audience simply agreed to pretend there was a performance, and we all went for a beer instead?

I look at the program: Julia doesn't appear until Act II.

There are seventeen numbers in Act I.

I turn to Silent Al.

"Can I get a drink here?"

"There's a water fountain," he offers.

"How about a bourbon fountain?"

He shrugs. Al isn't picking up what I'm laying down. Julia once told me, "I love Al. Al is *me*." Gotta work on this guy.

At halftime we all wander outside into the warm spring air. The sun is just setting. The air has that fresh suburban smell. Like stuff actually grows here.

"Though," says Duane, "ever been to a rethital before?"

I'm sitting next to him on a low concrete wall. The dad starts chatting with Julia's dance partner, Carla, who just got engaged. I follow the playbook and compliment her rock.

"One point oh two," she brags.

A large ant has appeared between Duane and me. I crush it with my shoe.

"Nah, nooo," Duane says with dismay.

Julia comes out in a hideous red-and-black-plastic cocktail dress, a dress that shouts "rented costume."

"I know," she says, before anyone speaks. "Aren't these costumes the *worst*?"

"Give us a twirl," I say.

She does. The dress is backless. "Tra la," she says, and shrugs.

She's in the next number but she just learned it. She has some butterflies. Also, what she's wearing is a fire hazard. She sits down on the low wall across from the one Duane and I are sitting on, equidistant from each of us, adopting a neutral pose.

Duane is a possessory toucher. He springs up—boing!—and posts himself behind her. He is constantly stroking her arm, putting his hand on the small of her back, tugging her closer. Sometimes she resists. Sometimes she doesn't. I try to chat with the dad, use my peripheral vision to clock it all. Julia notices another ant next to her on the wall and stands up skittishly. Duane ever so gently brushes the ant away with a leaf. Rehabilitates it. Releases it on parole. I scan the ground hoping to get a chance to accidentally step on it next time I get up.

Below the backless part of her outfit there are some sexy crisscross straps. Which is where Duane's hand is now. I'm not looking, but I'm looking.

I'm talking about the Microsoft case with Julia's dad. I'm not looking. (Touching, rubbing, holding.) We talk about the recession, about his job in the computer software sales business. We talk sports, and I'm not looking. (Grabbing, stroking, *mauling*.)

Back in my seat for the second half. Have you ever seen your girl, the girl you most like to look at, dance? About fifteen girls are out there for a "There's No Business Like Show Business" that's twenty-four-carat zircon. Julia is one of them. She's in vinyl. I'm in heaven. She's a little out of step. Her arms swing a quarter of a beat off. At one point she turns right when she's supposed to turn left, briefly hip-checks Carla, and giggles. I'm loving every second of it. The things she can do with her legs, the way she arches her back. What a waste. This body, reserved nightly for an ant-loving lisper.

The choreography on the number is so ha-cha-cha ridiculous that I'm not prepared for the one that comes next. There are forty dances listed in the program, but this one is the only one she choreographed. It's set to cool weird instrumental music and has cool weird costumes—sexy tight tops, loose Turkish harem pants. Half of the girls are wearing red and half blue. And as Julia moves and writhes and runs and spins and stands on one leg with the other pointing toward the gods, I get some sense of what I came for, some sense of why Julia is Julia: the mystery. In five minutes it'll be all over and the stage will give way to a bunch of four-year-olds lisping along with "Happiness," from *You're a Good Man, Charlie Brown*.

But for now, Julia is beyond beautiful. She is the thing itself. She holds the copyright. It's like finding a Matisse at a garage sale. When she's done, everyone else in the family gets up to go outside again. I just sit there alone for a minute.

When I wander outside, the family is there. Julia is there too. She's relaxed and damp with sweat and Duane's clutch is coming at her from all directions.

We go back inside to see the big finale, "One," from *A Chorus Line*, and Julia joins the kick line and we applaud dutifully and then we wait in the corridor. Duane and I stand side by side.

"So," I say. "Shall we settle this like men?"

Except I don't. I don't say anything. I just wait.

"Though, what kinds of books do you like?"

Time for a little detective work. I find out his work schedule (he's on nights, which is why Julia always seems to be available for the evening), discover that he's taking her to Mexico in September (not if I can help it, buddy), learn that when she went to Portugal last year ("The only time I was ever on an airplane," she explained sheepishly, the night I met her), he was the one who took her. I go back and mentally rewrite all of the stories she has told me. For "I," kindly read, "We." "I" live on 121st? No, that, according to Duane, is where "We" live.

I inquire as to his future.

For the time being, he's trying to claw his way into a job in the city. He wants out of Connecticut. His ambition is to become a generic general assignment reporter, a guy who chases fires and waits in the shrubbery, for one of the metro rags. In other words, the kind of job I had years ago and graduated from years ago. And he expects to support her in the style to which she's become accustomed (from me)?

Sure, he gets to sleep with her and all, but there are a couple of facts I am aware of, things that have come out with the gin and the wine Julia and I have shared.

1. He wants to marry her.
2. She "isn't sure" she wants to marry him.

"Are you," I say all friendly like, "going to propose soon?"

"Hi." Julia's back. I gape. This time it's a spangled red top, snug as a suntan, with a denim skirt. She still isn't wearing a bra, and she still looks amazing.

What must we look like to her, standing so close to each other and chatting so amiably? There we are. Two guys she's known rather well. Does she look at us and think: that one tastes great, that one's less filling?

Duane goes up to her. Whispers something in her ear. She smiles. And then he presents her with a cover-all-bases greeting card ("Congratulations on your special achievement") and a clump of dirt out of which poke a few dejected weeds and one fresh daisy. He must have picked it out of the ground behind the school. Being broke, he could have played up the po' boy thing with a thoughtfully constructed collage or a poem. He couldn't be bothered, or it just didn't occur to him.

She laughs, tries to look noncontemptuous, passes the card around. I look at his signature. His name, it turns out, is spelled D-W-A-Y-N-E. A Jew named Dwayne. Unbelievable.

There's some sort of plan for a bunch of dancers and our bizarre love triangle to get together later for a celebratory quaff.

"When is the last train to the city?" I say.

"I think it's about one," Julia says.

Back at the house. Mother has laid on another spread. Cold teriyaki chicken. The train schedule clings magnetically to the fridge: the last one is at 11:07. I look at my watch: 11:00.

"How long a drive is it to the train station?" I say, nervously.

"About fifteen minutes," Julia says.

Uh-oh. Everyone graciously starts arranging for me to be comfortable tonight: I can have Al's bed; being in his look-at-me-I'm-weird stage, he always sleeps on the couch anyway. But the gloom is settling in. I have had to watch Dwayne paw her. I have had to watch him kiss her. Am I going to have to listen to them doing it in the next room? Spare me the squeak, I think.

The three of us head out to Julia's dad's car. Julia gets in the driver's seat. Dwayne takes shotgun. Hurrah. A night of revelry is planned. We pick up Carla and Joe and head to the "hip" section, to one of those self-consciously "collegiate" bars where they give you a Bud in a plastic cup and the juke plays Bon Jovi and "rowdy" youths carve their names in wooden tables and attempt to practice philosophy without a license on Saturday nights.

At the saloon we all get Coronas and settle in with some other dancers from the show who show up coincidentally. Apparently this is the only decent bar around. It's called The Olde Cottage or The L'il Cabin or some such.

Dwayne starts talking about hockey. Figures. For a hockey fan, the guy's a genius.

"I'm more into basketball," I say. "I like that team from Philadelphia. What are they called again?"

"Theventy-thixers," he says.

"Who's that point guard they have that's supposed to be so great?"

"Allen Iverthon."

"Tom?" Julia says.

"We're talking sports," I say.

She slaps my knee under the table. I pinch her thigh.

And then it happens. No shit. The juke. That guitar line.

DUMB-dumb-dumb-dumb-DUMB-dumb.

Someone is playing "Jessie's Girl."

And I go all queasy again, thinking of what horrors await me back at Julia's house. It's one story and a basement, three dollhouse-sized bedrooms on the main floor. *Spare me the squeak.* Oh please, please, spare me the squeak.

I spend the rest of the evening looking down the barrel of my one-and-done Corona getting pointedly not drunk. I drop out of the conversation. Joe is wearing a T-shirt that says GET HOOKED ON A BOOK AT THE RED HOOK LIBRARY. There is a drawing of a huge fish getting baited, and thus doomed, with a book, which seems an excellent way to scare children out of reading. Joe is sitting next to Carla. Both of them are between conversations with other people so they look at each other. But they can't think of anything to say. So they start to cuddle. They're all caressy smoochy.

Before we get in the car for the drive to Julia's house, she gives Dwayne the keys.

"You're driving," she says.

I resume my backseat position, and this time Julia clambers in beside me, sacrificially taking the hump seat. Her thighs press up against mine. Carla is on the other side of her. Joe is in the front seat. As we go around corners, Julia leans into me a little. I can smell her. Can she smell me? Do I still smell nice?

Back at her house, Dwayne hits the bathroom first. He and Julia run into each other outside the door.

"The toilet won't fluth," he whispers urgently.

A toilet is possibly the least complicated piece of machinery in the house. There is not much that can go wrong. You push on the handle. Inside the tank, the handle is attached to a chain, which in turn has a rubber stopper on the end. The stopper covers the drain. When you push the handle, you're pulling up the stopper so water can flow out of the tank, down the drain, and into the bowl.

I take the lid off the tank. The chain has fallen off the stopper. This takes approximately four seconds to fix. Dwayne is not even smart enough to figure out that toilet maintenance begins with removal of the lid. This is no ordinary dullard. It's as if he has an advanced degree in stupid. The guy could lose a game of one-card monte. On the other hand, he is clever enough to get himself into a situation where he is about to see Julia naked, which makes him the Bill Gates of this house.

I'm putting the lid back on the toilet when Julia appears with a glass of water. I look at her eyes and her skin and her hair and her body. What I want is a glass of her. My heart hurts. Not my heart-shaped heart, my Disney heart; no, my real heart, the thumping thing. My auricles ache. My ventricles vent. *Spare me the squeak.*

"Hi," she says.

"I fixed the toilet," I say. But this is not what I am really saying. I am saying: *I am a useful male! I can fix household items!* I am saying: *You are stuck with a dumb guy when a toilet-repairing visionary stands before you!*

"Oh," she says. "Wow. I brought you this."

I take the glass of water gratefully. I had thought it was for her. This is her small gesture of affection. Her secret signal to me. Or, possibly, the world's lamest consolation prize.

Julia ushers me across the hall to Silent Al's room; it's weird, like a snapshot of myself from fifteen years ago. There is a cheap stereo matched with expensive speakers. There are posters of alternative heroes, edgy achievers: Einstein, of course. Brando, Gandhi, *Goodfellas*, Carl Sagan, Jim Morrison, and . . . Big Al from *Happy Days*. This one I peer at more closely. "To Al, from Al." There's a bunch of newspaper clips about John Glenn's return to space, a poster for

Miller Lite, and, perfect for a guy who lives three thousand miles from California, another for Ron Jon surfwear (wasn't that an '80s thing? Maybe it's back in a retro-ironic way).

"I drew this," she says. There's a child's felt-tip drawing on a piece of construction paper fun-tak'd to the ceiling. Which is only about six and a half feet off the floor.

"It's Carl Sagan," she says.

He is standing at the window of a spaceship with stars in the background. One rubbery arm is bent up so that the legendary space authority can wave in that slightly disjointed way of kids' drawings. I can't tell whether she drew it fifteen years ago or yesterday, but either way it's perfect. It says family, it says loving big sister, it says closeness and warmth and two people knowing each other so well. All the things I don't have.

"It's nice," I say, but I'm looking at her.

And we stand there, for a second.

"So I'll see you in the morning?"

I nod.

Julia goes to join Dwayne downstairs, to sleep in the basement. I hear them talking in low voices.

When I turn the lights out, there are these glow-in-the-dark stars all over the ceiling and I think I have never seen anything so mysterious and wonderful. I stare at them for seven hours, waiting for morning. Listening.

But no squeaks do I hear.

I wait for everyone else to get up first. Then I creep into the kitchen, the sheepish monster, the undead thing everyone would prefer not to have to deal with. I have my bag in my hand.

Everyone's having bagels and coffee, all familylike.

Julia bounces up, stands next to me. Awkwardly close. Awkwardly far. "Do you want a bagel?"

The thought makes me queasy. I need: a shower, clean clothes, a gallon of mouthwash, an oxygen mask, sleep, a body transplant, persuasive evidence that anybody other than my mom cares about me, a Bloody Mary, something to scrape my face with, a deep-tissue massage, Visine, some sex, and a team of paramedics to carry me out of here. But not a bagel.

"Do you want a doughnut?" says Julia's dad.

I do not.

"Would you like thumb coffee?" says Dwayne.

I would not.

"I have to go," I say to Julia's ear.

I'm overhandling the train schedule. I move it from my bag to my jeans pocket to my shirt pocket. I have parked my bag ostentatiously in the middle of the living room, which is about four feet from the middle of the kitchen. It's a really small house.

There is munching. There is slurping. And I'm feeling really, really, deeply unwell.

"The train is in twelve minutes," I tell Julia's other ear.

And we're in the car. Soon I'll be free. Free to have a little breakdown.

"Traffic is light today," I say, stupidly. It's a Sunday morning in suburbia.

"It was nice of you to come up here," she says.

We talk about her chattering mother and her silent brother.

And I think: I wouldn't mind this. I could live with the she's-not-into-me-anymore thing. I could handle the she's-living-with-someone-else detail. All of this would not unduly trouble me.

If only she would continue having sex with me.

When we get to the station the train is already there. I grab my bag and prepare to bolt. She hurriedly undoes her seat belt, skootches over to give me a kiss on the cheek.

"I'll call you later," she says with worried eyes. "I *promise*."

And I'm gone. I get ten minutes of sleep on the train, bringing the cumulative total since Friday night to ten minutes. Back home I sleepwalk through the day for a while and then go by the grocery store, straight to aisle two, home of beer, soda, dip, chips: they call it aisle two but why not call it what it is? It's the Bachelor aisle. Unchaperoned men in the eighteen to thirty-four demographic skulk and loiter, toting their glum plastic baskets like lost Little Red Riding Hoods who missed their chance to be wolves. Sometimes I wonder what's in the other aisles. That reminds me: I need cereal.

Lite FM seems to be blaring directly from a box of raisin bran. Look at this. When I was a kid you had crunch berries. Little delightful nipple-colored nuggets of sweetness in a humdrum sea of Cap'n Crunch. You had to work for those berries, go spoon diving, you had to make *decisions*, dammit: devour them all at once? Try to apportion at least one to every mouthful? Pick around them so that you can finish with a giant berry crescendo of confectionery nirvana?

Today you can buy an entire box of *just the berries*. Kids today. They don't know hardship. *And* they have Super Soakers. *And* their little Emilys and Amandas start on the BJs in, like, fourth grade. You read these stories about hallway hummers: it's practically a phys. ed. requirement now.

And as I'm checking out, I'm under attack from Lite FM. You know you're in trouble when you start hearing oracles at the frequency of 106.7. It's playing Bread.

Bread say:

> *I would give everything I own*
> *Give up my life, my heart, my home*
> *Just to touch you*
> *One more time.*

I drop my can of artichoke hearts. When I pick it up, the can is dented. When you're in this state, the State, every song is about you. Manilow, Diamond, Fogelberg: *these men are prophets!* Cue blubbering.

Walking home, I think about The Dinner a couple of weeks ago. The plan then was, instead of the usual date—a meal out, a few drinks, a few more drinks, a few more few more drinks, and then an invitation for a midnight tour of my apartment—instead of this, there would be dinner in, drinks in, and behold: a fed, happy, drowsy, tipsy girl planted adorably on the sofa by nine-thirty. A clandestine romp and then she could, if such was her choice (not that I would encourage it), get dressed and be out of there by midnight.

"This is the operator?" I said when I called her. "I have a collect obscene phone call for Julia Brouillard. Will you accept the obscenities?"

"Put it through," she said.

Did she want to grab a bite after work? She did. Sushi? No. (Good. That was a test.) Chinese? Eh, maybe. Italian? Italian. Then, as a just-about-to-hang-up the-phone afterthought: oh, why didn't she just sort of, oh, you know, have dinner over *my* place?

"Hmm," she said.

"I must warn you, your insurance premiums may rise as a direct result," I said.

"Hmm," she said.

"You wouldn't even have to bring anything," I said. "Except of course a fire extinguisher."

She laughed.

"Okay," she said.

"Say six?" I said.

"Six."

I hung up mightily pleased, and only moderately horrified. I had made dinner for a girl only once before in my life. It did not go well. Besty came over to that apartment I shared with a gangly, bearded maniac on West 106th. This was back in my twenties, that period when everyone's girlfriends were turning into their wives. I made blackened swordfish. Also blackened garlic bread, blackened green beans, and blackened soup. The kitchen gadget I am best acquainted with is the smoke detector. (For me, every recipe begins the same way: disable all alarms.)

Besty forgave me that time. She even put out: there is no limit to the sympathy of women. Later, however, she advised me never to cook for her (or any other woman) again.

So the night I offered Julia dinner, I left work with a hard culinary glint in my eye. This time I wasn't going to screw it up.

Where to begin.

Not only did I lack the skill to be a cook, I lacked the *stuff*. My cupboard contained one all-purpose soup/cereal/salad bowl, four smallish plates, lots of immortal food—fallout-shelter food, really—and an armada of drinking glasses. I didn't even have any napkins.

First stop. Bourgeois Barn. Some cloth napkins. Ooh, and matching place mats. Did I need napkin rings? Let's not get carried away. There's a fine line between tasteful and gay.

Second stop. Glutton Mart. Reached for a shopping basket. No: *a cart*. Started in produce. Got stuff for salad. What was the most fashionable lettuce? What was this season's superstar tomato?

Second course. Fresh tortellini. With cheese, the real Italian way. Vodka sauce, she loved vodka sauce. Oh. What about smoothies for a predinner drink? With a surreptitious extra shot of rum for the lady. Back to the produce aisle. Bananas. Apples. Yogurt.

Steak. Two big sirloins. Yes. Why? They were expensive. *Let her see you waste money.*

Of course I needed dessert. Something light and tasteful yet unusual. Passion-fruit sorbet? Better get the coconut one too. One scoop of each. Oh, and a single square of Ghirardelli's chocolate to stick in the middle of a scoop. It's called *presentation.*

Back to the produce aisle: got a fresh lemon. That way, if she wanted a glass of water, I'd put a slice of lemon in it. Verrry fancy. Who could resist?

The checkout stand. It was like the line to get into a Knicks playoff game. But it was moving pretty fast. Only a few more minutes and—damn. Bread. Back to the deli section. Spent precious minutes squeezing the white paper sleeves, going, what's the difference between French bread and Italian? I went for the French. Anything French says sex.

Back in line. It had gotten longer. By the time I got through it, it was 6:12. 6:12! Got a cab. For an eleven-block ride? I was burning money, bleeding money. Too bad she wasn't here to see it. That was all right. I planned to casually mention all this foolishness later. In charmingly self-deprecating fashion.

Back home. 6:18. She had probably been here and gone. *No.* I had to stop thinking that way. Simultaneously got out the George Foreman grill Mom got me for Christmas, washed the arugula, chopped the tomatoes. (Shit. Forgot to buy another steak knife. That was okay. I'd give her this one and saw away at mine quietly with . . . no! Better! Cutely, charmingly, we'd share the steak knife! Pass it back and forth! Like two Paris bohos in the twenties disdaining materialist cutlery-obsessed society!) Heh, heh. Got some water boiling for the pasta. Too bad I had only one saucepan. How was I going to warm the fresh vodka sauce? The same way I warmed my bachelor Ragu: in the same quick-rinsed saucepan, while the pasta sat in my only bowl, with a plate over it desperately fencing in the steam.

6:26. Salad was done. The steaks looked as if they were going to take a hell of a long time. They were a fucking inch thick. Plus each one was the entire size of the George Foreman grill, so simultaneous cooking was impossible unless I put one in a frying pan, in which case I was guaranteed to burn it and by the way where the fuck was she?

6:29. The phone.

"Hey," she said. "It's me. I'm coming out of the subway."

"Cool," I said, transferring the steam of the kitchen from my forehead to my sleeve.

"I was just wondering if you wanted me to bring anything," she said.

I was shoving a corkscrew into a bottle of my best red while look-ing at the jumble of empty bags, the two pints of sorbet sweating atop the fridge, the place mats and napkins with the tags still on them, the bubbles starting to disturb the surface of the water in the saucepan, the arugula and tomatoes washed and chopped and shoved back in the plastic baggies they came in since I had no mix-ing bowl and I said, "I think everything's under control."

When I hung up I thought: shit. She likes *white* wine.

Wow," she said as she entered my apartment, which had actually been pretty clean half an hour prior. Now it looked like a food pro-cessor had exploded. "Just so long as you didn't go to any *trouble*."

Cue sheepish grin.

That's when she handed me the flowers.

"Thanks for these," I said. What the hell was I supposed to do with flowers?

"Do you have a vahz?" she said.

No, I didn't have a *vahz*. What kind of guy owns a *vahz*?

"Got something better," I said, rummaging in the cabinet. "This'll be perfect."

"Such taste," she said, and plunked them in an eight-inch-high pilsner glass reading PANAMA CITY SPRING BREAK 1989. IF YOU'RE NOT WASTED, THE WEEKEND IS! She put some water in them and put the flowers on the windowsill.

The salad, the steaks, the tortellini: I was a sweaty mess the entire meal, dashing madly back and forth from my two-seater din-ing table to the spattered stove. I don't really have enough plates for a gathering of more than one. I spent half the meal frantically wash-ing things. She picked listlessly at my feast. Ate one-sixth of the steak. This, I thought, must be what it's like to be a mom.

"Sorry," she said, catching my look. "I was pretty much full after the smoothie."

"Did you save room for dessert?"

"Of course," she said.

As I was getting dessert, she picked out a CD. "Hey," she said. "*Automatic for the People!*"

"Great disc," I said, slightly disappointed. Why didn't she suggest *Murmur*?

I picked up my napkin and . . . shit. That goddamn price tag. Surreptitiously I peeled it off under the table, as though this would make the price tag on hers disappear.

"So," I said, giving her my smiliest smile as she sat down.

"You all right?" she said.

"Try this wine," I said, pouring her a big glass.

"I really didn't expect all this," she said. "New *place* mats? Really."

"These old things?" I said. "Family heirloom. Passed down by my granddaddy Ezekiel Farrell."

When we were done I shooed her away from the dish Everest in the sink (yep, there they were, pretty much every dish I own) and sat on the couch, swirling a glass of wine.

She went back to the table and just peered at me. From three feet away. Three miles.

And we talked about R.E.M. for a while. And the Cure and Radiohead and Nick Drake and *why wasn't she coming over to sit next to me?*

"C'mere," I said.

Shooter say: *Do not ask. Tell.*

She came over. I kissed her. Kissed her some more. Something in the kitchen crashed extravagantly. She flinched.

"The maid will get that," I said.

Got my hands on her waist, up under her shirt, with ideas. She stopped me. Double elbow slam on my hands. Girl kung fu.

"Grrr," she said, ducking and pressing her head to my chest. We sat for a while hugging. Not long enough. She oozed away.

"I really have to go," she said. It was nine-thirty.

Michael say: *Everybody hurts sometime.*

*T*hat was two weeks ago. Today I walk home from the grocery store and shelve my dented hearts. I need something to take the edge off. When I've got woman problems, at some point I always turn to the thing that is guaranteed to please the senses even as it dulls them. It makes me feel better for a while, then it makes me feel worse. The next day I always resolve to put it out of my house and never use it again, but I know I'm lying to myself.

The thing I need is *Blood on the Tracks*, Dylan's thesaurus of pain. Maybe every guy's. I make it through "Tangled Up in Blue." No problem, that one's kind of funny anyway. ("She was married when we first met/Soon to be divorced." Love that.)

She doesn't call.

I have no problem with "Idiot Wind," either. It gives me courage even, because I hear a prophecy that never struck me before:

> *You didn't know it,*
> *You didn't think it could be done,*
> *In the final end he won the wars*
> *After losing every battle.*

Righteous.

She doesn't call.

I make it, in fact, all the way to "If You See Her, Say Hello." That's the one where you can hear Dylan's heart falling to the floor and being trampled by a pair of high heels.

Sundown, yellow moon, I replay the past
I know every scene by heart
They all went by so fast.

And that's when it happens. It's getting late. And she still hasn't called. I break down and let the eye juice roll. Where is it coming from? There must be a Big Gulp–sized reservoir of salty liquids in my head because the storm lasts forty-five minutes. I will bear any burden. I will pay any price. She's my Vietnam.

At eleven: the phone.

"Hi," she says. "It's me."

"Hi," I say, my voice like wet gravel. Do I sound casual?

"I just woke up," she says apologetically.

"Okay," I say soggily. The less I say, the better my chances of cloaking the bad thing in my throat.

"I just came back to the city and I lay down to take a nap and, out. For eight hours."

"That can happen," I say.

"I'm sorry," she says. "Can we do a drink thing sometime?"

"Okay," I say.

She half-laughs, in that dead-space-filling way she has. It says not, *This is funny*, but *This is embarrassing*.

But now that she has made a sound, the conversation has returned to my end. I have to say something.

"I thought," I mumble, "you just didn't want to see me anymore."

At the end of the comedy they'll make about life in New York in 2001, look at the credits. I won't be the leading man. I won't be the cynical chum or even Bartender Number Two. No, you'll find me ten thousand names into the crawl, under "Gaffer."

Because of the State. The State: You don't rise to it. You fall in it.

MONDAY, JULY 16

For lunch I skip the usual nutritious cafeteria meal of veal parmigiana and Yoo-Hoo. Instead I gnaw on a pasty turd of a PowerBar and hit the pain palace. The grunt gallery.

Why do I go to the gym? To look better naked. Yet here is a complete list of all of the people who have seen me naked since that one time with Julia:

1. The guys in the gym

Basically, I am disrobing for black men with SUV chests and sequoia arms. Isn't this a bit gay of me?

In the locker room I meekly undress, trying but failing as usual to spot my schlong under the overhang of my big quivering Hostess Sno-Ball belly. I peek at the midsections of the other guys: Iron. Brick. Steel. Titanium. The way I put on a T-shirt, it's like Handi-

Wrapping a bowl of mashed potatoes. But I know deep down I'm not overweight, not really. I'm just three skinny guys trapped in the body of a fat man.

I hit the floor, which is writhing with mystery optimism. You ask: Why can't women and men understand each other? Look to the gym, where, by using the exact same equipment, women hope to become smaller and men hope to become larger.

This gym is for professional Midtowners in our thirties, so as I stretch, its sound system blares demographically appropriate musical quizzes from our youth: "Do you believe in love?" No. "Do you really want to hurt me?" No thanks, I'm busy hurting myself. "Is she really going out with him?" Grrr.

Huge guys—guys in *costume*, spandex singlets—balance barbells on their shoulders, with comical, cartoon-sized weights on either end. They bend their knees, squat deeply, then wobble themselves erect. Repeat. That looks hard. Pointless, but hard. How many girls are telling each other over their Caesar salads right now, *I want a guy with huge muscles in his lower back?*

There are mirrors on every wall, mirrors on every side of every column. It's like a fun house, only for "fun" substitute "bone-cracking agony." Everyone is exhaling and clanking in moist, puffy-faced determination, but what they're really doing is checking out each other. Worse: they're just pretending to work out so they can pretend to check each other out so they can actually check out themselves. Every time you look in one mirror—and you can't look anywhere without looking into a mirror—you can see reflections from other mirrors, which reflect on still other mirrors, and so on, into infinity. It's a whole lot more of me than I'm in the mood for.

Men loiter by the free weights, their T-shirts emblazoned with corporate pride ("Depends Runoff Central Park," "Arthur Andersen Means Trust"). I slouch to the bench press, examining the dull silver bar with corrugations that seem to have no purpose except to leave calluses. These you can then define as weightlifting inflicted if a girl notices them in a bar. I have no idea how much weight I can lift. I'm a newspaper editor. When was the last time I lifted anything heavier than a paragraph? When did I last push anything heavier than my luck?

A big guy and his neck come up behind me as I'm pushing and gasping. His chest is pneumatic hardwood. He has a *shelf.* I've heard that taking steroids makes you grow breasts, shrinks your nuts to sunflower seeds. It makes you so much of a man, in short, that you start to become a girl. That's what you get for caring about your looks. How dare we even try? Only girls are supposed to look good. We are here to admire.

"Hi, guy!" he says. "Want a spot?"

I look up. Either there is something in his eye or he just winked at me. His crotch is a foot over my face. I have a feeling there are gay porn films that begin this way. George Michael starts mincing over the stereo. (How could anyone have ever believed *that* guy was straight?)

I don't want to be rude. I also don't want any witnesses.

"No thanks?" I say. And I lie there breathing hard. He stands there behind me looking down, smiley faced. This is as awkward as most of my dates.

"Mind if I work in?"

The song: "I Want Your Sex."

"No, no!" I say, overfriendly. I spring up, glad to get a break.

He slides my dinky bread plates off the bar with a thumb and forefinger and puts them back on the rack. He adds flying saucer–sized masses to each side and eases himself backward onto the bench, looking straight up at me. Now I'm behind him, trying to look at nothing.

"Spot?" he says, as he starts thrusting and pumping.

George say: "*Sex is best when it's one on one!*"

"Suurre," I say.

He does about twelve of them quickly, but by fifteen he's running out of steam. This is my moment to step lively. I'm supposed to help him get that one last rep up into the air and back to rest on the rack. However, since my arms are like linguine and he is bench-pressing the approximate weight of Norway, I foresee comedy ahead. Actually, he knows very well he should never have asked me for a spot. But he is being fair. He is making an effort to be inclusive despite how I look. He's admitting me to the fraternity of sinew in some sort of affirmative-action program for weaklings.

He's got that last rep a quarter of the way up. My hands are underneath the bar, ready to help.

"You got it," I say.

"Uh. UH!" he says. His elbows buckling.

"All you," I say, my palms grabbing the bar.

"Aw! AWWWW!" The bar advances another two inches. I'm trying to help lift it. It feels like a Buick.

"It really is all you," I say apologetically.

He emits loud vowels. Sweat jogs down his forehead. I'm putting my whole body into lifting the thing the last two inches (thinking, Cool. I can see the veins in my arms), but his spotter needs a spotter.

I lower my voice to a manful growl. "Let's do this thing," I say. All Lee Marvin.

And we do. Which is lucky because I can feel my forearm tendons starting to pull apart like the caramel in a Snickers commercial.

He gets up, exhales the breath of a man. "Thanks, bro."

"No prob," I say. We lifters drop the last syllable of our sentences.

"It was cool how you made me do it all myself."

Are muscle guys smart enough to do sarcasm? And if so, what are my options? Do I ignore the slight, or challenge him to a rumble?

"That's why I'm here," I say.

As he turns his back to add more weight to the bar, I slip over to a scary apparatus called the "lat pulldown." This time you sit upright and pull down from overhead a giant bar chained to a stack of weights. I pull the pin out and place it near the top of the pile. No. Nearer. A gum-chewing personal trainer leans against the windowsill nearby, his arms crossed insouciantly. His eyes don't leave mine. I haven't even sat down, and already his eyes say: *You're doing it wrong.*

"How ya doin'," I grunt.

He nods slowly, once. Doesn't look away.

And I'm thirteen again. My high school weight room. Sometimes I would stop in there at the end of PE, after a lazy sixth-period trot from the soccer field or the tennis courts. The weight room was right next to the locker room, so guys would stop in and do a few curls or presses: extracurricular activity for physical geniuses, just like I used to show off by doing more book reports than required. So there we'd be: the captain of the soccer team, the first baseman of the baseball team, a couple of quad- and delt- and trap-trapped footballers entombed in their walls of muscle, and me. I was only here to kill time until the coast was clear in the shower, where I did not wish to parade my pubic Sahara amongst a dozen dirty-joke-telling, towel-snapping adolescents happily brandishing their jungly topiary. Why the occasion of being near denuded genitals of your own gender was supposed to be the green light for such merriment always escaped me. My visible cringing at such moments, though, would earn derisive cries of "fag," which seemed ironic.

The varsity gang would be effortlessly moving their skyscrapers of weight this way and that while I stretched my calves. My hamstrings. My arms. My ankles: don't forget to rotate them. Oh yes, and the neck, waggle that one around for a while. When I ran out of things to stretch, I'd sit down and do some pathetic bicep curls. Gradually everyone else would stop lifting. They would wander over to form a perimeter of hilarity behind me. All of them would contribute unsolicited play-by-play.

"What is he d—"

"—to use his whole bod—"

"—have to rest after each r—?"

"—some sort of disabil—"

"—my brother lifted weights like that, but he was elev—"

"Think he gets a lot of pussy?" Sniggering all around. It would have bothered me less if it hadn't been the gym teacher saying this.

The personal trainer on East Fiftieth Street doesn't have to say anything, though. All he does is chew his contemptuous gum.

I pull down the bar for my first rep as he watches stonily. I do another, and another. Little sounds burble out of me.

"Eep," I say.

"Yaw," I say.

"Ayyyyye," I say.

"You're doing it wrong," says the trainer.

"Really?" I say, letting the bar slip out of my hands. Kuh-lank! Heads turn. "I looked at the diagram."

"No, man, I mean your *noises*. All wrong. You know, you don't even have that much weight on there."

"Aren't you supposed to be encouraging to your clients?"

A shrug. "You're not my client."

So: I have to hire this guy to shut him up. Personal trainers cost $50 an hour. It's not a lat pulldown. It's a lat shakedown.

"What's it to you?" I say huffily.

A nod over my shoulder.

And I turn around: several oxen have put down their weights and formed a whispering semicircle around me. This could potentially turn into "The Lottery" pretty quickly.

"Done!" I say, wiping my sweat off the seat.

I put in a few agonizing miles on the treadmill. By the time I'm done, I'm as wet as if I'd been dipped in sweat salsa. My juices are all over the machine. My perspiration is probably rusting the gears. Plus I'm positive some of my body Crisco flew off and landed on the pretty little Asian girl on the treadmill next to me. For something to do while I gasp for life, I press a button. The calorie meter. I have burned . . . a third of a Big Mac.

Stumble to the scale. I've lost six pounds in a week. This is why men go to the gym: because it's always good news. If you gain, you think: *I'm adding muscle.* If you lose, you think: *I'm shedding fat.*

"Love Is the Drug" on the sound system. No, love is the drugstore. And Julia's the pharmacist dispensing my Viagra, ether, speed, Valium, heroin.

Shooter offered me dinner. Anywhere I wanted, he said. Rao's? I said. The most exclusive restaurant in town. Seats about twelve, all of them celebrities or mobsters or both. Shooter gave them a call, but even he doesn't have those kinds of connections, so we settle for the Yale Club. Glum eight-foot portraits on the walls like something from Disney's Haunted Mansion, waiters with subservient mini-mustaches, big heavy oaken tables hewn for mead-quaffing Vikings. The average age of the members is: deceased. Men display important hair and ironed handkerchiefs. Their wives have ironed faces. Technically the club is open to everyone who ever went to Yale (or Dartmouth, or fratted for DKE), but it's really an endangered-species refuge for that dwindling minority, the nonironic big corporation white male who likes to chat about something he read in *Foreign Policy* over a lunch of boiled beef and boiled potatoes, which he washes down with a sidecar or a Rob Roy.

Shooter is in his element, issuing pronunciamentos on the thread count of the napkins, the relevance of the wine, the fortitude of the crab-cracking apparatus. Occasionally he slips into an absurd British accent. While he talks, I drink. He talks a lot. Chance may have brought us together, but alcohol made us friends.

"How's your crotch traffic?" he says.

"There's this girl," I begin.

"Stop right there," Shooter says. "I know what this is."

I wait for wisdom. Shooter will straighten this out. Shooter knows all. I take another sip of wine. Fortitude.

"It's Perrier," he says. I turn, and the waiter is behind me. "I ordered Pellegrino."

I turn in my seat. A hapless immigrant in a tux, his shoulders rounded, his neck bent in subservience. "I'll see, sir."

"And take this with you," Shooter says, handing him the glass.

Shooter has just sent back a glass of water.

"Shall we utilize some wine?" he says, opening the wine list. It's the size of a world atlas.

"Utilize . . . ?" I say.

"Come on. *The Sun Also Rises*?"

"I've been meaning to read that," I say. This statement is not quite true. I remember when I bought the book, but I didn't get to it right away; there was a lot of good stuff on HBO that year. Since then I have taken it on vacation with me, optimistically stuffed it in backpacks and carry-ons with every intention of reading it, or rather of at least being spotted pretending to read it in an exotic cafe in the Piazza Navona or the Khao San Road. After a while it acquired such a wonderful beaten-up look that I figured it was unncecessary to actually read it.

"Basically, it's a book about drinking," Shooter explains. "Except that there are so many drinking scenes he has to keep making up new words for it. Like 'utilize.'"

"Good word," I say.

"Isn't it? It really gets across the importance of drinking as a tool. We don't consume it; we *build* with it."

"And, occasionally, drive with it."

"If you can't hold your fill and drive home without inflicting heavy damage on a tree or others," Shooter says, "you are not a man."

There are times when I wonder whether Shooter's advice is absolutely the finest counsel a guy can receive.

"You know, except for your haircut, you look good," he says suspiciously. "Not as good as me, but."

Shooter knows he looks good. Big stevedore shoulders, a waist like a girl's. His arms are thick and gnarly. His legs are toned by decades of soccer. His skin is unblemished mahogany, his shoulder-length dreads pulled back into a ponytail. He appears not to be aware that he is black. He almost never alludes to it. When I walk down the street with him, every girl laser-locks on his eyes. He smiles back at them. I am invisible, of course. He once told me he had never gone more than two weeks without sex. This would be a preposterous claim coming from anyone else I've ever known. I am a skirt chaser; Shooter is a skirt catcher.

His clothes are Italian. His watch costs more than any ten things I have ever bought, combined. I was with him when he bought it, in Florence. The figure in lire was a phone number. With area code. Shooter put it on his AmEx without a second thought. He isn't so good with math. I'm pretty sure he never did figure out what it cost. On the same trip he bought a pair of pajamas that cost more than my best suit.

"Your Pellegrino," says the waiter, returning.

Shooter nods like a Roman emperor as the waiter pours.

"What've you been doing with yourself?" he says.

"Been working out," I say. "Eating less."

"Drop another twenty pounds," he says. "Maybe I'll let you have some of my hand-me-downs."

"Clothes?"

A roll of the eyes. *"Girls,"* he says.

Then he tells me why the British should never get rid of the House of Lords. For forty minutes. He is strongly pro class system. He thinks America will never be truly great until it devises a better means of separating the lowborn from the mighty. When he was at Dartmouth, he founded a student newspaper that was so right wing he probably would have been cordially invited to transfer elsewhere if he had been white. But he carved himself a niche: the reactionary Rastafarian. *60 Minutes* did a piece on him once. He was nineteen.

"Speaking of. Viddy well, lit'l brotha. Viddy well." He tips his head suggestively.

On occasion Shooter and I lapse into *Clockwork Orange* speak, especially when we're trying to encipher our hornier moments amid polite surroundings.

I turn. A long blonde slinks by in painted-on pants that don't reach her hipbones. This is the Yale Club, so I guess you're not allowed to expose your belly, but her shirt just barely reaches the tops of her pants. We leer at her thong print as she bends over to kiss some geezer. Could be her father. Or it could be her daddy. Either way, she is hastening his timely demise with a big heart-attack-inducing smooch. Possibly she is giving tongue.

"That," he says, as if we've been discussing the subject all evening, "is a bubble butt. Rrrrrah!" He says, doggily, with a giant smile.

Shooter is a manboy like me, only he's a *man*boy and I'm a man*boy*. Unlike me, he owns things. He has a car (a Range Rover. It's fire-engine-colored. It's fire-engine-*sized*.) and a Hamptons love shack bought from a third-tier celebrity (there's a heated swimming pool, a frog pond, and 1.7 acres of dog-friendly land so densely surrounded by pine trees that you can't see any other house from anywhere on the property). Shooter does not work. His work ethic is: it is unethical to work. Instead he is getting a head start on his inheritance, the two-hundred-proof inheritance of an only child of only children. His father is the coleslaw king of the Midwest. You can't get coleslaw without putting money into Shooter's pocket. Coleslaw comes, unbidden, and goes, untouched, along with every meal you get in the big-eater family restaurant chains, the ones where they serve food by the trough. (When you go to the salad bar, please use a clean bucket for each trip.) Who knew that one of the world's least-requested foods ("More of that yummy cabbage and mayo, please, Mom"? I don't think so) could be as profitable as a midsized casino?

Shooter worked for his dad for a couple of years, but his big idea—a costly deal to include coleslaw with the Grand Slam breakfast—ate up a few mil in development costs. Shooter's dad decided his scion would drain the family treasury at a less alarming rate if he were gainlessly employed (studying painting, studying history, volunteering for quixotic political campaigns) and parked safely out of harm's way, in New York. Not that Shooter isn't creative about spending money: when I was at his apartment one time, he asked me if I wanted a coffee. Sure, I said. He called the deli downstairs and had one sent up, as his three-hundred-dollar German coffeemaker stood at forlorn attention on the titanium counter. His dog Alpha drinks only Evian. And he once left the AC on in his Upper West Side apartment while he went to the Hamptons for two weeks. Intentionally. "I dislike a stuffy flat," he sniffed. I turn my air on for three miserly hours at a time, silently calculating the kilowatts in my head.

At the rate he's going, Shooter figures he'll run out of money by the time he's sixty, but he has often vowed to outflank that problem by drinking himself into an early grave. Moderate alcohol consumption actually has been shown to be linked to long life, Mike once pointed out to us (I think he was reading aloud from an article in *The Wine Spectator*). But there is nothing moderate about Shooter.

"So there's this girl," I say again as the waiter starts sweatily decorking a second bottle of Bordeaux. I tell him the story of the weekend of my discontent, edited for embarrassing details.

"What's your next move?" he says.

"Don't know. Hang around her some more," I say. "Maybe familiarity breeds consent?"

"How far have you gotten with her?"

"Certain things have happened," I say.

"Good," says Shooter, and gestures with his right hand, which is the one holding his glass. About eight dollars' worth of wine sloshes onto the tablecloth. "What you need to do is tell her what the fuck the game is here. You have to stop being such a pansy. Tell her, look, this guy is a total loser and what the fuck is she doing with him anyway? The guy is never going to amount to anything. He's a newspaper reporter in Connecticut? Give me a goddamn break! He can't be making more than thirty-three! This guy sounds *stu*pid, he sounds *weak*, he is not going to be able to support her, he is not going to be able to get her into any cool parties!"

"That's right," I'm saying. I sit up straighter. "I can get her into parties." Movie-star wingdings. Music-industry revels. Book jamborees. Where she can meet lots of interesting people! And, possibly, leave with one of them.

"Tell her you are not going to be her fucking doormat anymore and that if she doesn't dump this *re*tard, then you're just going to find someone else. You have to make it clear that she cannot go on teasing you indefinitely."

I'm not liking where this is going. "But isn't it better to be tortured than not to get to see her at all?"

"No!" He makes a fist. In slow motion I watch as the fist rises all the way up over his shoulder in preparation for slamming the table, but instead, he catches the tuxedoed Mexican in the solar plexus. The waiter coughs a little. Shooter scowls at the waiter as if to say: *What the fuck are you doing hitting my fist with your stomach?*

"For dessert we have a mud pie, profiteroles," says the waiter.

"If she won't drop-kick this guy, then you need to show her you're a fucking man! Are you wearing frilly lingerie or what?"

"Isn't that taking a chance?"

"Lemon meringue pie, key lime pie, ice cream . . ."

Some men seethe quietly. Not Shooter. When he seethes, the guy two tables over has to wipe Shooter's saliva off his tie.

"Yeah," he says to the waiter. "Ice cream. My friend will have the TUTTI-FRUTTI!"

I look around nervously, wondering if any gay people present might possibly find this last remark to be offensive. But we are in the Yale Club, after all. Nobody is going to stand up in his pin-striped J. Press suit and polka-dot bow tie and say, Uh, excuse me, I happen to be treasurer of the American Queer Love Association.

"I will be a man," I vow, or predict, hesitantly. I've always thought there would be some defining moment that caused me to shed my adolescence. It always involved me kung-fuing a mugger, though, or possibly leaping at the far corner of a Super Bowl end zone to pluck the winning pass out of the stratosphere.

When I ooze my way home with a bottle and a half of wine sloshing around in me, I look at my watch: it's now 1:15 A.M., July 26. Boot up the computer. I've got mail!

sender: wayoutthere
subject: chicks on dicks

sender: salespro2001
subject: MANBOY33, DO YOU NEED $500 A DAY????

sender: hotaxx
subject: INCREDBILE!!! GIRL MEETS GOAT

sender: greetings etrade.com
subject: Happy Birthday, TOM FARRELL!

Zap. Zap. Zap. I double-click on the last one.

date: 07/26/01 12:01 A.M.

There's a cartoon of a slice of cake with a candle sticking out of it. The words are in chubby-hilarious cartoon font:

We would have sent you a cake, but were afraid the frosting
might get stuck to the computer screen. Best wishes, E*TRADE

So now computers have automatic programs to send automatic e-cards to their automatic customers. If I set up my computer to respond automatically to these messages, they could dispense with the me part entirely. And then the two computers could get into an infinite loop of well-wishing. "Thanks for your birthday e-mail." "Thanks for thanking me for your birthday e-mail." "Thanks for your response to my thank-you note for your birthday e-mail." Aren't manners one of the useless things that you would think computers would be able to cut out of life? Instead, the ATM barfs out its twenties and flashes, "It has been a genuine pleasure to serve you." Computers have taken us one more step toward the complete feminization of American life. You have to remember birthdays now. Because what excuse do you have for forgetting? "Oh, sorry, I didn't think you were important enough to enter into my Yahoo! date book."

Which might raise a question or two about why no one has called to wish me happy birthday. But I won't think about that today. I'm tired. It's two in the morning. Tomorrow's another day.

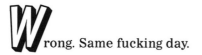

Wrong. Same fucking day.

The obligatory birthday party in the back room at Langan's. We're only supposed to have the room until nine, at which time we give way to a group of rowdiness-starved Wall Streeters who have apparently hired a belly dancer for some PG-13 fun. I pinged practically everyone in my e-mail address book. Those who show up bring people I don't know. Who are these people?

I wade into the crowd with false frivolity, counterfeit mirth. There are about seventy guests. My view of a party is, you should invite a lot of people you barely know, who will arrive and see a lot of other people you barely know, and start to believe that you must be really popular, and if everyone thinks you're really popular, *aren't* you, kind of? I e-vited 140 people, including some people whose business cards I obtained at parties for the express purpose of inviting them to my party so they in turn would invite me to their parties.

So I could meet girls.

Liesl is my date for the party. Gave me a present and everything: a paperback novel. I have no intention of reading it. I've already seen the movie. Ten minutes after we arrived, she found a half-German guy to talk to. They're sitting over there comparing schnitzel recipes or discussing lederhosen or lebensraum. She's supposed to be decorating me. I need arm candy, arm *armor*, to defend myself when Julia shows up. Luckily everyone is buying me balm for my Julia-flayed nerves, and every glass of don't-give-a-shit goes down easier than the last one. Everything looks so much prettier in the haze, don't you think?

A well-rounded figure is surging past at a speed that suggests you could easily wind up with Rockport tracks up the back of your shirt if you tried to stop him. The most dangerous place in New York is between a thirsty hack and the bar. I reach out into the center of the blur and hook him by the elbow.

"Eli!" I say. "Great to see you!"

"Tom!" he says. "Happy birthday! Get out of my way!"

Trailing behind off his left paw is Hillary, looking more stunning than ever. She just smiles and nods. And they slip away in search of succor.

This is when Rollo shows up, his eyes crinkly with hilarity. He glides smiling through the cacophony as if to the sound of a standing ovation only he can hear. All at once I am struck by a deep and abiding love for his scandal-loving smile, his buzzing tabloid heart.

"Hail," I say, doing something extremely vague with my hand that resembles a wave, a salute, and an obscenity. "Thou wobbly knight of the dark arts."

"Buy us a drink, lad, I'm skint," he says. "Your shout." I'm well lit, but even I can tell he's soaked to the gills. It's evident by the way we sway in harmony. Beautiful, isn't it?

"My shout? That's not my shout. Here's my shout: YOU CHEAP FUCKING BASTARD."

I laugh at my own line. This gets me some worried looks.

"Your day, you pay," Rollo says.

"That's in England," I say. "This is an entirely different country now. We won the war. It was in all the papers."

"Come on, boy, what was it Shakespeare said? For a taste of your whiskey, I'll give you some advice."

"That was Kenny Rogers."

"Right," he says. "Shakespeare, Kenny Rogers. Pair of hacks, scribblers, ink monkeys like us. Let's toast 'em."

"Serving girl," I say, giving a slow overhead wave to a classic Manhattan drinks duchess in a leotard and a leather skirt. Waitresses are the royalty of this town: they're great looking, they're dumb enough to be inbred, everyone's afraid of them, and they make more than any three hacks I know. Too late I remember hearing that waitresses put Visine in your drink to give you the shits if you mistreat them, but isn't a good colonic going for $150 in your better spas?

"That's it, Bingo, some happy juice for the pair of us," Rollo says.

"Don't you make a lot more than me?"

"Got a wife, haven't I?"

"Whose fault is that?"

"Come on, don't be such a tit."

The girl makes her way through the crowd, gives me a nasty look.

"My lovely," Rollo says, winking hard. "How do you do? And when will you do it to me?"

She waits, looking as if she wishes she had some gum to snap.

"The gentleman is celebrating the anniversary of his birth," he says, "and has agreed to defray expenses. Two double gins on ice. And what're you having, Zimbo?"

"Gin and tonic," I say. "Shaken, not stirred. With a maraschino cherry."

"And one for yourself," Rollo tells the girl as she turns around. She tosses him a coy little smile over her retreating shoulder.

"That all it takes?" I say.

"The world was built on money and bollocks, Zembla," he says. "One or the other will do."

I turn around to check the door again, rising to tippytoes. Nothing, although I do spot an out-of-focus version of Liesl. Is she talking to *two* guys? Crazy tabloid headlines crash through my brain. "HEARTLESS WENCH IN JOYLESS BAR." "FLOOZY FRAULEIN FORSAKES FLOUNDERING FELLA." Who invited unauthorized men to my fiesta?

"Looking for that special someone?" Rollo says. "Been overrun by cupid's tank? You look like a dog who wants to bury his boner. Who is it then?"

"Your wife."

"You don't mock a man's wife," he says. "The Geneva Convention specifically forbids torturing captives of a hostile nation."

"Is your wife beautiful?" I say.

"She's a trophy wife," he says. "A Westminster Kennel Club trophy."

"Tell me," I say. "Always wanted to know. Why do men get married? I know why women get married—all the home decorating and picking out baby clothes—but why do men get married?"

"Why indeed?" he says. "Why walk the plank? Why run away to join the two-ring circus? Better dead than wed, we used to say when we were tadpoles. Tell you, son, I was in the army, and that's exactly what getting married is: there's no privacy, you get orders barked at you all day long, and you get about ten inches of space to hang up all your clothes."

"So why'd you sign up then?"

"Because it drove me absolutely barking mad to think of her shagging anyone else. Marriage quiets the lunatic voices. It's that or become a serial killer, I'm afraid."

The waitress comes back. She hands Rollo two highball glasses and a 120-proof smile.

"*Bellisima!*" he cries, and tosses off the first drink. "Take this one whence it came, and bring me its twin," he says.

She gives me a G and T but stiffs me on the cherry, which, by the way, I really did want. After momentary consideration of whether to tip her, I fork over the industry standard and get no eye contact in return. She does leave a full bowl of peanuts on the mahogany drink-resting shelf. I scoop up a handful of dinner. "Want some?" I say. A confirmed sighting of Rollo eating would earn much newsroom marveling.

He raises an eyebrow. "I do not take food with my meals," he says.

"Uh-huh," I say through my munching. "Tell me a joke."

"Sadist and a masochist go out on a date," Rollo says. "The masochist says, 'Aren't you going to hit me?' The sadist says, 'No.'"

"Funny," I say, my eyes lashed to the door. "Tell me one I don't know."

"I know this," he says. "You're looking for that copygirl."

"Where'd you hear that?" I say, trying to read a message in the white pinstripes of his suit jacket, like chalk body outlines, racing up to his lapels, splitting to run away at weird angles.

"How d'ya think I fucking know?" He's rapping his emphasis finger on my collarbone. "My solid [tap] gold [tap] sources [tap]," he says.

"Rollo," I say, putting my drink down and clutching his lapels to make the chalk stripes stop moving, "you don't have sources. What you have is imagination."

"Isn't it obvious in every glance and sigh?" he says.

"Rollo," I say. "Who told you this?"

"Dearie," he says, "nothing transpires at Langan's without my knowledge. I'm here every night. I was here the night you met her. Valentine's Day, wasn't it?"

"I thought I saw you down the bar," I say. "I assumed you were unconscious."

"Good reporters blend into the surroundings," he says.

"You were blending into a coma. I've seen geraniums that moved more."

He lifts a witchy index finger to his forehead. "The third eye," he says. "It's always open."

"Yeah," I say. "Or Ciaran the bartender told you."

He ignores this. The mystique of the hack legend. No one must know how he knows what he knows, because if they did, they could cut out the middleman. "So will you be seeing this young sweetie tonight?" he says.

I shrug. "She has a boyfriend. It's a long story."Actually, it isn't, though, is it? It's a short story. It's a fucking *haiku*:

secrets over drinks
some sweaty naked Twister
enter lisping putz

"You are unschooled in the seducer's arts," Rollo says. "Here, write this down," he says, knowing that I, like him, like all hacks, have a notebook on me at all times.

I'm taking notes at my birthday party. There are times when my life seems a little weird, even to myself.

He pauses, puffs out his cheeks, empties his drink, and slams it on the shelf. Now he's talking at the speed of drink.

"Tell her how you feel. But she musn't feel threatened."

"She musn't," I say, looking around, hoping Shooter isn't hearing any of this. But Shooter is doing shots at the bar. With three blondes and a redhead.

"Tell her this. Start out by saying, 'Look, it's obvious you're not going to marry him.' "

"Is it?" I say.

"You'll be confident. She wouldn't be going round with you if she wanted to marry this chump, would she? You'll tell her, 'I know this must be difficult for you.' You'll ask her, nicely, 'What can I do to help you make a decision?' Make sure you tell her, 'I'm not going to rush you.' Underline that."

I underline.

"Give her *safe*. Give her se*cure*."

Write, write.

"Don't be negative. Be supportive. Act as if you're with her and it will happen," he says. "Act like a boyfriend and you'll become one. Make it easy for her."

"That easy?" I say.

"That easy," he says. "And one thing more," he adds, pulling my ear close to his flammable breath. "Girls like having smutty propositions murmured in their ears."

"Right."

"To the bog for me. Another drink will be required upon my return."

"Will any of this work?" I call after him.

"A great load of bollocks, all of it," he roars, over the heads of the crowd. "Of course it'll work."

As he walks away I notice for the first time that Rollo looks a little like my father. A guy who took with him whatever advice fathers are supposed to give sons.

Check the watch. 9:15 and she's not there. At 9:21 she remains absent. At 9:25 there is no sign of. And 9:27. And 9:28. And 9:29. She's not coming. Another routine rejection. I've been cut down more than Michael Jackson's nose.

That's when Brandy shows up. She isn't alone.

"Tom," she says. "This is Katie Swenson."

Former coworker of Bran's. She recently quit the intensely

competitive, back-stabbing world of TV news to . . . go to law school. But. Cute cheeks, streaky Cameron Diaz butterscotch hair, Midwestern honesty, like my mom. (Ugh. Make a note not to think of Mom when I think of Katie.) I like Katie. I also like Bran, and this way if I flirt with one I get to fire up the other one's competitive streak. Perfect. When it comes to relationships, scratch a girl and find a combat-hardened field marshal.

"Did you bring me a present?" I ask Bran.

"No," she says. "But Katie did."

"Oh?"

"Got it right here in my bag," Katie says. "Voilà."

It's a pack of tarot cards.

"Let me tell your fortune," she says. "It'll be fun."

I put down my drink.

A guy I know named Doug is standing there saying he doesn't get psychics.

"Like, take TV psychics. If they're really good, they tell you things like, you've just lost a family member/a job/a boyfriend. Things you already knew. For this I'm supposed to pay four ninety-five a minute? What good is that? Tell me what Cisco's going to do in the next six months."

"But maybe we can tell you something you didn't know about yourself," Katie says. "Tell ya what I'm gonna do. Let me read your aura."

She takes my left hand and peers into it. Strokes it a bit. Then she does the same with my right hand. Possibly she is flirting with me. She really is a tasty package. She's got hair like summer and a voice like three A.M.

"You're facing this huge obstacle," she says. "And you're not sure whether to confront it. But you will. And at first it will seem like a disaster. But after a while it'll get much better."

I feel a drop of sweat on my forehead. I look at Doug, a TV writer whose idea for a wacky show—it's about a bunch of slackers who keep plotting to steal from each other the talking urn o' ashes of Kurt Cobain, who razzes them every time they do something stupid—just got rejected by MTV, Comedy Central, and even Showtime.

"What about this guy?" I protest. "He's got obstacles. Everyone's got 'em."

"Okay, I'll tell you what's in your refrigerator," Katie says.

"What?" I say.

"Mmmm. Muh. May. Mayonnaise," she says.

"What are you? The oracle of Hellman's?"

"Well?" she says.

"That is so dumb. Because everyone has mayonnaise in their refrigerator. Except me." I'm still rattled, though. She got the obstacles, right off. Her next remark could reveal my masturbation habits.

She looks sad.

"I've got mustard," I say.

"That's right," she says, brightening right up. "Mustard. It was the *m* that threw me."

Thank God she doesn't know what that *m* really stands for.

"And I see some kind of . . . lunch meat."

"Absurd," I say. Every guy has lunch meat in his fridge. Except, as it happens, me. Just the stuff I use to make a Bloody Mary takes up practically a whole shelf.

And that's when the waitress breaks in to tell us time's up.

"That's it," I say. "Gotta go."

"Wait," says Bran, looking more smug than usual. "She hasn't read your tarot yet."

"Tell me some other time," I say, thinking, This girl can see right through me. Just like Neil Diamond, Dan Fogelberg, and Bread.

"Five more minutes?" Katie asks the waitress, and gives her this sweet smile. The waitress shrugs.

"Okay," she says, and deals me four cards. "You're the Questioner. We're going to read them left to right. First card." She turns it over. "Eight of cups. Interesting. It means a beginning, in the relationship sense. Traditionally, a blond woman could be of some assistance to you."

She gives me the kind of little smirk only blondes can do. This girl is cute, no doubt about it. But I'm thinking about Julia's dirty-blond hair. Come to think of it, Liesl is a blonde too.

"It's always about the blondes," says Bran, shaking her dark head. "The world is so . . . blondist."

"Two," says Katie, flipping again. "The knight of swords. Okay. This indicates a clever, charming man, a trusted adviser you consult with regularly. But he could be unreliable. He could bring excitement, or trouble, into your life."

I try not to look at Shooter, but at this very moment he and Rollo are sitting next to each other on an overstuffed sofa. Both of them have a girl sitting on either knee. Rollo is whispering obviously dirty things to one of the girls. The other one he's tickling. The girls on Shooter's knees are . . . well . . . I believe the word is "undulating."

"Three," says Katie. "The two of swords. Stalemate, a dead end. Things drag on endlessly."

You know how you never think about your armpits until you notice something is going on there? I'm thinking about my armpits. I don't need antiperspirant. I need a couple of Maxipads.

Snap, snap. Katie, with the fingers. "You ready?" she says, fetching me back to earth.

"Pay attention, Tom," says Bran, looking highly entertained.

"Four," Katie says.

It's a guy with a moronic giggle carrying a stick on his shoulder and wearing bells on his hat. A dog is chasing him, pulling his pants halfway down so his butt sticks out of his pants.

"Now," says Katie, "I have to caution you, this one is something of a misnomer. See how he's marching forward, and he's got his traveling stick? This is the card that generally indicates new beginnings. Fresh starts. A new job, or a journey of some kind."

"You can't argue with the cards," Bran says. "Tom, you're the fool."

Always take a personal day to follow the birthday. Sleeping in. So nice. And the dreams. I had an excellent sports fantasy: championship bowling, a record-breaking score; also, for a ball I was using Dwayne's head. Then up for some toast and tea, a languorous morning wielding the TV clicker, and now I can get on with the serious business of the day: not calling her.

I'm not going to call her, I'm not going to call her.

I'm not going to call her.

Outside it's 80 degrees, and 80 percent stupidity. But I'm not going out there. Why take a chance?

I shower and "blow out" my longish hair. It's starting to look like something that should be seen only on a member of the New York Islanders. In the attempt to cultivate flowing poetic-mysterious Johnny Depp hair, or at least interestingly demented-wavy Beethoven locks, I have created a formidable humidity mop. Something must be done.

When I turn off the dryer, the phone is ringing. I get there too late. My machine clicks off and the phone goes dead. A hanger-upper. Julia is a hanger-upper, a machineophobic. Instantly I hit *69. Well, not instantly. Can I afford to waste the 75 cents, plus the roughly 150 percent tax that mysteriously seems to apply to everything telephone related?

I get a pleasant morning-chat-show-type voice. The number I am calling cannot be reached by this method.

It's ten A.M. Obviously it was her, calling from work—*Tabloid* blocks the number on all outgoing calls, natch—and how kind of her! To worry that I might still be asleep. That's why she hung up.

I don't dare leave the apartment lest the phone ring. I wonder if I'll be able to last the entire day without going to the bathroom, though.

One P.M. The phone.

"Hello?"

"Hello? I don't know if you remember me, but . . ."

My relief tank is refilling rapidly, making cheerful glug-glug noises.

"You sound," I say, "like a girl I used to like."

She half-laughs. "I know. I know!"

"Did you sleep through it?"

"Yup."

"Poor sleepyhead," I say. And she's done it again: she's turned me. I am the one offering sympathy. When she slept through my goddamned birthday party.

"I woke up at eight and I thought, 'It's okay, I'll just take a cab downtown.' Then I fell asleep again."

I half-laugh. And I can't help it. I get a plate and prepare to load it up from the self-punishment buffet.

"Do you want to hang out after work?" I say.

"Okay."

Get dressed. Suck in. Psych up. I want to be everything for her. I want Tom Cruise's smile, Bob Dylan's poetry, and Elvis's swagger.

Instead I have Tom Cruise's height, Bob Dylan's hair, and Elvis's liver. Cinch the belt one notch more than usual. The pain is not, as I expected, Satanic; it is merely excruciating. One more notch and I can throw this belt away. I have lost some pounds.

I'm there at five on the dot to pick her up. We go see a movie about a guy who can't create any new memories. Whatever he sees, whatever he hears, whatever information is shoved right in his face, he just forgets. There's a scene where his girl is really mean to him, knowing that five minutes later he won't remember a thing. Some guys, they just don't learn.

"Let's go to the park," I say. "We have to take advantage of these summer nights. The snows will be coming in, like, three weeks."

"That," she says, "would be lovely."

I have prepared for the occasion. I've got a backpack containing a bottle of wine, two plastic glasses, a corkscrew, and a sheet. We go to the park and sit under a tree. The Sheep Meadow is alive with chirping. Not birds. Cell phones. Daddies are playing with their little girls all around us. Julia looks wistful.

Fifty feet behind us, a couple is making out. Fifty feet in front of us, a couple is making out.

"Reminds me of a Dylan song," I say.

"Most things do," she says.

The lyrics just leak out of me.

> *"They sat together in the park,*
> *As the evening sky grew dark,*
> *She looked at him and he felt a spark,*
> *Tingle to his bones."*

" 'Simple Twist of Fate,' " she says.

"Correct." I smile gratefully. This girl is so much fun to talk to, it's like talking to myself.

Dusk is already happening. This, too, is part of my plan.

I open the wine without getting any cork in the bottle (hooray) and we sit on the sheet and I pour her a little more wine than I pour myself.

"I loved your note," she says.

Her first byline in the paper today. To celebrate, before I left work yesterday I left her a funny card and a bottle of champagne. Also a long-stemmed rose.

I know. Don't tell me.

"What did you think when you saw the rose? Did you think some copy editor was stalking you?"

"I knew it was you the minute I saw it," she says.

She is sitting up. I'm lying behind her. Adoring the cello swell of her hips, the fascinating smallness of her waist. She's wearing a tight little sleeveless number that rides up above the small of her back. My fingers take a walk.

"You have all these little white hairs on your back," I say. And she does. It's like chick down. It's adorable.

"I know. I used to shave my back. I'm so hairy!"

"It's okay," I say.

I fill my lungs. She notices.

I sit up and move nearer. I pick up her hands. We've had two glasses of wine each.

"I'd like to say something," I say.

After the roller coaster has finished creeping up its steepest incline and before it begins its descent, there is that moment. Of absolute stillness.

She winces a little. The uh-ohs are etched into her forehead.

I pause for a long time. Partly this is a dramatic pause. Partly it's the pause you use when you don't want to know what's going to happen next.

I hunt for non-clichés, but there aren't any. Everything I feel has been felt before. Everything I have to say has been said better. But this could be the last chance I have to tell her these things she already knows.

"I want to thank you," I say. "For being you and sharing as much of yourself as you have."

Her eyes are desperate. We're sitting close. You couldn't slip a Frisbee between us.

"But the thing is," I say, "it's obvious you're not going to marry him. And I know you've been thinking, 'Am I a bad person?' You're not a bad person. If anyone would think you're a bad person, it'd be me. And I know you're a . . . kind, thoughtful, generous person. You just made one mistake."

Her face goes all damp. "You don't have another bottle of wine, do you?"

"And you thought maybe you'd fall in love with him after a while, but you didn't," I say. "You don't want to hurt his feelings. But you're not doing him any favors if you wait another two or three years before you tell him. You're torturing him, Julia." Aren't I a great guy? He's living with a sexy, sweet, smart woman. And I want to save him from all that.

Big pause. The sun is setting. The broiling has ended, leaving an absolutely perfect summer evening. Red wine is starting to spread over the horizon, the plaid light of dusk arriving filtered through the leaves. People are starting to pack up their beach blankets and their beverage coolers and their footballs and their dogs and children. But everyone moves slowly. Everyone is clinging to the day.

Julia is really crying now.

"You're right," she says.

And I think, This is going rather well.

"I think you just moved in with him because you needed a place to stay in the city," I say. I try not to remind her that she has never, in all of our conversations, mentioned this scrap of information.

"It all sort of happened at the same time," she says through the tears. "One time I tried to tell him. We went out for coffee and, I told him I didn't want to go on, but he just started crying. So I said, 'No, no, I'm not leaving!' "

Zip. Boing. This is news. I wonder what was happening between her and me around that time.

"When was that?" I say.

"A couple of months ago," she says.

A couple of months ago. I think back to what was going on between us a couple of months ago. And just like that, it's like adjusting the knob on a pair of time binoculars.

"He's always saying, 'I know you're going to leave me someday,' " she says.

I'm trying not to touch her, trying not to turn this into a sex thing.

"I want to take care of you," I say.

Shooter say: *Don't ever let her catch you caring.*

"You're going to regret this," she says, "when I'm sitting on your couch every night crying for a week."

"My couch," I say, "is Scotchgarded."

And I'm holding her. I'm stroking her hair. And I pull her down so she's half-reclining in my lap. Her head is nestled in the crook of my arm and her eyes are closed and I'm looking at her soft cheek thinking, This girl is ridiculously beautiful.

But she only does the nestling thing for a couple of minutes. And then she pops back up.

"I've always had a boyfriend," she says. "Since I was fifteen. I don't know what to do without one."

Does that mean I'm not her next boyfriend?

"Do you ever wish," she says, not looking at me, "that we could skip over this part?"

I just wait for her to finish.

"I mean," she says, "skip to however it ends up."

We watch the darkness crawl in. A firefly wanders into the wine bottle. I cork it back up and we watch the bug turning on and off. We can hear crickets. They sound like Dylan to me.

Flowers on the hillside bloomin' crazy
Crickets talking back and forth in rhyme
Blue river running slow and lazy
I could stay with you forever and never realize the time.

She picks up the wine bottle. Takes out the cork. But the firefly won't leave.

"Come on," she says gently. Tapping on the bottom.

"It's just a bug," I point out.

"No," she says, tapping. It takes a while to get the firefly out.

"Yay," she says, as the firefly darts away drunkenly.

She wouldn't hurt a firefly. Full-grown adult human males are another story. Us she stomps on.

TUESDAY, JULY 31

Back from lunch. Got the sweaty gym bag, the red face from the workout, and the sandwich (sad salad on stale bread) growing bacteria in its sad sack. Check the phone messages.

"Hey, it's me."

A sigh oozes out of me like a slow leak. Her voice. Her soothing radio-talk-show-host voice. Her talk-a-jumper-off-the-Brooklyn-Bridge voice. Her impotence-happens-to-everyone voice. Suddenly I'm relaxed.

"I was just wondering if we're still going to this party thingy tonight."

I have refrained from badgering her. I invited her to this party a couple of weeks ago, and I mentioned it to her again last week. She has a habit of canceling things at the last minute, but tonight I figure I have a little ace in the hole. How many girls get invited to parties with the president?

Well, not *the*. A. Clinton. He's going to be at this party at the apartment of one of these toothless literary lions who haunt the Upper East Side. Apparently, one of Clinton's aides got him to contribute a chapter to a book about famous people and their childhood memories about sports.

I call her later at home and we arrange to meet down the block from the party. She's across East End Avenue when I clock her: she's changed out of the khakis she wore to work today. Now she's in a shimmery salmon summer dress. She looks ultrafeminine, a Super Bowl commercial for beauty. At work I can boss her around. She's a copygirl; everyone is her boss. But when it comes to sexual authority, she's General Patton. In complete command—ten *hut!*—of my privates.

She's pacing around, looking at the sidewalk, having a cigarette. She's a little nervous. She always is. I find this a little irresistible.

I'm stuck across the avenue waiting for the light to change. So I pull my camera out of my bag and hold down the telephoto lever and I snap a couple of pictures. She smiles.

Across the street, I don't go for the big kiss. There's a little kiss, a little hug. And off we go.

I give my name to the PR bunny at the door, and she checks me off her list. But there are no metal detectors. There are no hired mugs or Secret Service gorillas either, and no one asks to check my bag. Obviously the president is not here. And I have let Julia down once again.

We go upstairs, where the women have faces stretched like the Joker's and the men wear rep ties and talk about what prep schools their grandsons are going for. There are a few people our age but not many, and I don't know any of them. So we find a couple of plush chairs by the window and slowly start to drain the bar of its wine supply.

The apartment looks like the kind of place where capital-I Intellectuals meet to swap hot gossip about the 1952 presidential campaign. Obesely overstuffed chairs, books on the shelves whose dust jackets have gone crispy with age. Fat Persian carpets. You could land a helicopter in the book-lined living room, and then there's the book-lined study and the book-lined bedrooms, and . . . wait a minute, I didn't even see a bedroom. Maybe the bedrooms are on a different floor entirely. This place is a mansion. How can you not be an accomplished writer, living in these digs? The brandy and quips probably came with the lease.

We make fun of the various "characters." A gossip girl from the *Daily News*'s Rush and Molloy column working the whole Holly Golightly thing, complete with elbow gloves. Liz Smith and Cindy Adams, each making sure everyone is noticing how she takes no notice of the other. There's our "downtown" writer, a dandy in a cream-colored three-piece linen suit with matching fedora and, possibly, spats: in other words, he's a typical Bennington graduate. In the corner is the swashbuckling, grenade-lobbing Elvis of gossips, Richard Johnson. The guy's about six-four, better looking than the people he covers. He stands as still as a maypole as publicists and sycophants do their little dance of fear around him. Occasionally he laughs his evil laugh.

While I'm at the bar I look out to the foyer and see a familiar face.

Coming back to our chairs, I figure not many guys ever get a chance to hit a girl with a line like this.

"The president," I say, "is here."

He's trying to move through the crowd but to them he's Moses in a light brown suit, canary shirt, not-cheap tie. He's heading down the three steps to the sunken living room, at the moment of peak attendance.

Julia is acting all shy. "Come on," I say. "This may be your only chance to meet him."

The crowd is pressing in on all sides, but I'm pressing harder, pulling Julia toward him. She's in handshake range and reaches out to touch his beefy paw. I'm snapping pictures wildly but people are jostling me from every angle. I need to back up to get them both in the frame but there's no room. So I take wild-ass shots, trying to get Julia in the foreground while the big He surfs on the adulation. He takes her hand, looks her in the eye, looks her in the body. I'm flattered at first, but then I remember his taste in women.

Eventually we return to our original position, backed up to the far corner.

Clinton begins to speak, tells us this long boring story about how the guy who edited the book was one of the first volunteers on his campaign staff back in '92. And he's off telling us how it was back in those early days, back before he became the pope of politics, back when there were only 100 phones and a few million bucks in the bank and the interns were nerdy Jewish guys instead of needy Jewish women and on and on it goes and I'm not really listening because I have decided to put my hand on Julia's ass.

I start with the small of her back, all civilized like, but three glasses of wine and a stance within groping distance of the most beautiful girl in the world can play tricks with a man's judgment and my hand takes all of three seconds to work its way down to her left rump.

I'm teasing, not squeezing, just running my nails over the cool curve. And I discover two very nice things:

1. Julia is wearing a thong.
2. Julia is enjoying having her ass stroked in front of the forty-second President of the United States.

She's leaning into me and Clinton is regaling the crowd, so I just keep regaling her ass. She puts her head on my shoulder and moves in close. Nice. God, her ass is so sweet and round and perfect and I will never stop stroking it. Until this moment, I never thought I was much of an ass man. (What's the big deal? I've got one of those.) Now I just want her ass for breakfast, lunch, and dinner.

Clinton wraps up and the crowd starts to follow him out the door.

"Time for the next adventure?" I say.

"Mmm-hmm," she says, and it's a yummy sound. A stroke-me sound.

"So," I say, whispering conspiratorially, "how do you like being molested in front of major heads of state?"

And she laughs.

We stroll lazily uptown looking for a place to eat. Turning on East Eighty-fourth, I notice it's a quiet block. It's a pleasing night. And I'm as horny as Rosie O'Donnell at a WNBA game.

"Look at this," I say rakishly. "A doorway. Let's go check it out."

The doorway is down some steps, five feet below street level, and marked REFUSE STORAGE AND PICKUP in a big red triangle. The bottom step is cement. The door is metal and locked. There is no garbage around.

I skip down the stairs and toss my backpack on the ground. She stands on the top step warily, hovering. Waiting to be talked into something, like Eve.

And then she's down the stairs and she's in my arms and I'm all over her. Pawing her waist, rubbing her back, drinking her lips, squeezing her ass, hickeying her neck. I want to publish my lust right there above her collarbone.

And my mind is exploring options.

I've got one hand under the hem of her dress, my nails on the soft valley behind her knee. She flinches a little but I'm already well on my way to the destination, determined to make her do some arriving of her own.

She starts to turn around but I hold her tight with my left arm.

"Don't worry," I whisper in her ear as my right hand goes to work. "No one's there. People walk by and they keep walking."

A few people have strolled by already. They glance quickly, but then they look away.

"Nobody can see anything," I whisper. "Your dress is hanging down in back."

I'm working. And playing. Touching, circling, teasing.

Her eyes are closed. All of her body weight is leaning on me.

She still hasn't let go of her shoulder bag.

"No one's going to make off with this, I promise," I say, and take it and put it on the ground next to us.

And I'm back to work.

Hello, upper thigh.

"Does it feel nice?" I say.

And in slow motion, with her eyes closed, she nods and nods again.

Hello, thong.

"We could meet on the West Side sometime . . . ," she whispers.

My neighborhood. That sounds like an invitation. You could hang wet laundry on my schlong. I could do push-ups with no hands.

And I'm bringing her along.

And then I bring her right on home.

Her mouth is all over mine in gratitude. I want every cell of her. There isn't any part of her I don't want in my mouth. The voluptuousness of her kneecaps. The lubricity of her toenails. And I pull her away for a second to get a look at her face: it's a bog of sweat. Her hair is hanging down as if she's just gotten out of a hot shower.

Then we're back at it.

And I'm panting, "I have to see your thong."

Then I'm on my knees, a supplicant to love, worshiping at the church of Our Lady of the Holy Fucking Hot Thong.

"I have others," she whispers.

It's red.

SATURDAY, AUGUST 4

I'm at Shooter's house in the Hamptons, sitting by the pool in my swimsuit with a book I am not reading and a drink I am not drinking. She's at the Jersey Shore. With her mother, her father, her brothers, and her boyfriend. You just know they're playing *Frisbee*. As punishment for this treachery, I am not calling her. I have this week obtained a cell phone, my first ever, for the specific purpose of not calling her. Of course, she might want to call me.

The hunt is continuing but she always dances just out of range. I'm the chaser and she's the chaste. We go to parties together. We drink our drinks together. Complain about our jobs together. We drink, we whine. We drink, we whine. Blather, rinse, repeat. We go to movies. We go to dinners. They all end the same way. Every evening is a seminar in cruelty. Not an exercise in frustration: an entire workout. She's like a personal trainer, except one of them would cost me only $50 an hour.

At the end of every evening, we share the cab. We run our lines together, in our taxi theater: "Come up." "I can't." I worship her from anear.

I woo her with food. I woo her with booze. I woo her with goo-goo eyes and stolen kisses. (Stolen? I paid for these kisses, bub. Oh, how I paid.) I woo her in the park and I woo her in the dark. I woo her until my woo-woo is worn and then what do I do? I woo her some more. She is woo-proof. She is unwooable. Woe is my wooer.

Back at the pool, Alpha Dog emerges first, at 12:15. As usual he goes straight for my balls.

"Hey, Alfie, how ya—ow, don't stand on my testicles, boy. Yes, I love you too." My face is covered in dog spit, but who am I to spurn unconditional love? Alpha's tail is operating at a thousand wags a minute. If he could figure out the angles, he could probably use it to rise vertically, like a helicopter. Then maybe he could fly around the neighborhood and discover there are lots of other guys' balls he could be stomping on.

"Heh, heh, heh," says Shooter, coming down to the side of the pool and sticking a foot in the water. He's working on a large Bloody Mary, possibly not his first of the day. What a degenerate. Which reminds me. I reach down and take a gulp of mine. Ahh. How could I have forgotten? When I find myself in times of trouble, Bloody Mary comes to me.

Shooter sits down, his feet in the water up to the knees, and pats Alpha's rump. "Get a room, you two."

"Pardon my screams," I say. "I just wasn't in the mood for a savage nut crunching on this particular day."

"You don't use 'em much anyway. Consider it exercise. Are you thinking about that girl again?" Shooter asks.

"You caught the dreamy look in my eye?"

"Yeah, that," he says, taking a sip. "Plus the huge boner."

Oh.

"Unless it's for Alpha, you sick fuck," Shooter adds pleasantly. He chuckles into his drink.

"I need help. This girl, she's everywhere," I say. "She's oozing through every cell of me. She's got a hold on every sector of my body."

"Can't help you there, sport. I'm a lover, not an oncologist."

"This girl is harder to get into than Rao's."

"Listen," Shooter says. "What did the wise old brain surgeon say to the rookie brain surgeon?"

"I don't know," I say.

" 'Relax. This isn't rocket science.' "

"I know it isn't rocket science. Rocket science makes sense. Earth's gravitional field doesn't pull things in on Tuesday and push them away on Sunday."

"Been having a lot of Sundays?"

"*Hola,*" someone says.

Another Bloody Mary enters the yard, followed closely by Mike. Last winter he and Karin bought the house next door to Shooter's in Amagansett. Mike's house features a screaming infant and basic cable. Shooter's has a pool and seventeen movie channels. I spend more time at Shooter's.

"Hey," I say.

"How's the water?" he says. Mike's also carrying a magazine and a boom box. He puts the radio down and plugs it in. It's tuned to the FM station for people who iron their jeans.

"Up to standard," Shooter says.

Mike takes his *Wine Spectator* and gets on a float. He paddles his way around the pool as he reads, the magazine propped on his belly.

The radio: the most overplayed song since that annoying Sheryl Crow tune about the guy peeling the labels off his bottle of Bud.

Now she's back in the atmosphere,
With drops of Jupiter in her hair, hey, hey,
She acts like summer and walks like rain,
Reminds me that there's time to change, hey, hey.

"I love this song," Mike says.

"You don't, really," says Shooter.

"What's it called?" Mike says.

" 'Drops of Jupiter.' By Train."

"I'm gonna get the CD," Mike threatens.

"That's a little extreme," Shooter says.

"Please don't," I say. The next thing you know, he'll be falling for that song that sounds like Superman talking to his shrink.

"Why?" Mike says.

"There's nothing to it," I say. "It's a string of nonsense—'since the return of her stay on the moon, she listens like spring and she talks like June'?—what's that? It's just killing time till you get to the chorus."

"Love that chorus!" he says. And here it comes.

Na na na na na
Na na na na na na na-aah-a-aah!

We listen.

"What's that line?" Shooter says.

" 'Man, heaven is overrated'?" Mike says.

"No," I say. "I think it's, 'Manhattan is overrated.' Don't you get it? It's an anti-New York song." Sometimes people don't get New York. The place is dirty and dangerous and crowded and costly, and every other place is even worse.

"Do you want to come over for a movie tonight?" Mike says.

My mistake: I agree. So hours later Shooter and I sit down with

Mike and Karin for some nice TV. The baby, having been "put down" (apparently this doesn't mean given a lethal injection, just as animals who are "put to sleep" won't be needing a wake-up call), isn't available for an in-person performance, so we watch a video of the baby.

In the video, the baby is getting a bath. That's it. This isn't any special bath; it isn't My First Bath or My First Shampoo or My First Breaststroke or anything; it's just A Bath. For fifteen minutes. Mike sits on an ottoman about six inches away from the TV, almost directly in my line of sight, peering at the footage as intently as Stanley Kubrick in his editing room. I consider telling him he's blocking my sight, but then again, what am I missing?

We watch A Bath.

"The film quality is pretty good," I say to Mike.

"Yeah," he says tersely, in a shushy kind of way, as though I were chattering away during the climax of *The Godfather*.

"But I guess you can't edit on these video cameras, huh?" I say.

"Actually," he says, "I edited out the part where I admit I've never changed Alexandra's diaper."

Ah, I get it. So this is not the rough cut. This is the finished drama of A Bath, edited down to its essence. Which consists of a mom splashing water around on a confused-looking little person who looks as if she's considering submitting a complaint to Amnesty International.

"So pretty," says Karin.

"Isn't she pretty?" says Mike.

"Pretty," says Shooter, dutifully.

"Actually," I say, "the phrase that comes to mind is below average."

Except I don't.

"Yes," I say, because it is the easiest thing to say. I wonder, when did people stop cooing over me? Or, given that I am Manboy and my mother can't deal with me as an adult anyway, is she still talking about me this way? "Oh, Tom, he's great. He's 397 months, 180 pounds, 5 ounces. Got a big, full head of hair!" Well, that last part isn't exactly true anymore. Let's face it, I was much cuter then. That's why it was so much easier to get a breast in my mouth.

My cell phone goes. I knew the calls would be rolling in soon.

"Tom?" A female voice. Nasal and impatient.

"Well, if it isn't," I say. I try to hide my genuine delight under a layer of sarcastic delight.

"I'm bored," says Bran. "You bored?"

I admire a girl who admits she's bored and home alone on Saturday night. "Yeah," I say. "Only I'm not in the neighborhood. I'm in the Hamptons."

"You dit'int invite me!" she says. I love the way she says "didn't."

"I'm sure," I say, "that I can make it up to you. Movies on Thursday?"

"Yeah. Hey, I may have a girl for you."

"Is it you?"

"Show up and find out," she says.

"Would this person have deep and abiding contempt for me?"

"I don't have contempt for you."

"Aha! So it is you."

"You're pretty cocky for a guy who sucks in his gut when he's trying to hit on girls."

"Girls adore my gut," I say. "Makes 'em feel thin." Besides, my gut is shrinking. The swim trunks are getting baggy.

"Um, *oh*-kay," she says. "And girls like ugly guys because they make us feel pretty. And girls like short guys because they make us feel tall. *That's* why Danny DeVito is such a sex symbol!"

"Wow," I say.

"What?"

"Nothing. Just. Give me a second." Sniff, sniff.

"Tom, you okay?"

"Sort of," I say. "No. I mean. You just, kind of hurt my feelings."

"I'm so sorry! Really?"

"No. In your face, Lowenstein!"

"You twat," she says, and laughs. "I'll see you Thursday."

My friend couldn't make it," Bran tells me.

"Oh really."

"Yes, really," she says. "How does this thing work?" She's push-ing buttons on a computer monitor. It beats dealing with the minimum-wage drones who sell tickets in person. But nothing is happening. When she touches the button saying "9:30 P.M." nothing happens. Nothing happens the second time. Nothing happens the fiftieth time.

"This fucking thing," she says, looking around for someone to berate. I'm a little fearful at these moments.

"Let me," I say, being all manly about it, assuming control. I fig-ure if the screen gizmo happens to work for me, I'm a golden god, her box-office hero. But if it doesn't, she can't very well blame me, can she?

I haven't seen Bran for a while, but looking at her now, with her cool flowy black hair and her just-about-to-laugh mouth, I start to remember why I used to phone her every other day, why I thought for a long time, Would it be so bad if I ended up with Bran? Before I gave up and accepted my demotion to non-potential sex partner, to Him? Oh, He's Just a Friend. Last spring we went to a play. Afterward we stopped by Langan's to get companionably drunk. She told me about the coolest moment in her life: when she was a college sophomore and just aching to become one of those Serious Young Journalists, she went to a job conference crawling with other Serious Young Journalists and met Barbara Walters. I laughed. She said I was mean.

I've been nice. I took her to many dazzling parties, got her drunk. Even got her high. What I did not get was in her pants, nowhere near. Yet we make each other laugh. We're like a married couple, except we're still attracted to each other. My problem is, after an evening together, I get all warm and cuddly like and I start cutting out the self-censorship button, the way I do when I'm with my guy friends. Guys make fun of each other mercilessly. Do it with a girl and . . . you can forget about doing it with that girl.

We talked about relationships that didn't work out and we got drunker. And lamentier. We had a nice cab home together since she lives a few blocks from me. "Thank you for being my friend," I said, with barroom sentimentality. "I'm glad we've gotten closer," she said. We went into the clinch. It wasn't a phony see-ya-later hug. It was a real boy-girler.

At the Union Square manyplex, we stroke the screen, we tap the screen, we rub the screen, we press the screen. Two college graduates are unable to win the rights to buy tickets to a movie.

"Do you really want to see this stupid movie?" I say.

"Of course not," she says. "I thought you wanted to see it." "Are you kidding me?" I say. "You thought I wanted to see a movie about a ditzy blonde with a passion for designer labels? How gay do you think I am?"

"In those pants? Not very," she says.

"What's wrong with my pants?"

"They hang loose in the back," she says. "How am I supposed to check out your butt? And the less said about the mustard stain, the better."

"This? No one can see this. It's really small."

"No, you're right," she says. "Only *you* can see it. It's in*vis*ible to everyone else."

We're strolling down University Place. She pulls up in front of a Korean flower shop slash deli.

"Ooohhhh, I *love* these," she says, sticking her whole face in a big barrel of flowers. "Lilies of the valley are the *best*. Remember that."

"You want to go back to a time when if a guy liked you, he'd keep sending you flowers. I want to go back to stewardesses being chosen primarily for their looks. Unhappiness reigns everywhere."

"Tom, can we be real for a second?" she says as we head back down University. "I'm worried about my friend Sharon. She might get fired. I've known her since I'm eighteen!"

"I like that, 'Since I'm eighteen,' " I say.

"Are you making fun of me?" Her eyes are blazing.

"I just said I liked it!" I say.

"What did I say?" she says. " 'I've known her since I was eighteen.' "

"No, you said, 'Since I'm eighteen.' It's a very New Yorky way of talking. People didn't say that in Rockville, Maryland."

"Jesus, you are such a snob," she says.

"What'd I say?" I say.

Bran and I often have conversations like this. Things are going perfectly smoothly, I make some light remark, she takes it as an insult, she scolds me for a while, my balls become Grape-Nuts and my A-Rod turns to shrimp cocktail.

There's a giant pile of garbage outside a dingy office building on University. This being New York, casual mountains of garbage are not news, but in this case, a dozen young hipsters are going through the refuse. It's mostly paperwork and vinyl records in blank white paper sleeves. Every so often a bored-looking middle-aged blue-collar white guy comes and adds another barrel or bag to the dump.

"There's a noodle shop around the cor—," I am saying when I realize I have lost her. Unlike me, Bran is a real reporter: she actually wants to go and see what people are doing with their lives. Me, I prefer not to think about it.

Bran is talking to someone sifting through the paperwork and records.

"You know what this is?" she says, sparkling. "This is KK-Killuh's garbage!"

In Manhattan below Fourteenth Street, it's the equivalent of finding Princess Diana's used tiaras. And it makes sense: as Mr. Killuh is, according to tabloid news reports, currently an involuntary guest of the state of New York, what use does he have for an apartment on University Place? You know how they say people comb the obits looking for apartments that have suddenly become vacant? Maybe they should start checking *Vibe* while they're at it.

Bran is going all Lois Lane on me. "This is a 'Talk of the Town'!" she says.

"You need to know someone at *The New Yorker* to get into 'Talk of the Town,' " I say. Wait a minute: I actually do know a couple of people at *The New Yorker*. A girl I went to school with and her friend. You know how they always say you have to know someone? I'm somehow one of those someones.

And see how far it's gotten me? I start picking through the garbage on the off chance that I might get paid to write about what I find. This puts me below the level of garbageman: they at least *know* their interaction with trash will earn them money. I'm collecting garbage on spec.

The site of a well-dressed twenty-nine-year-old woman picking through garbage, even in New York, even in this century, is unusual. People stop to stare. Some figure this must be really good garbage, and they start picking through it as well. Soon half a dozen well-dressed New Yorkers with degrees from top eastern universities and 401(k) plans are trawling through the detritus of an illiterate criminal from Staten Island.

There is a black guy next to me. We rummage together, joined in our celebrity worship.

"You like K-Cube?" I say.

He looks at me, gives me a little pat of recognition. "You all right," he says. "Can't judge a book by its cover."

I happen to know the etiquette on the matter of Mr. Killuh's name; he is addressed as K-Cubed (pronounced "K-Cube," of course), never as K-K-K. If you call him that, you're a racist.

"Look," I say conversationally, showing him a booklet. "Blank deposit slips."

"Give 'em here," he says, his eyes twinkling with bank fraud. "No, wait. Never mind. You see any withdrawal slips?"

Bran is running around interviewing people. I help pore through the pile.

I'm finding ICM contracts, riders listing demands ("Artist will travel in first class at Promoter's Expense"), scripts for music videos ("This video will be about the NOTORIOUS CRIMINAL KK-Killuh. We want to make it as THUGGED OUT as possible."), lists of producers and songs, and a long, tangled exchange between KK-Killuh and some party promoter about whether or not his mother was treated with the deference due a woman of her stature at some awards dinner. Bran is talking to the guy who was standing next to me a minute ago. It turns out he's a rapper too; he's doing a gig at Joe's Pub tonight.

"Why don't you get with me instead of him?" he whines. "Look," he says, rolling up his sleeves. "I got bigger arms than that guy. Feel."

Is this how people ask each other out in the 'hood? So much simpler. On the other hand, if I were black, I'd get no dates at all.

A guy who looks like he invests in socially progressive stocks is rustling through a box of blank fax sheets. Bran grabs him for a quote. "I don't know if I feel bad about being here, or if I feel bad about not being here soon enough," he says. "You should never be late to a good pillaging."

"Bran," I say. "We gotta eat something."

Bran and I gather up a bunch of documents and records and stick them in a box. She carries it proudly in front of her belly: her baby. We go to a diner for a burger.

Bran is humming the latest Madonna song. Producing a TV news segment involves months of work to put together a twelve-minute collage of pictures. This, though, could be an actual written story to be printed in a magazine next week. Her name in black ink. She doesn't get to see that often.

"Do you think it's a story?" she says.

"It's a story."

"I'm going to stay up all night writing it. I'm so excited."

"Bran," I say. "It's a five-hundred-word story." I take my cell phone out of my backpack to make sure it's still on. You never know when Julia's going to call.

"You shit," she says. "What are you doing with my phone?"

"My phone."

She starts pawing through her five-gallon bag, the one I mockingly called "fake Fendi" the first time I saw it even though I, obviously, can't tell the difference. It turned out that I'd stumbled onto the truth. She didn't talk to me for a month after that.

"So what's that?" I say, as she unearths a scratched Nokia.

"You got the exact same phone they gave me?"

"Looks that way," I say.

"You have to get a new one, then."

"Uh-uh."

I pay for the grub, then Bran and I head across the street to one of those cool old-fashioned quasi-Irish pubs, with carnival glass and conspiratorial little booths and beer by the pitcher.

"You're buying this time," I say, sitting at the bar.

"I don't have any money," she says, and opens her wallet. This is the cartoon moment when the moths fly out, but she's right: she's busted. Girls never have any money. Girls get away with a lot, if you ask me. I hear the Kennedy kids walk around without cash too. And royalty.

I order a Guinness. She looks at the beer list as if it's written in Urdu. "Stella Artois," she tells the waiter. I grimace, involuntarily.

"What?" she says, all defensive. "I've never had one. I want to see what it's like. Why do you have to always insult me?"

"I'm not insulting you," I say. "I've had every one of these beers." Many times. "I could have described them for you."

Bran is tall, looks taller in her gray wool suit. Wide lapels, shoulder pads, baggy pleated pants. Girls dressed this way for a brief moment, in the late 1980s. Then they came to their senses.

"You're looking at my suit," she says.

"Where did you get it?" I say, dodging.

"It was the first suit I ever bought!" she says, brightly. "It was three hundred dollars. Then the next week it was on sale for a hundred and fifty so I returned it and bought it again."

She's still wearing the first suit she ever bought. In the late eighties.

"This girl at work asked me if I was a lesbian," she says morosely.

"You do dress like Ellen DeGeneres," I say.

"Why are you always saying such hurtful things?" she says. "You're such an asshole."

Gaffe! Backtrack. "All I'm saying, you're a cute girl. Dress like one."

"How?"

"You're wearing, like, thirty percent too much clothing," I say.

I give the bartender a bill. Bartenders like me. I always overtip them. Give them an extra buck, they give you an extra six-dollar drink. What goes around comes around. It's barma.

She takes a sip. I drink half of my pint in a gulp.

"Do you ever think," Bran says gently, "that you drink too much?"

"Actually, since it hasn't started working yet," I say, "I was thinking I should up the dosage."

The J box starts up with "Tangled Up in Blue." The strumming hits me like intravenous beer. Ahh. Muscles going slack with joy.

"Did you know that in the original version of this song, the one on the New York sessions bootleg—" I say.

"What song?" she says.

"This song. On the original version, it's—"

"What song is this?"

" 'Tangled Up in Blue,' " I say.

"By who?"

"Oh come on," I say. "Dylan! It's the first song on *Blood on the Tracks!*"

"What *century* is it from?" she says. "Don't they have any new music?"

Let it go. "Anyway," I say, "on the original version of this song, it's all in the third person. *He* was married when they first met, soon to be divorced. *He* helped her out of a jam *he* guessed but *he* used a little too much force.' On the Minneapolis session, the one that was used on the commercially released album, it's all in the first person. Makes it so much more personal, don't you think? More powerful. And the language is so beautifully economical. Instead of saying, I met her, we cheated on her husband, I talked her into dumping him, he just says, 'She was married when we first met/Soon to be divorced.' And then he kills her husband, but Dylan never comes out and says that. It's just, 'Helped her out of a jam I guess/But I used a little too much force.'"

The idea of shooting the other man has a certain desperado flair, no?

"Tom," she says, "I don't know what you're talking about."

We wind up on University looking for a cab. We've had only one drink but I notice Bran seems to be walking awfully close to me. Leaning on me a little. I send a tentative arm slithering out on a reconnaissance mission to her waist. Normally when I do this I'm in for a nasty remark or two, like, *Tom, how many times do I have to tell you I'm not interested?* After three years of failure, one tends to scale back on operations a little.

But at the moment Bran seems to like having my arm around her. For the first time ever.

A few notable rejections by Bran:

1. The first time I met her. We were at a birthday party for some guy I'd never met at a grim little Bowery apartment filled with people I didn't know. Bran and I made each other laugh. I asked for her phone number. She gave it to me. Then she started dropping hints: hints that she wasn't interested. I called her anyway. We talked for forty-five minutes. I made her laugh some more and then I asked her out.

2 The first time I ever took her out: the premiere of the hot
    HBO show of the year, on a January night in John's Pizza in
    Times Square. We saw one of the tough guys from *Goodfellas*
    there and hung around him quoting lines from the movie
    while his eyes swept the room desperately for Security.
    Then I tried to heist a kiss off Bran as I was putting her in a
    cab. She turned her cheek: frostier than the January air.

3. The time we got dinner in the West Village in the summer a
    year ago and I bought a pot pipe. I had secured a little
    wacky weed a couple of weeks before, so I invited her to
    come over and partake. First we got drunk on red wine. We
    smoked a little, listened to eighties tunes, cuddled. When
    Spandau Ballet's "True" came on, I got her locked in a
    slow dance. Then I tried to kiss her. It was like trying to
    catch a butterfly. I gave up and we sat back down on the
    sofa and she lay down with her head in my lap listening to
    the eighties. I stroked her long black hair for a while until
    she went home.

4. The time her parents took us to see a Broadway play. Her
    father's first words to me were? "Tom? You're a genius."
    Apparently Bran had been saving my e-mails to her and
    forwarding them to her dad. Her parents brought their own
    food to the show: a quart Ziploc of trail mix. It was pretty
    tasty stuff. Afterward I walked her home and tried to kiss
    her again as a freezing wind blew off the Hudson. "Don't,"
    she said.

5. That time she came to my birthday party. She and her best
    friend, Sharon, were the last ones left, and we all sat on the

couch talking until four. When Sharon was in the bathroom, I whispered in Bran's ear, "Why don't you stay?" She laughed. And left.

I rub Bran's back a little as we walk. "You're tense."

"See those yellow cars going by, Tom?" she says. "Can't we get one?"

All of the cabs are occupied. We wait on a corner. My arm is around her. This would be an ideal moment for her to put her head on my shoulder, but she can't, as that would require contortions. She is one inch taller than me.

"Maybe we're not such a bad fit," I say.

"Tom," she says. "Men are like a black dress. Any woman could go shopping with a guy and try on a hundred black dresses, and he may say, 'They're all alike.' But to her there's just something missing from each one."

Ouch. But I think of those lines in "You're a Big Girl Now": *Oh I can change I swear. See what you can do. I can make it through. You can make it too.*

In the cab I go for it anyway. She breaks off after about thirty seconds.

"Tom," she says. "What the fuck are you doing?"

"I am trying," I say evenly, "to sex you up."

This earns me a) a laugh and b) another kiss. But there is a buzzing in the backseat.

"Is that my heart?" I say.

"Shut up, you idiot," she says, and pushes me off. She digs her phone out of her backpack. She's thinking: News! Sources!

I'm going for my phone thinking, Obviously Julia sensed me making out with someone other than her and she's mighty peeved. Heh, heh.

But it's Bran's phone. She hits the talk button with Serious Young Journalist urgency.

"Yeah, Stuart," she says, then covers the mouthpiece. "If you're going to have the same phone as me you have to at least change your ring tone," she orders.

"So that means you want to see me again," I say.

But by this point she's so annoyed that we don't touch for the rest of the cab ride. I don't change my ring tone.

I'm at work editing gossip, crafting headlines, throwing away press releases. But mainly I'm avoiding Julia. Not calling Julia. Ignoring Julia. She filled in for Hyman Katz at the noon features meeting, which I spent courageously not looking at her. She was not looking at me. But I was trying very hard not to look at her, whereas she did not seem to be trying very hard not to look at me. I know this because I was looking at her the whole time. Has she forgotten me? This ignoring game, it isn't much fun.

The phone. It's Bran. Do I want to come out for margaritas and bingo tonight?

"No," I say. I want to go home and stew in my own fetid bachelorhood. Seems like a nice night for it.

"Come on," Bran is telling me. "I'm bringing Katie."

Katie. That cute blonde who told my fortune at my birthday party.

"My schedule," I say, "just cleared itself."

So we head to the West Village in the rain. Bran looks pretty good in a tight blue tank top and a clingy black skirt. I let her get the cab for once.

"I always pay for everything," she whines. Girl arithmetic. Like when the check comes and it's $41 plus tax and tip and the girl, saying, "I want to pay my share," lays out a ten and three singles.

"I read your *New Yorker* piece," I say.

"Thank you *so much*," she says. "I couldn't have done it if you had been stamping your feet and saying, 'Let's go, blow this off.' But you were so patient with me, you helped me sift through everything, and then you were supportive of what I wrote even though I'd never written anything before."

You get girl points for the strangest things. Basically, I a) stood there like a potted plant on the KK-Killuh night; b) read her first draft of the story. It was good. I told her so.

"It was all you," I say.

"And thanks for giving me the name of your friend at *The New Yorker*," she says.

"It was nothing," I say.

"I really gained a lot of respect for you that night," she says.

"I lost all respect for you when you didn't recognize 'Tangled up in Blue,' " I say. This is not meant to be taken seriously. But. Here. It. Comes.

"Why would you say that? That's such a mean thing to say. I had nothing but nice things to say to you, and then you go and attack me again. You're a prick."

"What'd I say?" I say, incredulous. I spend a lot of my time with Bran in a state of incredulity. Nobody, with the possible exception of the collections department of the Columbia House Music Service, is so hostile to me.

"Why do you always have to be so mean?" she says.

"I wasn't mean!" I say. Was I? Come on, guys, you be the jury. Mean: Hitler, Nixon, Martha Stewart. Not mean: Fred Rogers, Oprah, me.

Katie is waiting in a cocoon of cuteness at the bar. She waves us over. She seems glad to see me.

"I didn't know you were coming!" she says.

So I get the exclamation point.

We're eyeing the pitchers, and I'm thinking expensive tequila.

"Patrón?" I say.

"I'm a student," she pleads. "I'm about to go to law school, I don't have that much money. Let's get the cheap tequila."

"You're a *law* student," I tell her. "It's not like you're going to study Renaissance Poetry. You can pay."

Katie and Bran both look utterly shocked.

"See," Bran says. "He's always being mean."

Gaffe! Delayed arrival.

"You think I'm mean?" I ask Katie.

"You're very, direct," she says.

We get a table, and I slide into the booth first. Katie slides in next to me. Bran is across. Well now. Wouldn't it be nice if this were really happening? Wait, it is happening. Pay attention. Make it keep happening.

We're playing bingo and working on our fourth margaritas. Katie *drinks*. And Katie is small. This is good news. Both of us are losing when some tool yells, "Bingo!" and skips to the front of the room.

I look at Katie. She looks pretty good to me.

Bran is talking to some chick she seems to know at the next table.

"You have big cheeks," I say to Katie.

She is mortified. "Why would you say such a *hateful* thing?" she says. "I *know* I have big cheeks. They used to call me Dizzy Gillespie in school."

"Is he being mean?" Bran says, turning around.

"He's mean," Katie agrees. But she's smiling. She leans over to me while Bran goes back to talking to the girl at the next table. "Tequila shots at the bar?" she says.

I wonder if I have gone so far into the *Gaffe!* zone that I have gone through a warp in the cosmic fabric and come out the other side: instead of being a doofus who can't make his mouth say socially acceptable words, I am, to Katie, the galactic opposite: The Total Bastard. The Guy Who Doesn't Give a Rat's Ass. The Man Who Calls 'Em as He Sees 'Em. Have I stumbled through a trapdoor and found myself in Shooterville?

We do a shot at the bar.

"I heard you called her Ellen DeGeneres," Katie says.

"Not in the lesbian sense," I say. "Merely the looking-like-a-lesbian sense."

"She's a little touchy about that."

"She asked what I thought," I say. Why do girls do this—Are my thighs getting fat? Do you find that underwear model pretty?—when they know that they will either get an honest answer or a lie that proves they have turned us into cringing castrati?

"There's this woman who keeps hitting on her," Katie says. "That's why. But after you told her she looked like Ellen, she went out and bought some skirts."

Suddenly Bran is behind us.

"Okay, you guys," she says. "Time to jet."

We go to the Art Bar to hook up with a friend of Katie. The Art Bar sounds like some kind of Eurosnob hangout but it's actually cool: if you go in the back room, you can find some old couches built before the primary functions of a couch were to be sleek and stylish and uncomfortable. These are plain old regular couches with all the styling touches of the ones I remember from Rockville: shabby cushions and threadbare arms.

My meanness trial is continuing.

"Why do you have to be so mean all the time?" Bran says, and begins itemizing my faults. What is she saying? I have no idea. I have to admit, I don't really listen well at times like these.

"Uh-huh," I say, picking up her right hand absently and rubbing it with both of mine. I'm watching Katie chat with her friend Ginny across the table. Ginny is tagged. A sparkly look-at-me-I-got-a-rich-guy ring. She is married, and has taken the corresponding 50 percent IQ cut. Everything she says is about "Josh." Where Josh just took her on vacation. Why Josh and she are moving to Japan. What Josh thinks of her piano playing. Where Josh is, right now, at this very second. It turns out this woman is fluent in Japanese, is a concert-level pianist, and is training for the marathon. Yet she can spend ten minutes discussing the curtains she bought—today! this very day!—at Bloomingdale's.

"Are you listening to me or are you watching Katie?" Bran says.

"Whose hand am I holding?" I say.

Katie shoots me a ferrety glance.

Ginny and Katie talk about how Katie, when she first came to New York from Iowa, stayed with Ginny, who also grew up in Iowa.

"Why'd you come to New York?" I say.

"It seemed so exciting," Katie says.

"It can't compete with Des Moines, can it?"

"You," says Katie, "are such a bastard."

But her eyes are flashing. Not with boredom.

I sink back into my seat and drift out of the conversation, wondering if I can get away with it: Can I be a Total Bastard? Will anyone buy it? From a guy who has reached only the Minimum Acceptable Height for an Adult Male?

Bran goes to the bathroom and I get up and sit next to Katie. She takes out her cell phone. She's a little sloshed.

"Give me your phone number," she says, and she adds it to her database. She wants my home number and my work number too. I enter hers into my phone. Now I've got her on call. Didn't even have to be the first one to ask. Total Bastard mode: you should try it some time. It's 99 percent humiliation free, since you never give any hint you care about anyone.

"Bang me on my cell," I say, as Bran comes back. "Anytime."

Now Bran is giving me a glance. "I'm gonna go," I say. Be the first to leave. Cool.

"I'm going too," Bran says, and all the girls do their hugging-and-kissing-good-bye routine.

But I don't. I hang back. When I kiss Katie, I don't want it to be a cheek job. And Total Bastards don't do hugs. All of those troublesome greeting-and-departure rituals are eliminated! I just lead Bran out the door and into a cab.

"You *like* her," Bran says in the cab. We're approaching her block.

"She's likable," I say.

"You're going to ask her out," she says.

"You never know," I say.

"It's all fun and games until someone loses a guy," she says miserably. And before she gets out, she grabs me and kisses me viciously on the mouth.

FRIDAY, AUGUST 24

Julia took the day off. She and her whole family are driving the little brother to the University of Wisconsin for freshman year. They volunteered to help Al unpack, no doubt to his undying horror.

And Rick, a young man who just happens to be at Wisconsin vet school? He was merely Julia's boyfriend from ages sixteen to twenty-two.

"Are you going to see him?" I say to her on the phone.

"Yeah, I called him," she says. "He gave me that voice he used to use on other people who called him when we were dating. That 'It's so good to hear from you!' voice. With exclamation points."

Rick broke up with someone last spring. He was in New York. But he never called her the whole weekend he was in New York. Possibly he has tired of her.

"Broke your heart?"

"No," she says. "He just dented it."

"Does he have a girlfriend?" I say.

"*Probably*," she says, disgustedly. He's the kind of guy who snaps his fingers, and girls waft gently out of the trees to land at his feet.

"You're going to hook up with him," I say.

"No," she says.

When she hangs up I immediately start dialing another number.

"Help," I tell the phone. "I need a lawyer."

"Any lawyer in particular?" Katie says.

"I'm thinking of someone I know with an intuitive sense of jurisprudence and a nice butt," I say.

Her laugh is low and naughty. "I'll let you know if I meet anyone like that," she says.

"How's the paper chase?" I say.

"We just had orientation," she said. "Mandatory fun, happy hour. They actually made us wear name tags."

"How were the boys? *L.A. Law* types?"

"I don't know, did they have a spinoff called *L.A. Khaki-Wearing Money-Grubbing Dorks?*"

Exactly what I need to hear right now.

"It doesn't even start until next week," she says. "And already I've got homework. *And I'm behind on it.* I'll never pass the bar."

"I never pass any bars without stopping in. Care to join me at one of them tonight?"

"I really shouldn't," she says. "And I really need a drink."

"And some dinner to wash it down with," I say. "If you're going to uphold the cause of justice, you'll need to eat your broccoli rabe."

"I know this new place on Columbus," she says.

So we meet at seven at one of those joints where waitresses with pulled-back hair wear tight black ass pants with white shirts and a skinny black tie tucked insouciantly into their shirts. Katie is thirty but at the bar, in a cranberry pleated skirt and a white twin set, she looks like a cute undergraduate. She's halfway through a legal tome and three-quarters of the way through a glass of red.

I sidle up next to her and take a seat. "I've come to examine your briefs," I say.

"Huh-huh," she says in that low way that makes me tingle.

When we sit down, our waitstaffer grandly opens our menus for us before handing them over: that's class. Then Katie issues a preliminary injunction.

"I'm not that hungry. And do not," she says, "get me drunk. I have to get through forty pages tonight."

Menu girl is waiting with a local-TV-newscaster smile that says: *Sure, I don't care if you guys walk out of here with a $23 tab. I do this job because it is my calling to serve.*

"We'll have a bottle of the Burgundy," I say. I love this place already: the most expensive bottle on the menu is only $40.

"Be right back," says the girl.

Katie narrows her eyes. "You total bastard," she says. But she can't help smiling.

"Who said you could have any of it?" I say. "A man's got a thirst."

The girl comes back and stages her little bottle theater. Presents the label (I peer, squint, mouth the words, finally nod solemnly), wrenches out the cork and pours me half a sip. Now it's my turn to star. I swirl, hold the glass up to the light frownily and swirl some more. Then I get into that whole sniffing business.

"Oh, just drink it, nancy boy," Katie says.

"Please. I'm checking to see if it has legs."

She tries to kick me under the table but she has little legs. I grab her ankle and hold it, running my hand up her calf.

I sip. Give the girl a nod.

"You don't need to check out *my* legs," Katie says. But she relaxes her leg and I hold her calf for a minute. Her sandal falls off.

"Ticklish?" I say.

"Don't you dare," she says, and her leg is gone.

"D'you ever get tired of dating?" she says.

"Yes. No."

"I know exactly what you mean."

"It's like a job interview," I say.

"Okay, interview me," she says, and sits up, all straight and perky. She starts to drink her Burgundy.

"Can you describe your last, um, position for me?"

"Huh-huh," she laughs, in that low, growly way of hers. "I won't tell you the position, but I'll tell you the guy. His name was Fred. The second time I went to his apartment? He had weird food. And that was it."

"Weird food?"

"Goose fat. Smoked turkey necks. Endless cans of clam juice. *Weird food.*"

"Everything else about him was okay?"

"Seemingly."

"But you dumped him for this."

"Yup."

"There is no limit to strangeness when it comes to dating, is there?"

"Him or me?" she says.

"Both. He could have turned out to be a great guy."

"He turned out to be a serial killer."

"Really?"

"Well. Not *yet*. But I'm watching the tabloids. I mean, the man had frozen squab. Pork hocks. Oh, and Vegemite. He wasn't even Australian."

"You tell him the reason?"

"*God*, no."

"Why is it we can never tell each other the real reason for our breakups? Why won't we grant each other this single moment of honesty when the other person needs it most?"

"What fun would that be?" she says. "Another time I broke up with a guy because I came home and he was, in*volv*ed, shall we say, with some porn. I caught him red-handed."

"Caught him with his pants down. As it were."

She laughs again. "Come on. What's the weirdest reason you've ever broken up with someone?"

One time this girl stayed for the night. In the morning she poured herself a pint, a *pint* of fresh-squeezed orange juice bought for the occasion in a moment of anticipatory exuberance and then had, like, one sip. I had to throw it all out, of course. Sex is one thing, but backwash is another. Nobody better use my toothbrush, either. Then there was the girl who, when we were talking about our favorite Simon and Garfunkel songs, insisted hers was "Cecilia." That was pretty much the last conversation I ever had with her.

"Just the normal reasons," I say.

"Liar," she says. And kicks me. I like a girl who can detect my lies.

When we finish the wine, it's a little awkward. I live south of here. Katie lives north of here. But just a few blocks.

"Can I walk you home?" I say.

"Yes please," she says.

There's another awkward moment when we get to the entrance of her building, the doorman eyeing us.

"I have learned much about you, T.F.," Katie says, not inviting me in. She's twinkling with merriment, though.

"You better keep it to yourself, little girl," I say, putting my hands on her waist.

"Or else what?" she says.

"Or you're in for it," I say, and tickle her.

"Agh! Stop!" she says. "Uncle!" And she smiles.

The kiss. It's a kiss that says: give me three solid, entertaining dates, and *maybe*.

SATURDAY, AUGUST 25

Eight-thirty at night. I'm home watching *Goodfellas*, just in case I missed anything the first twelve times.

My cell phone politely clears its throat. First time it's made a sound all weekend. Secretly I was hoping that the thing just wasn't getting reception in my apartment.

"Hi," says a female voice. Standard girl greeting. Why do girls always do this? I have no idea who it is. How am I supposed to tell based on one word?

"Hey!" I say, stalling. "How's it going!"

"Fine." Two words. I still have no idea.

Then it hits me like a mouthful of sauerkraut: Liesl. Haven't talked to her in weeks. I thought we had both more or less silently agreed to just let things slide. Into the quicksand.

"*Wie geht's?*" I say. We have this thing, the German and I, where I pretend to be able to speak the language—I picked up a few phrases from a Bavarian copy editor at work—and she pretends not to notice I'm pathetic.

She gives an answer that sounds like "*Selbstammerungenfrauverkaufkenkrankenschwesser*," and I give the audio equivalent of a nod.

"Well," she says. "I was just finishing up some stuff at work." Like this is the most normal thing for a person to be doing with her Saturday evening. "I figured you'd be out drinking and I could come have one with you."

"Actually," I say, "I was just watching a movie."

Gaffe! She doesn't know I'm home. This is my *cell* phone. Right now I could be hoisting beers with literary lions or horny actresses, for all she knows. Why do I have to clutter up my scheming with random acts of honesty?

We agree to meet up at Cafe Frog in forty minutes. It's a ten-minute walk from here. Perfect, I think: I have enough time for a nice relaxing game of Snake on my cell phone, then I'll change.

Fourteen minutes later I tear the game out of my hands with pangs of regret—I'm convinced that tonight I have a shot at beating Bran's best score—and dress in three minutes. (Out come the Banana Republic shirt in a darkish shade of blue, the Banana Republic pants in black, the Banana Republic shoes in black. When the pollsters call to ask about my party affiliation, I will answer: Banana Republican.) Then I'm dashing down the street just like I did when I was a kid: always late. Except now I don't have to allow time to lock up my bike.

Uh-oh. I forgot something. I hurry back upstairs to the apartment and paint my nails with Bite Me. No way am I going to bed the German if she sees me biting my nails.

I arrive, red faced, fifteen minutes late, just in time to spend ten minutes waiting for her. Meeting up with girls, in my experience, is a lot like having sex with girls. I always get there first.

We have some food, some drink. We "catch up."

"What did you do last weekend?" I say.

"Oh," she says. "I was with Gigi and Seb, you know them, we all went up to New Hampshire to hang out with Ramona and Bethany, I've told you about them, and we went to visit Shakira, Dora, and Colette, the ones I told you about with the little beach house, and then on Sunday I went to a dinner party with Mariel, Antonio, Robin, and Whitney."

Who are these people? Being with a new person, it's a memory workout. You try to track the names of her bestest friends and her worstest boyfriends and her siblings and where they live and what they do for a living and who their mates are and what they named their kids. (When uncertain, just guess Alex. Works for either gender, and your odds are about one in three.) That's not even counting everything you have to remember about the girl you're dating. Her allergies. (Once I dated a girl who was violently allergic to every kind of nuts. I kept forgetting. Suddenly everything I ordered seemed to have nuts in it. She took this as a sign that secretly I wanted to kill her, or at the very least, didn't want her to share my food.) Her boss's name. Her dress size. Shoe size. What she likes in bed. (Okay, that one isn't so tough.) How to get to her apartment. Her phone number. Her other phone number. Her other other phone number.

Of course, I have no problem remembering any of this stuff about Julia.

"That sounds great!" I say. I'm past the point where I can ask who these friends of hers are, because the German has explained all of their lives to me in great detail. I just didn't retain any of it. There is very little room left in my hard drive, what with the Bugs Bunny plots, Bogart one-liners, and football statistics stored there.

"Let's stay out all night," I say. I'm trying to be Impetuous Guy. With a German.

"All night?" she says. "I was thinking, maybe twelve."

We go to a corny grope shack on Columbus called E-Motion. I pretend I haven't been there before. In front there are tables in little nooks; in back there are giant, comfy, velvety couches. They stretch so far back that people get a drink, take off their shoes, and hurl themselves into the cushions. It's like your parents' basement, minus the carved Polynesian barware and the dusty fondue set that was always missing a fork.

So we have our gin and tonics and let our shoes thud to the carpet. We're leaning back. She's not far. She's not touching me either.

"You're in a very vulnerable position," I say.

"Oh?" she says.

"I could kiss you at any moment," I say. Can I drop a hint or can I drop a hint?

She smiles. And I kiss her. But only for a second. Because she bursts into giggles.

"Uh-uh," she says. "We can't make out here."

It takes me a while to digest what she's saying. What the hell is she saying?

"Do you want to go back to your place?" she says.

When was the last time anyone said that to me? Has anyone ever said that to me? Breathe. Nod. Calmly. That's it. Just nod.

And I reach down to put on my shoes.

She's got the giggles again.

"But," she says gigglishly.

This is funny?

"But I don't necessarily want to have sex," she says.

So we go back to my place and she is as good as her word: we don't necessarily have sex. What we do is a whole lot of very frustrating sweaty stuff in my bed. For two hours. Until finally we're asleep in each other's arms. For one minute.

"I have to get up at nine," she says, nudging me.

I get up to set the alarm, which I keep on the far side of the room. If I could reach it from bed, I would just hit the off button and go back to sleep. On the way, I notice someone has neatly folded and hung up the German's pants and bra. How did that happen?

"Sex," Liesl says gravely in the dark, "is very intimate."

No argument here.

"I guess I haven't kissed anyone this much in about, five years."

And a big bag of sadness falls on my shoulders. Here is a very pretty, very smart young woman. And she is, possibly, even more miserable than me.

At work, I reread the priceless e-mail from Monday:

From: LIESL.M.LANG@femail.com
To: FARRELLT@NYTabloid.com
Subject: Friday

You said you wanted to see a movie Friday night, but since it seems we have very different tastes in cinema, I think we should start planning now. I suggest. . . .

She suggests an Icelandic fishing saga, a French cross-dressing comedy, a Chinese soap opera. What is it with chicks and foreign films? The same ones you see creasing their foreheads over the mysteries of the horoscopes in *Marie Claire* suddenly are all brains when it comes to the manyplex. When was the last time you saw a foreign film that wasn't overrated? Okay, *Enter the Dragon*. Surprisingly, though, she wouldn't mind seeing the new Jackie Chan flick.

Maybe she's compromising, i.e., suggesting we do what I want to do? We hash out an agreement to see it next week as though we're signing an international peace treaty.

As I'm walking out of my building in the dying sunlight, I'm calling Julia to see if she's free for a drink before she leaves. She's going to Mexico with the Dwayne this weekend, and I won't see her for a while if I don't see her tonight. But instead of getting her on her cell, I get Darth Vader telling me, "The Verizon customer you are seeking is not in the service area." Why does every corporation think it's such a cool idea to have that guy do their voice-overs? He blew up Alderaan, for God's sake, not to mention slicing up Obi-Wan.

As I'm putting my cell phone back in my backpack, though, I have my own persuasive black guy to deal with. Shooter is walking across the plaza, his dreadlocks pulled back neatly in a ponytail, wearing a black suit, white shirt, skinny tie. He looks like a Rastafarian Reservoir Dog. Mr. Black. It takes me a second to notice that he has a companion on either side of him: Mike Vega and Eli Knecht. Both of them are trying hard to look ruthless.

Shooter removes his Churchill-sized Cuban from his mouth and blows a vast plume of smoke at me. "Seize him," he says.

Mike and Eli grab me by the elbows and hustle me into a dark-windowed limousine.

"What is this?" I say. "Have you signed up for the Mafia? Is it prom night?"

But Eli and Mike shove me in the middle of the back bench and take up guard-dog positions on either side of me. Shooter settles imperiously into the row of seats opposite. Then a guy in uniform comes to shut the door. The sound of the street is completely cut off.

"Fellas," I say, "I'd love to hang with you, but I've got to see Julia tonight."

"That," Shooter says, "is precisely the point."

I look at Mike and Eli, knowing full well that shameful things could happen tonight. Shooter inhabits a place where there are no rules, some sort of private Amsterdam of the soul. "What's the gag?" I say.

"Call it what you will," says Shooter. "It is what it is."

"It's an intervention," says Mike.

Shooter raps on the glass. And we're off.

Shooter reaches under his seat and locates a concealed fridge. He takes out a bottle of Bollinger. "And what is this?" he says. "We must utilize it."

"Yes, we will utilize it well," says Mike, who has located the champagne flutes in another hidden compartment. He makes a surprisingly inspired henchman, I have to admit.

"We will utilize it to the last drop," says Eli. Am I the only one in this town who hasn't read *The Sun Also Rises*? So many young men get their likes and dislikes from Hemingway.

When we pull up to the velvet ropes, there's a guy with a mustache and a tuxedo standing at the ready. There are really only three kinds of guys who wear tuxedos anymore. And this guy doesn't look like a headwaiter or a groom.

"Welcome to the place where men are men," says Shooter.

"And women are surgically modified," says Eli.

"Come on, guys," I say as the driver opens our doors. A spotlight sweeps around trying to create some drama on the red carpet between the ropes. "I don't need this. I have a girl to call."

"Girls, did you say?" Shooter says. "I'll show you girls."

Shooter confers with the guy at the rope for a minute. There is discussion as to where we will be seated. There's the VIP area (the entire club), the VVIP area (all but the back two rows of tables), and then there's the Executive Chamber, which is the front, and the Bull's Eye, which is described as a zone of such mighty exclusivity it consists of a single raised table surrounded by burgundy ropes and dedicated staff. Mike and Eli steer me discreetly by the elbows.

They're both spiffed up a little, wearing jackets and ties. I'm wearing wrinkled old Gap pants and scuffed shoes. I look like some kind of derelict or graduate student.

"Shooter," I say. "I'm not dressed."

"That's okay," he says. "Neither are the girls."

Then he pulls out a single bill and hands it to the velvet-rope wrangler. I didn't know President McKinley was on the $500 bill, did you?

"Looks like a special night," says Eli as we make our way through the corridor to the place where the colored lights swirl around madly. The music is deafening.

"It's Bad Girls night," says Shooter, giving me a little wink.

Gorillas in monkey suits crowd around us, fawning and mewling with tip lust, depositing us at the best table. Shooter and Mike distribute cash to the waiters while Eli looks the other way. Mike gives me a little glance.

"Don't look at me," I say. "I didn't ask to be here."

Shooter confiscates my cell phone and gets a round of double Scotches. And here come the girls.

A guy at the edge of the stage pats down his toupee and hits us with a comical Cockney accent.

"All right, lads, all right? I'm your host Ken Talent, here to remind you that history is being made tonight at Stallions Gentlemen's Club. Literally."

I can never figure out why they call these places gentlemen's clubs when they cater exclusively to our most primal grunting baboon urges.

"I love this guy," Shooter says. "He's the Robin Leach of titty bars."

Cue the opening guitar blast of the Beatles' "Revolution." Talent yells, "The women you are about to meet are scantily clad Satans, devils with the blue dress *off*, each and every one of them a tempest in a D cup, the *most evil girls* in all of history! Please give a snarling Stallions welcome to . . . Marie Antoinette!"

Enthusiastic hisses ensue as a lady emerges from behind the tinselly curtain in full 1789 dress. The big hoop skirt. The flouncy frills. The powdered wig. The saucy beauty spot.

Shooter is whistling with his fingers in the corners of his mouth. I wish I could do that. He pounds his Scotch and another appears at his elbow. I haven't taken my first sip yet.

Shooter gives me a look. "You look like a lump of something."

"Bad mood," I say.

"You'll be dead a long time," he says. "No need to start practicing now. Drink your medicine."

"Alcohol is not the answer," I say.

"No," he says. "But it'll keep you busy until you forget what the question was."

I take a sip. It rips a black trail of fire all the way down my gullet. Which feels good.

"I don't want to use booze as a crutch," I say.

"It's not a crutch," he says. "It's a life-support system."

"Now, lads," says Talent, "is that all you have to say about one of history's cruelest women? Marie's crimes include marrying for money, starving the masses, trying to escape the people's justice, and tacky interior decorating! What do we have to say about that then?"

"Boo!" shouts Eli, giving me a wink.

"Please," I say. "Do not wink."

I look around the club. The place is empty except for seven or eight desolate-eyed men with receding hairlines trying valiantly to be crazy. A lot of them are yelling and booing and nudging each other. Most of them are wearing wedding rings.

The temptress on the stage is wearing one of those little black ribbons around her neck, the ones that look like dog collars, with a little pendant hanging from it. She's fingering the collar suggestively. As if we've never seen a naked neck before.

"You know, lads," says the announcer, "I do believe that collar is the only thing what's keeping her head on!"

The three guys at the table behind me are chanting. "Off with her head! Off with her head!" But only until one of them comes up with, "Off with her clothes!" and they all pick up on it.

"The dress looks uncomfortable," says Mike.

"Stiff. Starchy," says Eli.

"Probably got on a whalebone corset underneath," says Mike.

"So constricting," says Eli. "Like a prison. Like the Bastille."

"Political prisoners," says Mike, "must be freed."

Marie's got one foot up on one of those Frenchy-looking chairs that clutter the sets of talky period movies, and she's pulling up her dress to expose an endless leg in a pristine white stocking. It takes hours for her to reveal the little black garter on her lovely lean thigh. It has a nice cloth rose on it.

The guys behind me are in a frenzy. "Let her eat cake! Let her eat cake!"

The garter comes off first. Marie twirls it around on her index finger, which has a long bloodred nail. She looks around for target possibilities and notices Shooter. She gives him a little smile that looks suspiciously unstaged, and flings the garter in his lap.

The guys behind me make wolfy noises. "Let her eat me!" one of them shouts.

Marie has both stockings off and is running an index finger along her décolletage when Ken Talent breaks in with a breathless update.

"Lads, bad news, I'm afraid. The queen of France has been too tightly stitched into her corset. It just may be that Marie Antoinette will need a little help getting out of her kit tonight."

The red curtains are already parting behind her.

"That's why it's a good thing she has friends like Lucrezia Borgia!"

Lucrezia is dressed in the hottest look of the fifteenth century, much simpler stuff than Marie's getup. Just a modest stiff cone of a white robe, like a giant coffee filter with red borders. The thing weighs about 50 pounds and, like Marie's, it's floor length. No need to unpack the goods too soon. She and Marie fix their gazes on each other.

The queen of France is reaching up to her powdered white wig and taking it off, shaking out her long red hair so it cascades down her neck. I have to admit, I'm paying attention.

This time the song is "Papa Don't Preach."

"Daddy's girl Lucrezia got married at age thirteen," Talent tells us. "But her father, Pope Alexander VI, didn't like the boy so he had the marriage annulled. Then Papa Pope had her declared a virgin while she was six months pregnant. Wild days, then, in a time they called the Renaissance!"

"They seem well acquainted," says Mike.

"Old friends," says Eli.

"Kiss each other hello," says Mike.

"And good-bye. And every occasion in between," says Eli.

"Too bad it's hot in here."

"So hot. Brutally hot."

"Taking off something might cool her down."

Talent is leering over his microphone. "Her first husband said the baby wasn't his; in fact, he said even Lucretia didn't know who got her pregnant, because it could have been either her father or her brother! But poor Lucrezia didn't get to keep her baby, boys!"

The crowd answers as one man. "Awww!" they say, as Lucrezia starts to slow-dance with Marie.

"Sadly, the boy was raised in secrecy," says Talent, "but Lucrezia consoled herself by killing her second husband and rising to the title of history's most evil woman!"

Cue new song. Familiar piano chords. Wow. This one sends me somewhere. I'm thirteen again.

"Yeah," I say, nodding.

"That's the fucking spirit!" says Shooter. "You like what Lucrezia is doing with Marie's sash, don't you?"

"I meant the song," I say. "I love ELO. It's 'Evil Woman.' " Hearing this on the club's stereo was worth the trip. So few of the neighbors in my apartment building have signed off on allowing me to play late seventies art rock on a four-thousand-watt system.

The guys behind me are stomping their feet and whistling. They look Italian. Maybe they carry a grudge. They like the idea of a nice clean Vatican. Why should popes go dating their daughters when there are plenty of perfectly healthy altar boys?

Marie and Lucrezia are peeling away each other's inhibitions and getting pretty creative in the kissing department too. But Ken Talent is back on the mike to ask us if they look lonely. Meanwhile the deejay takes off a great song and replaces it with that insipid synth-pop torch song from *Top Gun*.

"While Marie and Lucrezia are celebrating a new era in Franco-Italian cooperation," Talent tells us, "little do they know that they're being spied on by a lusty lady in lederhosen, the frisky fräulein who couldn't find a boyfriend who wasn't a mass murderer! Give a weak *wilkommen* to that heil-raising Valkyrie vixen: she's bad, bad, Eva Braun!"

"This could take a while," says Mike. "I'm going for another round before anyone gets naked."

"What's the name of this stupid song?" Shooter says as guys slap their tables and stomp their feet. One guy gets up and goose-steps around the back before a gorilla can chase him down.

" 'Take My Breath Away,' " I say.

"The fuck?"

"By Ber*lin*," I say.

Shooter motions one of the waiters over to our table urgently, stuffing twenties into his pockets.

"For the love of God," he says, "play some music for men. This isn't a tea party."

"And what is it you'd like to hear, sir?"

"Stones. 1968 to 1978. And don't try to sneak in any of that crap from *Their Satanic Majesties Request*."

Marie and Lucrezia are helping untie Eva's pigtails and fussing with her dirndl when I decide to stretch my legs. The Stones' "Some Girls" comes on within seconds. I gotta hand it to Shooter. Seeing money spent at close range is almost as much fun as spending it.

The bar is off to the side, away from the floor show in a dim little corner with TVs bolted overhead. Mike is on a stool surrounded by three girls not his wife. They appear to be looking straight at his crotch. They're making little cooing sounds.

I order a glass of water while Mike grins at me.

"Here she is at four weeks," he's saying.

The girls are shedding their neon-fired veneer, melting into little pools of hair extensions and silicone. One of them touches his knee fondly. Another one puts her head on his shoulder for a second.

"I'll bet you're a *great* father," one of them says.

"The *best*," agrees another.

The one with her hand on his knee puts both hands on his cheeks and gazes deeply into his eyes. "You are every woman's dream, you know that?"

"Let me show you the little princess on her horsie," he says, arrogantly. Really, who would have guessed that this would ever be a hot pickup line?

"Oh," says one of the girls with a sharp orgasmic intake.

"My," says another.

"God," decides the third, completing the thought. Silently I wonder how to broach a delicate topic with Mike. Surely, as a good friend of many years' standing, I have earned the right to have my name put forward in a serious discussion of the possibilities of weekend baby rental? I mean, one stroll in Central Park is all I really need to refill my little blank book. I could pick up one phone number approximately every 100 yards.

Eli comes over to the bar. "It's been amusing, *fellows*. But I have someone waiting for me at home."

"Come on, stick it out," I say. "Your blow-up doll can wait."

"I'm not the one," he says, "who will be doing the blowing tonight. Peace," he says. And he's gone.

What am I doing here? I mean, besides watching the TV over the bar, where a guy named Sven Olaffson, or possibly Olaf Svensson, is picking up a seven-hundred-pound log and stumbling a few tortured yards with it before dropping it in the sand. Thank God for all-sports networks.

Shooter appears beside me. "Double Laphroig," he tells the barman. "That chick who plays Lucrezia Borgia is a pretty good actress too," he says. "She was the star of this whole series of pornos based on Bob Dylan records."

"Dylan?" I say.

"Oh yeah, very artful, you know. *Forever Hung. Blonde on Blonde on Blonde. Blowjobs in the Wind.*"

"Please," I say. "Can we go? It gets so boring. They're all the same."

"This is the point," he says. "Consider this your reeducation. You have to get over that girl. You're going to allow yourself to be hung up on someone just because you like the way she tickled your giblets? There are a lot of girls besides her, and they're all built with the same equipment."

"I want her equipment," I whine.

"Listen," he says, knocking back his Scotch in one, "if I had that attitude, where would I be?"

"Can I join your coffee klatch?" says Mike, settling in next to Shooter.

"This round's on me," I say, and we all reload. Shooter gets another double. And a Corona chaser.

"Tell him," Shooter says. "Tell him about women."

"They're all the same," Mike says. "Except for my little girl. She's the most beautiful girl in the world."

"Oh shut up," I say.

Now a guy named Thor Orgenborg or something is pulling a Dodge Wrangler. With his teeth. Half a dozen supermodels in bikinis are dangling their feet off the back of the flatbed and waving to the crowd.

Shooter looks up. "Always go with the Samoan in these things."

"I'm betting on Sven. Or Olaf," I say.

"That sumo wrestler is looking good," says Mike. A couple of the girls he was talking to earlier come up behind him and start whispering suggestively in his ear. Then he gets up.

" 'Scuse me," he says. "Something about a private, um, exhibition they'd like to show me."

"What about us?" I say.

Mike shrugs. "They told me I'm special."

Shooter and I stare as the girls giggle and lead Mike away, one on either side of him. They all head for a little curtain of beads, where another doorman stands at attention and unlocks something for them. What wonders is Mike about to experience? There are no girls left at the bar.

"You really are social ebola," says Shooter.

Thor is doing well, though. He makes it about sixty yards.

"Concentrate," Shooter says. "A hundred on the Samoan, but Thor has one of those slashes through one of the *o*s in his last name. He might be worth a side bet. Thor over Sven. What do you say? Fifty bucks."

I take a gulp of my drink. It is always your rich friends who cost you. Somebody said that, I'm pretty sure.

The Samoan bends over and starts to grunt as he tries to lift a giant wrought-iron seesaw. It's perfectly balanced, with a rotund white guy sitting on one end and a "big-boned" black woman on the other. Both of them are familiar faces to the tabloid man.

"Shit," Shooter says. "Tough gig for Aretha. Who's that guy on the other end?"

"It's the latest fat guy from *Saturday Night Live*," I say. "They try to have a porky cokehead on staff at all times so he can die prematurely and they can sell lots of prime-time Best Of specials and memorial videos." *Tabloid* broke the story, of course.

"What is that?" Shooter says. "In Aretha's left hand?"

"Looks like a bacon cheeseburger," I say.

"If you fast-forwarded the tape, you could actually see her butt get bigger," he says.

We watch the Samoan stumble and totter. The sound is not turned up, so we can't tell if the judges are deducting points every time his stutter stepping makes Aretha spill her chocolate milk shake.

In the main room, Talent is babbling something about a history-making Jell-O wrestling event between Medea and Lizzie Borden.

Voices behind me. I turn around. It's the three guys from the table behind ours.

"Samoan has it all over the Swede," Shooter tells them, clipping a cigar.

The three guys all start betting with each other and ordering drinks. This bar is built for about four guys, and there are six of us crammed in here.

"Is there anyone left out on the floor?" I ask the guys.

"Coupla Japanese businessmen, that's about it," one of them says.

I finish my Scotch and let it slosh around in my brain. What's wrong with us? Offer us a choice between sex and sports, and we'll say: depends on who's playing. Happens to every guy. You're trying to watch a football game or something, your girl is crawling all over you trying to get your attention, nibbling your ear, whispering unusually dirty things—is there some kind of girl hormone that only kicks in on Sunday afternoons?—and even though the Broncos are up three touchdowns with five minutes to go, you're sitting there thinking, Get out of the way! I must know whether the Raiders beat the spread!

The Samoan tops Thor, so now it's up to Olaf, or Sven, to stand and deliver.

"There is no way," says Shooter. "Can't be done."

The Swede picks up a Volkswagen Rabbit with a backseat full of kegs of the sponsor's beer. He moves it an impressive twenty yards.

Another voice behind me. "Who want action?"

Now the two Japanese guys are here too, backing the sumo wrestler.

The Samoan manages to move the car five feet. The sumo guy can't even pick up the car. I win.

"*Fuck me,*" Shooter says. A Japanese dude pays him, and Shooter pays me. I can't remember the last time I won a bet with him. Must not be his night. He sways a little, his eyes going feral. "Back to the floor, mate." Suddenly there are four empty bottles in front of him, and he springs for a couple more beers to last us through our walk back to our table. The guy is going through Coronas like his Range Rover goes through Exxon super premium. Rarely have I consumed this many drinks on a weeknight, but then life with Shooter is a series of miracles.

"Packets of evil don't come much tinier than our next girl," Talent is saying. "She graduated from the Manson family to strike a courageous blow for seventies feminism when she became the first woman to try to assassinate a president of the United States! True, it was only Gerald Ford, but let's give freaky Squeaky Fromme a big roar!"

And whoever is running the sound system can't resist the urge to take this cue to drop the Stones and give us "I Am Woman."

"God *damn* it, where is that little homo?" Shooter says, looking around wildly. "I give that guy three bills for Helen Reddy?" I'm well lit, but in his present state he has the crackling wattage of that eighty-foot Coke sign in Times Square. You know what they call those giant neon monsters? Spectaculars. That's Shooter's state now, a *spectacular*.

The waiter comes over and Shooter uncorks on him. "Are you sucking each other's cocks back there?" he says. "Seriously, I want to know. You and the sound guy, you *are* butt bandits, right? 'Cause, just *tell* me. I want to *know*. If this is a *gay* tit bar, my fucking mistake. I'll find another establishment to patronize. Did I not specifically ask for the *Stones*?"

The waiter doesn't say anything. But he gives me a little eye roll. Uh-oh. He's working some sort of voodoo, I can tell. I don't feel so good.

Up on the stage Squeaky has come out. The Helen Reddy goes away, replaced by "Monkey Man," all lust and apocalypse slam-dancing together. It's one of the Stones' best but it gives me a vague memory of unease. Something about this album used to make me sad. As for Shooter, he seems to have entered a trance. He's gone absolutely still. Squeaky is this little blond waif, nothing special if you ask me, not much of a bod, hair conspicuously unstyled, scary makeup. She's got a little derringer in one hand and she wanders around in her bell-bottoms and hippie peasant blouse as if she's never done this before. She looks volatile and sarcastic, like she doesn't need a gun to hurt you.

The song makes me think of the first time I ever saw a monkey house. My grandparents, who then lived in New Jersey, took me to the Bronx Zoo. At the time the Bronx was running a surprisingly competitive second to Cambodia as the worst place on earth, and I was looking in the cage logging crime statistics in my head, thinking, Okay, that's a rape, attempted rape, assault, public masturbation. I hadn't been to New York before. So I thought, This city is so tough, even the monkeys are criminals. They deserve to be behind bars.

"Monkey Man" begins on the piano and ends in the jungle. In its finale, the guitar is like bullets being fired overhead and Mick Jagger has lost the power of speech. He's disintegrated into pained lusty yelps, nothing left of him but shriek and holler. This was his greatest moment. When he loses it, gives himself over to chaos in the fadeout, you can actually sense him tumbling down the evolutionary ladder, dropping a species or two. The room is heaving and teetering around me, but in my mind the meaning of "Monkey Man" is utterly clear. That level of intensity can't be faked. Mick was reaching deep inside for that one. And a question seems very important to me. What could have made a monkey out of even Mick? It wasn't drugs. The man was clean. It was something more dangerous. And if it made a monkey out of Mick, it could make a monkey out of any of us.

Shooter says nothing. He just wags his head at the stage.

It's when the next song starts that I remember why "Monkey Man" carries a built-in payload of dread. Because anyone who's ever listened to *Let It Bleed* knows what follows. The churn of the wild slips into aching prettiness. A dazzling feint, then a sucker punch. Mick was just setting us up with his horny baboon cries. Why did the

Stones choose to end the album with those two songs, in that order? They were trying to tell us something.

The children's choir. The acoustic strumming. And Mick starts to tell us one more time about the girl he saw. Today. At the reception.

A cloud passes over Shooter's face. I've never seen this expression on him before. It's as if all the confidence has been leached out of him.

"Shooter?" I say. "Shooter."

"That girl," he says. "She's . . ." his voice trails off into a strangled row of consonants.

"A skank?" I say.

This remark seems to angry up his blood. He gives me a foul stare. Then he leans in close and puts a hand on my shoulder to make sure I'm paying attention. "She *looks like Allison.*"

Mick say: "You can't always get what you want."

"This *song*. That *fuck*ing waiter," Shooter says. He's trying to wave the guy over from his corner, but the waiter has his smirk carefully aimed at a spot about ten feet over our heads.

Allison is a girl Shooter does not mention when he is sober. They went out years ago, when he was living in Boston. From what he tells me, they had nothing but bitter arguments and incredible sex. She cheated on him, he cheated on her, remarks were punctuated by flying objects, disagreements were re-explained in the weary four A.M. presence of duly-appointed officers of the law. They broke up, they got back together, then broke up some more. I've never met her in person, although of course I've seen the naked pictures of her he shows everyone. I listen carefully when he talks about her, trying to piece together the story, but I am not necessarily at my sharpest at these moments. "The problem with Allison." "The reason Allison dumped me." "Maybe I should have made it work with Allison."

"That psychotic bitch Allison." For a girl he hates, he sure has a lot to say about her.

"Come on," I say. "Don't be this way. Shooter? I need you not to be this way."

"This is not right," Shooter says. "Dammit! How can we not have a couple of girls to fuck? That's not how it's supposed to be."

"Well," I say, "I have a date next weekend. This girl Liesl? She's kind of growing on me, and—"

"I'm talking *right now*," Shooter says. "Let me ask you something: have you ever fucked a whore?"

Talking to Shooter, one does get asked the strangest questions.

"No," I say, vaguely embarrassed. And embarrassed by my embarrassment. *I'm ashamed because I've never slept with a prostitute?* "Don't really want any diseases. Or anything."

"That's idiotic," Shooter says. "The whores I'm talking about are a thousand a night. And you know *I will pay* for you. Because I don't give a fuck. These girls will do *anything* we want."

Oh? I wonder if they'll be willing to lie for me. Because I have no intention of going where ten thousand men have gone before. It's not the girls I don't trust. It's the guys.

"Real men don't go without pussy," Shooter says.

"Okay," I say. "Call one for *you.*"

We don't say anything for a while. And then he slams a bottle on the table, hard. Fizz erupts from the top of the bottle. Bouncers turn. This is the portion of the evening when anyone who has a weapon is stroking the handle.

"God DAMN it!" Shooter shouts. "GOD IS A FAG!" Surely that isn't him on his feet, his arms jerking spasmodically? Certainly, he can't be con*duc*ting the music? And that can't be him rumbling toward the stage. It isn't him, negotiating—whoops—the steps. It can't possibly be his body shimmying up next to little Squeaky/Allison. Pumping his shoulders and clawing at her waist. I'm pretty sure you are not supposed to do this in a strip joint, and I really want to help him avoid trouble, but I want to see what happens next even more.

Squeaky, staying in character with admirable persistence, is making little mousy noises. The staff men start whispering and gibbering, scratching their asses and hatching a plan. Once they get their team together, they move pretty quick. Six guys are all over Shooter while he's telling the girl she needs to go home with him, now.

"Sir," says the perspiring manager, trying to suck up and kick out at the same time, "as an honored guest, Stallions would like to invite you to utilize our luxury automotive service, with our compliments, and, uh, on the house." The bouncers are making Shooter their bouncee. It's only two steps back to earth, but his legs go comically wobbly and he almost loses his footing about five times. For some reason there are hands on me, too, and without any locomotive energy on my part I seem to be gliding out the door one step behind Shooter.

Our limo starts up. We pour ourselves into it and head for Shooter's apartment. He finds another bottle of champagne in the cooler.

"Want some?" he says.

"No thanks?" I say, hoping this is an acceptable answer.

"Pussy." He guzzles it heroically fast, straight out of the bottle. Then he finds the stereo and turns up Elvis Costello to a volume that enables any fans of his who may be in Queens tonight to listen. Shooter's head jerks spasmodically. He spills champagne all over his pants without noticing. When we pull up to his apartment he stays in the car.

"Is that all for tonight, sir?" says the driver.

"Yeah," Shooter says. "Just wait a second." And we sit there for about three minutes letting Elvis's "Allison" rattle the windows.

Then he puts his hand on mine. And he puts his other hand on my shoulder and pulls me in close.

"I do love you," he tells my ear. "You know that? Because you *list*en."

Which is not something I wanted to hear.

"I've seen another side of you tonight," I say.

"But you haven't," he says. "The other side of me is chaos."

The rest of the evening passes harmlessly enough in Shooter's apartment. Shooter on the couch. Shooter off the couch. The coffee table falling over. Things breaking on the floor. My large glass of hangover-repellent water. His (larger) glass of Jägermeister. Me thinking, How can anyone fall off a *couch*? Shooter fumbling through his phone book. Shooter saying: I could have plates— plates!—of cocaine here to*night*. Me checking my watch: 4:40 A.M. Me thinking, Can I creep off to bed now? Shooter giving up on finding the number, flinging his business-card wallet into the air and resting his head on the floor beneath a gentle flurry of white cardboard, just resting, plotting his next outrage. Me thinking, Run!

As I head for the door, though, there's a gurgling sound.

"Shooter?" I say.

He's out. But his tie is wrapped around the arm of his couch. He might be snoring, or strangling himself. A headline flashes through my brain. "HACK DUMPS FRAZZLED FRIEND IN DRUNKEN DEATHTRAP."

I creep up to Shooter and undo his tie. His head slumps over. His entire body follows, collapsing into a weird Raggedy Andy heap on the floor. I put a pillow under his head and tiptoe toward the closet to hang up the tie. In his bedroom I flick on the light switch next to a hand-carved wooden sign that reads, *MI CASA ES MI CASA.* The light stabs my eyeballs as I look at the entirely separate stereo system in his bedroom. There's a stack of CDs sitting there, with Dylan's *Desire* on top. "One More Cup of Coffee." "Hurricane."

"Sara." That's the one he wrote about the love of his life, the girl he wrote the entire *Blood on the Tracks* album for. The girl with whom, despite wealth, fame, and genius, he just could not make it work.

Shooter has one of those old-fashioned walnut armoires. I open the doors, and it's a dazzling sight. Pinned up to a corkboard on the insides of both doors is a riot of color, silk, cotton, lace. It's the Great Wall of Panties. Scores of them. I can't resist removing the pushpin that's holding a frilly black pair like the kind you see a supermodel wearing in *Randy*. I have to know. So I take a pervy little sniff. Yep, a girl was once in these. All the others bear signs of wear too. Some of them are brand-new thongs, others are ripped and faded Jockey for Her. I wonder how long he's been saving these up, and whether he hid their undies on them when they weren't looking or just came right out and told the girls they needed to give up a trophy if they wanted to stay the night. Probably he did the latter. Hell, they all take off their bras at Hogs and Heifers, don't they? Even Julia Roberts did it one time. 34B.

Suddenly I feel very tired. Shooter's lot in life has been to be grand marshal of a parade of writhing naked beauties that you normally can glimpse only by subscribing to the Spice Channel. And even he's missing something. Maybe the most important thing. Dylan had even more going for him than Shooter, and he couldn't get what he wanted. What chance do I have with Julia? Move on, sport. You lost. Try your luck at a different table.

I go back in the living room and this time I reach over the coffee table to turn off the reading lamp. There's a paperback of *The Sun Also Rises* that looks as if it's been pawed over a hundred times. I pick it up, running a finger along the cracked binding.

"Read it to me," Shooter croaks from behind sealed eyelids.

"What?" I say. Is he talking in his sleep? Sobriety is creeping up on me, or rather, less drunkenness, the way the sky gets less dark before it gets light.

"Read," he says.

"*The Sun Also Rises*?" I say.

"Just page forty-two," he says. "Please?"

He farts like a trumpet and rolls over. I turn to page forty-two and most of the page is underlined. There are asterisks and check marks all over the margin.

"Read?" Shooter says. Pleading this time.

So I say the words to him.

" 'We kissed good night and Brett shivered. "I'd better go," she said. "Good night, darling." '

" 'You don't have to go.'

" 'Yes.'

" 'We kissed again on the stairs and as I called for the cordon the concierge muttered something behind her door. I went back upstairs and from the open window watched Brett walking up the street to the big limousine drawn up to the curb under the arclight. She got in and it started off. I turned around. On the table was an empty glass and a glass half-full of brandy and soda. I took them both out to the kitchen and poured the half-full glass down the sink. I turned off the gas in the dining-room, kicked off my slippers sitting on the bed, and got into bed. This was Brett, that I had felt like crying about. Then I thought of her walking up the street and stepping into the car, as I had last seen her, and of course in a little while I felt like hell again. It is awfully easy to be hard-boiled about everything in the daytime, but at night it is another thing.' "

Shooter doesn't say anything, so I put the book down quietly and turn out the light. As I'm heading for the door, he makes a little sleepy noise. I'm not sure there is any language left in him.

"Shooter?" I whisper.

He coughs up some muck with a rumble that scrapes my eardrums.

"You're my only friend," he says.

I close the door behind me and go outside. On the walk back to my apartment, I think, That's it for the summer of horrors. I'm looking forward to fall. The new Dylan album comes out Tuesday.

I asked to be excused from jury duty. But in my pocket is a green slip folded to the point of falling apart. A little box has a typewritten X in it. Next to it is printed PREVIOUSLY EXCUSED EIGHT (8) TIMES.

While I'm getting an Egg McMuffin at Eighty-second and Broadway just before nine, WINS radio says there's a freak accident downtown.

"A small commuter airplane has just crashed into the World Trade Center."

My first thought is, I'm going to be in that neighborhood anyway for jury duty. I'll see everything. What fun!

By the time I get off the train, all the way downtown, it's nine-thirty. When I emerge from the Chambers Street subway station, I see the two buildings with giant black smudges on them. The smoke is out of control. Why are both buildings damaged?

There are hundreds of people on the corner, quietly watching. Every office building empties. Everyone is on the street, standing shoulder to shoulder, the workaday rush slowed to a crawl. It's weird how there isn't any sound. No traffic. No hubbub. People are making calls on their cell phones, whispering. Waiting for something.

There isn't a cloud in the sky. Once a guy crashed a B-25 into the Empire State Building, but that was at night, in a heavy fog. They reopened the building within weeks.

I ponder my next move. Ready? Set? Brag.

I punch up Bran on my cell.

"I'm at the trade center," I say proudly. Newshounds bathe in self-importance, which partially makes up for all the times we don't bathe in water. Proximity to important stuff, we figure, makes us important. We think we're lions but we're really the guys who clean the cages.

"The trade center?" she says. "What are you doing? Get outta there!"

"Huh?" I say. "It's kinda cool."

"That's nothing!" she says. "Now the Pentagon's on fire!"

"The Pentagon's on fire?" I say, processing the information slowly. Blip, blip, blip. One moment please. A coin falls. A conclusion forms.

Asian guy standing next to me goes, "Did you say the Pentagon's on fire?"

"Yeah," I say, arrogantly: I'm always the first to know everything. I'm in the *media*.

To Bran I say, "But this wasn't terrorism. It was an accident, right?"

"They hijacked the planes!" she says.

Planes, plural. Hijacked. Pentagon. Uh-oh.

"Oh," I say.

I put away my phone and start walking. Must get to Centre Street to report for jury duty. As I walk into the court building, I'm zipping open my backpack to dig out the notebook I wrote the room number in. Am I in the right place? One of the epaulets-and-badges guys is watching me.

"I'm here for jury duty?" I say.

He's windmilling his arms. "Cancel—"

But I don't hear the last syllable. Instead I hear a huge groan from the crowd on the sidewalk. I scurry outside. I look up at what everyone else is looking at. But all I see is dust.

"What happened?" I say.

A bald guy in a suit tells me: "The building just fell down."

Where the south tower of the World Trade Center stood for thirty years there is now a column of brown smoke 110 stories high.

I want my mommy.

I'm calling her on my cell phone, walking north, walking west, trying to get service. Everyone is jogging into the streets, looking over their shoulders. Cops and security guards yelling *Git outta heah, git outta heah.* Some people are crying loudly. More of them are just looking at the ground, walking uptown in utter, surpassing silence. Pedestrians fill up the streets. All the cars have disappeared or parked. Cops are putting up blue sawhorses at intersections. *Git outta heah, git outta heah,* they say. *Git away from the buildings. Git away from the buildings.* So people look at the row of neoclassical court buildings, normally governmentally boring and squat, now rendered potentially lethal. Security guards and lawyers are hustling away. Everyone is frantically punching their cells, or lining up for pay phones. There are forty people waiting for the first pay phone I see. All of them standing patiently. No one looking at their watches, tapping their feet, yelling "Hurry up." I'm walking, but I keep an eye on the other building. I'm wondering if . . . but no. It can't happen, what just happened.

Then it happens. In slow motion. It's like an elevator going down, only it makes each floor vanish as it goes. Story after story becomes vapor. For 110 floors. There's steel and glass: now there's smoke and particles.

When it's done, a cyclone of brown smoke and debris starts racing up West Broadway to where I'm standing ten blocks north. Maybe we should . . .

"Run!" yells a cop. "Run! Listen, if you see *me* running, you *know you* should be running. You get it?"

The cops all pair up like kindergartners and run hand in hand. Some of the lady cops are crying. Some of the guy cops too.

We all jog up West Broadway but the twister is coughing and sputtering and running out of gas. It's not going to reach us. Then there's another noise. This time it's one of ours. An F-15 ripping, spectacularly, the sky.

Parked cars in the middle of the street. Silence except for the car stereos. People gather around them listening to newsradio. One car isn't playing news. It's playing Train.

> *Tell me, did you sail across the sun*
> *Did you make it to the Milky Way to see the lights all faded*
> *Manhattan is o-verruled*

The city has never been quieter. I can't believe it. Are these the same guys who, after trying to blow up the same buildings in 1993 by parking a Ryder rent-a-van full of combustible cow shit in a cement-fortress underground garage, were swiftly nabbed after they went back to the rental place and *tried to get their deposit back?*

I gotta get the Desk on the phone. After a half-hour wait at a pay phone, I reach Max, who orders me back to the office. The buses are ridiculously overcrowded and the trains aren't running, so I trudge up Seventh Avenue. Outside St. Vinny's, there's a sight nearly as amazing as what just happened: New Yorkers patiently waiting on line to give blood. It's like the line for a superblockbuster outside the Ziegfeld, multiplied by about twenty. And no one is griping or perturbed. Just resolute.

It takes me an hour to walk back to Midtown. The street is as quiet as a Sunday morning. In the city room, there is no noise except for the blare of CNN. People are standing in front of the bank of seven TVs, watching fireballs. Nobody is cracking wise.

The Toad comes in behind me, reporting in unasked six hours early.

Max claps him on the shoulder, gives him an awkward little half-meant manhug. I wonder if I've ever seen Max touch another human being in a nonthreatening way before.

"Irv," Max says. "We haven't heard from Eli Knecht."

Occasionally we pay a penalty for taunting the animals of the world, for poking a stick in their cages, and one of them flicks a lightning paw at us. Or maybe we've just discovered we live in the cage, and the whole time we've been stepping on the beast's tail and pissing in its kibble.

Almost everyone is gone, out covering the story. I stand there with the copykids and Max and Irv and a couple of rewrite people and we all watch TV together in silence, all of us embarrassed by the idea that chasing a good story might result in accidental martyrdom, that a newsroom that smells vaguely of feet might secretly be infested with honor.

"Rollo?" Irv asks.

"He was at Langan's when it happened," Max says. "So he knew about it immediately. He went down to the site with a cop friend slash drinking buddy."

"Is he all right?" Irv says.

"He was right there when it collapsed," Max says. "He and the cops were all running away together. He fell, says he sprained his foot."

"I hope it wasn't his writing foot," Irv says.

"So he's going to do a column when he gets back," Max says. "Did you page Eli again?" he asks Hyman Katz.

"I paged him a hundred and six times," Hyman Katz says.

"Page him again," Max says.

Hoff from rewrite creeps up and nudges Max, "Hey, boss. Does this mean we get free pizza?"

Stacks of pizza boxes sometimes appear in the newsroom—hack bribery—only during selected national disasters.

"Hyman Katz," Max says. "Call Patsy's. Get half a dozen pies."

A cheer seems inappropriate at the moment but everyone looks relieved.

Something snaps Max out of it, and he starts lobbing commands in every direction. "Hoff, you're doing the scene at the trade center, the scene in D.C., and victims' families' reax. Rita, international reax, the airports, the FAA, the scene in Pennsylvania. Burkey, the whodunit, the political angle, what Bush's going to do. Who's that leave?"

"I could pitch in," I say.

"Tom," he says. "Your pages are all locked down?"

I nod.

"Good. Do a ticktock. Of the whole day."

I go to my desk and start checking the wires, pulling exact times everything happened for a minute-by-minute rundown of all the events. Like the newsman I used to be.

The Toad limps over.

"We haven't heard from Eli yet," he says.

"I know," I say.

"We need somebody to be, uh . . ."

"To be?"

"Pre*pare*d," he says. "Pull clips."

"Clips on Eli?" I say.

"You know," he says.

"Should I make some calls, or . . ."

"Not," says the Toad, "just yet."

"How, uh, long?"

"Page lead," says the Toad.

"Page lead? Twelve? That's it?" I say.

I give him a look but he shakes his head and says, "I know." Then he does the Quasimodo shuffle back to the Desk.

Twelve inches. A sidebar. Any other day, a *Tabloid* reporter killed in the line of duty is page one in our paper, and probably every other paper in town too.

So I call the library and get the clips. I've written a lot of obituaries. I've written obits on people who weren't even dead, just to be sure. ("No obit is ever wasted," the Toad likes to say.) My Bob Hope obit has been ready to go for five years.

I've never written an obit of someone I know. And usually when you do an obit, you have to get reax. That means one of the hack's grimmer duties: calling the wife, the mom, the cousin, the next-door neighbor, the coworkers, and telling them, as softly as you can, that you're preparing a "tribute." You don't say obit. You say a "story in his honor. Something to remember him by" and wouldn't they like to say a few words about what the loved one meant to them? They never refuse. They sniffle, they catch their breath, they talk.

The library brings me Eli's bylines, hundreds of them, years of work. But they don't even fill the shoe box that contains fifteen little four-by-six manila envelopes stuffed with tattered newspaper stories. What to say about the author of such modern prose classics as "STRAPHANGERS RESIST MTA FARE HIKE" and "HIZZONER

SEEKS ALBANY ALLIANCE IN BOARD OF ED BATTLE"? All of it, for the present purpose, junk. There isn't a clip headlined "ELI PROBE REVEALS SECRET LONGINGS, PROFOUNDEST JOYS." I realize I can't remember Eli's sister's name. Donna? Dina?

I'm wrestling with the lead when the Toad yells over, pressing a phone receiver to his chest. "Tom," he says. "I got Eli, he claims he's not dead. He's got stuff to dump."

"Let's do it," I say. My phone goes.

"Tom," says a voice. "Christ, it took me half the day to find a phone that works down here. What was your lead?"

"Huh?" I say.

"Your lead. Read me your lead."

" 'Amid the horror of yesterday's attacks, award-winning *Tabloid* reporter Eli Knecht sacrificed his life on a hero's errand when he was caught in the World Trade Center collapse after racing to the scene and filing the earliest reports from the catastrophe.' "

"Whoa, whoa, whoa. 'Award-winning'?" he says. "Who says I got awards?"

"Like someone's going to call up and sue me for being too nice?"

"My obit's going to have lies in it?"

"Why should it be any different from any other story that ever had your name in it? I also said you had a big schlong."

"Plus I didn't file any reports either," he says. "Fucking cell phones are out."

"None of the other reporters is going to call you a liar if you're dead," I say. "We're talking posthumous Pulitzer here. Thought I'd do something nice for Diane."

"Diane? Debbie!"

And I'm back in the rewrite groove: phone a weird appendage jammed between the shoulder and the ear, debriefing hacks in the field, discovering that I can still type as fast as a fast-talking reporter can talk. Without a word, the Toad takes a seat at the computer next to me and pitches in on rewrite. Instead of pressing the phone between his shoulder and ear, the look that says hard-boiled, he puts on a goofy little phone headset that makes him look like a girl telemarketer from Phoenix. Our chubby fingers slam the keys together, making mad music of the day.

"Remember the view up there?" he says.

"Yeah."

"You could see the Statue of Liberty," he says. "And all the bridges. At night they looked like strings of jewels."

"It made you remember why you moved to New York in the first place."

We're all hanging around the Desk watching CNN at about seven when Eli shows up. Rollo hobbles in right behind him. Our word warriors, returned intact in all their inky glory. Everyone bursts into applause. Momentarily trapped in our sincerity.

"Pots of coffee," Rollo says. "Instantly."

We all stand around looking at each other. No one does anything. Someone coughs.

"Good on them," Rollo says, the shoulder pads of his charcoal pinstripe looking deflated. "Round one. Caught with our knickers down, that's one up the arse. All fine. Knock us down. End of over-ture. Curtain up. Act one, scene one. Our story begins. Civilization and savagery. Ultimate confrontation, good versus evil, apocalypse now. Our shout now. We'll roast 'em to a turn. And the toll? How many'd they get?"

"Maybe ten thousand," Hyman Katz says.

"Only two things left to do, then," Rollo says, counting on his thumb and forefinger. "Lock, and load."

Eli brushes some dust off his leather jacket. He looks at all of us and shakes his head like a man who has weathered a personal insult. "Can you believe those motherfuckers?" he says.

Everyone works past eleven, when the Metro edition comes up, and most of rewrite goes when Max finally checks out at one A.M., the last deadline for the Late City Final. The other papers are late coming in, though, and if they have anything important we don't know about, we can steal it and make last-minute changes by stopping the press run until three A.M. There's really no need for anyone but the Toad to wait that long since he's Night Desk, but a few stalwarts buzz around anyway, playing with our shard of history. Someone has turned down the volume on the bank of TVs and the copykid who is supposed to answer the phone has put his head down on his desk.

I hadn't realized Eli was still here, but he comes over to take me aside for a word.

"If anyone was going to write my obit," he says, "I would have picked you."

"Yeah?" I say.

"Hoff would have spelled my name wrong," he says.

"Thanks, Ignatz."

"Good night, Pappy."

And my first thought when I wake up in the morning is, Buildings crashing. Lethal explosions. Fire. Devastation. Horror.

My second thought is, *Cool. I'm not thinking about her.*

I'm not due in until three this afternoon. Today's like an evil snow day. Everyone on the Upper West Side has the day off. Even the bark and snarl of the streets has been tranquilized: most of the bridges and tunnels are closed. Nobody wants to come in anyway. At last, the day has come when you start to understand the point of New Jersey. There are hardly any cabs on the street: cabdrivers are often Muslims. Driving a cab in this town is dangerous on a good day.

Haven't heard from Julia. At least she must be safe: she's in a third-world country where there isn't much to blow up. That's okay. There's no reason for her to call me. There was no reason for me to have been downtown. I call Liesl. No answer. Weird. Couldn't get hold of her yesterday either. Call Bran. Maybe I'll tell her about how I've been thinking about her. What with everything that's happened. Have I? Well, sort of. I mean, the mere fact that I've been thinking about telling her I've been thinking about her must count for something.

I get her on her cell.

"Bran," I say.

"I can't talk," she says. "I'm in Boston."

"People talk in Boston," I say.

"Haven't you been keeping up with current events?" she says. "I'm on *a story*."

Boston: where two of the planes took off. Oh. I'm an idiot.

"About the airport?" I say.

"Yeah!" she says. "I gotta go, all right?"

And she does.

So I call Katie. If circumstances warrant, I could just dump my Bran speech on her.

"Are you all right?" she says, sounding genuinely worried.

"I'm fine," I say. "I've been thinking about you."

"Me too," she says.

"Were you down there?" I say.

"Please, I was three blocks away!" she says. "You know where my law school is."

"So was your building damaged?"

"It's inaccessible," she says. "What am I going to do?"

"You'll have some time off," I say. "Might as well make the most of it."

"I want to go back to class," she says.

"I thought you hated your classes," I say.

"I do. That's why I want to get them over with."

"So what are you doing today?" I say.

"I've got to work on this paper," she says. "It's due next week."

"You would think at a time like this people wouldn't be so interested in working obsessively," I say.

"I'm not obsessed," she says. "I'm just looking to catch up."

Sigh. Is everyone in New York thinking this way? Major terrorist attack = a once-in-a-lifetime opportunity for extra credit?

I join the slow-moving throngs looking for newspapers on Broadway. A sign of the times: there is no sign of the Times. Everyone wants printed validation of the absurd Jerry Bruckheimerness of what we watched yesterday. Every newsstand has hand-lettered SOLD OUT OF signs, with lists of the names of pretty much every paper. Even the *Amsterdam News.* People are saying "Please" and "Thank you" and "Have a good day" to the Arab news vendors. *Poor things,* everyone thinks. Not their fault. Hope they don't get blamed.

I check a dozen newsstands but all they have is magazines, their covers now looking as up to date as the Edsel. Heading back home at West End and Eighty-third, I see a blue *Times* delivery truck heading north. On the southeast corner there is a freshly filled metal *Times* box. "U.S. ATTACKED," in *Tabloid*-sized headlines. Events have raced past hyperbole, lapped it. I feed the box three quarters.

Mike invites me over for lunch and commiseration. Over our sandwiches we watch CNN. Odd gurgling noises emerge from the bathroom. Not the baby. The mother.

"Kuh-wee! Kuh-wee!" comes the sound of Karin dunking the baby.

"Not the same world as it was yesterday, is it?" says Mike. "At some point, you start to get the idea that no one likes us."

"Living in New York," I say, "you really have to learn to love having your heart broken."

Karin returns, bearing an overswaddled child. "Bubbie! Aw, blub-blub-blub!" The kid is going to develop brilliantly. She'll be speaking fluent gibberish at fourteen months.

"Kind of a compliment, though, isn't it?" Mike says. "They hate us the most. Like when your ex-girlfriend starts calling you in the middle of the night just to hang up on you. It drives you nuts, but then you brag about it to everyone."

"Yeah," I say. "We're number one."

Karin has a different take. "Shooo, shooo, shoooo. Ah-dubba-dubba-dubba. Pish, pish. Joopie? Joopie?"

This woman has an MBA. One baby and she's Jar Jar Binks.

"Which reminds me," he says. "I got an e-mail from Nina."

"Really?"

Nina was Mike's college girlfriend. All four years, nonstop. The guy majored and minored in nooky. Sometimes the two of them would show up red faced and smirky at *lunch*. On a *week*day.

"She said she was thinking about me when she watched the news," Mike says.

"You didn't tell me that," says Karin, rejoining the adult world.

"When was the last time you heard from her?" I say. I haven't heard from Maggie or Besty or anyone else I ever used to date.

"Couple of years," he says. "She has a baby now. Another one on the way."

This attack, it's like a *69 for the whole city. Quick: redial your last conquest.

"You heard from her two years ago?" says Karin. "We've been married for four years."

"I always liked Nina," I say.

"I know!" says Mike. Winkity-wink.

"What was so great about her?" Karin sniffs.

"Of course I like you better," I say.

She beams.

I'm back on the street when my cell phone bleats.

I figure it's Julia, desperately worried about me.

"Hey," I say.

"Oh my God," Liesl says. "Do you be*lieve* this?"

"I called you at work all day yesterday," I say.

"I know, our whole switchboard went down."

"Did you go home right afterward?"

"Well, I had some pleadings to copyedit," she says.

"So you worked a full day after the biggest terrorist attack in U.S. history?" I say.

"Didn't you?"

"I'm a journalist!"

"Well," she says. "Not really."

It's the unintentional insults that hurt the most.

"Of course I am. I work at a newspaper."

"But. Don't you do the fluff?" she says.

"I—," Well, yes. Ours is a navel-gazing profession and I'm the lint. "I did my part, though," I say, grouchily.

Then I remember something from when I covered the story the first time around.

"Didn't your firm represent the guys who bombed the trade center in ninety-three?"

"Yeah," she says. "Our lawyers actually know a lot about all this from the guys who got convicted," she says. "Apparently they wouldn't stop bragging about the details. They just talked about all kinds of stuff. Which obviously I can't discuss."

"Attorney-client privilege?"

"Yeah," she says. "I guess there are just boxes full of transcripts."

"You weren't home last night, were you?" I say. "I called a few times. You okay?"

"After work I went down to see if I could give blood," she says. "They didn't need it. And I ran around trying to find someplace I could volunteer."

"You sound shaken up," I say.

"Where were you?"

"I had jury duty," I say. "So I was downtown. Saw the whole thing."
I have to learn how to say this without sounding like I'm proud of it.

"Oh my God—are you hurt?"

"Wasn't that close. I was on Chambers Street."

"When do you think they'll start finding survivors?" she says.

"Liesl," I say. "There aren't going to be any survivors."

"There have to be," she says. "I'm going down there tomorrow."

"I don't think they'll actually let you, y'know, *sift through* the rubble. They have unionized emergency workers to do that. And they're getting the biggest overtime bonanza of their lives."

"How can you *say* such a thing?" she says. "I'm going down there tomorrow."

"Be careful," I say.

We hang up.

At work I boot up my computer and am greeted with one of those magical little fairy-dust whooshy sounds.

*T*he Internet user EMonahan582 has sent you an instant message. Do you accept?

EMonahan582: *Tom? It's Betsy*

Manboy33: *Hey, Besty! Was just thinking about you*

EMonahan582: *Can u believe this???*

Manboy33: *I was downtown. Saw the whole thing*

EMonahan582: *get out! you all right?*

Manboy33: *Yeah. Stunned I guess*

Manboy33: *Havent seen you in so long*

EMonahan582: *i know just been so busy*

Manboy33: *What's new with you? Get married or anything lately??*

EMonahan582: *actually . . .*

Manboy33: *What?*

EMonahan582: *Vince and i got married a couple of months ago*

Manboy33: *wow*

EMonahan582: *felt funny about inviting you*

Manboy33: *thats okay*

EMonahan582: *it was a really small ceremony*

Manboy33: *you could have just told me though*

EMonahan582: *i know :-(*

Manboy33: *. . . .*

EMonahan582: *mad at me?*

Manboy33: *no . . .*

Manboy33: *i gotta go*

EMonahan582: *call me sometime?*

Manboy33: *ok bye*

SUNDAY, SEPTEMBER 16

Everyone in the city has been talking about This for five days. That's what we call it: This. "This is going to change everything." "I wonder if This will make the economy tank." "Do you think they're planning more of This?" I have spent the previous few days doing the following: Going to work. Hanging out at Mike's. Ordering in food. Listening to the new Dylan CD (which adds another classic Juliacentric line to the Dylanguage: "Gonna look at you till my eyes go blind"). And, occasionally, turning on the news. Which I can only handle in ten-minute disaster bites.

The German has spent these days doing the following: watching the news, reading the news, discussing the news, attending memorial services, lighting candles, writing heartfelt letters to the *Times*, and calling me, frequently, to ask if I'm okay. Never once does she mention the supreme charitable act she could perform that would hugely improve the morale of a New Yorker, and all she'd have to do is come over and take a shower with me. Much better than schlepping supplies, no?

"You all right?" I say on the phone.

"I don't know," she says. There is a wistful tone to her voice, though, and if I can't get lustful, I'll take wistful. Maybe when wist grows up it gets a tattoo and a naughty piercing.

There must be something happier to talk about.

"Hey," I say, for no reason at all. "When is your birthday?"

"Uh, tomorrow?"

I realize you're supposed to get this knowledge committed to paper as soon as you start seeing someone. On the other hand, if you don't know, you can't screw it up, with the Scarily Expensive Gift or the Lamely Chosen Trifle that shows lack of interest or the Wrong Color Gift that shows lack of attention to detail. Birthdays are a deal breaker for girls, no question about it. When was the last time you heard a guy say, "Oh, I had to dump her. She got me a Gap gift certificate for my birthday. Talk about a Weirdly Impersonal Gift!"

I put down my spy novel and pick up something far more difficult to master: a stack of *Randy*s. I turn to the sex pages. Okay, that's most of them, but specifically the how-to guides. This is because of the vague sense that *all my life I've been doing It wrong. Randy* will set me straight. *Randy* knows all.

After a few hours of devoted study, I take the train down to Midtown. Stop by work. See if they need any help. The Toad is on the Desk.

"You workin' today?" he says, holding a phone in one hand and chopsticks in the other. His hair is writhing on his head. It looks fake but rewrite rumor has it that it's actually real.

"Not supposed to."

"I didn't hear that. Take a seat. Louise's got some stuff to dump."

"What's that?" I say, nodding at his desk. There's a weird little wooden tray with a thin layer of sand. There's a miniature bush and a little rake. The sand is immaculate.

"Tom, please. We need you to translate Louise. She's all excited."

I extract the who-what-when-where-why out of the hoarse gibberish our third-string City Hall reporter Louise has gathered after following the mayor around all day and rewrite a couple of Reuters items. Around twelve I walk over to shoot the shit with the Toad. He's raking sand placidly, arranging every grain.

"Nice dollhouse," I say.

"It's a bonsai garden," he says. "Keeps me sane."

"Too late," I say.

"You hear about Max?" he says.

"No, what?" I say.

"He's going to the *News.* I did not tell you this."

"Why?"

"Remember that fight he had with Cronin last week? When they were screaming at each other and telling each other they didn't know shit about newspapers and told each other to suck each other's cock?"

"The one on Monday?"

"No, the one on Wednesday. Anyway, apparently Rutledge-Swope heard the whole thing."

Tyrone Rutledge-Swope is known to call in from his yacht or his jet or his Hollywood bungalow several times a day. The guy owns half a dozen of the biggest newspapers on the planet, plus a network and a movie studio, and still he reads every smudgy caption of ours. We're his baby.

"The big boss was here?" I say.

"No, he was on the phone. One of the copykids had him, was trying to get Max's attention but she couldn't. She should have put Rutledge-Swope on hold. But she's new. So Rutledge-Swope heard the fight. Anyway, he told Max to pack his bags. He said he's the only one allowed to call Cronin a shithouse bitch."

"You say that with a distinct twinkle," I say.

"Cronin called me in for a chat," he says. "Looks like Claudius takes over a week from Monday."

"The drooling idiot," I say. "Did I mention how fine you look in your Sansabelts today?"

"You're the best hack I have," he says. "Don't leave town, I may have some plans for you."

"Aye aye, Claudius," I say.

'm done with work for the day but Rollo is looming over me brandishing the *Times*. "Know why they did This?" he says. "Skirt! Guaranteed each other seventy black-eyed virgins in heaven!"

It's true, to a point. In the writings they left behind, they described heaven as a place sounding a lot like the Playboy Mansion. Everything men do, even This, can be traced to the need to get action.

"So what's that tell you?" Rollo says. "We were hit by virgins. Virgins, all of them! Who else's idea of cosmic sex involves a virgin, except another virgin?"

I'm beginning to feel like a black-eyed virgin myself when I leave the office. Outside, summer is on the gurney, wheezing and coughing. It's calling its lawyers and signing its will. It's already survived three days longer than it was supposed to, and autumn needs the bed.

Get a train to Brooklyn. It's a complicated borough to begin with: the subway map is merely theoretical, a starting point for the endless hidden agenda of breakdowns, reroutings, and service interruptions (Need to polish 100 yards of rail? Shut down ten miles of track.) that define Brooklyn living. Then there are the changes wrought by the attack: entire subway tunnels have been crushed. I wind up missing my stop and taking the super-express train to an obscure cranny of Brooklyn. It takes me half an hour to retrace the path back to Williamsburg.

Billyburg. Boho heaven. Sidewalk anarchists, PhD waitresses, organic-vegetarian soup kitchens, coffeehouse Commies, the Feminists That Time Forgot. Give it up for the twenty-six-year-old hipsters whose trust funds free them to live their lives in quotation marks, faithful parishioners at the church of irony, people who moved to Brooklyn because they're so downtown that downtown wasn't downtown enough for them. Even the dogs seem vaguely political. All those newspaper articles written by imported-car-buying white people about how much they hate oppressive genocidal imperialist globalist white people? They're written here.

I'm pushing my way through a crowd of men and women dressed as if it's always sophomore year (identical unisex jeans, chunky glasses, T-shirts with racing stripes) to where the German awaits prettily with daisies woven in her hair. She's at an outdoor table, surrounded by her friends.

"Hi!" she says.

I'm not sure what our policy on PDAs is so I go in for the cheek kiss.

"I got these for you," I say, handing over a bouquet I bought for Julia before I found out that she won't be back in the office until Wednesday.

"Gorgeous!" Liesl says.

There are balloons and a cake on the table. The German is chattering excitedly, introducing me to everyone. Some of them I have met before. Shake their hands. Shake, shake. People rearrange themselves a bit so the German and I can sit next to each other. I like that. Automatic boyfriend proximity. Which also means there is at least one side of me flanking someone I actually know.

On the other side are a couple of friends of the German. We're talking about how to seduce a woman.

"It has to be something specific," says Conchita, a grad student in Postmodern Mexican Feminist Narrative. Or something. "Like, 'You have a beautiful spine,' " she says.

"Did someone say that to you?" asks Malcolm, the multiethnic bond analyst who holds three passports, two of them from strange and terrible lands.

"Yes!" Conchita giggles.

Malcolm and I share a glance.

"Did it work?" I say.

"Kind of!" she says. "But only for a while."

Never once did I tell Julia specifically that she had a beautiful spine. I thought it was implied.

"Where does it end, though?" I say. "What if he tells you you have beautiful nostrils? Are you buying?"

Suddenly I'm pelted with something. I'm under attack!

It's some kind of crepe-paper party favor you blow on. As you do so, the streamer unfurls and flies at the target.

"You just got your first blow job from me, honey!" the German says brightly. *Loudly.*

I flash shades of scarlet and crimson. I can't believe she just told a table full of people that she has never given me a blow job. Actually, I would not have guessed the words were in her vocabulary.

"What's gotten into you?" I say. "Besides super-sized German beers?"

She just smiles, takes another sip.

As embarrassed as I am, I'm thinking, Must get some more of this brew into her. There's no telling what naughty little fräuleins can get up to when the lederhosen come off. If she can speak the words, imagine what else her mouth can get up to.

I'm blowing up balloons. We bat them around the table. Bat, bat. Hooray! We're so wacky!

The German's wound-one-turn-too-tight friend Nora bats one back at me like a volleyball player. It hits me on the nose with an amusing pop.

"Aggggh!" screams Nora.

"It's all right, I'm okay," I say. I touch my nose. "I'm not hemorrhaging or anything."

"No!" she says. "My ring!"

Great sentimental value, this ring. It's not a wedding ring: it was a cheap costume thing given to her by her big sister. Apparently, it was a size too big. Make that her dumb sister. We move chairs and tables aside, get down on our hands and knees, and conclude: yes, for certain, the ring must be somewhere in Brooklyn.

People are picking up pieces of popped balloon, birthday candles, wrapping paper. We stuff them into plastic trash bags and crawl around some more. This is no longer terribly interesting after an hour and fifteen minutes.

Back on my feet, I talk to the German's Irish friend, Molly. She's the only one not still pretending to search frantically. She stands smoking, coolly surveying the scene.

"Can I get you another pint?" I say.

"Love one," she says. "So d'you like her?"

"I like her," I say.

"Listen, a bunch of us was thinking, there's one more birthday present she's wantin'. We'd like you to give it to her later," she says naughtily.

"Um, want to go look for the ring some more?"

After an hour and forty-five minutes, Nora is bleakly going through a trash can full of empty beer bottles, soggy napkins, and discarded food. The German and I are edging closer to our getaway.

"Do you want to come over tonight?" she whispers, pleasingly enough. I nod.

"You seem different," I say.

"I guess I feel closer to you," she says. "What with, everything that's happened."

"That's nice," I say, and look in her eyes with what I hope is a Meaningful Gaze.

"Nora," says the German, "we have to go. But I'll come by here in the morning and look for it. The light'll be better."

Nora sobs "Okay!" She gives a tragic wave, like a brave leukemia victim.

And off we go. It's a long walk to the German's apartment. It's in a tumbledown building, hidden behind a foreboding black door next to a kosher Chinese-Mex takeout joint where a bunch of Haitian-looking fellows are listening intently to a polka.

The apartment's on the second floor: Door that won't close all the way, 50 percent of the locks on it inoperable, one room, kitchen sink in the middle, battle-scarred linoleum, dire rumblings upstairs (is someone *bowl*ing?), two wobbly bikes taking up most of the available floor space, yellow paint cracking on the walls, small futon instead of large comfy bed, tiny "living alcove" just big enough for a love seat, startlingly miscellaneous stuff scattered on the floor. One bookcase, books sorted by size.

"What do you think?" she says.

"It's Brooklyn," I say.

"It's not very nice, is it?" she says.

"I guess you'll probably fix it up a little when you've lived here for a while," I say.

"Yeah," she says, looking around with fresh eyes. "Yeah. Definitely. Although I have been here six years."

Looking at her CDs: Everything Annie Lennox ever did. Plus the Indigo Girls. A bit of Parliament. Some PC world music for show. Must put something bearable in the stereo before she can take charge. Girls have cheap stereos and expensive bedding, I muse. Except . . . ho, what is this? Denon? It's a portable, a rack job, it's tuned to NPR of course but still: quality merchandise.

"Who got you this stereo?" I say.

"Oh," she says. "An ex. How did you know?"

"Hunch," I say.

We kiss for a while. My hands wander over her little short-sleeved shirt. The sleeves have tiny little slits. I love sleeves. They make me think of upper arms. Which make me think of shoulders. Which make me think of straps. How I love straps. Strapless bras: really dumb idea. Bras with *extra* straps would be the thing. I read somewhere once (probably in *Tabloid,* probably in my own section) that strippers have learned it's really important *not* to have that even, all-over body tan like centerfolds. No, *you have to have tan lines.* Your tips will be much bigger. Why? You're showing straps *and* you're naked at the same time. It's a helpful reminder: guys, these bits are supposed to be covered *by clothes.*

And what are all these things underneath? There's the bra strap up high, but there's another one down low, and some kind of camisole thingy . . . God. I will never be uninterested in women's underwear. She breaks off. Smiles.

"Thirsty," she says, and goes to get some soy milk.

I go to the bathroom. Midget bathtub. Desolate shower curtain. Steady drip. Indelible rust stains. Encouragingly, girly makeup stuff is piled everywhere, little bottles and tubes, even on the toilet tank. (Then why doesn't she wear girly stuff? Does she wear invisible girly stuff?) I wouldn't want to date a girl who didn't have some girly stuff.

When I come out she is—what a lovely surprise—topless and changing into a filmy nightie. I strip down to my uptighty whities and we lie in bed talking. Well. In futon.

"We don't seem to have much in common, do we?" I say.

"Nothing at all," she says.

"But I like you," I say.

"I'm glad," she says.

The phone: it's Nora. I wait.

"Whoo-hoo!" the German says. "Where did you find it?"

Apparently Nora took home all of the garbage bags we shoved birthday refuse into. And in one of these bags she found success. On the third try.

The German is in a fine mood when she returns to the sheets. The lights go off. We cuddle for a while. I figure, Why not?

"I'm so happy for her," she says. "But I was worried. I'm still a little on edge."

"Well then," I say, throwing my voice into the lowest, growliest, purringest gear it'll go into. "We'll just have to get you off."

"Tuh-hee!" she says. But she's game.

I'm going over my notes like a quarterback returning to the huddle. The end zone. The G spot. The trick with the pillow. Where my index finger should be, exactly. How much time to spend on each play. Ready? Break.

I get her naked straight off, give her a nice rubdown. Her eyes are closed. Good sign.

Randy say: Do not touch her just there. Touch her there, there, and there.

Randy say: However much time you are taking, on her clock you are still rushing.

Randy say: Get comfortable. This may take a while. She won't be able to concentrate if she thinks you're off balance.

Rub, rub, rub, rub.

Knead, knead, knead, knead.

Stroke, stroke, stroke, stroke.

Randy say: Once you have gotten near, retreat. Then go back. Then go away again. Repeat as necessary.

Rub, rub, rub, rub.

Randy say: Do not flick your tongue. Use it like a dog.

Slurp, slurp, slurp, slurp.

Randy say: Let her hand guide you.

Her hand ambles into the area, then disappears.

Randy say: It won't happen if she isn't relaxed. She can't relax if she thinks you are getting bored.

Moan, moan, moan. That's me. She hasn't made a sound. Am I doing this right? Hello?

But I keep doing it. I'm right in the area, I'm moving tantalizingly closer, then I'm prancing away again. I turn up in surprising locations, launch new approaches from distant shores, creep back to HQ ever so slowly. Then I'm gone! Wherever did I go? Whenever will I return?

She just lies perfectly still. And my manhandle? It's aching, but it isn't anywhere near the action. Only the face and hands are on duty here.

An hour and fifteen minutes have gone by when she finally starts making some noises. There's some quaking. Some vibrating. Then there's . . . something. Was that it?

Still I have to ask. I'm an idiot.

"Did you?" I say, lying next to her.

"Yeah," she says dreamily.

"How was it?" I say.

"Wonnnnderful," she says.

"It's tough for you, isn't it," I say.

"Usually I only have them when I'm by myself," she says. "But they never feel like that."

My nose is kinda stuffy.

"Tell me how it felt," I say, picking some pubic floss out of my teeth.

"It was like, all these colors," she says. "Burnt oranges and browns and reds," she says.

I need to unclog my nose.

"I felt," she says, "like I was in Turkey. Or Morocco."

It's really dark in here. I can't even see her. She can't see me!

"It was like I was in some tent, in the middle of the desert," she says.

I poke a finger up my nose. Ahhh.

"And it's like I was being initiated," she says. "It was like a rite."

"C H-T?" I say, rootling.

"I-T-E," she says.

Pick, pick. Much better now. Except it's all . . . juicy. Was hoping it would be a dry one I could just flick away into the night.

"It was like some kind of sacred, mystical ritual," she says.

I'm feeling around the edge of the futon. It's totally jammed up against the wall on two sides. And I'm on the wall side. Land-locked! I roll the evidence between my fingers. Roll, roll. Into a dry little ball.

"It was like centuries of women passing this knowledge down to me," she says. "I mean, I kept thinking, You don't know me. You don't know my body. How did you know all those things about my body?"

"It helps," I say (roll, roll), "if you just let a guy know what you want." Which she didn't, by the way. I was flying on instruments, in the dark. Look where that got JFK Jr.

"I didn't know!" she says. "It's like you know my body better than I do."

Really? We aren't talking about a landmass the size of Wyoming here. I just did the standard stuff, only for a really long time. But apparently this girl has had lousy lovers. So I keep my mouth shut. Let her think I'm Merlin of the mattress.

So I just roll lovingly on top of her and gaze into her eyes as I drop the evidence on the floor.

I sigh. Check the clock: 4:03. Gotta get some sleep.

"I'm just so happy," I say (gaze, gaze), "that I made you happy."

"Usually I have to help out," she says. "It was just never like that before," she says.

"Never ever?" I say.

"Never evvvver," she says.

"So, are you ready to go to sleep?" I say.

"Um," she says. "No?"

Ahhhhhhhhhhhhhhhhhhhhhhhhhhhhhhhhhhhhhhhhhhhhhhhhhhhh. hhhhhh.

I've just pulled Rollo's dissertation on *Training Day* up on my screen, preparing to get it in shape for next Friday's paper, when the author himself appears.

"You couldn't help us out with this one a bit, could you, mate?"

I look at him. Unbelievable. A lime-green single-breasted with a blue shirt and a red handkerchief big enough to bullfight with.

I shield my eyes. "Jesus," I say. "You get more Runyonesque every day."

"The structure is there," he says. "I mean, not the structure but the idea, the blueprint, do you know what I mean? Not that at all, of course—bollocks—but the mood, the milieu, the flavor, the *music*, I mean, it's right in front of you, you just have to fill in the notes, do you read me, Houston?"

I look at the review, which reads, in its entirety:

Denzel Washington's cop drama *Training Day* is

"I don't want to tamper with what you've got," I say.

"It'd be a great favor to me," he says. "It's just that with the excitement, you know, the news, the axis of evil, I've been making preparations, sharpening my pencils, getting fit, making the rounds, having a laugh with old mates, one last lap for victory, isn't it?"

"You've been going to Elaine's more than usual?" I say.

"Allow me to breathe one word to you. *Stans.* A-Stan. P-Stan. Unreadable stamps on the passport. Secret checkpoints, foreign intrigue, clash of nations, John le Carré, search for the killers. They're sending me. With the troops. Need I say more?"

"Why don't you just talk about the film for three and a half minutes?" I say. "I'll copy down every word and that'll be the review. It's not like this is a real newspaper or anything."

"Problem," he says. "Small one, admittedly, but it's there, a tip-toeing buggerer, wanking in the shrubbery—try to keep up—testing the perimeter, slouching toward Gomorrah and that—"

"You haven't seen the film," I say.

"'Course not," he says. "Except in this case I haven't seen the trailer."

"You've been reviewing trailers?" I say. That explains the digression-filled vagueness of the last two or three reviews.

"'Course not, 'course not," he says. "Just the last nine or twelve. Has anyone complained?"

"No," I say. "But I might be the only one who reads your reviews, and I wouldn't do it if they didn't pay me."

Blank look.

"I'll give it a shot," I say.

"Cheers," he says. "I know you'll make it sing like Caruso. Oh, and just put my byline on it, that'll be lovely, wouldn't want to rain dismay on the loyal readership and that."

Training Day was supposed to come out September 14. They already delayed it for three weeks because they figured newspapers were still too full of real news to start treating every movie opening as a bright new hope for the republic. The studio has been previewing it for weeks. Even I've seen it, and I've got lots on my mind. Such as.

"Well, look at you."

Julia smiles over me. "Hiya," she says. "I just got in last night."

Little gray skirt, tight black top. And a really nice tan.

We freeze for a moment, but then I get up and we're having a nice hug. A real one. There is no one else invited to this hug.

"I was worried about you," I tell her cheek.

After work we head downtown for a drink. And I notice she's wearing a ring. Left hand. Second finger. Not her ring finger.

Don't ask.

Mexico was nice? Mexico was nice. Flight back was terrifying? It was. When did she hear the news? That night. They were glued to CNN.

It's a cheap ring. I think. The jewelry equivalent of a clump of weeds and a daisy.

"By the way," I say, "did you have e-mail in Mexico?"

"Yeah," she says. "I checked it once in a while."

She never sent me an e-mail. I couldn't send her one. I've seen her naked, but I don't have her home e-mail address.

Heading down Fifth, the sun seems to be going down too early. The farther downtown we go, the darker it gets.

"What's that smell?" Julia says.

Acrid, like burning tires. The wind is blowing uptown.

"It's still burning," I say. "You can only smell it when the wind is right."

A hand-lettered sign on the West Third Street basketball courts says WE'RE STILL HERE. Xeroxed fliers are Scotch-taped to walls. "Do you know of an animal whose person is missing?" says one. And there's one you see on virtually every block. A businessman. He worked on the 100th floor. There's a full-color digital photo of him on a notice carefully spell-checked and centered and laser-printed on high-quality rag paper, neatly posted in scores of locations. "Have you seen this man?" asks the flier. As if the guy simply forgot to call home. As if his absence is just another challenge to be solved by a PowerPoint presentation and a high-res printer.

"This city has changed," Julia says.

"Yeah," I say.

"I hate change," she says.

"It's still Manhattan," I say.

"Manhattan is overrated," she says.

Quatorze Juillet is another one of those frog theme parks. Everything about it screams, "Real French bistro!" The weather-beaten marquee saying "Cafe-Journaux-Tabac-Jour et Nuit." The drink menu written on mirrors. The ineffectual ceiling fans rearranging the cigarette smoke. The beaten-copper bar. I ask the barkeep for a carafe of dry white. He recommends Sancerre. I take one sip: blech. It's about as dry as Hawaiian Punch.

"Tell me tales of Mexico," I say. Traveling can be tough on a relationship.

"We were both cranky," she says. "We had a fight."

"Oh?" I say, giving off a friendly vibe of mild interest, when I feel like a hawk spotting a field mouse on crutches.

"Dwayne has this reputation for being a little *cheap*," she says. "And everywhere we went he was always trying to save a few *pesos*. So while we were hiking up this hill, he refused to stop to get something to drink and I got all pissed."

"So what happened?"

"I sort of threatened to leave," she says.

"What did you tell him?"

"I said, 'Maybe you'd enjoy this more on your own. I'll just fly back tomorrow.' "

And lazily I picture the joy if she had called from JFK a week before she was due back: *Hi. It's me. I need a place to stay.*

A couple of days later, though: the attack. They watched TV news for two solid days but after that Dwayne "just literally went from town to town finding a place with a TV set. So I got bored. I didn't want to watch that shit."

"Exactly how I felt," I said.

"Exactly," she says. "So I went out and wandered on my own for a while."

"Did that bother you? Being by yourself?" I say.

"No," she says. "It was kind of nice."

Good answer.

She orders some food but I'm not hungry after my typical late, post-workout lunch.

"You should eat," she says. "You've really lost a lot of weight."

"You noticed?" I say.

"You look kinda great, actually," she says sweetly.

I take my sustenance in liquid form. After a carafe, I'm fairly drunk. So I order another. Her drinking pace slows to nothing.

I reach under the table to find her right ankle. I prop it on my right knee, slowly slide her sandal off. She's wearing the cute gray ones with the little ribbons on them. I start running my nails up and down her calf: smooth. Unlike Liesl, she shaves conscientiously. Unlike Liesl, she smells all girly.

She closes her eyes, blows smoke in my face. "I'm a sucker for scratching," she says.

"Feel nice?"

"*So* nice," she says. "Your *nails.*"

The Bite Me worked. I actually have fingernails now, for the first time since I was eight. And with my Bite Me–restored leg scratchers I move up and down her calf, scaling to knee and descending to ankle. Surely this counts for something. It isn't sex, but on the other hand, if Dwayne walked in he'd be plenty pissed. This seems to be my new standard: whether my actions, while not sexually satisfying to me, would at least annoy a person who isn't there to see it. Dwayne's newspaper has sent him down to interview people near Ground Zero. Not far from this very neighborhood. Why can't he just stroll by some night while we're like this? Maybe Julia is hoping also.

"So nice," she says, swoonily.

"Almost as good as sex," I say.

"Nothing's better than good sex," she says.

"Define good sex," I say.

"Sex in which I have an orgasm."

"What's your batting average?"

"Seventy percent," she says.

Wow. A circuit breaker in my brain flips over.

"Seventy?"

"For guys, it's a hundred and ten percent!" she protests.

"You little minx," I say. "I had no idea."

Dwayne is getting her off three-fourths of the time. Or, optimistically, call it two-thirds.

"Especially when I'm ovulating. I'm ovulating now. And I've been so horny the last two days."

That she would tell me this, unbidden, connotes very good or very bad news. She would share this information with a lover. She would also share it with a gay hairdresser.

"Only, sometimes I have trouble with a new person," she says.

"It takes a while to get used to someone new," I agree, wondering if my face is burning visibly in the dark. *I didn't ring her bell.* I didn't even come close. And she is possibly the most orgasmic girl in the city of New York. At least there was that time in the doorway. Does that count for anything? Does she think about it?

"Talk to Rick?" I say.

"No," she says. "But I wrote him a letter."

I would love it if you wrote me a letter. Instead she wrote to him.

Scratch, scratch. Up calf. Down calf.

"See, when we were in college, we agreed we didn't like e-mail. So we used to write these letters, on real paper, when I was at Bowdoin and he was in Pennsylvania. So I thought I would write him a letter again."

"Oh?"

In Manhattan there are these moments. You cross the street twenty, thirty times a day. Almost all of the streets are one way. You're careful. You wait till the light has changed, heed the command to WALK, and you step off the curb thinking about a girl or what's on TV tonight, keeping a wary eye on the eight-ton delivery truck rumbling down the block to make sure it's stopping and then— *whoosh.* The eight-ton truck waits lawfully at the crosswalk but while you were watching it your life has almost disappeared. From your blind side, a demon delivery boy misses you by inches as he hurtles by in a cloud of moo-shu pork, going the wrong way on the one way, just him and his tanklike iron Chinese bicycle. A death machine that has to move fast because someone exactly like you is waiting for his dinner and is more than willing to stiff an Asian immigrant for being three minutes later than promised.

"And I, basically, told him I love him."

Whoosh. Didn't see that one coming.

"And." I say it quietly.

"And he didn't e-mail me or call me."

"When did you send it?" I say, genuinely worried. The attack might have slowed mail service.

"I, I mailed it from Mexico," she says.

Boom. Crash. Crack. Shatter. She destroys me, this girl. She's relentless. The original title of Elvis Costello's *Armed Forces* album was *Emotional Fascism,* did you know that? I always thought it was a better title. Maybe I'll use it myself. If I ever record an album about the Saddam of South Norwalk.

"When?"

"Last Saturday. After all, This, happened? I was just thinking, if I lived in Madison I could be with my brother, who I love—"

"And Rick," I say.

She doesn't say anything.

"You must feel so bad," I say.

"You're the only one who knows this," she says. "You're literally the only one."

"I know," I say, scratching and stroking.

Whir, rattle, clunk. I'm in third place. But Dwayne is dwoomed and *Rick doesn't want her.* Does he?

"You were wearing a ring earlier," I say.

"I was?"

"On your left hand," I say. "You kept fidgeting with it, hiding it under your elbow," I say.

"Oh, I took it off," she says.

And I muster a joking tone. Give her a little comedy prosecutor's scowl. "Did you get engaged?"

"No," she says. With a half laugh. "It was just something I bought."

Oh.

"I have to get out," she says. "It's a problem of logistics. I don't know where I'd go."

The temptation to leap to the feet, to pump the fist, to reintroduce my mouth to hers, is there.

Randy say: *Play angel's advocate.* Make her talk herself into it.

"Are you sure?" I say. "It can't be salvaged?"

"On the way back he brought It, up."

"Marriage?"

A nod.

Bastard. I've been hoping for months that he would do it officially, spring out of the shrubbery with a $300 Zales ring and a fresh bouquet of weeds. And she would say no, and that would be it. Instead the little wuss has been edging his way up to it, asking her without asking her, searching for a signal. Dragging it out.

"So what'd you say?"

"I said I wasn't ready."

Yes, she flakes just like a woman. She's just a girl who can't say no. Women have no problem rejecting you; they just can't use the word. If she had said no, maybe he would have thrown her out of the apartment that day.

I get the bill. Another $72. My plan to hold down expenses this month would almost certainly require unloading one or more of the girls I keep taking out.

We're walking to the corner of Fourteenth and Ninth in a heavy rain. Her poor tootsies are soaked. Her darling little sandals. I've had two carafes of wine on an empty stomach. In case I forget, my head will remind me of all this tomorrow.

It takes a while to get a cab. I put my arms around her and we get good and soaked. When we finally flag down transportation and head toward the West Side Highway, she takes up residence in the southern corner of the backseat.

"Get over here," I say.

And I pull her over and she buries her head on my chest and this is nice. And not only because I have the loveliest view down the front of her tank top.

I think for a second about that line, the wrongest line in the history of pop music. It's from a Beatles song on *Rubber Soul,* "You Won't See Me":

I wouldn't mind if I knew what I was missing.

I know, I know. And I mind, I mind.

The cabbie is a Lite FM addict. Maybe he's got woman troubles too. Maybe he just kissed his girlfriend good night. Or maybe he just has bad taste. The radio plays Mariah, Celine, "Rikki Don't Lose That Number."

"I love this song," Julia says.

And she moves away. A little.

Rikki. I get it. Of course. Why else would she like Lite-FM-quasi-jazz-geezer rock? The time I spent getting mentally ready for this date. The suit. The tie. Researching the restaurant. I feel like the kid who comes to the SATs with a fistful of impeccably sharpened number two pencils in his hand and all the wrong answers in his head.

"It makes you think of him," I say

She doesn't say anything.

"Because you're hoping he calls you," I say.

She doesn't say anything.

And I hold her all the way home. When I get in my apartment, I head automatically for the bathroom. I want to whack off. But there's no interest. My hand has a headache.

DENZEL'S LATEST: THIS DAWG HAS HIS "DAY"

by Rollo Thrash

Tabloid Senior Film Critic

Viewers who arrive thirty minutes late to the new drama *Training Day* may be confused by the sight of Ethan Hawke, he of the weedy unshorn chin and poetess-slaying blue eyes, getting a back-alley beating by a pair of miffed Angelenos. Surely this is a documentary? And the two gentlemen rearranging his teeth must be film critics exacting their revenge for being forced to suffer through Hawke's puppy-eyed simpering in *Before Sunrise*, *Reality Bites*, and *Great Expectations*?

Actually, though, the film is a police drama that takes place on a single day in the life of Jake (Hawke), a young straight arrow with a wife, a baby, and nineteen months on the Force who, aching for a detective's badge, agrees to try out for an "aggressive" street-crime unit led by Alonzo Harris (Denzel Washington). Jake is no wimp: settling into Alonzo's "office," a bad-ass Monte Carlo with a chain around its license plate, he'll have us know that he once played strong safety for North Hollywood High, though his delicate looks would appear better suited to a somewhat less physical position on the gridiron, say third clarinet in the marching band. Soon he's learning how to recover crack vials from the digestive tract of a wheelchair-bound dealer—a ballpoint pen jammed in the back of the throat works nicely—and search a home at gunpoint with a rolled-up Chinese food menu serving as a field-expedient search warrant. It's all in a day's work when it comes to protecting and serving the citizens who greet him alternately as "choir boy," "rookie," and "punk-ass, bitch-ass, crooked-ass cop."

By the time Alonzo gets his innocent charge limbered up with such early morning exercises as perp robbing and unnecessary force deploying, not to mention drinking beer in the car without any apparent effort to recycle the cans, it should begin to occur to Jake that Alonzo is as dirty as Oscar Madison, and South Central is no place to be Felix Unger.

Instead, soaking up Lorenzo's advice that "it takes a wolf to catch a wolf," Jake hangs in, hoping to learn street wisdom while still playing it by the book. Unfortunately for him, that book seems to be *Police Work for Dummies*; before long he will be tricked into smoking PCP and surrendering his service pistol to a well-armed trio of thugs with whom he inexplicably sits down to a game of cards. "This s———t's chess, it ain't checkers," Alonzo tells Jake, who appears more ready for a nice round of tic-tac-toe.

Messing with Jake may be a pleasure for Alonzo, but it turns out to be business as well, and his scheme to use his new partner to settle his own scores is where the plot begins to kick in.

At times it kicks a bit like *Mannix* with a hip-hop soundtrack, what with cops leaping from balcony to balcony and swan-diving onto the hoods of fast-moving vehicles, all in an effort to meet some shadowy gentlemen awaiting receipt of (exactly) one million dollars, "by midnight and not a minute after." For the sake of jamming many adventures into the same day we are asked to believe that officers present at the shooting death of a suspect would immediately be free to get back in their car and resume cruising the streets. (Surely there would be *forms* to fill out?) But director Antoine Fuqua and screenwriter David Ayer have an eye and ear for lots of scary, and entirely realistic, situations (not the least of which is the prospect of riding a municipal bus after dark), and there are grimly hilarious moments. At one point, a fellow is thrust into a bathtub by some citizens who aim both to shoot him and minimize subsequent cleanup time; the victim's life is unexpectedly prolonged, though, because the killer keeps tidily closing the shower curtains while an onlooking compadre, pleading for a better view of the action and possibly credit for an assist on the job, keeps yanking them open. Fuqua and Ayer have pared the action down to a shiv's point—there are no scenes of Hawke's missus staring dreamily at the phone and only for fleeting moments do we sense Ayer scratching away at dialogue like Jake's declaration that police work "is all about smiles and cries. You gotta control your smiles and cries, because that's all you have." Hawke, well cast as a naif, gives a performance that makes the most of his doe eyes, and Washington, who has been coasting on Righteous Dignity longer than Jesse Jackson, hot-wires his stalled talents, issuing his "Dawg"s and "It's like dat"s with spellbinding malice. "You gotta have a little dirt on you for anybody to trust you," he tells Jake. Dat's what *I'm* talkin' 'bout.

• • • • •

I'm at my desk when the Toad comes over wielding a galley of Rollo's review. He betrays no hint of noticing the office topic du jour: that the perfect tableau of his bonsai garden has attracted a visitor. Somebody has added the little silver dog from a game of Monopoly. A modified little silver dog. His doggie leg has been cut off and resoldered on his body in a pissing pose. The mini silver terrier is taking a miniature leak on the tiny bonsai tree. Definitely a sign of rewrite at its best.

"Rollo's gotten good," the Toad says. "Which surprises me because I thought he was a drunken has-been who couldn't fill a cocktail napkin with actual coherent sentences."

"I combed out a few knots. Smoothed out the split ends. Put in some styling gel."

"You wrote it," he says.

"Only the part from the headline on," I say.

"So why is that blowhard's name on it?"

"He's the superstar. I've been tweaking his stuff for months."

" 'Tweaking'? Joan Rivers has had less work done to her. You know he's going to Afghanistan next week. Who were you going to have write his reviews while he was gone?"

"My orders were to just keep on keeping on."

"Orders from who?"

"From Rollo."

"If his byline says he's in Kabul, he can't have his name on the movie reviews too."

"Maybe he saw the movies before he left? They screen these things pretty far in advance."

"Wait one second," he says. And I watch him limp the galley down to Cronin's glassed-in office at the other end of the floor. The Toad gives Cronin the galley. Cronin looks at it and the Toad keeps talking. He points at something on the sheet, and they both laugh. I got a laugh! A silent one, but still. Then the Toad comes back to my desk. He puts down the galley.

"Cronin says you're very talented," he says. "Take Thrash's byline off this. Put yours on."

"With a photo?" I say, dazed.

"No, with an oil painting," he says. "Get a headshot taken. Try to give them your good side. Wait, you don't have a good side. Put a bag over your head. Get plastic surgery. I don't care. You're our new film critic." He does the sign of the cross over me.

I'm touched. I don't know what to say. Except.

"Do I get a raise?" I say.

"Jesus Christ," he says, leaning into me and whispering. "You ungrateful piece of shit, you are the biggest ballbuster I ever saw. I already discussed it with Cronin and you're not getting more than—"

He then names a sum that raises me twice as much as I would have thought to ask for.

I wonder if this means I'll have to start wearing better clothes. If they'll get someone else to clean up the messes in Features from now on. I wonder if I can even do this job.

"Oh, and Tom?" the Toad says, shuffling away. "Don't fuck it up."

Liesl and I are walking up Broadway after dinner.

"Do you want to go camping in Utah next week?" she says.

"Camping?" I say incredulously.

Liesl sketches a vision of what this odd activity entails. Hiking. Biking. Sleeping under the stars. Me, I'd rather sleep under the roof. Isn't not sleeping under the stars kind of the point of western civilization?

"Actually," I say, "I'm an indoorsy kinda guy." Say what you want about New York, but rarely do you get bitten by a rattlesnake.

"That's too bad," the German told me. "I was hoping we could go camping sometime."

"My personal prediction," I say, "is that it is not going to happen."

She scowls at me. But we're right in front of my favorite grocery store. Time for a change of subject.

"Hey," I say. "Let's go in."

"Do you need groceries?" she says. "Isn't it kind of rude to do your shopping when you're with me?"

"No, it's not that," I say.

"Then what?" She's putting down roots in the sidewalk. It's going to take a backhoe to dislodge her.

"It's a surprise," I say, as teasingly as I can. Girls love it when you say this, even if the actual surprise turns out to be nothing much.

I'm in luck. Inside, the light over the produce aisle is out again. At some point you have to start getting suspicious that there is an organized campaign of sabotage. Maybe gangs of young romantics are creeping around here to shoot out the lights with BB guns. It's the New York version of carefully managing your fuel gauge so as to make certain that you'll run out of gas on your date.

I lead her by the hand through the dim. A couple of Japanese tourists with funky blond hair loiter by the Fuji apples. Two septuagenarians get friendly among the Granny Smiths.

"Everything's so juicy, isn't it?" I say.

"What do you mean? Isn't fruit supposed to be juicy?"

"Close your eyes," I say.

"What?" she says. "Why? What are you doing?"

"Just trust me," I say.

"Are you going to buy something, or?"

"No, I just—"

"I kinda wanted to get home early tonight," she says, checking her watch. "*Friends* is on soon."

"Give me just a second. Surrender to the moment."

"I don't get it," she says.

"Here," I say weakly, and present her with a strawberry.

"Ew," she says. "Has that been washed?"

"Never mind," I say, and I eat it myself. It doesn't taste right. This isn't the season.

"Did you pay for that?" she says.

W̲hen I walk by rewrite everyone is talking at once. They're all telling the same story. Apparently someone got poisoned by some specks of white powder when she opened a letter, had to be taken to the hospital, the works. "We got 'thraxed," is how Hoff puts it. The stuff is supposed to be lethal but apparently she only got anthrax lite, the Sanka of anthrax, the kind that only gives you a skin rash. Of course we're wooding with it tomorrow: "TABLOID UNDER ATTACK!"

"Who was it?" I ask Hoff.

"I don't know. That hot little assistant with the belly shirts?"

Burkey laughs. "She has a name, Hoff. Hillary, I think. St. Luke's says she's in Stable. She'll be all right."

"Hillary? Eli's, um . . ." I can't bear to say the word.

"Fiancée," says Hoff.

Ouch. So he went for the upgrade. I didn't know that.

"When did that happen?"

"Ever since This happened, love is in the air," says Burkey.

Really? I thought the only thing in the air was spores of chemical warfare agents. A couple of guys in space suits walk by us and head for Editorials. They start sealing off the area with large sheets of plastic and duct tape. This seems to accomplish the opposite of its intended effect, and terrifies all of us into brooding silence for a few minutes. News isn't so fun to chat about from inside the body bag.

"Who was it addressed to?" I say.

Burkey doesn't know. "The police impounded it. Evidence. Who knows? She opens everybody's mail."

"I bet it was me," Rita says. "My hard-hitting Al Qaeda coverage."

"Yeah, right," Burkey says. "I wrote that thing last week about how we're going to bomb Afghanistan out of the Stone Age."

"No, no, no," Hoff says. "It had to've been me. I've gotten more death threats than any of you."

Burkey holds up a hand. "Please. I've gotten all the best death threats." She starts ticking them off on his fingers. "The Zodiac killer, Colin Ferguson—"

"Wait a minute, the Zodiac I'll give you but Ferguson's was addressed to all of us."

Burkey is rolling her eyes. "Yeah, right. Al Qaeda targeted the Senate majority leader, the chairman of the Senate Judiciary Committee, and the guy who broke the exclusive about the lady cop who stripped down to her utility belt for *Playboy*."

"Get outta here, that was a good story!" Hoff says. "I even wrote the hed."

"Come on," Rita says. " 'THIS IS A BUST'? About ten people thought of that simultaneously."

"Tom Farrell," Hyman Katz calls out. "Mommy's on the phone."

The other hacks make derisive mama's-boy comments as I retreat to my desk and wave at Hyman Katz to send the call over.

"Honey," she says. "Aren't you worried about the anthrax?"

"Not really," I say. I pick up a mass-produced corporate leaflet ("NEW YORK NEEDS US STRONG") that has just been dropped on everyone's desk. Its conclusions for unlocking the secret of post-September 11 health: get lots of rest and drink plenty of fluids.

"Didn't they hit NBC?" she says. This is a good sign: she hasn't heard how they got us yet. Why tell her? This is a woman who worries aloud whenever she sees me opening a package of Hostess cupcakes with my teeth, insisting that the chompers perfected by millennia of biology for ripping into mastodon flesh will be "ruined" if I employ them on cellophane packaging.

"Yeah," I say.

"You're not anywhere near there, are you?" she says.

"They're way over on the other side," I say, looking out the window at the deco NBC STUDIOS neon sign on the other side of the street.

"Just be careful, honey," says my mom.

"I'll cut down my breathing to the bare minimum," I say.

As soon as I hang up there's another worried female on the phone: "Oh my God, are you okay?"

"Never better," I say. "What are you up to?"

"Page forty-nine of *Civil Procedure*," says Katie. "If you've read it before, don't spoil the ending."

"Have you learned to think like a lawyer yet?" I say.

"You mean attorney? Every day is a new exercise in dread. But I have no one to blame but myself. I got into this *sua sponte.*"

"Sua sponte, yum. I had one of those for dessert at Carmine's last week," I say.

"Huh," she says. I miss the way she used to say "huh-huh." But you can save time if you limit your laugh to one beat, can't you?

"Can you spare a few billable hours later?" I say.

"I don't know. I have a lot of studying to do. I mean, a *lot.*"

"Maybe I can help."

"Stipulate as to how."

Somehow the instinct to protect a lovely soft sweet female dwindles when said female begins to bark like Alan Dershowitz. On the other hand, Katie still has a great ass. Which is a fact that, it occurs to me, I'd better never mention to her again unless I feel the urge to put my nuts into a Clarence Thomas–sized vice. She can't stop me from looking, though. That's the nice thing about asses; every time you take a peek, she has to be looking the other way. Why'd they have to stick the breasts on the front, though?

"Promise me you won't try to make me drink," she says.

"Send over a notary," I say. "I'll sign anything."

We meet up at Cafe Frog. She's in a rush. I'm sitting on a banquette working on my second beer.

"I'm eleven minutes late," she announces.

"Approach the bench," I say, and give her a kiss. At least, I'm kissing. She keeps talking. "I can give you seventy-five minutes," she says. "Are we going to eat or just drink? Because if we're eating, we need to order right away and we have time for appetizers or entrée, but probably not both."

I respond to this in the most dignified way possible, i.e., by jerking my head around crazily trying to pin my mouth on hers. Fifteen years ago when I was in the same situation with a date, her head would have been bobbing in mad catch-me-if-you-can circles because she was nervous about not having kissed many guys, or she wasn't sure we had reached the moment of most perfect specialness in the relationship, or a guy she liked better was at the other end of the prom with Linda Mazzucchelli, who was just like this total *slut* who probably had six kinds of VD and serves him right anyway and was he at least *look*ing over here to see what he was missing? Girl crazy, it never goes away, does it? It just keeps mutating into strange and terrible forms. Today she's got a thing for My Little Pony, tomorrow she's getting up at five so she can spend several hours waiting in line at the Hervé Chapelier sample sale to see how this year's extra-plain nylon handbags stack up against last year's.

The waitress comes over, nearly tripping over a crack in the floor tiles.

"Tort!" Katie says.

"Excuse me?" she says, in a thick French accent. Possibly she thinks Katie just said, "tart," which would have been pretty close to the mark too.

"I wasn't talking to you," Katie says, and grabs a menu. I can almost hear the waitress hawking up a loogie with which to flavor our drinks, so I hasten to explain that my friend is a lawyer and keeps an eye open for any excuse with which to crush a hapless small-business owner such as whoever runs this joint.

"This afternoon there was hot coffee? That spilled on my arm," says the waitress. "Look."

There's an almost indiscernible pinkness there, about one-tenth as bad as the average Indian burn we used to give each other in seventh grade. It was the thing in seventh grade. Sixth grade, the thing was to give each other flats. You'd sneak up behind a guy as he was walking and step on the back of his sneaker so hard that the heel of his foot came partway out of the heel of the sneaker and then landed on it, crumpling it underneath. So he'd have to stop and, cursing his attacker, take the shoe completely off to fix it. We got Bucky a record thirty-six times one day on a field trip that year. I know for a fact that he never completely recovered from the trauma. Now that I think about it, grade school was the history of escalating violence. It's lucky we discovered girls, because otherwise by the time tenth grade rolled around, we probably would have spent after-school time chasing each other playfully around the soccer fields with chainsaws.

"Oh . . . that's actionable," Katie says, examining our waitress-plaintiff. "You should see someone about that. I'm not an attorney yet, but if I were I'd definitely look into your case."

While she's in the bathroom, I order a bottle of wine for the both of us. The waitress is uncorking it when she gets back.

"What is this?" Katie says, holding up a wineglass as if it's Exhibit A.

"Is there anything sadder than an empty glass?" I say. "Let us utilize it."

"I'm going to have to estop you from doing this," she says.

"Estop?"

"You already stipulated that you wouldn't try to get me drunk."

She orders one of those no-alcohol beers even reformed alcoholics won't drink. Who would ever drink Budweiser if it weren't for the alcohol? Even with the alcohol, it's pretty gruesome.

"So," she says. "What have you been up to? Why haven't I seen you? How's your job? How are you emotionally?"

"You used to read tarot cards," I say.

"That was a long time ago," she says, rearranging her cutlery.

"Three months. Your classmates couldn't believe it when I told them."

Now she looks up. Her expression is as blunt as a gavel. There aren't many pretty gavels. "Who have you told?" she says.

"It's a joke," I say.

"Have you told more than one person? When did you tell them? Exactly what did you say? What was the context?"

"I wasn't being serious," I say.

"What do you mean?" she says. "Either you told them or you didn't."

"I was kidding," I say.

"When? Just now or when you told them?"

"Just now. And before. I made up the whole thing. I never told anyone anything," I say.

"Oh," she says. She scans her watch, which she now wears to face inward. She has also strapped it around the outside of her sleeve. She must be reaping a bonanza in saved wrist-rotation and sleeve-retracting time.

"But now I will!" I say. Winkity-wink.

"Listen, Tom, I've *got* to make law review, okay? Something like that could be really deleterious to my chances."

Not long after that she releases me on my own recognizance.

"I'm really sorry," she says as we're walking out. "I've been stressed about this test I have coming up. I just have to do some studying tonight. I'm not really like this. I'm just, *non compos mentis* tonight. You know?"

"Ah," I say. "That happens so often."

"Good night, Tom."

"Good night, Katie."

"Oh, Tom? It's actually, um, *Kate,* now."

"Kate."

"That's right."

There is no kiss.

Liesl got back from Utah Thursday night. She didn't call me. Last night we spoke briefly. She informed me that she was attending a party Nora was giving. There was no mention of inviting me to this little fiesta, though.

"So," she said.

"So," I said. "How about tomorrow night?"

And this pause really stretched out and made itself comfortable.

"Actually," she said, "I have plans tomorrow night. Another friend of Nora's. Another party."

This would be a perfect moment to invite me along.

"Maybe I'll see you tomorrow afternoon?" she said.

"That sounds nice," I said. Afternoon?

So today I'm sitting around feeling slightly queasy. Could be the flu shot. Everyone is so scared of anthrax that they've been getting flu shots to feel secure. That way, if, say, a month from now you feel like you have routine flu symptoms? Having had a flu shot, you'll be comforted to know that you're actually dying of anthrax instead. Only, the flu shot itself seems to have given me an off-off Broadway version of the flu. My stomach is doing the rumba. My skin is like the inside of an oyster.

Getting dressed, I think, What do you wear for a breakup? It's somewhere between a wedding and a funeral. Black is always correct. The official color of New York. So I do the black jeans. Mousse the hair, try to make it artfully messy. Unfortunately, my hair isn't wet enough and I wind up with artlessly messy hair. I look thirteen. On the other hand, do I care? Maybe playing the pathetic card—the King of Schlubs—will earn me a sympathy fuck?

Instead of coming over, she calls from the subway stop, tells me to meet her at the coffee bar. When I see her, I don't go in for the kiss. Neither does she. We hi each other. She has on thick woolen pants. Flannel shirt. A down sleeveless vest. Knit cap. She's practical. And practically a lumberjack.

We sit in the corner so I can stare at Cafe Frog behind her and think about the times I took Julia there.

This seems pretty civilized. She takes off her pea coat and she's wearing a loose khaki sweater covered by a sleeveless fleece vest seemingly calculated to rob her figure of any feminine connotations.

We sip hot chocolate. Too sweet. It's like molten Hershey bars poured into a glass of hot Quik, with chocolate sprinkles. I don't want to finish it. On the other hand, it's expensive: yes, you can pay $4.50 for a cup of cocoa in this town. I can picture my mom sitting there next to me going, "Why did you order it if you didn't want it?" I make myself drink it. To shut up my mom.

I tell a story about the Toad.

"So I was asking him, when do you think the love-in for the fire department is going to end? And he says, 'Probably when they figure out that they're the ones who stole all those Tourneau watches from the mall under the trade center.'"

Liesl makes a sour face. "Why would it be the firefighters?" she says.

"It had to be them, or the other emergency workers," I say. "Everyone else evacuated the building. They were, y'know, *fleeing*? For their lives? And then security blocked off the area. No one got in after that."

"Don't you think it was just regular criminals?"

"Why would anyone stop fleeing for their lives to hatchet their way through inch-thick windows to take some watches?" I said.

"I don't think criminals are very smart," she says.

"But criminals wouldn't have had time to get there," I say. "The building was full of ordinary office workers running for their lives."

"Well, *some* of them were probably criminals," she says, her brow darkening.

"Who forgot to bring their crime axes to work that day," I say.

She glares. The cocoa is in motion in my guts.

"Never mind," I say.

Our appetizers arrive. She takes a bite. When she looks up, she looks different.

"Your eyes are all shiny," I say.

"I was thinking, when I was sleeping in the desert in Utah," she says, "we don't have much in common. Which we've discussed."

"Hmm," I say.

"What do you think we have in common?" she says.

Apart from sex, nothing. On the other hand, why deprive yourself of sex just because you think the other person is a bore?

"Not much, I guess." The manboy manual is quite clear on this case: time to sulk. But simultaneously act as if you don't care.

"And your cynicism really bothers me," she says.

Can you ever really be too cynical? I mean, look around.

"And I feel you look down on my lifestyle," she says.

I shudder involuntarily, thinking about her apartment. The TV spastically blinking "CH 03" in the top right corner. The shower head hissing out one minute's worth of hot water. The tree-bark toilet paper. The muttering ruffians lurking at the bus stop outside her window. It's not her lifestyle I disapprove of. It's her borough.

"Check please," I say.

"Do you think this is going anywhere?" she says.

"Not especially," I say.

"I've been in other relationships that weren't going anywhere that lasted a long time," she says. "I don't want to do it again."

She did it. She got me. In a public place. She knows I'm not going to make a passionate argument in defense of continuing my apathy with her. She saw my torpor and raised me with inertia.

How did we get on this subject? She's moving to Düsseldorf next spring. Couldn't we have just let it drift until then? I've got holidays to deal with.

"Okay," I say. And then she does an amazing thing. She *lets me pay.* I'm thinking, I'm spending the last five minutes I will ever spend with this person. I walk her to the subway on Central Park West.

"Safe trip home," I say.

She smiles and kisses me. On the mouth. I give her shoulder blades a little rub. And she makes a big show of kissing me again. Lips on lips. As if to say . . . what? Who can figure out these girls?

" 'Bye," she says happily, and off she goes.

" 'Bye." I give a wave and turn around to delete her numbers from my cell phone.

I recalibrate my sex odometer, silently confessing to myself. Forgive me, Father, for I have not sinned enough. It's been eleven days since my last lay.

I had always thought the smallest fraction in existence was the percentage of net worth Bill Gates spends on haircuts, but now I realize that an even smaller number is the chance that I will ever again unhook a bra without paying for the privilege.

So I hit speed dial 8.

"Heyyy!" Kate says. "Good to hear your voice! I thought you were mad at me. I haven't heard from you all week."

"Gosh, you know," I say, wincing. Gosh? This is my idea of how to speak to a Midwesterner? "Busy at work."

"Possibly exculpatory," she says. "What are you doing tonight?"

"Are you hungry?" I say.

"Let's just say, *arguendo*, that I am. Would you be up for sushi?"

"Um," I say.

"Don't you like sushi?"

"Well," I say. By what leap of faith do we suddenly trust raw fish just because it's served by stylish-looking people in a slick room, with a cute little designer lump of wasabi? If oily men in overalls named Zeke were serving it in roadside Texacos and calling it "raw just-kilt sea critters that by the way *we have not cooked in any way*," would you eat it?

"How about eight o'clock at Sushi Zen?" she says.

"Um," I say. "Cool?"

"Oh, but I can't stay out late," she says. "I have to be in by ten to work on my torts."

"That's okay," I lie. Shit.

We hang up. I hit speed dial 7.

"It's Mr. Sunshine," I say.

"Tom!" Bran says. "I never hear from you anymore."

"I saw that piece on airport security you did. Fantastic."

Actually this was sheer coincidence. While channel surfing one night, I came across a breathless TV news story on airport security, vaguely remembered she was working on same, and connected the dots. I watched for thirty seconds, got bored ("In fact, the FAA said damning things about airport screening systems in this! 1999! Report!"), and switched to *Road Trip*.

"Did you really?" she is saying. "I am so proud of that piece. You have no idea how much work it took."

"You have to tell me about it," I say. "Can we go get a drink later? Say, around ten?"

"Yeah, okay," she says. "I just have this source who's supposed to call me."

"How about if I stop by later? I'll bring you some dessert."

A confection from the Columbus Bakery won't cost more than four bucks. One drink is $5.50 at the Dublin House. Plus I am unlikely to be invited to knock boots with her at Dublin House.

I go home and, since I will be going out for sushi, eat a full meal. There's some hamburger in the fridge. I haven't eaten at home all week, so I give it a sniff: it smells. Not a good thing. But isn't this a bit unfair of me? It's a dead animal: will I smell this good a week or two after my demise? What should I expect? Anyway, I've had worse. And what is cooking for if not to kill germs? If I don't eat it, I will be conceding that when I bought the hamburger on Sunday, I was stupid not to freeze it. And I can't let myself be proven stupid. So I decide to eat semi-rancid meat. Just to make sure I kill the germs, though, I turn the flame up high on the frying pan. Which leaves me with a burger that is thoroughly charred on the outside, pink and cold on the inside. I do not discover this until after I take a bite, however. Ugh.

I put on my tight new sweater and paste my hair down with a petroleum-based substance and put on the good shoes and I'm ready to go. It's eight. I'm supposed to be at the sushi place at eight. It takes five minutes to walk there. Damn. I've got time to kill. So I sit down and waste fifteen minutes watching *Cops* as the hamburger and the chocolate and the flu/anthrax/breakup microbes reenact some of the world's wildest police chases in my guts.

When I walk in the sushi place, every table is full of happy Upper

West Siders. Kate is sitting at the front table. Coincidentally, so is Bran. They're smiling daggers at me. There are slimy piles of raw fish everywhere. Uh-oh.

Silently, I take a seat. Somebody should be banging a gavel.

"We already ordered," Kate says.

"Let me explain," I say. But my brain is not in service at this time. Try again later.

Luckily the two of them are not strapped for words.

"You are truly *sui generis*," Kate says.

"That's Latin for asshole," says Bran.

"I would have invited you," I gurgle. "You said you were busy."

"You double-booked us," Kate says. "You are *so* busted."

"You said you had to be home by ten," I say. This evening, I am starting to think, was a good idea that doesn't quite work in practice. Like those hand dryers in the men's room.

"You wouldn't even know Kate if it weren't for me!" Bran says.

"I prefer to be called Katherine," Kate says.

Bran ignores her. "And you were just going to go out with her behind my back?"

Katie-Kate-Katherine and I lob looks at each other. How much does Bran know?

"What?" says Bran. "What does that look mean?"

"Is that a California roll?" I say. "Yum!"

Kate looks guilty.

"After what happened between you and I?" Bran says.

In my stomach it's like the KKK and the NAACP accidentally booked the same dance club for their fall fund-raiser.

"Actually, I think it's correct to say, 'Between you and me,' " I say, throwing up a smoke bomb of grammar. Which fails utterly to distract anyone.

"What happened?" Now Kate's defensive.

"Tom and I had a thing," Bran says.

"I wouldn't call it a thing," I say. "Thing*let*, thing*y*," I say.

"You guys had a thing and neither of you told me?" Kate says. "You're joint tortfeasors!"

"I can't talk," I say. "Mouth full." I pop a California roll in my mouth. Yup: it tastes the same as ever. Like wet uncooked sea rodent.

"Don't change the subject," Bran says. "I'm going to the bathroom and when I come back, you *will* talk."

Kate and I look at each other while she's gone.

"You don't look good," she says.

"I think I have the flu," I say. "You know: that disease with anthraxlike symptoms?"

"I'm disappointed in you, Tom," she says.

How do you explain to women what it's like to be a guy? For them, picking out a mate is like picking out a bra. Is it sexy? Is it a good fit? Will it support me? If they don't find the right one, they keep looking. They don't care if they get a bra today. They can try Bloomingdale's next week.

For a guy, though, looking for a girl is like sitting down in a restaurant with your throbbing hunger. You look at every entrée and wonder, is it tasty? Will it go down easy? You want steak, but if they don't have one, you'll settle for a hamburger. You'll settle for sushi, even. Why do men cheat, even if they've got a beautiful girlfriend? Who wants sirloin every night?

But in the real world you can't count on a girl to show up on a plate just because you want her. The sexateria is more like a diner in Moscow in 1965. You order the steak *and* the hamburger *and* the sushi because chances are they might be out of something. They might be out of everything. The main thing is, you have to eat or die.

The sushi and the overworked simile jump into my guts as my

tummy cycle switches from Tumble to Agitate. As for my mouth, it's in Spin.

"I hope you understand how painful a position you're putting me in," I tell Kate, putting a tender hand on top of hers and aiming a gaze at her. "I didn't call Bran because I wanted to have a nice dinner, just the two of us."

"Which you were going to finish by taking her dessert?" she says.

"Katie, it was just going to be a regular dessert," I say. "Not an éclair wrapped around my schlong."

"It's *Kath*erine now. Did you really think we wouldn't find out?" she says.

We? Are they suddenly pulling some kind of sistahs-against-the-world act on me? "Look, I thought *we* had an understanding that *we* weren't going to tell Bran every single time *we* went out." Meaning: *I thought we had a gentlemen's agreement to act like sneaky little rats.* "You know how weird she can be."

"I'm starting to discover how weird you can be," she says. "It's the deception of it." She looks as if she's about to file a motion to strike me.

I think of all the sneaky things I've done in my life. Nah. This really doesn't rate.

My phone is sitting on the table. It goes off. Saved!

"Hey," I tell the phone.

"Ah—Tom?" says a familiar voice.

"Yeah, who's this?" I say.

"It's Liesl! What are you doing there?"

"What do you mean? You called me," I point out. I've got her there.

"No I didn't," she says.

"This is my—" Uh-oh.

"I called *Bran*," she says. "Do you know Bran?" And as my gastrointestinal revolt begins to emit audible pops and moans like distant gunfire, I'm picturing the conversations that will ensue between Bran and Liesl. Bran: How do you know Tom? Liesl: Well, actually, we've kind of been, y'know, going out for a few months? Bran: Well, that's very interesting, because he and I just kissed a few weeks ago. When he wasn't busy hooking up with my best friend.

"We're, sort of, old friends?" I say. Create a diversion! Think! "How was your, um, subway ride home?" Excellent.

"Tom." It's Bran, looming next to me. "What the fuck are you doing with my phone?"

And I pat my jacket pocket. Yep. My phone. Still there.

The waitress comes over. Lurks behind Bran.

"Uh, it's, uh, for you," I say, handing it over.

"Hey, who's this?" Bran says. And I watch her. Oh. So this is what angry looks like. That other? Just a dress rehearsal.

"Everything okay?" says the waitress. I look up at her. She's smiling. Then frowning. Scowling. It's my ex-girlfriend Maggie's big sister, Stephanie, the waitress/failed actress. How much of the preceding conversation did she hear? In a moment I'm frowning too. But I can do better than just a frown. For example, I can, I discover, also send a fire-hose-strength fountain of vomit over Stephanie's shoes. And the taste of my puke? It's so disgusting, it makes me want to throw up. So I do. And I do. And I do. My abs are convulsing muscularly— it's a pretty good workout, I am dimly aware—and my gut bucket is emptying out across the floor. I sense people knocking over bottles of soy sauce, scuttling out of splatter range, making noises that I hope but doubt are expressions of sympathy for my plight.

When I look up Kate is handing me napkins with a blank expression. People are calling, "Check, please." Bran is still on the phone. "Tom just ralphed," she says. "He's such an idiot. There's nothing wrong with this sushi."

"Would everyone excuse?" I say, as a speck of barf flies out of my mouth and lands on some sushi. "Not feeling well."

"Hold on," says Bran to the phone. To me she says, "You owe me fifteen for the sushi."

I'm not in the mood to argue, so I pay. Bran is scowling. Kate is scowling. Stephanie is scowling. Liesl's scowling can be inferred. I've just hit some sort of anti-grand slam, like the Bugs Bunny baseball cartoon where he throws a pitch so slowly that three different batters each take three whiffs at the ball before it gets to the catcher's mitt.

I slink home alone nursing only one hope: that I have anthrax. That'll show 'em!

When I get home, I flip through the TV stations. I stop to watch a little Mick Jagger piece on prime-time news shows. There's a guy we can all look up to. What is he, fifty-six? And still shagging everything in sight.

Before the break, the announcer starts with the bloodcurdling urgency.

"Next up, an exclusive. Inside! Evil Incorporated. We'll clue you in on what the cold-blooded murderers who plotted the 1993 World Trade Center bombing told their lawyers—and about how their! damning! statements! are linked to the thugs who masterminded September eleventh. When we come back."

So I sit down with my Doritos and watch. It's Bran's TV show. It's Liesl's law firm. So that's how they knew each other. My Eva Braun turned out to be Mata Hari. If I had known she was the kind of person who would risk her job to leak documents to the press, I would have found her so much more interesting.

Except at work, I haven't seen Julia for two weeks. She always comes up with a reason to cancel. Waiting for her at the Marriott Marquis, I think, Wouldn't it be great if you could take someone to relationship court? Plead your case before a neutral observer with the power to make someone quit acting unreasonably? Hate crimes are severely punished. How about love crimes?

Last night I stayed up far too late sifting through evidence: her old e-mails. You can chart the whole history of a relationship on them, can't you? Push a few buttons and they're right there on your screen, like the news ticker on CNN.

Number of e-mails I got from her in February: 9.

In March: 78.

In April: 94.

In May: 105.

In June: 97.

In July: 70.

In August: 22.

In September: 8, all of them in response to mine. Except, I sent her 25.

In October: 2.

In November: 0. In November I stopped e-mailing her. It was too depressing, waiting for her to not answer.

But if I ever get her in front of the nooky judge . . . Isn't it true, Ms. Brouillard, that on a winter day at precisely 5:37 P.M. you sent, *unsolicited,* the following e-mail to the plaintiff?

From: BROUILLARDJ@NYTabloid.com
To: FARRELLT@NYTabloid.com
Subject: snow

I heard about this e-mail thing and figured I'd give it a shot although if you ask me, it's a crazy fad that won't last. I had fun yesterday; I hope I didn't keep you out too late. The only bad thing is, I woke up with that Sir Mix A Lot (is that the name?) song in my head. It was my morning shower song of the day. There's always a song stuck in my head when I wake up, and it's never a good one. Anyway, have fun in the snow tonight when you're going home. It's actually quite lovely out there, and the snowflakes are sparkly and perfectly formed. (I just spent a rather long time outside staring at the flakes that landed on my coat. It was the highlight of my day.) Okay. I won't subject you to my babbling any longer. Talk to you later. Julia

And *by the way,* Ms. Brouillard, were you being completely candid when you sent this memorable note a week later at 4:28 P.M.?

From: BROUILLARDJ@NYTabloid.com
To: FARRELLT@NYTabloid.com
Subject: dinner

Hi there. How are things in editor-land today? Everything's going
smoothly in my part of the hovel, you'll be pleased to know. I was
wondering, however, if you don't have plans tomorrow night,
if we could do our dinner thing then. I'm kind of feeling like hell
today and really just need to go home and get some sleep. The good
news is that I'll be moving in to my new place next weekend, so I
will no longer have to make that pain-in-the-ass trek to Connecticut
every night. It ain't Paris, but it will most certainly do.
Julia

And precisely how, Ms. Brouillard, do you think a reasonable
person should have reacted when you sent such nothings as this one
on March 9 at 5:44 P.M.?

From: BROUILLARDJ@NYTabloid.com
To: FARRELLT@NYTabloid.com
Subject: you

Will you visit me before you go home today?

Isn't it true, Ms. Brouillard, that you fully knew the effect you
would be having on an innocent young man when you engaged in
this saucy March 23 exchange?

From: BROUILLARDJ@NYTabloid.com
To: FARRELLT@NYTabloid.com
Subject: fleeing

I'm terribly restless today. Want to run away with me?

From:	FARRELLT@NYTabloid.com
To:	BROUILLARDJ@NYTabloid.com
Subject: Re: fleeing	

To get a coffee or to, like, Fiji?

From:	BROUILLARDJ@NYTabloid.com
To:	FARRELLT@NYTabloid.com
Subject: Re: Re: fleeing	

More like Fiji

Ms. Brouillard, you have been found guilty of emotional battery of a man who was already socially crippled when you met him. I sentence you to five minutes to life with the plaintiff. He has plenty of room in his apartment, you know.

My cell.

"Hey," I say. "Are you here?" You never know if she's coming. She forces me to ask the same questions repeatedly, like my mother. Can't be sexy. Can't help it.

"I'm at Forty-seventh and Broadway. All my trains were late."

"I'm at Forty-fifth. I'll meet you at Forty-sixth," I say.

So she isn't canceling tonight. Not because of me. Because it's the National Book Awards. Hosted by Steve Martin.

Walk north one block. And there she is. All buttoned up in her cute yellow coat. Fishnet stockings peeking out beneath. Don't tell her how fine she looks.

"Hi," I say.

"Don't hate me," she says.

"It's okay," I say. She's fifteen minutes late. I don't really care.

Up the escalators of the Marriott Marquis, all brass and glass.

Check-in is on the seventh floor. I help her off with her coat and rake my eyes down her front. She's wearing a black wool sheath. She has nicer dresses.

"I'm underdressed," she says. "I was having a fat crisis."

"Oh?"

"I changed to this one. The other was too tight," she says.

"I would have preferred that."

"Yeah. I know."

Time to find the bar.

"Who are these people?" she says.

I don't know. But Steve Martin is standing right behind me.

Julia goes silent.

We have two glasses of wine. Julia is smoking a cigarette, but she looks as if she wishes she had a second aperture to inhale through. Unfair, isn't it? Two lungs, but only one mouth.

"You look pretty spiffy," she says.

"I do?"

"You've lost a lot of weight since I met you."

"Forty pounds, actually," I say. The vomit diet served me well, although I turned out not to have anthrax.

"You're a catch," she says.

"Thanks. You're a knockout," I blurt.

"Aw," she says.

"So I almost didn't make it tonight," she says.

A look of hurt darkens my brow. I can feel it.

"Why?"

"I was in this bodega buying cigarettes, and this man—he didn't look like he was homeless or anything, he was just a normal guy in his thirties, leather jacket. Well groomed. He just started to cry."

I'm running my various sympathetic faces, thinking, This guy's suffering. I'm sorry about that. Why should that mean I have to suffer with him?

"It really got to me," she says. "That, plus I saw a dog get run over the other day. And the owner just stood there wailing. It was so haunting. It's all just too sad."

"If the guy was crying in his apartment, that wouldn't have bothered you," I say.

"I know!" she says. "That's what's so wrong about New York. So communal. I can't breathe."

"Did you cry too?" I say, creasing my eyebrows and hoping I don't look like a smarmy talk-show guy trying to suck out some Nielsen-friendly pain.

She nods. "I was really shaken," she says. "I just stood outside for a while, thinking, I can't go to dinner now."

"I'm so sorry," I say. "It's really nice to have you here though."

"Do you think I'm a muppet?" she says. "My brother called me a muppet."

"I do not. I think of you in black and white, in the early sixties, seen through a rainy windshield. Wearing a shiny three-quarters-length raincoat with matching boots. And a wistful look," I say.

Yes, I sometimes do talk this way around pretty girls. And empty wineglasses.

She gives me her crooked half smile.

"I thought about you the other day," she says.

That one is like slamming a double Scotch. Her thinking about me is such a rare occasion that it merits a mention. Did I think about her the other day? Did I breathe air the other day? Since I met her I haven't gone two hours without thinking about her.

"Yeah?" I say.

"I was walking down the street. And I was thinking about how you have this *im*age of me. As this, *person*, with, all of these characteristics. Like in a novel. And I was thinking that you're one of the only people who thinks of me that way," she says. "Doesn't that sound stupid?"

"No," I say. "To me you are a walking novel."

She doesn't say anything. Her eyes look shy.

"Heard from Rick?" I say.

She slumps.

"Just informational e-mails," she says.

"You don't discuss the letter you sent?" I say.

"No," she says. "He hasn't mentioned it. Except to say he got it."

"You still love him."

"I think I'll always," she says. "I've really realized it this fall."

Yep, sports fans: you never quite get used to hearing that the girl you want is permanently woozy for someone else. She's hopelessly infatuated with someone who has made it clear in a hundred ways that he doesn't want her. Why doesn't she just give up the chase? Can't she see what she's doing to herself? Who could be *that* lame? Who could—Oh. Never mind.

"What did you love about him?" I say.

"He could always, just, *see* things. Like that guy in the bodega. He would have been really upset by that too. He would have felt it."

Memo to self: start seeing things, and report all sightings to Julia at once.

We sit in the press gallery where they serve cold sandwiches. The swells are downstairs eating $1,000 a plate filet mignon. Steve gives a fabulous introduction to the awards. "Earlier today awards were given out in some technical categories," he says. "Best glue binding . . . best page numbering." The crowd loves it. Book celebrities aren't really celebrities. Here is an actual celebrity, celebritizing the nerdiest art form. A roomful of myopics has never felt so cool.

"The National Book Award is the most prestigious prize a book can receive and still be unknown," says Steve (wittily, *damn* him).

I start to give Julia's arm the treatment with my nails. She gives a half turn. Smiles.

"The competition has gotten really dirty this year," Steve is saying. "One of the nominated poets actually went to the printer of one of the other nominees to insert an extra iamb into his meter."

Julia looks at me with a swoony face every time the guy says something brilliant.

I laugh, smile, hate. The guy's a genius. I don't really measure up. I drink some more wine. Ready. Set. Brood. Occasionally I stroke her back. Mmm. No bra.

There's a long break for dinner. Then the awards are given out. We clap. Steve gives a brief wrap-up. We go.

At the end, we get our coats, go down to Forty-sixth. Cabs and tourists are thrusting in every direction, pummeling the air. Julia looks overwhelmed.

"Let's. Just. Stop," she says. She lights up.

I wait. She smokes.

"A nightcap," I say.

She doesn't say anything. She just follows.

We go to Mystery. The same bar we went to that frigid night in March when she got adorably lost and everything seemed ready to happen.

"So I had a little chat with Dwayne," she says.

"Oh?"

"It wasn't as bad as I thought."

"Took it like a man?" I say.

"Yeah. He said it wasn't a surprise. He said, 'If you've been staying with me all this time out of guilt, then that's fucked up. You deserve to be happy.' "

"So that's all set then," I say. "Good for you."

She shrugs.

"What are you going to do now?"

"He isn't kicking me out right away," she says. "He said I could stay as long as I want."

"If you need a place . . . ," I say. Then I stop.

She lets it go.

"I want to read that book on depression," she says.

The depression book won for nonfiction. The guy who wrote it lives in an old-money Fifth Avenue apartment with twelve-foot ceilings and elaborately book-lined walls. What has he got to be depressed about? He hasn't even met Julia.

"You can still be depressed if you're rich," she says.

"Are you depressed?"

She nods.

"When did it start?"

"When I was nineteen," she says.

"You remember it that precisely," I say.

"Uh-huh. I just started having these panic attacks."

"And now?"

"I just sort of feel vaguely unhappy. All the time. Like, there's so much *wrong*. You see it every day. Like that guy crying in the deli. And there's nothing you can do about it."

"It can't be that bad," I say.

"Plus I'm starting to think everyone is a bomber. Like today, I was smoking outside the building and I saw this, hairy guy go in the bank next door. He looked like he'd just been laid off or something. And he had this box under his arm. I was sort of edging away the whole time. I feel so helpless."

"What are you going to do?"

"Flee," she says.

I give her a look.

"Shouldn't everything have been fine with Dwayne?" she says. "I had someone who loves me extravagantly and takes care of me. Shouldn't that be enough?"

"There's just that thing," I say. Thinking, Extravagantly is my adverb. Dwayne rates no better than *doggedly*.

"There's just that *thing*, missing," she says.

"The mystery," I say.

"Maybe."

We drink silently for a while. I wonder if just possibly she is unaware of how I feel about her. Maybe I should unload.

But she's too quick. That's why I like her, isn't it? She can figure things out.

"Shall we?" she says, motioning to the door. It's only eleven-thirty.

"In a second," I say. "How do you think I feel about you?" I say.

Finding something fascinating to examine at the bottom of her glass, she says quietly, "I think you've said."

Bob Dylan say: *I offered up my innocence, got repaid with scorn.*

I've said too much. And yet I haven't said what I want to say. Because she doesn't want me to say it.

There are questions I want to ask her. Questions I don't want to know the answers to. Because they'll take me closer to the point where I know I'll have to give up.

"My brother called me up yesterday," she says. "We talked for an hour. He said he went to the library and ripped out all of the articles I'd ever written for *Tabloid.*"

I hold thumb and forefinger up to the waitress and sign a pretend check. "He's the one?" I say.

"Mmm-hmm. He's just . . . *me*," she says.

"You don't feel that way about any of your friends?"

"With all of my friends, there's something missing," she says. "Like we don't communicate on some level."

"So what's missing with me?" I say.

"With you," she says, "I communicate on all levels."

And now I'm perfectly bewildered. Has she just said I'm her only real friend?

We're back on Forty-eighth Street, walking out to Eighth Avenue. We go by the parking garage, the one where she stole up behind me in March, that night. That night I caught her in midsneak, bear-hugged her, scooped her right up and whirled her around in the air. And she laughed and laughed.

"Remember that garage?" I say. "You coming up behind me?"

"It seems so recent," she says, and something occurs to her. "It's been an adventure."

And as we pass the corner and wait for a cab I give her: "Why do you hang out with me?"

"What do you mean?"

"I mean, what's the point?" I say.

"You're my friend," she says. "You buy me drinks."

Even then, as she heads for her getaway cab, I worship the ground she walks away on.

The day before Thanksgiving. The director's cut, the extended remix of holiday weekends, the four-day reprieve, the time you see your family for the first time in months, the signal to begin your patriotic holiday shopping orgy. At the office everyone is in that hurtling holiday mood, smiling at each other in the hallways, being visibly *nice*. I have grown used to anticipating general misery around the holidays. If you go through life expecting bad things to happen, you will rarely be disappointed.

I call Bran's cell.

"Why are you calling me?" she says.

"Bad time?" I say.

"Tom," she says, "don't you know I'm working on This? The attacks? The airports? The anthrax?"

"Sorry," I say. "I thought maybe you only worked on it twenty-three hours and fifty-five minutes a day."

She sounds like she's having four other conversations.

"What?" she says. "Never mind. Gotta go."

"Hey, Bran?" I say.

"What?"

"You know how in the movies, when the guy sometimes doesn't get the girl you thought he was supposed to get? The girl he thinks he wants? And how sometimes he instead just gets together with his best female friend? The one who you knew all along was just perfect for him, except they couldn't see it in each other? They squabble; they stop speaking to each other. It takes them a while to see why they're perfect together. Didn't you ever think we had that kind of thing? Can't you see us putting everything aside and just admitting we have feelings for each other? This is me being honest."

"Tom," she says. "This is me hanging up."

"Give it some thought," I say.

"Tell it to the dial tone," she says. "And Tom?"

"Yes?"

"Don't ever call me."

"Ever? Ever is a long time. What if I get cancer?"

"Okay. Exception. You can call me if you get cancer. But only if it's terminal."

"How terminal? What if I have a disease that's bound to kill me in the next forty years?"

"I'm hanging up."

"You're hanging on."

"Up."

"Can I call you next week?"

"Next week? No. I'm beyond busy next week."

"So I *can* call you. Just not next week. What about next month?"

"Next week is next month."

"Next *year*. Come on. My final offer."

"Next year?"

"Next year. Five weeks of suffering. Of pining for you."

"Okay, *why* should I let you call me again, ever?"

"Because you were the first one I called on September eleventh."

Where did that come from? This thought has never occurred to me before, but as soon as I say it, I realize it's true.

"Now you're just cheapening something a lot more important than you and me," she says.

"Of course I am," I say. "But look around. Everyone in this city has been acting crazy lately. People opening their mail wearing rubber gloves. People buying gas masks. People buying a lifetime supply of antibiotics. People who have lived here twenty years moving to the suburbs."

"So what?"

"So. You're not leaving town. I'm not leaving town. You're not buying a gas mask. I'm not buying a gas mask. We're sticking. Why? What have we got in common?"

"Okay, what?"

"We love the chaos. Chaos is sexy. Anybody who can't see that deserves to be living next to a strip mall."

She thinks about this for a second. "You never did send me a huge fucking bouquet, you know."

"Is that your price?"

"Send me one and find out," she says.

And then she really does hang up, before I can ask what her favorite flower is. But in a second, I realize I already know. Lily of the valley.

I'm holding on to the receiver with a stupid look on my face when a voice comes parachuting out of the fluorescent lights.

"Here he is, right where I left him. Simba. A lion of the word game, pacing in his cage, bloody of claw. Give him a wide berth, ladies and gents, beware the fanged carnivore in preparation for All Gluttons' Day, thinking about carving up some turkey and Ethan Hawke."

"Mr. Thrash," I say. "How was Afghanistan?"

"Brutes, can't get a drink there, strictly BYO, bombs away, corruption, devastation, detonation. The horror, the horror. Murder and move, fold your tent and run, shivering in the desert, sudden movements with the troops, thump in the night, saddle up, lads, and here we go, move on to the next hole in the ground."

"You loved every minute of it," I say, having already seen the expense sheets showing he spent every night but one in the presidential suite at the Islamabad Hilton. We ran the photo byline every day: Rollo, in his Kevlar and flak jacket, looking like a man who can't wait to get bombed.

"Nothing in life so exhilarating as to be shot at without success," Rollo says. "Winston Churchill said that, boy."

"Or maybe it was his rewrite man," I say.

"Yeah, cheers," he says. "My invisible friend. Your services have not gone unnoticed, except outside this newsroom."

"So what's next for you?" I say, gingerly.

"Can't go back to the movie reviews," he says. "News on the march. Back to the thrice-weekly column, real reporting, rattle the cages, bang it like a gong, mate. Also, Cronin told me your reviews were better."

The phone. A voice I don't recognize.

"Tom Farrell?"

"That's me," I say. Rollo looks impatient. I tell him to hold on a sec. He drifts away to regale rewrite.

"Hold for William Winterbottom, please."

Winterbottom. Name's familiar. An editor of some sort, somewhere.

"Mr. Farrell?"

"Yeah?" I say.

"William Winterbottom, executive entertainment editor, the *Daily News,* and how are you today?"

"I'm fine." A newspaperman. One of us. This could be good, but it's starting out like America's Most Boring Telemarketing Calls.

"Excellent. It has not gone unnoticed that you have been on your way to achieving something of a reputation in the criticism community," he says. I'm picturing the city room as being larger and better decorated than ours, but what is that sound in the background? It's hard to identify. Oh yeah: silence. No phones, no fights, no CNN. The guy could be calling from an assisted-living community in Boca.

"My gratitude for taking a charitable view of my talents," I say. Where are these words coming from?

"Would it be possible for you to envision honing your skills so as to befit the nation's third-largest newspaper?"

"You're asking me to cross the street?" I say. No one's ever head-hunted me before.

"We feel certain we can offer an attractive compensation package, superlative benefits, and the respect that comes with writing for 1.1 million paying readers every day," he says.

"Every day?" Let's not get carried away here. "I'm a film critic."

"Yes, no, you're right, I envision your criticism running on Fridays, along with more in-depth examinations of trends in the film industry, perhaps on Sundays? As you know, we offer our writers up to two thousand words to afford them the freedom to explore issues of interest."

Two thousand words. Of real writing. No more hit-and-run six-hundred-word pieces. Analysis. Criticism. Ideas instead of puns.

"I like where this is going," I say.

"Of course," he says, his voice humming like a Mercedes, "we are not *Tabloid*. At the *Daily News,* standards of decorum prevail. You would be expected to fine-tune your material. I myself, as you may be aware, began my career at *The New Yorker.*"

"But the *News*, well," I point out. "It is a tabloid."

"*Tabloid* is a tabloid," he says. "At the *Daily News* we prefer to think of ourselves as a newspaper that happens to be printed on reader-friendly stock. Otherwise we consider that the two papers are no more similar than *Hustler* and *Architectural Digest.*"

I've never spoken to upper management at the *News* before, but this explains the unfocused quality of their stories, which cover the same ground as ours but eschew the crackling monosyllables, the all-caps headlines, the rakish wordplay. I'd always thought they were trying to be like us and missing the point, which is why we always call it the *Daily Ruse.* Turns out they think their way of doing it is actually better.

"What sort of compensation are we talking about?"

"We have been discussing a figure of—"

And here William Winterbottom of Nyack and Martha's Vineyard reads me a number that I associate with other professions entirely. Like international jewel thief. My voice sounds like I'm on helium.

"I think that would be acceptable," I say.

"Perhaps you could stop by the office today?" he says. "I've got a few quibbles, of course, notably with your *Training Day* review, which I thought may have crossed the line into mean-spiritedness about Ethan Hawke. His publicist is a long-standing friend to this newspaper, of course, and I remember running into her at a party and discussing with her some changes in tone that she felt would have been appropriate. I couldn't disagree with her. After all, it is not our business to be gratuitous, is it?"

And speaking from the forty-second floor of the house that gratuitous built, I say the words, "No, sir."

The next time the Toad shuffles by I stop him.

"Guess what?" I say.

"Guess what. What kind of question is that? What are you, four?"

"Okay, enough. I just got an offer from the *News.*"

"For Christ's sake, you don't want to work there. I talked to Max just the other day, he's miserable. When they hired him, they said they loved him, told him they wanted him to keep doing what he'd been doing, but they piss on all his ideas. He's not even city editor anymore, he's deputy assistant managing editor for information or something. Not news: information. It's like working for the UN."

"Can I just tell you how much they're offering me?"

"What?"

I tell him. The Toad can't believe it.

"That's it," he says. "Go. Clean out your desk."

"Aren't you going to make me a counteroffer?" I say.

"Look, we're a mom and pop operation, they're Bloomingdale's, we can't match it. That's more than I make. We're not in this business to make money."

"So why are we in it?" I say. "The artistry? The thanks of a grateful nation? The view of Fu Ying?"

"We're in it because we're a club. We're a club for people who hate people who join clubs." And he walks away.

I'm thinking about that when the phone rings.

"Hey," says Julia.

"Hey," I say.

"What are you doing for the weekend?" she says.

"Going to my grandparents' house in Maryland," I say. "My mom'll be there. But before I get there it's hours of I-95 hell on the bus."

"That sucks," she says sympathetically. "I'm heading for Grand Central."

"What time you leaving?"

"The 4:14," she says.

Check the watch: 3:32. She didn't leave a lot of time for this conversation.

"I just wanted you to know," she says. "I quit my job."

"Oh," I say. I'm wondering if this is going to be the worst sixty seconds of my life.

"You're moving, then," I say.

"On Saturday," she says. "I'm going to Madison."

"Here's an idea," I say. "Don't go."

"Huh," she says.

We don't say anything for a minute.

"I just feel," she says. "I have to be there with him."

Horrible as it is, I don't want this conversation to end. But there is nothing to say.

"So good-bye," she says.

"Yeah," I say.

And she hangs up.

The Toad comes by my desk as I'm about to call Winterbottom back.

"Look," he says. "Don't cross the street. We found another ten grand a year for you. But you have to take it in expenses. Expenses are fully tax-deductible for the company, right? So you get yourself a book of receipts from a restaurant-supply store, charge us two hundred a week, you get reimbursed in cash, tax free, no questions asked, everyone's happy."

"Irv," I say. "It's not enough."

"What?"

"Look, I'm packing my stuff."

"What else can I give you, partial custody of my cats? Read my lips, I have *nothing left to give*," he says.

"But you do," I say. "That." I nod over his shoulder.

He turns around. "That's it?" he says. "Done."

And for the first time in my life, I have an office. A real columnist's office with a sofa and a TV/VCR combo, one that they were saving for a personage of rank. Irv says I move in Monday.

My entire department is out the door by five. I linger till six-thirty, reading the papers, killing time. Just to punish myself I decide not to take the subway. Instead I head out into the thrust and teem of the concrete carnival. The city is simultaneously emptying and refilling. All of us who live and work here are going to meet our relatives in the suburbs. All the bored families in the suburbs who haven't sent their children to live in the city think, Let's go into town to look at a big-ass dead pine tree propped up in Rock Center.

I head for Port Authority on foot in the cold, in the dark. I've got a lot, but I don't have Forty-eighth and Eighth. I walk by it shivering and stand there for a minute. I can't get into the parking lot. It's closed. There's a blue painted scaffold around it. A sign says it's about to be torn down to make way for an apartment building.

My scarf is in my pocket. I leave it there. My gloves are at home. Right by the spot where I waited for her that time, there's a poster for a movie that quotes a witticism I came up with a few weeks ago. I wrote it to impress her.

The things I can't tell her. More than the times we undressed each other, more than the times we snacked and snorfled and slobbered on each other, more than the time in the park when I told her how I felt and she cried to hear it, more than the one and only time I slept with her in my arms, I remember Forty-eighth and Eighth. In the multiplex of my mind, it's always playing on one screen, in an endless loop. She is tiptoeing up behind me on an unfairly cold March night, in a little yellow coat much too thin for the weather.

Because she wants to be with me.